Buttermilk Book Publishing

Myrtle Beach, South Carolina

Typecast in Times New Roman

ISBN 978-1-7365555-0-7

Dedication

While this is a fictious tale, much of it is based on facts, opinions and speculation. For this reason, I offer my thanks and undying respect to:

All those lost to Covid 19, a coronavirus that devastated the world's population.

The first responders that performed above and beyond to save those they could and to protect those that could not protect themselves.

The Mom-and-Pop businesses.

The restaurant and fast-food owners, cooks and servers.

The truck drivers.

All essential personnel deemed unessential.

Those who produced a vaccine in record time.

A president that never gave up despite the odds.

The churches and those persecuted for their religious freedom.

God who saw us through the worst of times making believers out of nonbelievers.

It is easy for us to forget God's presence and power when we face uncertain and difficult times. Our faith can falter, and we can doubt God's presence, sometimes even doubting that He is real and who He says He is. We can forget that God understands when we struggle with our unbelief in Him and of His miraculous ways. When we begin to doubt, we should read Bible verses about believing and pray that He will renew our hearts and minds to remind us of who He is and who we are. We must be encouraged as we see God move through all circumstances in life to grow our faith. He has a purpose and loves and protects us under the worse of circumstances. Only He can perform miracles and protect us from evil. Our job is to forever believe in Him and never forfeit hope for despair. He truly works in mysterious and wonderous ways.

I will lift up mine eyes unto the hills, from whence cometh my help. My help cometh from the Lord, which made heaven and earth.

Psalm121:1-2

Covert 19

2020 A Devil of a Year

*Confinement, isolation, and loneliness can sometimes take its toll on
one's morality and dignity. Home is supposedly where the heart
belongs, or so I always thought. I never envisioned home as being a
prison or worse, a tomb. My perspective on much of what I had
previously grasped has been completely shattered. Belief is a
wonderful concept. Believing everything will be fine. Believing
everything will eventually work out for the best can be a pipedream
given unforeseen circumstances. I am not quite broken just yet but
being on the brink can be just as devastating. One thing for certain,
one can never be too prepared for the worst-case scenario. We
thought we were, but our confidence was chiseled away one painful
piece at a time, an agonizing process to endure.*

*I sound as if I am painting the ultimate scenario of gloom and doom.
Maybe I am. If it isn't, it's a close second. No. I am no quitter. Yes. I
have considered tossing in the towel more times than I dare count. It
is not my nature though. Somehow, I have managed to persevere, an
amazing accomplishment given what has happened...what continues
to happen. Yes, isolation and loneliness can wear down the best. I
am far from the best being beaten, battered, demoralized can test
one's faith and belief in God. You can find yourself slipping,
questioning where He is and why hasn't He intervened. It is a
vicious circle. I pray. I curse. I pray some more. I ask why. I blame. I
even find myself hating. None of it gets me anywhere. What I face is
still here. It has not gone anywhere. If anything, it has tightened its
grip, its foothold, its destructive force to tear me down; to destroy
me once and for all. Somehow, I battle back. I reach deep and find
just a bit more fight left in this old body. Maybe prayers are being
answered after all. I cling to it. That's all I have left.*

*Eighteen months ago, everything was much different. It is tough to
fathom that the entire collapse happened in this short time. Riding
high and then plummeting to the lowest of lows. It began gradually,
a slow burn, unbelievable to grasp but we remained vigilant and
were positive everything was temporary. That's what they kept
telling us. Do this. Do that. It is only temporary. Why wouldn't we
believe and trust what was being said? I am highly skeptical now
though. I am equally suspicious of the motives behind it. Even so,
who can I tell? Who would listen? More importantly, who would do*

anything to reconcile it? I fear reconciliation is not in the cards. This has been thoroughly orchestrated. Conspiracy theories run rampant. I certainly have my fair share. Accusations at my level mean little. Accusations elevated can have deathly consequences, so I have heard. It's tough to hear much though. Everything is being precisely filtered. Only propaganda exists. True or not it is all we have.

I do the only thing I can do at this time. I record my thoughts, my suspicions, and my theories. It is risky using a computer. My laptop provides too much evidence if it falls into the wrong hands. Sometimes I gather my thoughts the old fashion way…pencil and paper. I am discreet. I have not shared my thoughts with anyone lately. I really have no one to share them with even if I wished to do so. Retirement was supposed to be blissful. It was for a few precious years. We did the things we always said we were going to do. Tomorrow is never promised. That mantra has made a believer out of me in the worst way. Cherish every second has never loomed larger. Once it is gone…once they are gone…there is no recapturing what can't be recaptured. Time is valuable…more valuable than I could have even conceived. No. This is no pity party. Pity was sucked out of me long ago by way of an endless whirlpool of emotions. I am well beyond the pity segment. I am pissed. I become more enraged every passing day. Somehow…someway…my goal is to get to the bottom of this…to find the truth. Will it set me free? Doubtful! Will it change anything? Probably not! Little old me cannot right this wrong but there are those who can. Question though; is there any fight left out there? Is the opposition too powerful to squash any resistance? No. I am not part of a counter movement…not yet.

1
Three Months Earlier

George and Camilla Ritchie were waiting in the terminal for their plane to arrive. The connector would be the last leg in their journey after a month long across country vacation. Camilla had finally convinced George to retire six months ago from his construction business. It hadn't been easy though. As a matter of fact, she had been working this angle with him for almost three years. She had won out but not under the best of circumstances. George had suffered a mild heart attack requiring a quadruple bypass. Having had a medical background, she knew how to care for him and keep him on track with a regimented diet mixed with the correct blend of exercise. George was fit as a horse anyway. Tweaking his daily do's and don'ts had not been difficult.

Retirement though had been a tough and awkward transition for her hubby. He had sold his business to his closest friend and still monitored it regularly. Melvin Meeker looked up to George like a father and never let on if the constant looking over his shoulder ever bothered him. He often lunched with George and then walked him through active construction sites appreciating his insight and opinions. Camilla did her best to wean George off his previous life by constantly finding home projects to keep him busy. George was almost 75. She was ten years younger and had retired at age 52, burned out and ready for a change from her stint as a virologist. She remained active in the community volunteering at a homeless center run by their church. She served meals in the soup kitchen and offered a free medical clinic for those in need. She had been doing it three days weekly until George retired. She had now cut it back to one day. She missed her time there but figured if she had talked George into retirement, she should cut back on hers to spend more time with him. George would have probably preferred her still working those other two days. It would have given him ample opportunity to sneak away to his previous life.

A voice came over the airport's PA announcing the arrival of their flight. It was on time and on schedule. They were seated at the gate's terminal. They'd be back home and in Rochester, New York soon enough. Camilla had been born in Elberton, Georgia, rural America. It hadn't been an easy adjustment for her transitioning to city life. Rochester with over one million people is the third largest populous in New York State behind New York City and Buffalo. Elberton by comparison had a population of less than five thousand. This was a Green Acres moment in reverse for Camilla. She had already completed medical school when she and George met, and had begun her medical practice in Athens, Georgia. Athens was the sixth largest city in Georgia, with an estimated population of just over two hundred thousand. Her brief time there had given her a taste of city life, even though she resided in the country on her uncle and aunt's farm while commuting back and forth into the city.

George grabbed their carry-on and ambled along behind his wife until they located their seats. He was itching to get back home. Travel was more important to his bride of thirty years than to him. Still, he would not deny her happiness. It was just tougher on him to follow the sheep herd of tourists. He had been a Shepherd of men, not one of the flock. Leaders make difficult followers. He had done the best he could. Those heart problems had taken a bit of a hitch from his normal steps. He carried nitroglycerine tablets in his pocket just in case the need arose. Luckily, so far, he hadn't. George didn't embrace having something like this hanging over his head. He had never ever had any medical concerns until the heart attack, out of nowhere, had given him a close call and a reality check. Still hell bent on living life to the fullest, George balanced risks with rewards. Often Camilla called his decisions too risky and reckless for her taste. George would just console her, telling her not to be such a worry wart or party pooper. Pills in pocket, he would simply be fine if disaster struck.

Life of retirement had gone better than George had expected financially. This new president had no political obligations. He had said what he was going to do and had done what he said. The economy was booming. Unemployment was at a historical all time low. The stock market seemed to be breaking records regularly.

Their portfolio was flourishing. He and Camilla had managed not to kill one another having begun the new faze in their lives, both being at home instead of having had working careers to keep them busy and go their separate ways. She had her hobbies and little escapes. He had begun developing his.

George still missed his construction business though. It had been his life. His life now dwarfed in comparison. He loved his wife but needed something to occupy his time for him and her. Home projects and fixer upper chores would last just so long. Camilla had done her best to fill his honey do dance card. He worked the list enjoying the little projects but that void still existed. George had tried his hand at golf. While those rounds did occupy the days he mustered the gumption to play, he just didn't embrace the game's concept. Besides, he was not a golfer. In the short time he had been playing he had hit almost everything conceivable with that little white ball. Included on his list of accomplishments were a condo, a car, a golfer, a homeowner, and a swimming pool. He was wondering when they were going to ban him from playing. He never shared these accomplishments with Camilla. He just pretended he was having a swell time. Sometimes he just sat in the golf resort club house until four hours expired and then returned home. If Camilla asked how the round went, he would just reply that the course was in good shape. Leave it at that. She never asked what he shot, so technically he never lied to her.

Camilla didn't hover over George. She wasn't a wife that wished to crowd her husband or push him to do things he really didn't enjoy doing. They attended church regularly and both enjoyed the fellowship offered there. Pastor Moony and his wife Abigail were regulars at their dinner table. Monthly they had the pastor and his wife over for a meal and a game of scrabble. Pastor Moony had just turned 80 and was fit as a horse. Abigail, 78 was just the opposite, frail, and a bit needy for a preacher's wife. Roy Moony had gotten George interested in fly fishing. George would take him up on it when Roy's schedule offered a time for them to fish. Lately times had been few and far between. Abigail had developed some serious medical issues requiring Roy to devote any spare time he had to her. George was not one to venture to their favorite fishing spots alone.

13

Life in the not so fast lanes coasted along. George and Camilla made it work. At least a couple times a week they would dine out. At least once weekly they would attend a movie if something less risqué was appearing and suited their mutual taste. Camilla enjoyed long walks. George preferred riding his bicycle. His was not one of those fancy multi-speed versions. He had purchased it at a yard sale for 20 bucks. It was a one speed and went as fast as George felt like peddling it, which wasn't fast. Camilla had insisted that he buy it saying he needed the exercise. Exercise had not been an issue when he was still working. While he wasn't obese, he had put on a few extra pounds since engaging in this retirement bliss. He justified the transformation saying growing old it was expected to pack on a few extra pounds.

Children and grandchildren were an important part of their lives even though they didn't reside close by. George Jr., his wife Nara lived in Atlanta. They had two boys. Greg was single, in the army and stationed in Hawaii. Paul was married to Shay and lived in Texas. Daughter Margie and her husband Louis were in Vermont. She had just announced they were expecting their first grandchild from their only daughter Mimi who lived with her hubby in Washington, D.C. Thanksgiving was a big deal for family gatherings. Most times they would pick a getaway rental and meet there instead of having them at one of their homes. It had become a tradition. This year would be spent in Orlando. That would be nearly a year from now though. They had spent the holiday with them before taking off on their extended vacation.

They were both looking forward to being back home. The trip had been wonderful from her perspective. She wasn't so sure George had embraced the experience as much as her. She could tell he still struggled a tad with retirement. He never complained but she could still tell. He had been a workaholic. You can't make a transformation from that in a blink of an eye. She did her best to help him find a happy balance. She knew that the heart condition had made more of an impact on him than he would admit. She monitored his condition covertly. She refused to be a worry wart and meddler believing George needed breathing room and his own space. Still, he was her husband, and he did have a medical issue that must be monitored.

While they were on the backside of life, she refused to give in to the old people scenario. They had much yet to do.

After the redeye special, they were finally home. Upon gathering their luggage, they hailed a taxi to whisk them home. George didn't trust Ubers. He felt using one was unsafe, a robbery waiting to happen. Within an hour after landing, they were home. Rochester never looked better than after returning from a month-long vacation. At least George was glad to be back. Camilla loved their home as well but embraced the adventures of traveling. She hoped this trip would be the first of many that she and her husband would be sharing. They deserved happiness ever after.

George stood on the sidewalk breathing in the view of the modest ranch style house they had called home for over 40 years. Camilla gave him a nudge signaling him to help with the luggage. He smiled and gave her a little wink. Once inside Camilla brewed them a fresh pot of coffee while George carried the heavier luggage to the bedroom. His joints snapped and crackled as he sat on the edge of the bed for a little breather. He was feeling his age but that didn't keep him from thinking about his construction business. No. It was no longer his business. It was Melvin Meeker's. Melvin had been doing a fine job keeping it going in the right direction. He had taught Melvin well and he was making him proud in return. A little twinge on the left side of his chest woke him from his daydreaming. Darn old ticker thought George. It wants to be the center of attention. Just as quickly as he had felt it, it was gone. George smelled the coffee and eased off the side of the bed heading to the kitchen. The aroma of the brew made him crave a cigarette. Coffee and a smoke once went hand in hand. One just didn't seem complete without the other. George's doctor had advised him to give them up after his heart attack. She had insisted he keep the promise he had made to her. So far, he had. He had almost given up coffee as well. One without the other was almost sinful.

"George, are you, all right?"

"I'm fine. You worry to much, woman."

"Your color is a bit pasty. You should sit and rest awhile. We can unpack tomorrow. Here. Drink your coffee."

"Wish we had some donuts,"

"Tomorrow you can stop by Regan's Bakery and pick up your favorites. Make it a half dozen though. I know how easily you can inhale a dozen fresh ones."

"Wish I had them now."

"It's late and that's decaf. Donuts would have you tossing and turning all night."

"Fine then. I'm about ready for bed. It has been one long day."

"Next time we should probably break the return up and not travel all day."

"Next time?"

"Of course, there will be a next time."

"Spare your details tonight. You'll have me tossing and tumbling."

"I'll let you pick the next one, Honey."

"Honey might decide to spend his right here."

"Oh George, we've only just begun our golden days."

"Best time of our lives…so you have said."

"Every year we spend together is the best. Drink your coffee now."

"Wish I could wash down a donut with it."

"Put the cup in the sink when you've finished. I'm going to get out of these travel clothes and shower before bed. I love you."

"Love you too."

2
Present Day

Pastor Roy Moony and his wife Abigail had just departed. They retained the scrabble championship for another month. It had been nice to see Abigail doing a bit better since church Sunday. She was still feeble though. Roy did his best to conceal his worry. Neither George nor Camilla pried. It wasn't their business. They would just keep them in their prayers.

"George, I know I told you to pick our next trip but…"

"But what? I know that look. Just drop the suspense and tell me."

"I've been thinking."

"Thinking…this can't be good."

"Winter renters should be out of our condo in a couple of weeks. It would be nice to go to the beach. I miss South Carolina. It would be like going home."

"You're from Elberton, Georgia. South Carolina has never been your home. Besides, what are we going to do at the beach? We are no longer sun worshipers. We hardly ever even dip our toes in the Atlantic anymore."

"You could take your golf clubs."

Golf clubs…I should probably tell her. Nah. She would just bug me to take up something else to fill my time. "We haven't been home long. Isn't it a little too soon to take off again?"

"We're retired silly. What is time to us?"

"You're not going to let this go, are you?"

"Just for a couple weeks…it will be fun."

"Fun for you, you mean. Sorry. That didn't come out right. Let's think about it."

"Fine. You think about it. My mind is made up."

"This is supposed to be my choice. Must I remind you yet again."

"Then pick somewhere, George."

"I'm not ready to pick somewhere. It's too soon."

"Okay. It is your choice after all and I will abide by it, even though you know where my heart lies."

George hated it when she spun that guilt trip on him. He would at least think about it. He wasn't ready to commit just yet, but he would give it careful thought. He just wouldn't tell her he was considering her proposal. Who was he really kidding? He knew she knew he would be doing just that. She could read him like a book and knew darn well all she had to do was plant the seed.

The next day began like in other day in their household. Uneventful. Routine had become the new norm. It didn't bother George, a creature of habit. Rising at the same time, coffee while reading the old fashion way a newspaper instead of internet, then a light breakfast, worked simply fine for him. Now Camilla could deviate from the norm in a blink. She seemed to embrace spontaneity. George credited this to her having been so organized and structured in her career. She found her rebellious and risqué side once she exited the profession. It would be a long while before he ventured over to the wild side from his years in construction. He wasn't even sure he could be converted to her way of thinking. He wasn't sure he even waited to be set free like that. He didn't like surprises. His life had always been calculated; the risks included.

"What do you have planned today, dear?"

"No golf if that is what you are wondering. Think I'll work some in the shop. I have plenty of projects out there that could use a little TLC."

George had built the shop years ago. The building contained an assortment of equipment perfect for almost any need or project. He enjoyed woodwork and could make about anything imaginable. Metal fabrication was his wheelhouse though. As long as he was working with his hands, he was a happy camper. Today he would finish the bookshelves he had promised his wife.

The afternoon flew by quickly. He had lost track of time, consumed by his creative activities. Eventually, Camilla had halted his production saying dinner would be served shortly. George sighed, not yet willing to give into calling it a day. His shop was his escape from the boredom of retirement. He missed his business and the guys on his crews. Darn broken ticker had forced his hand on giving up what he loved to do; that and his beloved's persistence beckoning him to hang it up. Oh well. No need crying over spilled milk. It is what it is he reminded himself.

After dinner, George sought out his comfy Lazy Boy leather recliner. The president was supposed to be giving his state of the union address tonight. George had always been a political hound even though he despised the political bureaucracy. He followed politics closely and liked the current president. He was a 'no nonsense', get it done, hell or high-water type guy. The man played by his rules and not those of the career politicians. He owed no one favors and stuck to what he said he was going to do. George admired men of that fiber. He was cut from the same cloth as the man in charge. Promise no one. Owe no one later. Follow the rules when you can. Break them when you had to do the right thing. Put God first, the people second and everything else in the backseat. Yep, he liked this guy.

Ten sharp, the president took to the podium. The biased media hung on his every word looking to twist anything they could to fit their narrative. Most thought he would address the one-sided political impeachment witch hunt being tossed at him. George figured the head guy would destroy those seeking to remove him from office during his speech, but to everyone's surprise, and to the disappointment portrayed by the media, he never mentioned the proceedings targeting him. He stuck to his agenda, his administration's accomplishments, and goals ahead.

George looked over at Camilla and asked knowing she was a virus expert, "What was that Covid-19 thing he mentioned? He said China was dealing with some kind of medical crisis."

"Coronaviruses are a large family of viruses. They are common in people and a variety of animals. Rarely do any found in animals infect people or can be passed from person to person."

"Then why would he be compelled to even mention it in his address?"

"Not sure. Guess it could be reaching pandemic stages in China maybe. The world must always keep an eye on what happens in other countries. The 1918 Spanish flu infected about one third of the world's population. It was estimated that 50 million people died from it."

"I guess that makes stuff like this worthy of keeping an eye on then."

"Those were tragic times back then though. We are more advanced now. Medically we are better prepared for anything like that ever getting out of hand."

"It is curious though, why he would mention it then."

"We're talking about a ruthless communist dictatorship."

"Do we have any more of the key lime pie?'

"One slice dear and it is yours for the taking. Sit tight and I will bring it to you."

"You are the best, C."

"Always remember it and you'll do just fine."

Days later, the media and political opposition were put in a tailspin by the president's announcement. He had decreed a travel band on all flights from the communist regime. He was called a racist and xenophobic. The virus had begun wreaking havoc on the communist country. Under advisement the president had acted swiftly to prevent it from spreading the United States. He was literally crucified by those that hated him.

"What do you suppose this is all about, C?"

"I'm not sure. Precautionary I assume. I wouldn't worry."

"You're the expert. If you're not worried, neither am I."

"I'm retired and far from being an expert. It is probably more political than medical. These are troubling times. It's difficult trusting Washington or the bias fueled by the media. Enjoy your lunch. Have you given any more thought about going to our beach condo?"

"Come on C."

"All right, sorry I asked. What do you have on your agenda today?"

"Why? Do you have something in mind?"

"Berkley texted me. He hoped we would join him for brunch."

Berkley Jay Patrick was their black author friend. He was the same age as her, 65. They had been friends for almost 30 years. More friends with Camilla; George could tolerate him in small spurts. Berkley was a nice guy but too much the intellectual for George's taste. He utilized Camilla as a sounding board for his writing projects. She had even proofread a couple of his books. He and George just didn't travel the same circuit. George talked manly topics. Berkley talked the worldly stage. His views and George's were not very compatible. Berkley was not a liberal or global warming nut, but he could be a tad too philosophical and lost in the weeds for George's taste. It was time for diversionary tactics.

"Actually, I had planned to drop by one of Melvin's construction sites. He wanted me to look at the progress of the project."

"He wanted that or do you, George?"

George shrugged. No need admitting or denying anything.

"Fine then; say hello to Melvin for me. Invite him over sometime while you are at it."

"You know how busy he is."

"A man has to eat and a bachelor like Melvin doesn't get many home cooked meals."

"I'll mention that to him. Tell old Berkley hey for me."

George exited the premises as quickly as possible to avoid a further inquisition. Melvin wasn't expecting him, but he figured that didn't really matter. Male bonding required no formal invite. He strolled into Melvin's office like he still owned the business. The receptionist smiled as he passed her desk. Two quick knocks on the door and he walked inside. Melvin stood, smiled, and offered George his hand. After a manly handshake, George flopped down on the old leather couch that he had bought 25 years ogo. He was glad Melvin had hung onto it. Looking about the old office felt shrine like. Not much had changed in the short time of the changing of the guard. George felt homey and comfortable with the surroundings.

"How's the world treating you, Mel?"

"I can't complain. We are almost done with the Spencerport project. I just started a new crew in Brighton and quoted another job over in Honeoye Falls. I'm going to give Ken Wolf a shot at foreman if that one falls in place."

"Ken is a good Joe. He can handle anything you toss at him. Oh yeah, I am supposed to ask you to join us for dinner when you have a dry spell."

"Tell Camilla I would love that. Maybe next weekend if that suits you guys."

"Name the day. Saturday or Sunday and time. We'll make it happen."

"Sunday is church day for you. Let's make it Saturday."

"You bet. What do you think about this virus kicking China's butt? The president halted all flights from there."

"It must be some bad crap for him to do something like that. They say it isn't that contagious though, no person to person spreading. If that's the case, why the travel band I wonder."

"You know the drill. Everything he tries to do is made out to be political. I'm so damn tired of these politicians bickering and getting nothing done for the people who put them in office. It is all about what they want. Not what we want and need. Taxes and regulations …don't get me started."

"Amen to that brother…getting a simple permit in New York is a hassle. Requesting a presidential pardon is easier."

"I never trusted China on anything. They took our jobs and our faithful leaders just sit back and let them. They handed over the American economy to them on a silver platter. Our tax dollars at work, taking our hard-earned money, and giving it away to the world instead of making things right for the Americans. There is something terribly wrong when people live homeless on our streets and veterans are not taken care of, and we take care of other countries first. That money should be used here. When we have fixed our problems, we then offer help to others. Don't even get me started on these border jumpers."

"You're mighty fired up today George."

"I'm like this everyday since I've been retired and cooped up watching the news. If you really want to call it the honest truth that is. These networks tell us what they want us to hear. Trim the fat and doctor the narrative to suit their agenda I'm telling you. Take this virus. Media says it is overblown and the president is just lying to us. That means there is probably something to it then. They always paint it the opposite of what he says."

"You need to calm down, George. Your ticker doesn't need to get so over worked."

"My ticker is just fine. I've never felt better. I should never have retired. Sorry, I didn't mean it the way it sounded. You're doing a fine job with the business, Mel. I never doubted you would."

"No offense taken. Would you like to go out to the potential new site?"

"I would enjoy that immensely old friend."

****

Camilla and Berkley were enjoying their brunch at The Owl House.

"Tell me Berkley, what's your latest book project."

"Oh, my dear Camilla, I have found myself stifled in a dreaded writer's block; my first time ever I must add. I am struggling to visualize a concept for a new novel. My creative juices are suffering terribly for whatever reason."

"Don't fret it. I'm sure it must be temporary."

"I certainly hope so. Neither my agent nor my publisher is happy with my floundering. They seek their greedy overreaching percentages. Blood from a turnip does not fly with them. Money talks. Everything else walks."

25

"Is there anything I can do?"

"Please inspire me Sweetness. Surely with your medical history you must have experienced something quite sensational or heart rendering."

"My life was boring in comparison to yours. Germs and viruses won't lure in your readers."

"I agree. You can only go to the well just so many times with zombies and apocalyptic sensationalism. Speaking of viruses, what is your spin on that Chinese virus that has halted flights from that horribly oppressive country?"

"Not sure. Our president seems to think it is of some significance. A political firestorm has certainly resulted from the actions he has taken. Most are opposed to his actions."

"Politics make me want to puke. Us against them, does it ever end? Talk about fiction; tune into the news and get your fill. Most journalists have crossed over into the fictitious genre. They no longer report the news, they peddle their opinions instead. Bias has never been more bias and them painting only their narrative has never been more important to them. Toss the truth out the window with the bathwater and do what is necessary to destroy a president that has no loyalty to any politicians on either side of the fence. Especially those swamp dwellers that have made careers out of deceiving those who keep putting them back in office. Well. That's my observation. I avoid those 24/7 news channels like the plague, especially UBN."

"Tell me how you really feel but I do agree. The United Broadcast Network is possibly the most liberal and biased of them. You may be passing up on some ideas for you next greatest novel. Communism and socialism creeping into the lives of those occupying the free world."

"Fake and Bake, now for the Rest of the Story, not a book title for me. Nope, I think I will seek inspiration elsewhere. I do not have the constitution, no pun implied, to digest what the media is serving. Covid-19…why haven't I ever heard of the other 18 Covids?"

"If you've seen one, you've seen them all, Berkley."

"So, you don't share our president's sentiment then?"

"I deal in data and I haven't seen the data to support the concern yet. I must confess. I haven't researched its validity. I've been out of that loop for a while."

"You were such an expert in the field. I find it difficult that the mere mention no longer interests you."

"Blissful retirement has its perks."

"Bravo," Berkley clapped his hands and then saluted her. "Has George not driven you completely batty yet?"

"George has done better than I could have ever envisioned. He thinks I'm not onto him, but I know he isn't playing as much golf as he would like me to believe. Every chance he gets he sneaks off to check in with Melvin Meeker. I just let on that I don't know."

"Oh dear. He is lying to you about it."

"I'm okay with that. It isn't easy weaning off something you have done all your life. Take me for example. Look how long I volunteered at clinics after I retired. It was my way of weaning off my profession. I get it and I don't hold that against George. Now, if he started hanging out there seven or eight hours a day I would step in and say something. He hasn't quite embraced retirement. It's a work in process."

"At least he's not doing something truly deceitful. Do you kids have any more epic adventures planned?'

27

"I would like to go to our beach condo for a couple of weeks, but George isn't too keen on the idea. He sees the condo as a rental investment, not a vacation luxury for us."

"What I wouldn't give for sun, sand, and the sea."

"Then go for it, Berkley. The ocean breezes and sound of waves might be just what you need to free you from the writer's block."

"I wish it were that easy."

"Brunch is on me my dear friend."

"Camilla, we do go back a ways, don't we? You have always been my rock and sounding board."

"And you have always offered me a shoulder when I need one."

"Peas in the proverbial pod we are. Next time it is on me."

"Go. Unlock the mysteries buried inside that brilliant mind. I could use a distraction. Give me something worthy of proofing for you."

"Deal. Tell that sneaky hubby hello for me. Twist his arm and bring him next time."

"Love you too, Berkley."

3

The president announced banding travel from and to other nations. This has upended the political applecart royally. His critics the media and the opposition party were launched into a feeding frenzy. It was tough telling a difference. Liberalism thrived over the airwaves from the newsrooms. The opposing party was in the middle of what some had dubbed a politic coup as they were ram-roding a partisan impeachment attempt. This had come on the heels of a nearly two-year accusation of Russian meddling in the election. Through it all the president remained as resilient as ever, unfazed by the roadblocks being tossed his way.

"What do you think now, C?"

"What do I think about what, George?'

"Is this virus the real deal? Shutting down travel from almost everywhere overseas seems a bit extreme for just one case of this alleged virus being reported here."

"Without seeing any concrete evidence of the dangers, I don't feel I can offer a reasonable opinion one way or the other."

"Come on, C. This was your wheelhouse…disease control and all. Surely you have a gut call concerning it."

"I'm not being recruited for my opinion, George. I'm sure the resident experts are on top of it and are advising the president the best course moving forward."

"I'd like to be a fly on the wall inside the White House to witness who is pushing our leader to make such outrageous calls. Shutting down air travel from communist China and now thgis some mighty big balls even for him."

"I must admit. It does seem a bit extreme when the evidence out there doesn't support it. Someone evidently knows something that the American public is not yet privy to, George."

"Scary stuff if you ask me. Why would he go this far? This is another example of why I don't trust government people as far as I can toss them. They never have our well being in mind for the most part. Too many hands are in too many pockets to suit me. They got into government as regular people and leave after 30 or 40 years as millionaires and billionaires. Tell me that there isn't something obviously corrupt about that picture. We need term limits for all of them. The president gets two shots. Why not the rest of them? And why does congress get the say so on when they deserve a raise and how much? Fox watching the hen house, I'm telling you. Retirement has ruined my way of thinking; too much time to watch all this junk on the television. And I am being polite calling it just crap."

"I love you, George. This just justifies why we need another vacation."

"Not that again."

"Your pick. I'm just saying it might be a refreshing escape from the political madness you've gotten yourself into."

"I can switch it off as easily as I switch it on. I am already over it. What's for dinner?"

"We're dining out; my pick."

'Fine, I'm ready for some Italian."

"That sounds like you are picking."

"Too obvious?"

"Rocco it is dear."

"Perfect."

The remainder of the evening progressed uneventful for the couple. It was exactly what had been needed to escape the political madness of the day. Unbeknownst to George and Camilla and the world, devastating troubled times were ahead. Some would call it historical. Others might refer to it as of biblical proportions. No denying it either way, it would be epic and plain terrifying.

A week later George dropped by Doctor Kyle Richardson's office for his six-month checkup. Richardson was a cardiologist and dear family friend. His wife Mildred worked as the reception for the private practice. She and Camilla visited while George was examined.

"How is George coping with retirement, Camilla?"

"You mean how am I coping with a retired George."

"Eloquently stated my dear. Care to expand."

"Not so eloquently I'm afraid but let's just say he remains in denial. I'm running shy on home projects to occupy his impatience. He finds excuses to slip off and visit Melvin Meeker and various construction sites. I pacify him by pretending I don't notice."
"It sounds as if you need a girl's retreat."

"That does sound like a wonderful suggestion."

Camilla and Mildred continued their chat while George completed his examination by Doc Richardson. So far, nothing alarming reared its ugly head. George's blood pressure and pulse were fine given his cardiovascular system. The doctor had found no irregularities. To say he was fit as a fiddle was the furthest from the truth though. Richardson informed him that he was doing as well as expected and left it at that. A new prescription for blood pressure meds was issued. The doctor had reminded him to always keep his nitroglycerin tablets on him just in case. And more exercise couldn't hurt as dropping a few extra pounds would benefit him as well. And just like that he and Camilla were on their way home.

Later that night, George remained glued to the news as an outbreak of the new mystery virus had been discovered on the west coast in an adult care facility. Three had died and a dozen others were infected. The president used this incident to support his decisions on the travel bands. The mainstream media and the opposing political party crucified the commander in chief over his comments, scoffing that he was blowing things out of proportion. Undaunted, he warned that this virus spreading from China should be taken seriously. He even indicated that he was forming a task force to address these concerns. Again, he was met with equal opposition, those opposing him painting the picture that he was a paranoid unfit leader. George didn't agree with their opinion but still couldn't wrap his brain around the proportionate concerns and banter. Camilla straddled the proverbial fence holding firm to her original statement, she had not seen any convincing data one way or the other. An infected nursing home in one city did not paint a picture for concern. As far as she was concerned, containment should be a cakewalk.

No warning bells were evident for most. America did not overact to viruses. The United States led the world in these matters. Technology prevailed. This was not the black plague of mid evil times. Still, this president continued to paint a different scenario. Banning international flights did seem to be a bit over the top, even for this presidency. Camilla's curiosity had been tested, but even she was not overly concerned. The world of politics can often distort almost anything. Unfortunately, the news media enjoyed fanning the flames if the fire could harm the president. Some things in life remained all too predictable.

4

News correspondent Paula Wise kicked off her nightly segment with word from China that the Covid-19 virus was wreaking havoc in the communist country. News was sketchy though. The communist regime controlled the news though especially if it could be perceived as negative or harmful to the country. Rumors persisted that this virus had become deadly, but outsiders had been banned from gaining direct access to developments. Foreign journalist had been all but kicked out of the country. Paula deemed this highly suspicious if there was no story to be had. It was a tough one to crack though. She briefly reported on the president's newly formed task force looking into the allegations that something of pandemic proportions were suspected. Other countries were not reacting with similar travel bans. China had not suspended any international travel. Something just wasn't adding up, thought Paula.

George switched to another channel after Paula Wise's segment. There was no mention of the so-called Coronavirus on that channel or any others he surfed. The top story on UBN had to do with hearings on foreign meddling and collusion in the presidential election. Congressional hearings were underway about an election that was over three years old. George perceived this as poppycock and waste of American tax money. His spin, if you do not like who is running the country or any office, just vote them out come election time. It really was not any more difficult than that. Politics, who needed it. He surfed channels until he located an old John Wayne western classic. Now, old Duke was one that could square things the good old fashion way. Kick butt and take no prisoners. Government needed more men like him running for office.

The phone rang. George almost let it go to voicemail but life of the retired could use any distraction, even some stranger trying to sell bogus goods. He enjoyed getting under the skin of those unsolicited callers, especially the ones wanting to extend his truck warranty. He pressed the button on his smartphone and readied for the pitch.

"Hey George. Just wanted to let you and Camilla know that we might have to pass on scrabble next week. Abigale is not doing too well right now. Doctor wants her to come in for tests."

"Sorry to hear, Pastor Moony. I will let Camilla know. Anything we can do?"

"Keep her in your prayers, George."

George ended the call thinking he sure hated to hear news like that. She had been going downhill for a while. Last time they had played scrabble she hadn't seemed too focused on the game. She had looked tired, and a bit spaced out, so George had told Camilla afterwards. Silly game, scrabble, thought George. He had allowed C to snooker him into playing, suggesting he needed an outlet after retirement, something to occupy his time. He didn't need anyone, including C, trying to run or ruin his life. He managed to do just fine filling his dance card on his own. If it weren't for his so-called bad ticker, he would be blissfully happy running his construction business. Falling into a bit of a pity pit, George cursed how his life had gone south. He was fit to still be running his business. It wasn't like he was doing any heavy lifting or anything close. C called what he did stressful. It was the furthest from being stressful. The doctor had sided with her. George had his suspicions though, the two in cahoots, a conspiracy indeed. John Wayne would not have quit and walked away. Real men persevered. Shaking his head, then what did this make him.

Golf, scrabble, vacations, who needed all these distractions? Retirement, worthless to a man not ready to be put out to pasture. He wasn't washed up by a long shot. Why had he given in to this without more of a fight? Double, no, triple teamed, C, the doctor and the kids had piled on. Playing the guilt card, saying he needed to be around for the grand chaps. Heck, they weren't even around, lived too far away. Besides, all of them were too young to play golf and scrabble. Who needed a vacation with the family at Disney World? Talk about stressful. Tourists of every nationality and the life wasting away standing in those long lines. All worthless for the sake of forced family fun. Bitter old man, George caught himself thinking. A bitter old, retired fool at that. Retirement was for old people, not him.

George couldn't stand it any longer. He scribbled a note to Camilla about Pastor Moony's call and then added that he was heading over to the driving range to hit some golf balls. This time it wasn't a little white lie. He felt compelled to take out his frustrations. Might as well be some of those stripped range balls. A lot of tension and frustration could be relieved in a bucket of balls. He hated golf but this wasn't really golf, whacking away at balls without worrying about a score or losing them. Plus, a drive in his truck seemed to be more what the doctor ordered. A man in his truck, cruising the highway had a way of clearing one's head. Might even have a little time to stop by the new construction site. What could that hurt, just eyeing the progress, and offering an opinion or two. Before he made good on his exit strategy, his cell rang again. Caller ID, the curse to end all curses. It was his son, Greg, incoming form Hawaii. He couldn't ignore that one.

"Hey Pop. What are you up to today?"

"Greg, you caught me on one of my slower days. How is big island life?"

"Always sunny and same old. I just wanted to check on the two of you. You know, with this Coronavirus and everything."

"Why would that concern you? I think it's just bogus communist propaganda myself. What says the military experts?"

"I'm not sure about bogus. Something is going on, but feedback and news is in short supply from our Chinese comrades. We take all threats seriously. It's the military way. Drop your guard and pay the piper. What does Mom have to say about it?"

"You know her. Deals in only the facts. She hasn't seen enough to support an honest opinion. Plus, she is happily retired."
"Like you, Pop."

"You said that, not me."

"Seriously, how are you feeling?'

"Fit enough to go hit a stupid bucket of golf balls."

"You hate golf."

"Finally, someone with a sensible perspective."

"Don't let Mom get to you. She is just looking out for your best interest."

"My best interest! Allowing me to do what I do best and…ah, never mind. Old news, lost arguments, blissfully enjoying my days in the pasture. Do I sound convincing?"

"No more than usual. Why don't you two plan a trip here?"

"Don't plant that seed in your mother's head. No ill intent meant, son, but she missed her calling. She should have been one of those trip planners. She thinks life is just one continual vacation now. If I'm too old to work, I'm equally too old to galivant all over hell and back. And if you tell her, I said that I will deny every word."

"Mums the word. I guess I'm wasting my breath then to convince you to take a few weeks and come here."

"Better idea. Why don't you get a leave or something and come here."

"I'll see what I can do. It's been a while, hasn't it?"

"You got it honestly."

"What do you mean, Pop?"

"Married to the army like I was always married to construction. When are you going to find a woman and settle down?"

"Don't start on me. You're sounding like Mom."

"Bite your tongue. I retract that last suggestion. Guess being in house confinement tends to wear a man down."

"Tell Mom I called and give her my love. Hit a few of those golf balls for me."

"Why? Do you hate golf too."
"That's why I want you to hit them instead of me. Think about what I said. You would love it here."

"And like I said, don't toss that suggestion to your mother if you wish to remain my son."

"Love you too, Pop."

George flopped back down in his easy chair. The notion to go to the driving range no longer interested him. Truth be known, it never had. He stared at the blank television screen for a minute before deciding to head to his workshop instead. There was nothing more relaxing than operating tools. Whether fabricating something metallic or wood, it brought out the man in a manly man. He engaged his press finishing a project he had started weeks ago. A slight twinge made him stop. He rubbed the left side of his chest and arm. It quickly subsided. Nothing but a mere spasm or something. Camilla might raise an eyebrow but what she didn't know couldn't harm him. The last thing he needed was her hovering about, watchful of his every move.

"Hawaii," he sighed. 'That's all I need right now."

It wasn't that George didn't miss Greg. He did like any father would with his son thousands of miles away. He just didn't need another long vacation right now. The president had already halted travel from almost everywhere. Who's to say he wouldn't ban it to and from the Hawaiian Islands too. Sure, it wasn't really international travel flying from New York to Hawaii per se but this virus thing might be ramping up everywhere according to recent news reports. News, he thought; who can believe anything they report? Suddenly he felt as if he was being watched. He disengaged the drill press and looked about.

"I didn't mean to disturb you dear. I was checking on you. Didn't know where you may have wandered off."

"Wandered off C! Makes it sound like I'm a dog or cat or something, forever wandering out of the yard and you having to heard me back home. I'm not a pet and I'm not a kid. And before you say anything, my ticker is doing just fine, and the doctor says I'm doing simply great."

"Sorry to step on your pride, George, but it is my job to worry about the man I dearly love."

"You need a hobby C, not me. Why don't you volunteer like you used to do?"

"Are you growing tired of having me around? I thought we had both retired and ready to enjoy life."

"Don't start. I'm not ready to go on another trip, not even Hawaii." He sorely regretted that little slip as soon as it happened. "Hawaii? Have you been thinking about visiting Greg? That would be a marvelous idea and simply wonderful treat, don't you think? We could surprise him."

Oh, it would be a surprise all right, he thought but dared not say it. "I didn't mention it for any particular reason. Just saying, I'm not ready to go there or anywhere else right now. You've seen all the travel ban restrictions. It's not a good time to fly anywhere with that virus looming."

"I have heard nothing about travel anywhere else. Hawaii is a state, not another country."

"Air travel is air travel. Takes a plane to get to and from there."

"Or a boat. We could take a cruise trip."

"But we would have to fly to the West Coast. What if the travel ban was extended while we were on the coast or worse, heading to or already in Hawaii? We could be stranded for who knows how long."

"Stranded in Hawaii doesn't sound so bad to me."

Stifle it, Edith, he wanted to say like old Archie Bunker to his wife, a character in one of his all-time favorite sitcoms, *All in the Family*. Now they didn't make them like that anymore. A world so focused on being politically correct would never condone a show like that now. What a waste. The world no longer had a sense of humor. This generation had become sensitive and fragile to every little thing. Anything said was picked apart and a person could be shunned and exiled if just one person was offended by it. George hated the world being destroyed by so few. It was like those in charge feared every little whinny weasel out there. The world, especially the United States had lost its backbone. You could hardly joke about anything now without hurting someone's feelings. He had heard the term 'snowflakes' used to reference those spineless fools; a generation worse than any he ever experienced in all his lifetime.

"George, I'm going to have Frances Farmer look into the options on Hawaii trips. She is an excellent planner."

"Research, plan all you want C. I'm not flying to Hawaii or anywhere right now, not until this virus panic has subsided."

"Since when did you all of sudden become so concerned about Covid-19? There were only a few cases on the other coast, and they were confined to one nursing home."

"Old people caught it. If you haven't noticed, we are old people too. Maybe it just goes after people like us."

"I've seen nothing to indicate that is factual. Diseases don't single out age groups, genders or races. A germ is a germ. A virus is a virus. Some people are susceptible to either. Immune systems vary."

"Sorry. Forgot. You are 'The Expert' in these matters, not me. I'm just a retired blue-collar grunt that watches way too much television. Still, count me out on any traveling right now. Been to Alaska. Don't need to check the Hawaii box right now."

"You're impossible, George."

Call it your mission impossible, he thought but didn't dare say. "If you don't mind, the old, retired coot has an important project he would like to complete while he still has his health and all his faculties."

"Dinner will be served in an hour. Piddle until then, dear. We're eating healthy tonight, salad and baked sweet potato."

"I didn't retire to eat healthy."

"The doctor suggested that you lose a few pounds. This meal will be excellent for both of us."

"Fine, have your way. A starving man is not a happy man."

"One hour."

George rolled his eyes thinking how she treated him like a little chap. Hopefully all the rhetoric about virus and travel bans would stymie her thoughts about Hawaii, airplanes, and cruise ships. He needed another vacation like he needed a hole in his head. Retirement wasn't cut out for those not ready for the pasture life. George was having regrets and second thoughts. Maybe he should consider a little part time work, two, maybe three times a week helping Melvin Meeker. Heck, Melvin didn't even have to pay him. He could tell Camilla that he was simply consulting, saying that Melvin had asked him for the favor. Yep. He would work it and make it happen and happen sooner than later before his sanity became more compromised.

5

The United Broadcast Network ran a segment during primetime hours about Senator Charles Paulson criticizing the president for the travel bans. In the interview, Senator Paulson framed the president as being a germaphobe, completely overreacting to Covid-19, adding that it was less evasive than the common flu. The United States was losing respect from its allies. He added that the president was overreaching and out of control, even questioning the leader's sanity. He painted the president as being unhinged and determined to cause a rift in the world and how other countries viewed the USA. Politics on the grandest stages, relentless and belligerent. The president had yet to address the accusations. Be warned though. He would in due time. His administration had been at odds with the opposing party and a handful of his own constituents as well. He was not a politician and didn't do things as predictable as career politicians are expected to react to situations. He owed no one any favors. He did what he professed to be the right thing to do for the American people, like it or not. This sent those threatened by his approach, including the mainstream news media, into a daily tailspin, no shortage of chest thumping and banter from either side.

Sadly, no one but the current administration seemed to be taking the virus threat seriously. The president was relying on feedback and guidance from a taskforce assembled of those highly respected in the medical field, specifically those specializing in infectious diseases. Still, the media and the opposing party played this up as paranoia and over reaction by the president, fear mongering propaganda. What did the president have to gain by spreading what they portrayed as lies about something perceived as no more harmful that the common flu? His approval rating was at an all-time high. This president had made good on most of his campaign promises. Those he had not been successful in completing had been blocked by those not wishing to see him succeed. There were those on both sides of the political aisle that feared and hated him. He didn't play by their rules and got things done; something the career swamp creatures had never accomplished.

Despite the critiquing by the naysayers, this new virus was beginning to show up in other cities, specifically the opposite coast. New York had begun seeing evidence of its arrival. Still, the president haters played it down, encouraging the people to live their lives normally and ignore all this foolishness. The mayor made it a point to be interviewed out and about around the city demonstrating just how safe it was. The Speaker of the House visited even Chinatown in her city, scoffing the legitimacy of the racial profiling of the so-called China Virus. He added that Chinese people were good people and would never unleash a wicked virus on the world. Germ warfare was something pushed by ruthless companies back in an era that no longer existed. Times had changed. No country played by those despicable rules UBN assured their viewers. It was an all-out assault on the president, whatever could be done to tarnish his imagine. As was his way, the president did not back down, held firm, waving off the critics that this was nothing to play around with. Still, the pushback continued; all lies spewing from a man not worthy for the office of the presidency. It had been this way since his inauguration. A nonpolitician was not supposed to occupy the White House. One thing for sure, try as they might, so far nothing tossed his way had stuck to the wall. Amor proofed, he had prevailed and stuck to his agenda, and he did it in an unorthodox manner, again riling those who opposed him.

This Covid-19 was on American soil, or at least in the air, no denying the fact. Reports coming out of the communist regime were sketchy and unreliable. The country's doctors had been banned from speaking publicly. Rumors circulated that some outspoken doctors had disappeared. Take that the way you want, said some reliable journalists. Speaking of journalist, foreign journalists had been booted out of the country. The president addressed this as suspicious, leaning toward some type of obvious coverup. Question, what was the communist government trying to hide and why? Scary stuff for those who honestly believed, but the media circus continued, chastising the administration, and pushing their narrative; fear mongering and racially motivated, just another way for this president to divide the country. There seemed to be no end to the rhetoric from either side politically. Sadly, this was not a time to play political cards so advised the president. Even those words were taken to mean he was making it political. Meanwhile, the coronavirus, an invisible enemy secured its foothold within American borders. Where would it end? Anyone's guess, for those willing to pose the question. Right now, few did.

Kitt Whitt, a young believer in democracy completed his podcast. He had a loyal following, those envisioning a free and prosperous America. Sometimes Kitt could be a bit over the top with his portrayal, but his heart was in the right place. Those opposing his views had labeled him Nitwit. Kitt dealt in data and facts to support his convictions while others spewed narratives not often backed by fact or data. They preferred a simple approach, repeat it often and sway the viewers and listeners by wearing them down, convinced that what they spread was indeed the gospel. Too many networks were using this playbook. It was Kitt's quest to debunk them by fact checking and producing data that contradicted their bias rhetoric. That required him expanding his audience though, tough so for an independent set on defeating the established bureaucracy.

"Hey Kitt, cool podcast today," commented his mentor and pal, Berkley Jay Patrick.

"I don't know, Berkley, sometimes I feel I am fighting a losing battle. There are more of them out there than me, the one-man gang."

"Come now. Your base has grown leaps and bounds. Think about it. Technology has allowed you to reach people that were unreachable years ago. Pod casts are indeed a unique format."

"And yet, you still won't give it a shot. You are an author. This would be a perfect tool for you to reach out to existing readers and connect with new ones."

"I'm too old school. I can barely text and tweet."

"I have offered to help you, remember."

"And I do appreciate your generous offer. Maybe some day I will have the gumption to take you up on it. Right now, is not that time."

"Does writer's block still have you in its grip?"

"Like a vice. My creative juices have become a dry riverbed. I have lost my way, short on inspiration for the next greatest novel. I compare it to any male confessing to his significant other that his failure to achieve an erection has never happened, the first-time honey; doesn't happen to me. I, too, am in denial about the inability to write for the very first time and I honestly mean it has never happened before," Berkley chuckled.

"Men are challenged to be the performers, so it seems. We fail and what happens is all our fault whether it really is or not. Blame comes easy. I say, why not use current events like what is happening in the political arena to freak free of that mental block?"

"Politics! Don't make me choke. I do not think I could stomach a political thriller. My dear friend, Camilla tried to convince me going there. I cannot wrap my brain around where to start such a manuscript."

"It's easy. Didn't you just listen to my podcast? Craziness is running wild. Conspiracy theories, attempts to overthrow the presidency, invasive viruses threatening us, fake news at its worse and politicians gone quite batty. It's all there. Plus, there is always the communism and socialism twist, Americans trying to reboot America in a way that will destroy it for sure."

"That's your wheelhouse, not mine."

"Piece of cake. I feed you the material. You develop the characters and spin the plot. And I get collaboration rights, maybe even co-author status. It would be another box checked in my young career, the revenge of the ultimate nerd."

Kitt certainly portrayed the perfect image of a nerd, huge round glasses, wiry red hair, a freckled boyish face, skinny physique, geeky

45

attire equipped with the trademark pocket protector. Yep. Nerdy as they come but he did not shy away from the stereotype. Instead, he used it to his advantage on his podcast, often making fun of himself saying nerdy was the new normal. He referred to it as his approach to being the ultimate chick magnet. He just had not convinced the chicks yet of his magnetic qualities. Well, at least not most of them. He remained as single as they get. He professed that there was no room in his life right now for romance. His podcast and dedication to this country were his equivalent of a loyal love life.

"Sounds intriguing, Kitt, but I don't know; it really isn't my genre."

"Your genre is fiction, thrillers to be more specific. Nothing is more fictitious than today's politics and with your unique touch added, your next greatest tale could be the perfect political thriller. Trust me. We can make it happen."

"No denying I could use the help, but…I don't know…sounds a little far fetched for me to concoct something that might interest my loyal readers from mere politics."

"Promise me you will think on it, Berkley. I think we could make it happen. Fiction based on fact blended with your personal touch, the perfect Berkley plot twist."

"I'll think about it, no promises though. You were really playing up that virus on today's show. Do you really think we should take it seriously?"

"Indeed, I do. This president takes it seriously. He doesn't need to fuel the fire for bad PR. The press already holds him accountable for every disaster manmade or God created. If he came up with a cure for the worst disease, the mainstream media would skew it, claiming he was trying to destroy the medical profession by eliminating patients and adversely impacting hospitals. They hate him that much. Time will paint the canvas I suppose. I prefer planning for the worst outcome and being thankful for the best. So, does he, Berkley."

"Mighty winded reply…a simple yes would have sufficed."

"Not my way. I must build the watch first. The time will follow. Tell your Camilla hello for me. Hope to meet this mystery woman of yours someday."

"Perhaps lunch when you can break away from your quest to save America from the evil doers. She would enjoy meeting you."

"Sounds intriguing. Might I remind you though, the downfall of this great nation will happen within, not from the likely suspects beyond our borders."

"You still don't buy the Russian conspiracy then?"

"Russia is minor league. Keep your eye on communist China."

"Thought you said the threat was coming from within."

"With the assistance of that sneaky regime. They control our supply chain and have bankrolled our government spending. They already own and control us. Toss in this Covid-19 and it might be the final nail. Some theorize the virus will devastate not only us but the world."

"Where do you come up with this stuff, Kitt?"

"Fact supported by hard data. We as a nation better wise up quickly. Just saying."

"Why do I always leave here in a stressful mood?"

"Look in the mirror my dear friend. Gloom and doom sells your goods, remember."

"Touché. Take care Kitt."

"See you on the other side, Berkley."

"I hate how you always say that."

"Just the facts, Dano. Or would you prefer my other favorite movie cliché…You can't handle the truth."

Berkley just smiled, knowing deep down that Kitt had nailed these situations more often than he had missed the mark. No denying it, thought Berkley, this virus had been dominating the news lately. The medical world was surely up for the task, combatting any virus tossed out, even something engineered in a foreign lab as Kitt seemed to think. Germ warfare, had it really been perfected this time? Time would tell he supposed. Spreading panic accomplished nothing. Being in denial could be equally as dangerous. Pitting good versus evil was always an element in his novels. In the end though, good always won over evil. Possibly it was time for a new Berkley twist, a novel where evil conquered all. Nope. Not a zombie apocalyptic adventures; those required survivors, heroes. What if even the hero didn't survive? Would his readers buy into total annihilation, a not so feel-good outcome? If so, he still required a catchy plot. Could Kitt be onto something, a political thriller with an unpredictable outcome? It had to be something completely different, something never attempted. Did he have it in him to deliver such a fictional novel? His creative juices were on the brink of flowing again. Any crack in the door was promising at this juncture. Berkley craved another lunch rendezvous with Camilla. She was after all his sounding board and she had posed a similar idea first. Political…the mere concept still concerned him. Could he pull off a convincing plot? To be determined.

6

Camilla had just gotten off the phone with her daughter Margie. She and her husband Louis lived in Vermont. She had received the latest update on the pending arrival of her first grandchild. Mimi, her granddaughter was five months away from bringing the child into the world. She and her husband resided in D.C. She had thus far endured a tough pregnancy having previously suffered two miscarriages. Supposedly, she was in no danger now but even the slightest pain sent her into a paranoid worry frenzy. So far, so good though. Camilla could hardly wait for the blessed event. She was already making plans to travel to D.C. to help once the baby arrived. That is if they were back from Hawaii in time, and that is if she convinced George to visit Greg. She couldn't be gone when Mimi had her baby, just that simple. Maybe the Hawaii trip was a push right now. Possibly she could play up the beach trip to their condo instead. Given a choice, surely George would prefer there instead. It was all in the presentation, she smiled, thinking this might just work.

She realized that George was suffering from a bit of melancholy right now, a setback to the forced retirement. She had done everything humanly possible to assist him in getting past it, but he missed work. He had been forced to leave and had not had the luxury of leaving on his terms, his timeframe. She had retired when she had chosen. She got it. Maybe her approach was the incorrect path. She shouldn't be trying to force the issue. After all, it was his to conquer and she should afford him the breathing room to overcome it his way. Her concern though, he might decide that retirement just wasn't for him and push for a return. If he did, what would she do? She had not forced him to retire. Kyle…Dr. Richardson had suggested it based on his heart situation. Sadly, even she realized, a man could die an equally horrible death from regret and feeling useless. Possibly he could work on a limited basis, short hours, part time even. She could not deny him the opportunity to be happy, even if it came with risks. Isn't life, any chosen path, a risk, she tried to convince herself.

She heard George meandering about in his shop. The sounds of his side grinder usually drove the neighbors bonkers. He promised them he would limit his use of the grinder to certain hours. The compromise had been agreed upon by all parties. This was George's primetime opportunity to utilize his man toy. She left well enough alone and allowed him to indulge without interruption. Camilla had the television on as nothing more than background noise as she prepped dinner in the kitchen. Dinner, she smiled, thinking how during her upbringing in Georgia this meal was called supper. She no longer resided in the south and gave into the local terminology. Dinner would be served promptly as always.

A news segment caught her ears, something about several large outbreaks of Covid detected in California and New York. The oddity as reported, cases on both coasts but nothing in between. The newsperson indicated that the president was blaming it on air travel, allowing the virus to travel great distances with contaminated passengers. Still, the word coming out of China and the medical authorities, this strain was not passed via person to person contact. Camilla wondered then how such outbreaks had occurred so suddenly. She suspected there was more to this virus than was being shared or there were yet too many unknowns. The segment ended after reporting a handful of deaths in that first infected assisted living facility. She pressed the remote's off button, escaping the daily depressing news. No feel-good stories were ever reported; only gloom and doom, tragic happenings made the cut in the daily programming. Bad sells. Good is ho-hum and drama less, harms the ratings. The world had lost scope of its priorities. Her cell rang. She almost allowed it to go to voice mail until she noticed George Jr. on the caller ID.

"George Jr. dear, what a pleasant surprise. Shouldn't you still be at work?"

"I am at work, Mother. Had just a few free minutes and thought I would check on you and Dad."

"We're fine as can be. How are Nara and those two sweet grandboys?"

"Everyone is doing great and I'm sure they would have sent their love if they had known I was calling."

"And how is everything in the peach state?"

"Not sure about the rest of the state, but life is always quite hectic in Atlanta and the burbs."

"I known you George, Jr. You don't ever call during a workday. Spit it out. What's really on your mind?"

"I can't pull anything over on you; never could. That's why I always got caught and my sneaky brother never did. Greg always had the perfect poker face."

"Odd, I can't see your face, but I can still read you like a book. Now, why did you really call, not that I'm not flattered."

"Not sure. I guess I was wondering if you were concerned about this new virus that allegedly originated in communist China? I heard that a few cases were reported in New York."

"Come now George Jr., why would you be fretting over a few cases of virus? Be honest. What's on your mind?"

"Okay, got me again. I have a friend in Hong Kong. She called me earlier saying we'd better be on alert. Sources there are telling her that this virus is ugly, much worse than has been reported. She claims that the outbreak and death toll being leaked is astronomical. She even referred to it as a pandemic. She thinks it is only going to get worse. The communist regime is hiding something, covering it up and keeping the world out of the loop."

"What makes your friend such an expert and so insightful?'

"She was a journalist and without explainable cause was kicked out of the epicenter supposedly where it started. She is convinced that this is much larger than anyone knows."

"Okay, but what does this have to do with your sudden urge to check up on us?"

"I saw where cases had popped up in New York."

"Less than a dozen. Those were in New York City. Dear, we are in upstate New York, remember. Rochester is over five hours from the Big Apple. Besides, a handful of cases does not equate to a pandemic."

"I know, Mother. You're the germ expert and these are not the days of the black plague. Maybe I overreacted a bit. Still, my friend seemed sincere in her concerns. She indicated that this had never happened, all foreign journalists being booted without viable explanation."

"She is a journalist. She is supposed to sensationalize the narrative and toss out as much wow factor as possible. They believe in bang for the bucks and out-scooping each other. That's what these news people do."

"Maybe so. But she didn't have to call me if that was her intend. What was there to gain by giving me a heads-up if she wanted to capitalize on the story."

"You know this person and her motives better than I do. I promise you. I will pay attention if indeed something worthy of concern occurs."

"That's just it. If it is a cover-up, you may never know."

"American is much different than China, dear. No one would hide a pandemic nor a plague in our country. Well, maybe a bias news media would if it offered a means to destroy our president."

"I didn't call you to discuss politics, Mother. From a medical perspective, please keep your eyes and ears attuned to what might be going on and be open minded to the premise she painted."

"I will. Please give Nara and the boys my love."

"Will do. Oh yeah, how is Dad doing with this retirement thing and how is he otherwise?"

"His retirement is still a challenge for both of us. Healthwise, other than losing a few pounds, Dr. Richardson gave him a clean bill of health during his most recent checkup."

"Love you. Give him my love too,"

Camilla stood in the kitchen, ringing her hands, something she did, a nervous habit. Covid-19 was becoming a common subject lately. It had reached a frenzy when the president issued the travel bans. That had been political and predictable though. No medical emergency should have been twisted as political. These were abnormal times. The current president had upended the political applecart. It seemed everyone was out to bring this administration down.

The sound of quietness meant that George was taking a break, calculating his next build, or was finished for the day. Camilla did not have to wait for that answer. Her hubby strolled through the backdoor and headed to the bathroom to wash up. She could keep pace with his location by his whistling a tune. Moments lately he plucked a bottle of water from the fridge and sat on one of the barstools.

"Did you finish your latest, greatest project?"

"Nope, my time had expired. I had to stop using the grinder. Got to keep these overly sensitive neighbors happy. You know how they get thinking I am operating noisy, heavy equipment. I need to take them to a construction site and introduce them to real heavy equipment. What has happened C? Everyone has become so fragile and combative. My business is their business and all they care about is ruining it for me. I stay out of theirs. Why can't they stay out of mine?"

"I was going to ask you how your day was going but I see I can skip over that. George, Jr. called earlier. He said to give you his love."

"In the middle of the day, a working day…what's wrong?"

"Nothing really. He was just concerned."

"Concerned about what?"

"It's this Covid-19. He saw where cases had been detected in New York."

"Why should that concern him? It hasn't concerned you. It's just a virus, right? Like any other virus, right? Well, that's according to the news and which channels you watch. The president seems to think differently but what do I know. I am just an old, retired shmuck doing the best he can to not annoy the neighborhood while attempting to blissfully enjoy my life."

"One of his friends living in Hong Kong painted this grim picture of an epidemic outbreak in China. She seemed to think it was severe and was being covered up."

"What makes her so knowledgeable about the situation?"

"She is a journalist. She told George, Jr. that all foreign correspondents had been ordered to leave the country, the immediate area where this outbreak supposedly was happening."
"Makes sense, don't you think? That's why this president got the jump on things. He must have had reliable sources, an inside track to what was really happening. That's what got him elected, putting the American people first for a change. So, what did Junior say we were supposed to do about this?"

"He didn't say. He just wanted us to remain careful and alert, just in case it worsens."

"And what do you think now, given the new information?"

"A few cases on the west coast and few in New York does not make this a pandemic or warrant reason to panic."

"I didn't mean that we should go into panic mode. It just seems a bit odd that at every turn we are hearing more and more about this germ."

"Virus, George, not germ; there is a difference."

"Sorry C, I build stuff. I don't deal with the boogeymen that can't been seen. I know that was a little over the top, but you know what I mean. If you are not worried, then I am not worried."

"Let's just wait until actual data indicates this is something significant. Besides, what can you or I do either way??

"Like I said, you are the expert on these matters, retired or not. What's for dinner?"

'Your favorite, baked lasagna."

"Perfect."

Camilla shrugged off the notion to worry with nothing evident to be sounding the alarm. Sure, Covid-19 was a new strain but how could it be any worse, any deadlier than any other? There just was not sufficient information to support making any assumptions. She knew full well though that the entire story was not being told. She had worked on the front lines in this world and had firsthand exposure to how it developed, what was shared and what wasn't. Maybe, she thought, it was time to call an old friend still employed by the agency to get his take on it. Not that she was overly concerned, just more curious currently. She would keep that to herself right now though. Her cell rang and she recognized the caller of course.

"Berkley."

"Hope I didn't catch you at a bad time, Sweetness."

"Not at all."

"Check your social calendar and see if you can pencil me in for lunch this week. My treat his time."

"Tomorrow if that works for you."

"What about The Orange Glory Café on East Main at 11:30?"

"That will be fine. Why do I detect a bit of urgency in your voice, Berkley? Are you all right?"

"Oh, I'm simply marvelous. I just need to pick your brain a bit. You are my sounding board after all."

"Writer's block gone?"

"Maybe. Depends on how our lunch chat goes. See you tomorrow and thanks for meeting me on short notice. Tell George hi. And for the record I am not slighting him by not asking him to join us this time. I just need a little one on one."

"I'm sure this will free him up to sneak off and check in on his partner in crime, Melvin Meeker. George is probably itching for an excuse to get his construction itch scratched."

"You are such a wonderful and caring wife. George is a lucky gent indeed."

"Save your flattery. I have already said I would meet you."

"Later then, Sweetness."

7

Unlikely friends, Senator Charles Paulson, a liberal, and Senator Aaron Breeze, a conservative, were breaking bread for lunch at their favorite spot, Pete's diner in Washington. Most politicians saved their theatrics for when they were in front of the camera or when rallying their base. Charles nor Aaron were not ones that preferred the spotlight. They were more intent on solving issues. This alone separated them from the pack. Both were considered good Joes as far as politicians go but this created a double-sided sword for both. Neither was considered beneficial when a critical vote was in play, especially if neither agreed with the bill being presented. It still didn't deter their conviction to stick with what they believed and what their supporters wanted. Trying to sway them otherwise just for the party vote was a waste of time. Most got it. Those that did not tried to make their lives on Capitol Hill a living hell.

"Are you voting for your party's bill today, the one tossing more money to the post office?'

"You know how I feel about it, Aaron. The government never had any business getting involved in the postal service. Let's face it. Government couldn't effectively manage a one lane toll booth between New York and Jersey."

"Got that right, Chuck. We've been in Washington, what, a decade, and have we seen the budget balanced a single time?"

"I have found myself too frequently lately asking why I chose to go into politics in the first place."

"Chuck, what we do now is not politics as politics were meant to be. Very few even try to work together. And most certainly are not looking to serve the needs of the people who put them there. There are too many egos here to suit me, egos looking to fatten their bank accounts. I have said it and will say it again, we need term limits."

"Right, and how do you suppose to pull that off? We consolidate our vote, take care of the people that put us here. These career leeches would never pass something that destroyed their livelihood. It's just a s bad on both sides."

"I'm thinking about opting out at the end of my term. I just cannot take this anymore. I am being lumped into the pile with all the rest even when my record says different. Our approval rating is at an all time low and if it gets any lower, we will be in negative numbers. My life is worth more than that."

'Funny you mention that Aaron. I have been leaning that way as well. I think I'm ready to try it in the private sector. I was even going to ask if you might consider us opening up a law firm."

"Surprised to hear you ready to toss in the towel. I do like the sound of a partnership but that would require one of us to relocate. You live in California and my home is in Florida. My wife and kids would never move to California. Mine might consider a Florida move if we were to live on the beach. It would be a tough sell though considering we currently live twenty minutes from the Pacific. Pipe dreams, maybe just a bad idea after all. Guess I value our friendship and will miss it when we do go our separate ways."

"Same here, buddy. Changing subjects, what is your read on the coronavirus?"

"Your president seems to take it seriously."

"My president?"

"Hell, I didn't vote for him. Be honest. Not many of the swamp critters like him. He makes everyone look bad."

"He is trying to do the right thing for the country."

"I guess I can't deny that, but I will never admit it beyond this table. And if ever you say I said it, our friendship is history, at least in front of my party members."

"I wasn't trying to bring the politics to our lunch table, Chuck. But seriously, what is your read on what we have been hearing?"

"Seems to be some credence to what has been leaking out of China. Scary if it is true, I reckon. Sounds like our communist pals are in a bit of a struggle if the facts pan out. I don't know that much about viruses."

"It is on our soil now according to reports. New York and your home state, along with Oregon have cases. There have been a few deaths as well."

"I'm sure it isn't something our medical experts can't contain. Your president might have had a knee jerk reaction with the travel bans though."

"Now you sound like the old guard establishment. The president would not have reacted as such if someone wasn't bending his ear. What would he have to gain by going out on that limb?"

"Makes good fuel for the fire in an election year. At least for my side so it seems."

"I hope for all of us that this has just been blown out of proportion."

"Sounds to me you are not sure, Aaron. Hope you're not going to be a Chicken Little, the sky is falling, the sky is falling."

"You know me better than that. I just weigh on the side of caution. At least the experts are saying no person to person spreading. That will make it much easier to contain in the worst-case scenario."

"Worst case, what are you envisioning, The Walking Dead?"

"I do love that series but no, I'm not painting a portrait of gloom and doom, end of the world as we know it. Forget it. Lunch is on me today."

"Very generous. It was your turn anyway. Restore that game face. We have to be convincing when we return to the floor."

"Yes sir. You should practice some vile cursing and ranting then, what your side does best."

"And you try not to push my grandma over the cliff today. Fighting words when you harm family."

Both laughed even if it really was no laughing matter. Concerns about the virus remained, even if neither was willing to admit their true feelings about it. Time would be the judge. No need to panic just yet. A few cases popping up here and there didn't equate to an outbreak. That is, unless you bought into the rumors of what might be happening in China. Indisputable evidence did not currently exist. Yet, the president seemed to be reacting differently. Most chalked it up to him always acting unpredictably and nothing more. Still, what did he have to gain? He surely was in jeopardy of losing a lot more if he was wrong. Lines in the sand remained drawn. Such was politics.

8

George could not believe that Camilla had given him a pass on joining her and Berkley for brunch. Usually, she unmercifully hounded him to accompany her. Maybe she had finally given up hope for his persistent pigheaded ways. It wasn't like he had anything against Berkley. He was a nice enough chap, but their conversation wasn't his cup of tea. Too cultural for his taste. Sure, the guy was quite the writer and had made a living from it to support his lifestyle, but with his background in construction there where as it opted few openings for enjoyable conversation. The man had soft hands a bit to womanly. No, George was not the judgmental type and he certainly didn't look down on anyone for their chosen lifestyles. He was just a genuine observer, good at reading people, and uncomfortable in situations outside his normal element. He would describe himself as a floundering fish out of water in those scenarios.

Why look a gift horse in the mouth. C had insisted that he visit Mooney today. Any other time he would have been cutting cartwheels if ever he could, but today he experienced a bit of apprehension and suspicion. No, he was not jealous or suspicious of their little rendezvous. Cheaters do not divulge their intent and Berkley didn't intimidate him from that perspective. It just seemed odd, C overly nudging him to do what she usually frond on him doing. Maybe she had come to accept that being around construction, even as a retiree, put him in a happier mood. What the heck? He was at the site now. May as well enjoy the fellowship and real man discussions. Tools and heavy equipment couldn't be beat. The smell of oily exhaust fumes and sounds of the earth movers were welcome to his senses.

Melvin Meeker wasn't on site. Ken Wolf was the site foreman. Ken was a good kid, proven and worthy of a shot. He wasn't a big guy, but he was a man's man, smart and ambitious. George liked that he was a square shooter and not the cocky know it all type. Ken didn't hesitate to ask questions or to seek advice. He would not risk failure by pretending to know something he didn't know. Ken stepped out of the construction trailer, plans tucked under his arm, tool belt around his waist with his ear glued to his cell phone. George could tell by his demeaner that he was not a happy camper. George bided his time until he saw Ken end the call. He then strolled over to where he stood with his back to him.

"Ken, I should probably have given you a call instead of just dropping by like this. I see you must have your hands full, understandably so. This is a huge contract and outstanding opportunity. Meeker and I were bidding heavily for it before I retired."

"Mr. Railsback, long time no see. No apologizes please. You are not intruding. You are welcome anytime. I think I owe you my gratitude. Melvin only gave me the opportunity to prove myself because of the good word you had given."

"Son. You proved yourself long ago. It was time that this company made good on rewarding someone of your stature. I'm proud as a new papa seeing you out here reveling in what I so sorely miss."
"Yes sir. We miss your presence as well. Are you considering coming out of retirement and joining in again?"

"Nothing would make me happier, Ken. But no. Once you decide, you got to stick with it no matter the consequences. Camilla and old Dr. Reynolds would pitch a double hissy fit if ever I even suggested un-retiring myself. The ticker would always be in question. Those two would double team me and make my life miserable asking if I felt okay. The Spanish Inquisition would have nothing on what they would put me through. Not my style. I can't live my life being under constant scrutiny about my health. What had you so rattled on that phone call earlier? Is there anything I can do to help?"

"Thank you sir, but I don't think so. It seems some investors are thinking about pulling out of the project."

"Pulling out of the project my ass. This complex is a no brainer, a sure thing if any ever were. Did they give a reason?"

"Not in so many words. It seems they think the bottom is about to fall out of this business. Frankly, sir, I see no signs to indicate it. What about you?"

"Same here. Construction and the housing market have been booming. I see no let up."

"A buddy told me lately that the construction company where he is employed has been hinting something similar."

"Did he say why?"

"Kind of sketchy. He seems to think it has something to do with this new virus. Beats me though. How can a germ impact us? Maybe it's like swine flu or something; people getting antsy that workforce sickness might slow things down. Not something I can wrap my head around. Might as well ignore it, right, sir?"

"I have been half ass following this Covid-19, and like you, I can not make heads or tails if we should take it seriously or not. I had the flu a couple years ago and except when I was running high fever for a day or so, I never missed a day of work. Camilla had advised that I stay home and away from folks back then to keep from spreading it. She is retired but was an expert on germs in her day."

"You're a lucky man, having someone under roof that can give you sound medical advice."

"Yes and no, I'll just leave it at that. What are the projections for completing the project? Are you on target?"

"Not far off. Rain last month did cost us almost a week. The storm was a brutal one."

"Always factor in a little wiggle room. Not saying that you didn't, just saying it is an unwritten law."

"We did just that. Mr. Meeker insisted."

George smiled. Smart kid. Can't trip him up. He didn't need a virus outbreak though to impact availability of workers. Not my problem. Been there too many times. Wrong side of the fence is never fun. Ken granted him a nickel tour of the site. George breathed in every sight and sound, a mixture of regret and envy ensued.

****

Seated at the Orange Glory Café on East Main, Berkley and Camilla had just placed their order. He had caught her up to speed on his latest endeavors. It had not taken long, mostly small talk between old friends. Berkley eventually got around to his real reason for inviting her. He laid out what had transpired between him and his friend Kitt.

"Conspiracy theories, some attempting to overthrow the presidency, an invasive virus knocking on our door, fake news and politicians gone plummeting over the edge. I agree, it is a compelling plot, Berkley"

"Don't leave out the push to communism and socialism, twisted anti-Americans trying to remake American in a way that will destroy it as we know it. Lot to take in and I am not convinced I can pull off a convincing plot."

"It would be different from your norm for sure and there must be a willing and ready reading audience for it. Humor me though. Isn't it taboo for an author to cross genres once his loyal following has been established?"

"It can often be. You know me, I am no risk taker. I make it a habit to remain within my comfort zone. Give me your honest opinion. Should I or shouldn't I?"

"I have no doubt that you can do anything you set your mind to do."

"I hear a but, don't I."

"Not exactly."

64

"Then spit out this 'not exactly.'

"One suggestion, why not outline it, maybe even write a few pages and then assess how you feel about the work."

"Intriguing, I did not see that one coming."

"What could it cost you, a little time? By trying something different, maybe it would cure your writer's block."

An alert chimed on Berkley's cell. He retrieved the phone from his pocket and glanced at the content. "News alert," he informed his brunch partner. "Seems there have been more outbreaks of this mystery virus. Most noticeably here, New York and Jersey. Others reported in Michigan and L.A. They are calling it a spike. Appears to be a few more related deaths. The president is planning a press conference at five this afternoon. Hope he doesn't ban the subway next. Covid-19 seems to be the new buzz word, latest disease flavor."

"New strain, I'm sure the experts have their eyes on the ball and are advising the president appropriately. Is that all?"

"Seems so. Brings me back to something Kitt said, 'Current events can sometimes captivate the public.' That is why he suggested that I capitalize on it, the information there for the taking. Add a little fictional twist and compelling characters and *Voilà*, his words, not mine."

"Interesting concept, allowing the news to set the tone and possibly paint your narrative. George already believes the news being reported is fictional. At least when it comes to the president or anyone associated with his administration."

"Can not say I blame him. I have bent your ear a time or two on how I see it. Politics…yuck…double yuck…cannot envision Berkley Jay Patrick, renown black author penning such poppycock."

"I always find it amusing that you refer to yourself as black instead of African-American."

"Why so difficult, Sweetness? I have never stepped foot in Africa. Born and raised on this soil makes me simply an American. Too many in the black community suffer from identity insecurities. Making a crisis out of being called this and that is simply too silly. There are so few truly genuine Africans now living in American, statistically speaking of course. Playing this color or race card is quite boring. It would be like you now wanting to be called beige or tan, being offended by someone referring to you as white. Defining people as a color or race is just the epitone of divisiveness. It holds as much substance as this preposterous slave and slave owner argument. Look around you. Have you ever known anyone who was a genuine slave or slave owner?"

"Are you going to profile that argument in your book? That is if you venture down that path?"

"I should forget this notion, don't you agree? A political thriller is just not my genre of choice. I think I would prefer permanent writer's block rather than ponder this ugly notion."

"Berkley, I say do what makes you happy and bury this conversation. I don't cherish becoming your therapist."

"And I would never burden you in such a fashion, Sweetness. I write because I embrace it. When it is no longer an enjoyable experience, I shall cast it aside and seek fulfillment elsewhere. Those wishing their percentage of my efforts might see it differently. I am a slave to my work I suppose, and they own me, confine me to the plantation. How is that for the sake of the argument?"

"Only you could perfect such a unique analogy, Berkley."

"Just wait. Might just belt out a verse of *Swing Low, Sweet Chariot*."

"You are impossible. That's why I love you so. Never a dull moment."

"Love you back. You fill an otherwise huge void in my ho-hum life. Black holes and black hearts need a little loving too. Should we splurge on some shamefully delicious desert? I'm all in for an abundance of sugar and countless calories."

"While that does sound scrumptious, I think I will have to pass this time and be on my way."

"Saving me from temptation once again. You are my alter ego and conscious combined. Very well. Indulgence cancelled. Maybe next time I will be successful in wearing you down for the greater cause."

"And that greater cause would be you, correct?"

"Can you think of any other worthier cause?"

Camilla just shook her head. Berkley stood and she gave him a parting hug and peck on the cheek. He bowed and then escorted her to the door, her arm looped in his. He did the gentlemanly thing and opened the door for her and walked her to her car before heading to his. Their relationship was indeed a special friendship. Neither would hesitate to do for the other without question or need for an explanation if a precarious situation existed. They had leaned on each other countless times, offering an ear or a shoulder as needed. Unforeseen or unpredicted circumstances ahead might forever test and impact their unique bond. That would entail another chapter in their lives and possibly send the world into uncharted waters. Unfolding events held uncertainty in its wake.

9

Weeks later…

Cases of this new virus had exploded, especially in New York, New Jersey, and California. The outbreak called for more extreme measures, an attempt to contain what was now being portrayed as a pandemic. Transmission theories continued to be conflicting, further muddying the waters. China had originally claimed Covid-19 was not spread by person-to-person contact. The medical hierarchy had supported and communicated this premise to the world. Now there appeared to be back peddling evident in this original assumption. Which was it? Person to person transmission potentially made this a new ballgame. Medical experts, bending the president's ear, were suggesting extreme measures to prevent the virus from getting completely out of control

The president had been mocked by the opposing political party and the mainstream media when he halted air travel from China and then later Europe. With a presidential bid at stake merely nine months away, his opponent took every opportunity to discredit him for reelection by calling him a germophobic, overreacting to a situation less threatening than the common flu. Mayors and governors mocked the president, challenging his handling of the virus, saying everyone should stay calm and live their lives normally. The Speaker of the House ensured his constituents that this president was feeding on their fears. To make his point he visited the local China Town, staging a video photo opt with hordes of people, beckoning tourists and locals to visit the sights the city had to offer. All was safe. The virus was not a threat to anyone.

"What do you think about this coronavirus now, C? I know, you don't have access to the data. Still, what do you think given what they are saying. I use the term 'they' loosely."

"Our president does appear to be concerned. Someone is convincing him that the danger is factual."

"Yeah, it is an election year and he is hoping for four more years. I don't see him as the type to muck up his chances by going out on a limb if he didn't believe there was something to this virus. Do you?"

"Previous administrations did not go to such extremes in similar situations. HIV, influenza, Cholera, nor Ebola prompted serious actions to be taken."

"Election year makes those politicians go crazy. Puts them in a feeding frenzy if they sense opportunities to discredit or upstage the other side. Maybe this is just another example of rhetoric and chest thumping. The economy is at its all time best and employment at its all time low for this president to jeopardize it all over a silly bug, right?"

"You have been watching too much television, George."

"Retirement! I must fill in the gaps by doing something. You know me, C. I am not a political hawk. But it is tough to ignore the sensationalism. Plus, one has to do one's homework to make sure one votes for the best candidate."

"Come now, your mind has been made up for nearly four years. I think we both know who your candidate is. Same one you voted for last time, correct?"

"Well, yes, but Americans are supposed to keep an open mind and be tuned into what one versus the other has to offer."

"Whatever you say, dear."

George wandered out to his shop in search of therapeutic intervention. While interested, possibly if a bit concerned, he was not the type to panic over anything, especially over something he could not control. It was best to leave it to the experts he finally convinced himself. Stick to being a craftsman. Camilla had wanted some birdhouses. While the thought of constructing birdhouses did not exactly prompt his creative juices, doing so would be a welcome distraction. His design would not be the common variety that could be purchased at a big box store. His would be unique, a George signature brand. First, he must ponder what that might resemble. He reached for his sketch pad. He thought about a sport's logo design, but he quickly dismissed the idea. This was for Camilla. It must be something she liked. Sports related would not do it. Suddenly, it clicked. He had it, the perfect birdhouse envisioned. He began sketching his masterpiece.

Once he completed the sketch, a trip to Home Depot would be next to purchase what he needed. Selfishly, this would pose and even better distraction. He could easily become lost in the aisles, killing more time, and quenching the boredom of what was supposed to be retirement bliss. He stopped in the house long enough to share his project plans with C. She eyed him suspiciously, but he had grown accustomed to that look. He smiled and kissed her on the cheek as Elvis exited the building. A birdhouse, why hadn't he thought of this before, he smiled. Plus, he would pass near one of the construction sites and might as well drop by for a little visit on his way. A perfect day indeed. Thank goodness for my feathered friends and their need for apartment complexes he whispered. A miniature construction business will have to suffice.

Camilla sipped a cup of herbal tea, caught in a web of ponder. The alleged pandemic did seem odd and out of the norm. Research as a virologist and epidemiologist had been her life. Not a braggart but colleagues had said she was one of the best in both fields. Her retirement had been discouraged by the leaders of the Global Virus Center lobbying what an enormous void would be left in her departure. Sure, she had regrets and had almost been persuaded to remain a few years more, but she had sensed it was the right time for her to step away. Long hours and tiring workloads had taken a toll on her. The GVN had offered to work with her, allowing as much paid time off as she required, if she would remain. In the end, she had to go with what George calls gut instinct and stick to her plan.

Her decision had been swayed by a center transformation. New leadership had an even newer envision of the center's role and a direction that did not inspire her. Lobbyist had deep pockets and were influencing studies and their outcomes, too much so to suit her.

The data never lies, but there was those that were insistent in skewing the data if it adversely impacted their agenda. Politics and monetary gain had invaded science and science was losing its credibility. Her integrity and credibility could not be bought by bureaucratic billionaires.

She had bucked the system so many times she was not sure why they were so persistent in getting her to stay. One thought had crept into her head. Just maybe they feared she would expose the growing corruption and by keeping her fat, happy, and paid well, it offered an insurance policy. These types practiced ownership, enslaving those under their rule. Hush money even in the form of substantial raises and highly paid incentives guaranteed loyalty to some extent. Once they had sunk their claws into you, there was no turning back or exposing the corruption. You were part of the corruption, bought and paid for.

A higher and more ethical road, she should have exposed the corruption and had given that avenue serious consideration. A colleague had talked her out of it, pointing to what had happened to another colleague who had attempted just that. The doctor had been ruined financially and his reputation had been destroyed. It had been achieved with such precision that no one believed his accusations. The man had lost everything, even his family. His wife had divorced him, the result of an alleged affair that never happened. The other woman had been quite convincing, paid handsomely for her lies. The poor guy had committed suicide as a result. Camilla could do as all the others did, stand by silently as it happened. Out gunned, there was no winning if others didn't band together to fight the injustices. Fear is a powerful deterrent. Camilla reluctantly remained quiet and simply walked away. Her colleagues that remained must battle the demons as they saw fit. Years had passed and wounds had healed. She no longer had the stomach to dig up old bones for any greater cause. She had not succumbed to the corruption but turning a blind eye had haunted her.

Until this moment, she had not ventured back down that sordid path. Now, she wondered. So many people despised this president that she doubted there was nothing they would attempt to ruin him and his

71

presidency. Was there a real pandemic or was it politically motivated? This Covid-19 was certainly a new strand, but had it originated in the communist regime of China as the president had claimed. Nothing was out of the realm, China, or something homegrown, the jury was out. She regretted having these thoughts. Maybe there was a remote possibility that the GVC had cleaned up its act. Doubtful but one could hope. Camilla sipped her tea and tried to shake the dark clouds invading her mind. This was not her war, no longer her battle to wager. Who was she kidding? She had never confronted it. She had simply washed her hands and walked away allowing the chips to fall where they may. Cowardice she whispered. Let it go. She was certainly not in any position to take on the bureaucracy, tossing tiny stones from the comfort of retirement. Besides, she lacked any evidence. Without data to support her convictions it didn't exist, no matter how much she knew it did.

Camilla shifted her thoughts to Berkley. If she shared what she suspected from her time with the center, he could spin it into a best seller for sure. She would have to remain an anonymous source if she even dared. Tentacles of corruption can reach long distances. She enjoyed her life too much to chance rocking that boat. If his fictious tale remotely mimicked the truth the bloodhounds would surely be unleashed. With the means and the money backing them they would turn over every stone until they found the guilty party. Nope. She had washed her hands. The time to have dirtied them would have been when she was an insider. Then she could have excavated the data to support her accusations. Even then, too risky. One must pick the battles if one is willing to risk it all to fight. That criteria did not exist. The risk was not worth any reward. She had George and her kids to consider. A failed attempt would most likely ruin it for everybody. Her family deserved better, even when doing the right thing might be at stake. Water had passed under that bridge long ago. "Leave it be gal."

George had pulled into an open parking spot within walking distance of the construction site. He had spotted Melvin Meeker's truck when he passed by the site. He hoped this did not mean something was wrong. Why would it he tried to assure himself. Melvin was like him, a concerned soul, one always wishing to show his crews that he was supportive of their endeavors. After all, Melvin had learned that trait from the best, him. All things considered, this construction project was indeed a biggie. It was the type of job that could make or break a reputation. Not that he was overly concerned that Melvin was not up for the task. He was and always had been a perfectionist. That is why he was George's righthand pick. Melvin Meeker, a class act, nothing slouchy or half-ass about him. George could not have been prouder if Melvin had been his son.

George had slipped on his hardhat, always keeping it in his truck just in case. There wasn't any security on this site which was a bit unusual for a job this large. He strolled inside the gate eying the perimeter as he did. Observation, there was not nearly enough activity for this time of day. He eventually spotted Melvin, jackhammering of all things. It didn't surprise him. Melvin certainly knew how to operate one, but it did seem odd, him being the owner of the construction business now. George cupped his hands and gave out a shout. Too noisy, and with Melvin wearing protective ear wear he could not hear him. He closed the few short yards and placed his hand on the back of Melvin's shoulder. He glanced back and spotted him, nodding as he laid the jackhammer aside and removed his googles.

"George, pleasant surprise. Hope you are here to lend a helping hand."

George let out a little chuckle and then answered, "Don't tempt me. What gives? You miss the everyday grind too?"

"Not hardly. Shorthanded. Real shorthanded."

"Not a worker's strike, I hope. Haven't heard any union rumblings lately."

"No. Nothing like that but more than half my crew have called in sick this week. Odd. So many coming down with flu or something like it all at once. I suppose one or two might have passed it on to others but peculiar and quite sudden."

73

"Yeah. Can't recall that ever happening on my watch before."

"Good people too. Reliable. This was not orchestrated as best I can tell. All of them are too sick to work."

"You don't suppose it's this coronavirus, do you?"

"Did cross my mind. The news is abuzz with it. I just chalked it up to a scam like most stuff they tend to broadcast. Maybe not."

"I don't mind rolling up my sleeves. Point me to where you need help."

"Thanks George. Not that I would not appreciate that, but Camilla would have my balls if I did. You know as well as I how she feels about it. What brings you out this way?"

"Picking up some wood for a birdhouse project. See how low I have sunk. Me, constructing bird condominiums. You know I must be bored out of my mind. Now, this is a real man's dream. I'm here. You might as well let me help."

"Your lovely wife might be a bit suspicious you being gone too long and then showing up a tad too dirty for a lumber run, don't you think?"

"You make a compelling argument, I hate to say. Don't you have any men to spare from another site?"

"Short on the only other job I have going on right now. Forman was one of them."

"Now that's where I could help, foreman. I think Camilla would understand if I told her I was helping you like that in tough times."

"Your call but I'm not jumping in the middle of it. A woman pissed off is not a pretty sight."

"I cannot catch a break, so it seems. I do hate leaving you like this, Mel. Maybe I can call in a few favors then and round you up a few warm bodies."

"That would be great, George."

"Done. After this Home Depot run, I will look through my contact list and see what I can do. You look a little pale, Mel and couldn't help but notice that persistent hacking cough. Are you feeling okay?"

"Fine, just sinus congestion. Jackhammer stirs it up. Plus, it has been a while since I have done any heavy lifting."

"The men don't need to see their boss go down in flames. I will call you if I have any bites. Take care of yourself, Mel," said George shaking his friend's hand a second time.

Melvin leaned against a front loader after George left. He wiped heavy perspiration from his face and neck. He felt a bit flushed and the day was crisp and cool. He didn't need to come down with anything right now and he did not have time to drop by the doctor. Suck it up he told himself. That's what leaders do. Lead by example. The series of convulsive coughs made for a compelling argument.

George had picked up what he needed for the birdhouse project, but he could not shake Melvin Meeker from his thoughts. Being that shorthanded could push him into a corner quickly. It was up to him to round up some help, even if only temporarily. Something else bothered him. Mel didn't look well. George hoped he wasn't coming down with the same bug that had struck his men. If need be, he would buck Camilla, make a compelling argument that Mel needed his help. Surely, she would see it his way. This was on the brink of an emergency. Even she should understand the severity of such a situation. George rehearsed his sales pitch out loud. The birdhouses might have to be put on hold. The birds would certainly understand. He hoped C would be as understanding. He pulled into the drive. Man-up time had arrived.

10

A couple weeks had passed since George had stopped by Melvin's construction site. Melvin had become dreadfully ill. He had been diagnosed with Covid-19 as had much of his crew. So many that the two crews had to be combined to one site. Camilla had conceded. She and George had met a compromise. George was helping two days a week but was under no circumstances to work the site. He was delegated to foreman. George reluctantly stuck to his part of the bargain. He had rounded up a few helping hands to fill the void left by those still too ill to work.

One of Melvin's crew had died. No word yet if it was the virus or some other cause. Dead was dead anyway you looked at it. Pete Allison was nearly sixty, a bit overweight and had type 2 diabetes. George had known Pete for fifteen years. He had always been a workhorse. Until now, George couldn't remember a time that old Pete had ever missed any work. Always dependable. His death had come as a shock. Melvin was in the hospital still. This virus was royally kicking his butt. Seemed that there were plenty of people coming down with it. Stories about the Covid-19 tended to change daily. Now the so-called experts were saying person to person might be a possibility.

****

Erwin Shipley Pod Cast...

"Well, brace yourselves folks. Cases and deaths are increasing at alarming rates. Covid-19 is being referred to as our invisible enemy by the current administration. Conflicting scenarios are being framed as to just how this virus originated. Communist China may have misled the world professing that it was no big deal, something easily contained and controlled. Information is always sketchy from the China propaganda machine. My sources are saying this did not originate in a Chinese wet market. It possibly escaped from a high-tech lab. There have even been suggestions that it might have been intentionally unleashed on a small community. Now why would the Chinese government do something to its own people? Simple. Test study. Determine how the virus performs in the population. Germ warfare communist style. It would not be the first time a communist regime has used its people as guinea pigs. Nazi Germany comes to mind.

Person to person contact makes this a whole new ballgame according to the medical experts. New York is being hit hard as are a few other large cities. The president has formed a medical task force to examine the data and share any recommendations. A task force, really? There are those accusing the president of fear mongering tactics. I say, why would he use these tactics when he is riding high on the best economy and lowest employment rate in history. We are ten months from the election. Sorry, the political pundits are way off base this time. I would expect this from the opposition but the president.

Guess we will find out this afternoon. The president has a news conference scheduled for five to discuss this coronavirus. What some are calling a pandemic in the making. Most people have no clue what a pandemic is. Why should they? The last one occurred in 1918, a much different time without the technology that exists today. The H1N1 influenza, the Spanish Flu as it was called, supposedly infected 500 million people, one third of the world's population. An estimated 50 million people died. Hard to wrap you head around numbers like that. It was even odder how the disease impacted certain age groups. Mortality was particularly high in children five and under, adults over 65 and oddly those in the 20 to 40-year range. There was no vaccine to thwart it or antibiotics to treat it. Best that could e done back then was through isolation, quarantine, promoting good hygiene, using disinfectants, and ultimately limiting public gatherings. And yet, 50 million people still loss their lives. Sounds to me these were all for naught. Guess you must try anything when you have nothing to combat it.

If that happened today, we would be better prepared. Our society could never be subjected to mandatory isolation, quarantines or prohibited from public gatherings. It would never be accepted. Luckily, the technology exists in our world to combat such viruses. The debate continues if the president should have halted air travel from China and even more so from Europe. Again, the president had nothing to gain taking such evasive actions. Leading the polls while doing something like that is unforgiving some say. Oh well, suppose we will hear what Paul Harvey would say, 'the rest of the story' during the president's news conference this afternoon. Until then, this is Erwin Shipley calling the balls and strikes as we head intra innings. Tune in tomorrow when I will be joined on my pod cast by a special guest."

Kitt Whitt always listened to Shipley's pod cast. The rogue journalist was a virtual political genius. Launching his podcast had been quite successful, reaching more viewership that when he was part of a nightly news segment for ten minutes here and there. He had built a loyal following, a no bull, tell it like it is, warrior. With the fall of the discredited news media of today it was refreshing to hear something different than the same orchestrated narrative, 95% negative against the president. Kitt could only hope to someday follow in Erwin Shipley's footsteps and spread the truth and nothing but the truth in his own pod cast. He wasn't there yet though; only in the dream stages but ambitions would be fulfilled.

Kitt commanded Alexa to call his friend Berkley.

"Kitt, I heard. Shipley is always ahead of the eight ball."

"Yeah. Figured you were tuned in. What do you think the president will have to say about this pandemic?"

"Epidemic, pandemic, another fabricated political witch hunt, who knows? Guess it is getting a bit concerning if the facts are factual this time. Plenty of cases are being identified. No denying it, this Covid-19 is dominating the networks. Every channel seems to work from the same script, use the same buzz words. I find it difficult to differentiate one from the other. I have been tempted to just ignore them all and just watch nostalgic flicks instead."

"Who do you suppose his guest will be tomorrow?"

"I can rule out a famed bestselling author."

"Pen something politically controversial and you can punch your ticket my friend."

"Why does everyone persist that I toss my hat into that disgusting arena, even if from a fictitious perspective? I have writer's block. I'm not that desperate."

"Forgot to tell you. Do you remember Guy Wheaten, an old college buddy of mine? You met him once at one of your book signings."

"Vaguely, name sounds familiar. Why?"

"Got sick last week, deathly sick. Ended up in the hospital over in Queens. I was going to drop by and check on him, but they were allowing no visitors. Couple days later I called his sister to see how he was doing; he died. He was only 43, healthy as can be other than high blood pressure. Meds had stabilized that though. I asked his sister what happened. She said that they blamed his death on the coronavirus. He had been on a ventilator. Blink of an eye and he is gone."

"Sorry for your loss, Kitt. Anything I can do?"

"No, thanks though. Do you think this virus is something we should worry about?"

"People die everyday from this and that. The common flu is just as deadly if not treated. We are born and then we die. It is the cycle of all living things. Worried. Not me. Death knocks at our door sooner or later; sooner than later for some. I just wish they had a cure for this darn writer's block. Every time I think I'm on the brink of a breakthrough, my old brain shuts down yet again. I always thought it was mere myth until it struck me."

"Due time, Berkley. You will break out with another best seller; I have no doubt. Guess I should let you go for now. Stop thinking about it and maybe the old thinker will kick start into something fabulous."

"One can only aspire, Kitt. Loves and kisses my friend."

****

"George, you aren't over doing it now are you?"

"C, I'm doing exactly what we agreed I would do; help out Melvin a couple days a week until he is back on his feet and able to return to work."

"How is Melvin?"

"Not good. This virus is kicking his butt. Says he has never had anything like it before. They will not even allow him to have visitors. He has been quarantined on a wing with others afflicted by it. What do you make of that, C?"

"It is not uncommon for infectious diseases. A friend at the GVC told me that they now think this could be highly contagious spread person to person. If so, it changes everything, including how it must be handled."

"Might hold some water. It has surely taken its toll on Melvin and his crews. One death and plenty of sick people."

"That concerns me, George, you being in contact with potentially infected persons."

"Now C. Look at me. I am fine."

"George, do you even know the symptoms of Covid-19?"

"Okay, if it will dismiss your worrying ways, let's go through the check list."

"Very well. Any fever or chills?"

"None."

"Cough?"

"Have you heard me coughing?"

"Noted. Shortness of breath?"

"Not unless my fat ass is attempting to outrun a bear or I am making wild passionate love to my wife."

"Me and a bear, how romantic? Fatigue?"

"Fit as a fiddle."

"Anybody or muscle aches?"

"I'm old, C, everything aches."

"Headaches?"

"Not from a hard head like me."

"How are your senses of smell and taste?'

"I can smell dinner in the oven, and I bet it taste scrumptious as always."

"Sore throat, congestion, runny nose?"

"Not even a sniffle."

"Nausea, vomiting, diarrhea?"

"Constitution of a bottom feeder, no upchucking from this guy and I am regular as the time of day and no more. Do I need to perform any tricks like a circus pony or to ensure I am not impaired to operate heavy equipment?"

"You aren't operating heavy equipment on the construction site are you, George?"

"Just figuratively speaking, my dear. Do I pass with flying colors?"

"If you were honest with me, yes."

"I never lie to you, C. Well, nothing big anyway."

"How much longer do you think Melvin will be hospitalized?"

George shrugged. "I heard on the radio that the president was having a big news conference this afternoon to talk about the virus. Let's plan to eat in the sunroom so we can watch."

"If you wish."

11

The president declared Covid-19 a national emergency. It had been recommended by the task force after consulting the nation's governors that a shutdown was imminent to prevent the spread of the deadly virus. Deaths were skyrocketing as the cases exploded. New York continued to be hit hardest. Rather than mandate a one size containment fits all, the governors were given the leeway to decide what actions were required after guidelines and recommendations were offered by the task force. The nation was reeling with these recommendations by their governors, mayors, and city leaders.

In most states school had been halted. Restaurants were ordered closed. All sports were impacted. Gathering in crowds larger than ten had been deemed as dangerous. Broadway came to a standstill in NYC, plays disallowed. Movie theaters, entertainment venues, casinos were all considered taboo. A fine line in the sand was being drawn between what was essential and what wasn't essential. Hair salons, gyms, even public parks were causalities. Amendment lines were being crossed when churches were warned to shutter their doors while liquor stores remained open. America in the 21st century in shutdown, impossible. How could government order this and furthermore enforce it? Would American stand for such silliness and invasion in their private lives?

The medical experts stood by their recommendations asking that everyone do their part and basically self quarantine for a couple of weeks. Social distancing guidelines were suggested. Death and doom were prophesied, spreading fear nationwide. A pandemic alert was issued. This couldn't be happening in America thought most. Even crazier it was happening worldwide. Comparisons to 1918 surfaced, deaths to millions a possibility. No cure, no vaccine, highly contagious and spread person to person were game changers. Grocery stores remained open, but panic prevailed. Soon there were shortages of toilet paper, paper towels, hand sanitizers and disinfectants. Hoarders prevailed. The world had gone mad in a blink.

Camilla returned from a grocery run. She shook her head profusely astonished by the empty shelves.

"George, we may have to ration bathroom tissue and paper towels. I visited three grocery stores and the local Walmart and there is none to be found anywhere."

"Why in the world, of all things, would people buy up all the toilet paper. Is nothing sacred anymore? Food I get, but toilet paper."

"Defies logic, I agree but the shelves don't lie. It was quite an unpleasant experience I might add. People shoving, arguing, worse than any Black Friday frenzy. The world has gone mad with this shutdown."

"C, it has only been a week. How can society collapse in just a week? And to make matters worse, we had to shut down the construction sites. I get it. It's supposed to just be for a couple of weeks but seems a bit extreme to me expecting everybody to just stop what they are accustomed to doing. Sacrifices to get this under control is what the experts are suggesting. My butt. Those telling us what to do are not doing it themselves. The rich and famous don't live by the rules they toss at us."

"Be patient. Two weeks will not hurt anyone. Life then returns to normal."

"You believe that C. Government just wants to control the herd. They always have."

"The president supports the recommendations of his task force."

"I like the president, but it doesn't make what we are doing the right thing to be doing. You are the expert. What do you think now?"

"Cases do seem to be on the rise as are deaths."

"In New York City. Rochester is over five hours from the Big Apple. Surely they can cut us a break."

"What is your friend saying at the Center? Is it real or concocted?"

"Mums the word. Not hearing much lately."

"Don't you find that rather peculiar. He has never been shy about dishing the dirt."

"I'm sure everything is ultra-sensitive with the situation lately. Leakers aren't tolerated, especially in such extraordinary circumstances."

"I heard on the radio that the president is holding a task force update meeting later. Guess we will here it directly from the horse's mouth. No filters from the news media and no false narratives. I liked it better back in the good old days when Cronkite gave it to us straight. Huntley and Brinkley reported it like it happened and we decided if we agreed or not with those doing whatever they were doing or saying. I don't need a bunch of pollical bias hacks pretending to be commentators telling me what I am supposed to think, and who I am supposed to like. I sure by damn don't need them telling me who I am supposed to vote for."

"Take a breath, George. No need you getting all worked up over it."

"Riled is more like it, C. The world has overdosed on crazy pills."

"I agree. We are tested regularly. If we hold onto our faith and pray God will protect us in our times of need. I will say this for our president; he does not exclude God when he speaks. Christians have a warrior in the White House, the likes no one has ever seen in our lifetime."

"Can't argue with that and it drives the opponents wacky. They have worked hard to remove the Almighty from every aspect of our lives. Funny though. The naysayers don't mind spending money that has In God We Trust printed on the bills. Same worthless pieces of..."

"George!"

"Ungrateful socialists burn our flag and attack innocent law-abiding people. Worse, they treat the military, especially the Vets, like crap. I served eight years in the army and it makes me sick to my stomach how these thankless bastards think."

"Do you act like this on the site? I hope not. You always say lead by example."

"Sorry. And no, we keep politics shelved at work. Got people on both sides of the fence on that crew and the last thing we need is them locking horns on these matters. They don't play nice about stuff like this."

"I will be glad when Melvin is back so we can happily retire you again."

"What? So, I can go back to building bird condos. Let a man enjoy life a little, C. Being there gets my juices flowing. Being put out to pasture isn't what it's cracked up to be, especially when the old bull still had a little life left in him. I feel alive again. Damn ticker is doing fine. Maybe we overreacting when Doc Richardson suggested I throw in the towel for my own good. My own good feels right spry and healthy as can be. Just when things were looking up, they go and mandate this two week hide and seek game from a virus."

"Two weeks might be all Melvin needs to get back on his feet."

"And then I am…"

"George, I want you to be happy. We agreed to you helping a couple days a week and I'll stick to that decision."

"Why don't you consider a little part time help?"

"I did that for a while. I am over my stint now. I am content enjoying my life with you. I look forward to us traveling to new places and experiencing what life has to offer."

There she goes again, thought George. Vacation planning to the ends of the earth. A man needs more. I need more. I am a worker. I make a terrible old, retired person. My butt doesn't sit well in a rocking chair. Medicare and social security are for old people. I don't feel old. Might look it but I certainly don't feel it. Richardson says my heart is the problem. Well, my heart is in construction. Flows through my veins. I cannot help it. My father worked until he was nearly 90 and he died a happy man. Everyone deserves to die happy. If I were old and decrepit, maybe suffering from Alzheimer's or something, then it would be different. I feel fine. It should be my decision, not Richardson's.

George ended the silent discussion and justification with himself and decided no need going there with his beloved wife. He would never win that argument with her. He was retired and the business, his business, now belonged to Melvin Meeker, end of story. Two weeks. Two wasted weeks. Two weeks he could have being running the show now down the drain. And, for what? A virus of all things. Shutting down the country for two weeks over a virus made absolutely no sense. What were they thinking? Had to be politics. Why did so many hate a president so much? The man had kept his promises, unheard of in the political arena. Maybe that's why they hated him so. He did not play politics. Republicans and Democrats and every version of politician in between were intimidated by his tenacity and record of getting things done when the career swamp rats never had. It was a compelling testimony for sure, a non-politician doing what traditional politicians had not achieved, and not because they couldn't; instead, because they had not tried. Job security hinged on the fact that chaos and unsolved issues reigned.

Later that afternoon, George, and Camilla, like millions of Americans, sat in front of their televisions listening to the grim picture the president was painting. Medical experts on his task force spewed data and statistics on the emergence of Covid-19 and its potential spread. Cases and death tolls were expected to rise exponentially. The proposed two weeks did not sound as if it would be enough time to suppress the invisible enemy. Experts were calling for an extension, maybe as much as a month. Even then the prognosis sounded grim. Worldwide, the virus unleashed by China, as the president framed it, was wreaking holly havoc on the world's population. Pandemic was indeed the new buzzword. Social distancing, washing one's hands and staying home, shut in as much as possible appeared to be the proposed defense mechanism for this cureless virus. Not much was making any sense to most, but the seed of fear had certainly been planted.

12

Senators Charles Paulson and Aaron Breeze sat in the diner, having just finished lunch. Still firmly on opposite sides of the aisle, they sipped their coffee while, as always, candidly sharing their thoughts. The obvious topic, the coronavirus remained center stage. Four and half weeks into the shutdown, the once prosperous economy had crashed. The lockdown was ravishing the nation. The United Broadcast Network, like many of the major networks, were now tracking the Covid-19 tallies on the screen for the viewing audience. Projected on a chart were the number of cases and deaths for the world and for the United States. The numbers were staggering for both. If ever the mainstream media wished to panic the public over the pandemic, it was working like an imposed occult curse.

"I despise how the networks are posting cases and death rates. Your party seems to embrace this fear mongering rhetoric."

"Sadly, whatever can be done to discredit the president, Aaron. I don't support it but what can I say?"

"You could say what you feel and support us for a change, Chuck."

"No denying it. It is wrong but you know how the game is played."

"This is not a game. This is serious business and no time to play politics. You know it. I know it. Those cheering on this just to divide the country and hurt this president is wrong on every level. Stand with me, Chuck. Do the right thing. This is clearly a nonpartisan issue."

"You know I want to, Aaron, but I would be crucified, devoured by my own."

"That statement alone makes for the perfect argument it is the right thing to do. Wishing the worst for our country and its people cannot be trumped by the necessity to play politics. We were elected to protect the people no matter which side of the aisle we are on. Who knows, you might instigate a movement for your constituents?"

"No doubt, I would instigate something. More likely the end of my political future. You have witnessed firsthand just how far my side is willing to go to take down this president. I have never seen anything that compares to it."

"You could always leave the dark side and convert to mine."

"Sorry old pal. I'm not there yet but try not to hold it against me."

"The voters make those decisions, not me. This shutdown is hurting everyone. They suggested two weeks and now there seems to be no end to it."

"Your president and his team of experts instigated this shut down. My party was firmly against it."

"Your party takes the opposite stance on everything he does. It is so predictable. The shutdown was an aggressive maneuver, I agree, but doing absolutely nothing might have worsened the situation. We are stuck now with the hand that has been dealt."

"My wife reminds me every day. She cannot fathom why we have a sudden shortage of bathroom tissue and paper towels. I can offer no sensible explanation or reasonable solution."

"Hope you are not blaming the president and the republicans."

"I would if I thought it would fly," laughed Senator Charles Paulson. "Unfortunately, my wife doesn't agree with everything my party does. She supports me and the party policies in public but at home we are somewhat divided."

"Communist China is to blame but I don't hear anyone from your party supporting that premise, only blaming the president."

"Not my narrative. I believe like you that they could have prevented the spread if only they would have made a full disclosure to the world instead of hiding it. I know I haven't vocalized my concerns on the floor. Sorry, Senator Breeze, you know how the game is played. Both sides play it well."

"Do you think it was intentional?"

"Wouldn't surprise me given how Your President has tossed all these tariffs at them."

"My President has balls. He is not shy about stating fact. China has been stealing our technology shamelessly for decades and no one had held them accountable. They do not respect any ownership of intellectual property. Don't get me started on job losses to them."

"So much for a leisurely and nonpolitical lunch. Guess it supports just how badly divided we have become as a country."

"Sorry. Guess I do take it seriously and personally."

"And you think I don't. Face it, Aaron, you and I cannot wave a magic wand and wish this away. It is much more complicated and too deeply seeded for our young asses to challenge the Washington establishment. We are out gunned by both sides. The old guard is in charge. There are too few of us yet to challenge them with our newfangled ideas and cures for what is destroying this great country."

"See. You are already sounding like a republican."

"I am just practical like you. Party has nothing to do with it."

"Well, guess we need to make our way back to the hill and climb into our opposing trenches for another fun packed day of accomplishing absolutely nothing beneficial for the American people."

"Remember. You said that, not me."

"In character already, nice going."

"And I despise it as much as you do, my friend."

Political lines drawn; the two senators returned to their thankless roles. The approval rating for congress was at an all-time low, barely into double digits. The downward death spiral of the economy and the mandated shutdown would adversely impact that meager percentage. Panic had reached feverish levels within the world. Medical experts were pushing for a second month. The president was doing his best to project a more positive tone and quicker return to normalcy. Death rates continued to climb despite the task force stating that flattening the curve was crucial. More controversies complicated an already too complicated situation.

****

"What is it, C? Wear a mask or not. Can't they make up their mind? The experts told us that wearing one would serve no purpose. Now they are saying everyone should wear a mask."

"Puzzling, I admit. I cannot fathom transmission person to person can be prevented by merely wearing facial covering and social distancing. It cannot be this simple."

"Like I have been saying, keep the flock in check. Or I should I say, too many Americans are just a bunch of blind sheep."

"Honestly, George, this pandemic is becoming more concerning each passing day."

"Why, because you are cooped up here with me, your fellow shut in? It is like the ultimate retirement plan. No frills, no company, no social life. Heck, since they declared us as the most likely to catch it, we are a like the black plague. Everyone is keeping their distance, our kids and grandkids specifically."

"I miss them too. Age and preexisting conditions are the mantra. We both meet the age threshold, and your heart makes you more vulnerable."

"Adds a new meaning to old and worthless, doesn't it? You always profess that the numbers never lie. Show me the data, right? People are dropping like flies according to those tasked with tracking them. Turn on any news channel. Staring you in the face like they are tracking donations for a telethon. Now if that doesn't boost your morale…"

"I agree. A little over the top to be doing that."

"More scare tactics to humble the flocks and herds. I hate this strategy, C. Read between the lines people. Big brother is doing what he set out to do, control every aspect of our lives. They are telling us to stay home. Don't go to church. Don't go to school. Don't be social at all. Where are we going to be social besides the grocery stores? They have boarded up the movie theaters, bowling allies and stopped sports, even for kids. Kids need to rip and romp. They need to be outside, at parks, tossing footballs, playing baseball and soccer, shooting hoops. Unamerican has arrived loud and clear, C. You want a taste of socialism or communism. Look around you. It is here. Our first sampling if ever anyone wanted to taste the Kool-Aid."

Camilla just nodded. She feared far worse ramifications given what she knew about the world in which she had worked her entire career. Something smelled rotten. Her gut, as George might call it, was on high alert. She could not support it with opposition data but no denying the feeling, an underbelly of corruption existed, and it was morphing, becoming stronger, more dominant, and was being utilized for all the wrong reasons. Her friend at the center remaining neutral when asked spoke volumes. This was bigger than even he feared and cared to admit. That or he had been bought off like so many. Enough hush money can often corrupt even those thinking they stood on high and moral ground. She had sadly witnessed it firsthand. No mask and now wear one was but the tip of this ugly iceberg she feared. What could she do? A mere minnow will only be taken and swallowed in such a large sea. She was in no position to challenge anyone, now a member of the civilian herd. Follow the rules, the mandates or else. George had been correct in his analogy. Her cell ringing broke her from her trance. Caller ID indicated it was George Jr. in Atlanta.

"Hey Honey."

"Hi Mom, just checking in to see how you and Dad were coping."

"We are fine. Your dad is stir-crazy as always. It's Junior, George, just checking up on us."

"Ask him if he has any toilet paper he can spare?"

"I heard him, Mom. Foraging here in Atlanta too. Crazy how it disappears off the shelves as quickly as it is restocked. Why toilet paper? I get hording food when the world is in panic mode, but toilet paper. Nara has been freaking out over that and not being able to find any paper towels and sanitizers. Oh yeah, just try to convince the boys to wear masks when we do venture into the real world. Seriously tough Mom, why is Covid-19 doing such a number on us?"

"I don't know dear. I have been out of that loop for quite some time. A new strain, possibly something created in a lab and not intended to be released to the public."

"Or maybe intentionally unleashed is what some think. I talked with Greg the other day. Without just saying it, I could tell he thinks it might be a military in origin, the communists trying to catch us off guard. I would not put it pass them. Nukes are not the answer so why not try something like this."

"You sound like your father. He is into all kinds of conspiracy theories. Too much time on his hands."

"Yeah. Thank him for the birdhouses. The boys loved them. Birds are not under house arrest, so we plan to get them put up this weekend. It will occupy the boys for a few minutes I suppose."

"Sorry we can't keep them here with us for a while."

"Maybe once this is over, we can plan a visit."

"Sounds marvelous, Junior. Give Nara and the boys hugs from both of us and tell them we love them and miss them."

"Will do Mom. Please tell Dad no more birdhouse right now."

"Not to worry, he just shipped three to Greg in Hawaii. The next ones are destined for Vermont."

"Mom, doesn't he know that Margie and Louis live in an apartment? Where are they going to use birdhouses? Never mind."

"Exactly."

"Stay safe. Love you."

"Love you too."

"Did Junior get the birdhouses yet?"

"He did and thanks you for them. The boys loved them."

"Toilet paper would have made a wonderful gesture. UPS is still considered essential to our livelihood."

"Thoughtful indeed if they had any to spare. Perhaps we should chance a trip to Costco tomorrow."

"I'm for anything that gets us out of this cellblock. Sick and tired of semi-solitary confinement."

Next they ventured to the big box store and almost immediately regretted the decision. Bedlam and total chaos greeted them. Shopping carts wheeled about like rush hour on Interstate 390. Shoppers frantically searched for the 'hard to find' items, toilet tissue, paper towels and anything sanitizer related. No common sense prevailed. It was worse than Black Friday and Christmas Eve shopping combined. George tired of the battle and stressful bickering among the members with self-imposed overreach privileges. They exited early from the unpleasant experience, opting to visit a local grocery store instead. The experience did not improve. More chaos and empty shelves of the treasured items were the common theme. Out of options after two more stops, they headed home.

"This is crazy, C. You would think we were in a third world country. I have never witnessed so much panic on the faces of so many people. Does toilet paper miraculously fend against catching the virus? What am I missing?"

Camilla could offer no reasonable response. She remained quiet allowing her husband to vent and hopefully get it out of his system. Concerned. Yes, she was genuinely concerned with the unraveling of America taking place. A pandemic and shortage of specific essential items was most troubling. Making a logical correlation between the two was confounding her even more. What could she do about either? Retired, she could not help where she could contribute the most. Covid-19 had arrived with a vengeance. People were dying. The medical community had thusly offered no sound defense against the virus. Wear masks, socially distance and gather in crowds no larger than ten. Stay home. Avoid people other than those within the immediate household. Suggestions only. No vaccine nor therapeutics were being mentioned short term.

The drive home was eerier, fewer vehicles than imaginable were on the roadways. People were taking the confinement to heart or were simply too terrified to venture out. Even scarier, most businesses were closed, especially the mom and pop establishments. How much longer would this madness last she wondered. People were not designed to live in this manner. Camilla feared what this might do to those already mentally impaired. Her heart ached for the children; a school year cut short. If the schools did not reopen what would become of the beloved proms and graduations? No answers or solutions were being offered by those in charge of making the tough calls.

George pulled into their driveway and then abruptly announced, "We cannot live like this, C. I say we take one of those vacations. You pick. I don't care. We can go to the beach condo, visit some of the kids, or just drive until we see something worth stopping."

"George, no denying it, I would love nothing more to do than just that, but…"

"But what?"

"Wherever we would go would just be more of the same. This is not restricted to Rochester or to New York. What is happening here is happening everywhere. Experts are suggesting the opposite. We are in the at-risk category. As much as I miss our children and grandchildren, it would be ill advised for us to be around them."

"Do you have data to support your decision?"

"This is no time for sarcasm, George. This is not a joking matter, far from it. Do I agree with everything being imposed? Certainly not, but I have no evidence to dispute these actions. I always err on the side of caution. The world is reacting the same to the Covid and the consequences. If it weren't real and weren't a serious concern, this would not be happening. I do fear that a pandemic could be in play, but I have faith in science to derive a viable solution. This is not the Middle Ages, and this is not the Black Plague. It is not the 1900's and the influenza pandemic. We are better prepared."

"Better? This thing has brought us to our knees and quickly if you have noticed. Modern technology and no toilet paper seem a bit too serious to me. If that isn't an eyeopener I don't know what is."

"George, please exercise patience. We will get through this and life of normalcy will return."

"I'll remind you of that when we are completely out of toilet paper. By the way, that will not be long. Better contemplate a backup strategy if this thing turns any uglier."

"Help me unload the groceries, Dear."

"Better cut back on food consumption. That's the only strategy I have for offsetting the TP shortage. Constipation has never been more welcome in this household."

Camilla just rolled her eyes and sighed. Inside though, her worries continued.

13

Mid-June…pandemic still raging over three months later…

Camilla stood shell shocked from the news after ending the phone call. Her heart ached for Pastor Moony. Abigail, his wife, had just died. She had been struggling for quite some time, but Camilla had not expected this. The pastor had not provided details, only saying she had passed this morning. She and George had not seen the couple since the pandemic had basically quarantined everyone and had closed the church. Poor Abigail had suffered from dementia and along with age had landed her in the higher risk category. Not wishing to jump to conclusions, she dared not speculate on the cause. George was in his shop. She ventured there to break the news to him.

"More birdhouses?"

"Not exactly. New design. I call this my bird condo combo. It is for nesting and it also has a feeder accessory. Boredom has inspired me to be more creative before I go completely Looney Tunes. Don't look at me like that, C."

"I am not looking at you in disbelief. Sit down, George. I have some dreadful news."

"It's not the kids or grandkids I hope."

"No. There a fine as far as I know. Roy just called. Abigail passed last night."

"Abigail! What happened? How did she die?"

"Roy didn't say. We have known she has been on the decline. Her dementia had worsened, and she had other complications, even long before this pandemic began."

"What can we do for him?"

"Maybe you should give him a call. Funerals are not being allowed right now, considered a high risk for gatherings."

"World gone crazy when you can't even take time to bury the dead. Isn't anything sacred anymore? I cannot imagine what poor Roy is feeling."

"Roy's faith is strong. I'm sure he has suspected this as a possibility given her numerous health issues."

"No. Nothing prepares you for something like this. I cannot fathom a world without you, C. It would be unbearable. You are my rock. I probably don't tell you that nearly enough."

"I love you too, George," she said leaning over and kissing him. "We are not promised another precious second in this world. Guess it is easy to take life for granted. We are all guilty of it. We are the lucky ones. We are grounded and even if unspoken, we know how we feel toward each other. You are my rock as well."

"I wonder if this virus did her in. Damn Covid is taking its toll. People are dropping like flies according to the posted numbers. New York is being hit worse than anywhere else in this country."

"Again, Roy didn't say, and I did not feel comfortable asking."

"Old people are being hit the worst it seems, especially in those nursing homes, and more so in New York. Numbers are skyrocketing. I am so glad we are not in one of those assisted living facilities. Damn shame too. They are not even allowing family to visit those folks, sick or not. This is America and yet everything being forced on us is so Unamerican. We are not a third world country for heaven's sake."

"Times are indeed troubling. I do like your creation by the way. You are quite the innovator, George."

"Birds might see it differently. Uninvited guests feasting too close to their living quarters might not be preferable. If nothing else, it might make an interesting ornamental or conversation piece. Maybe the grandkids would like it."

Camilla just rolled her eyes, hopeful that he would not ship it to any of them. Most importantly, it kept George busy. A healthy mind was half the battle in these challenging times. She thought about poor Abigail, having just turned 80 and unable to celebrate her birthday among friends or family. Roy was 80 as well, placing him in the higher risk category too. She said a special prayer for him and their family. She hoped George would follow up and give him a call later.

Doctor Kyle Richardson had been the Mooney's physician as well. Roy had called him when it happened. Richardson was old school and still made house calls when appropriate, especially if his patients were unable to visit the office. Richardson and his wife Mildred attended Roy Moony's church. It saddened him to see Abigail die so tragically. Death seemed to occur regularly lately. Still, some circumstances tend to impact you worse than others. Abigail's had certainly fit that scenario. Pronouncing one dead never got any easier, especially when the departed was a dear friend. He saved the coroner some trouble by filling in the cause of death. He sat with Roy until the ambulance arrived to transport her body. The man of God was handling it as best as one could expect, better so than most, given the circumstances. Still, losing a loved one had to be tough in the middle of this pandemic. Neither death nor life marched to a familiar drum beat right now. Even worse, there appeared to be no end in sight for the return of normalcy.

****

Governor Anita Ming held a televised press conference updating New York and the nation on the state's current situation of handling the pandemic. Although she represented the opposite party from the president, she spoke accolades of how his office had assisted New York. The president had supplied everything she had requested in this war against the deadly virus. Governor Ming professed to putting partisan politics aside to serve the people of New York. Yes, death rates and cases were leading the nation by a long shot, but New Yorkers were fighters she proclaimed for the viewing audience.

Mayor Francis Kowalski on a split television screen gave his account of how the Big Apple was coping under the tragic circumstances. Death toll was astronomically increasing daily. Hardest hit were the assisted living facilities, the older and weaker most vulnerable. The mayor offered no detailed plan to combat these deaths. He too being from the opposite side of the aisle from the sitting president, commended the commander in chief for offering the medical equipment and assistance where needed most. Flattening the curve became the common rhetoric by all. New York sadly was far from the right side of that curve.

Senator Aaron Breeze eyed the television screen as he conversed with Senator Charles Paulson on his cell phone, both viewing the segment from their residences. "See, Chuck, it isn't so tough working with the other side, is it?"

"Your president has performed nicely giving us what we need to save lives," replied Senator Charles Paulson sarcastically.

"It should be like this all the time, don't you agree?"

"In our dreams. It will never be this easy. You know it as well as I. Everyone cherishes their photo opts, all for the political greater good. Once we have licked Covid-19 the kumbaya moments will be history."

"You really think it will last that long, Chuck. This is an election year, and the gloves are coming off sooner than this pandemic will be over. Both campaigns are heating up, just readying for the right moment to one up the other."

"Well played. Your state, specifically New York City, is certainly being hit the worst. How will your governor and the mayor of NYC define and defend the statistics? Never mind, I know the answer to this one. When kissy time has expired, they will blame the president like they always do. The media will support the well-choreographed narrative I'm sure. Why is it, Chuck, that nearly 95% of most network coverage is negative toward the president?"

"Don't ask me. Ask your president."

"Right, lying and false narratives have nothing to do with it."

"Politics have never been pretty my friend. You knew that before you jumped in with both feet."

"Maybe so but I thought the drive by media would at least report the news fairly and accurately and allow the public to form their own opinions. Skewing it and then forming opinions is not what journalist are supposed to do."

"Who said they were journalists just because they appear on camera. The old days are just that. Gone forever. Cronkite, Huntley, and Brinkley were long before our time. And long before this 24/7 coverage. There is no waiting for the nightly news to find out what is going on in the world. Sensationalism and immediate on the scene reporting are the new wave."

"Forget checking out the accuracy of the story or reliability of the source, just toss it against the wall and hope it sticks, right? And if it doesn't stick, they still profess that it does. That is propaganda, not news."

"Preaching to the choir, Aaron. I cannot change it any more than you can."

"Why would you want to Chuck? Their narrative matches your party's narrative. It is all from the same daily play book."

"Aaron, why even go there? You are wasting your breath and my time. Make the best of it and just try to keep your constituents happy. Tell them what you know they want to hear."

"That might be your game, Chuck. I tell mine the truth."

"And if the truth hurts…"

"Honesty is my policy. Without it, I have no reason to be here."

"You are weak, Arron. Sorry for being so candid but you and your party are."

"Call it what you wish but I still believe we work for who and not the other way around like you guys do. Our founders warned us against this. Sadly, if things don't change, we are becoming what we fled in the first place. Government has been allowed to become too large and powerful. For the people and by the people has been lost in the weeds."

"The why don't you get out? Staying here just makes you part of the establishment, doesn't it?"

"Not if I fight to restore it, it doesn't."

"Huge dreams. Good luck."

"You've changed, Chuck. What happened to you? You were somewhat of a believer and fighter when we both arrived. You cannot be giving in to the swamp so early in your career."

"Maybe we should no longer have these discussions, Aaron. What do they say, friends should leave politics and religion out of their conversations if they hope to remain friends?"

"But we are politicians. We should be able to civilly discuss politics, shouldn't we?"

"Maybe not if we are on firmly on the opposite side of the issues. Like it or not, we are for the most part. I cherish your friendship. It has been a refreshing escape here in Washington. I fear though that we are talking shop too much when off the clock so to speak. Possibly we should leave it in the House when we are lunching. My side, your side, really doesn't get us anywhere socially. Truce?"

"Truce. Lunch is on me when this pandemic has subsided, and we can return to normal."

"Bribery?"

"Not hardly. You will have your turn in the rotation, Chuck."

****

"I called Roy. He seemed to be doing as well as expected given the circumstances. No funeral is planned anytime soon. He said she would be cremated, and he would be with her alone. I didn't have the heart to ask him what happened. She's gone. May as well leave it at that until he is willing to talk about it."

"I'm glad you called him."

"Me too. I called Melvin Meeker. He is doing much better after that tough stint he had in the hospital and on the ventilator. He is as stir crazy as the rest of us. State will not let him resume operations on any construction sites yet. He said they deemed him and his crew nonessential. Nonessential, what a load of bull that is. How do they decide who is and who isn't? I would love to see that play book."

"Glad to at least hear he is doing better physically."

'Mentally wacko like the rest of us though. I will be in the shop if you need me. Love you, C."

"Love you too, George. Make those birds proud of your latest creation."

"I think I will give it to Roy when the time is right."

Camilla Ritchie smiled and kissed him again for good measure. She wondered if this world turned upside down would ever right itself. Nothing good could come of this extended shutdown. People were not meant to do absolutely nothing, to remain at home in close quarters with family, no matter how loving you are. People require outlets, social activity, not confinement. Even she was succumbing to the forced social distancing and complete isolation. It mentally challenged even the best. Camilla had been researching the virus on the Net, keeping updated as much as possible. Peter, her contact at the center, remained closed mouth on Covid-19. This troubled her but she did not hold it against him. After all, that was what he was supposed to do. She shouldn't leverage her friendship to gain access to data. She could have remained employed instead of retiring if it meant that much to her. Selfishly she justified it by the facts that this was different, a virus unleashed on the world by communist China supposedly. Germ warfare seemed possible, but she hoped not. If true, it could mean a new deadlier war for all.

Not doubting it, this virus appeared more contagious than any she had encountered during her years with the center. It had spread beyond comprehension worldwide. Even more concerning, news of what to do or not to do, deviated too frequently. People, including her, were questioning the validity of the everchanging narrative of the virus. More concerning, politics were muddying the water. If anything should be off limits to politics, this should be. Unfortunately, everything was on the table where politics were concerned. A presidential election just magnified the consequences. Remaining on the sidelines had never been more uncomfortable thought Camilla.

14

Kitt Whitt remained skeptical of the virus and its downward spiraling consequences. He laid it on the line during his podcast. Covid-19 was being used politically to manipulate the nation. Obvious to him was how one party was using the virus to control every aspect of life for Americans. Sure, no denying it, the president had recommended the shut down but had only suggested two weeks. Two weeks became a month then two months. Clearly the United States was in the fifth month with no end in sight according to those driving this bus. The economy was in ruins. Unemployment was at record highs from record lows prior to the pandemic.

This president has been in the crosshairs of the opposing party and news media since day one of his presidency. Continuation of the shutdown could work wonders for removing him from office. No more partisan politics. Finger pointing and blame was in full force. Kitt pointed out how Governor Anita Ming and Mayor Francis Kowalski, who both praised the president for his actions supporting New York initially, had now turned on him as they began to catch flack for the high death tolls in the state and specifically the Big Apple. Death rates in nursing homes had offed the chart, specifically with news that the state officials had ordered patients with Covid to be returned to nursing homes instead of isolating them elsewhere. The president was to blame, not them.

The president was now being criticized for not reacting soon enough in his handling of the pandemic. Those same critics, pointed out Kitt, had been critical of the president's actions to suspend air travel from China and Europe, and the temporary shutting down of the country. No matter what he did, he should always have done the opposite so said the slew of opposition armchair quarterbacks, intent on bringing him to his knees. Kitt used a familiar quote in his podcast, 'If the president had come up with a cure for cancer, they would blame him for destroying the medical industry that depended on cancer patients.'

Kitt remained constantly under fire for his spin on the political arena and the bipartisan news reporting. He held back no punches, calling them like many saw it. His loyal following had grown by leaps and bounds as had his critics. Any PR was welcome PR so said Kitt professed Kitt. If the opposition was mentioning him in their broadcasts, it meant that they feared him. That was his spin anyway. People he had begged in the past to appear on his podcast now eagerly participated as guests. This spoke volumes to his growing popularity and loyal fanbase. Kitt did his fair share of conspiracy theorizing. He did so in a manner that relied on supportive facts and data. Sources, anonymous at times, fed him this information discreetly of course. Kitt beamed with delight that such sources were now contacting him instead of him seeking them. Sometimes he had to pinch himself to make sure he wasn't dreaming.

Remaining grounded was a constant battle for him. It was easy for a political podcast nerd like him to allow the swelling of his head override everything else. He had been an introvert much of his life until he had stumbled into his calling, a voice for the people, the underdogs, the often too quiet majority. He said what so many wished they had the courage to speak out loud. Kitt held back no punches when he clearly spoke his mind and mostly from the heart. He was not a fear monger. He believed in good over evil, the cream rising to the top, the best will always survive. He bled red, white, and blue, was vigorously against the concept of communism, socialism, and totalitarianism. Marxism had no place on American soil. Nothing came free, especially from the United States Government. Fact over fiction; the government has no money. The money was provided by the people for the people. The government just loves taxing and spending it frivolously by promising free stuff. Good work ethics trumps laziness. Nothing comes free. Kitt believed in capitalism and the right for people to keep their money and not be taxed to death. The American dream could be achieved by anyone willing to get off their lazy ass and work for it.

Don't even get him started on racism. He could put it in simple terms that most anyone should be able to understand. Perfect examples: Miss America Pageant. Not Miss Black America Pageant. There was no Miss White America Pageant, no Miss Asian American Pageant,

No Miss Hispanic American Pageant. Color blindness should be the American way according to Kitt. Equal opportunity for those willing to go the extra mile. Freedom of school choice should be a right for all. Some had suggested that Kitt run for office. Kitt had no stomach for that. He served the public better through his willingness to educate and do so at any cost. The truth was a powerful tool if you were willing to openly view it.

This Covid-19 reeked of corruption. On his Podcast he referred to it a Covert-19. Something evil swam just beneath the surface of this viral madness. Kitt had not assembled all the facts to support his suspicions. For now, he merely cultivated the seed. The plant would spring forth and flourish soon enough. He would not dig a furrow of unsubstantiated conspiracy rhetoric without the facts to support it. That was not his way. This is what made him different than most. As badly as he wanted to believe, he would refrain from doing so with his listeners until he had data to support it.

With fame comes the cost for it. A mere nobody had now gained enough notoriety to warrant frequent death threats. He had luckily avoided some close calls when in public. While attacks were not common, there were a few crazies out there wishing to make an example of him. Kitt took this with a grain of salt, realizing it just supported his popularity and substantiated that he was right and a threat to those undermining the democracy. Nope. He was not stupid. He had no desire to be plummeted by anyone and avoided in person conflict. Kitt was a decent judge of character and could usually detect an intended threat. Gut instinct spoke volumes.

He had just finished his podcast when his cell phone chimed. "Yes, this is he. Sure. I would be interested. I have never appeared on anyone else's show before. Will this be live or prerecorded? No. Live works fine for me, just asking. Tell her it would be my honor. Should I prepare for any specific subject matter? Fine. Spontaneity it is. Yes, that date and time slot should work perfectly. Thank you for the opportunity."

Kitt was beaming. This was his shot at the big time. He had apparently arrived. Never would he fathom Paula Wise would reach out to him as a guest on her syndicated show. She was a conservative, a straight shooter, not one of those extremists that would want nothing more than to do a hit job on him. He wondered what he had done to interest her in inviting him. To be determined he supposed when he appeared next week. He would obviously milk this PR on his next podcast. His only regret, he would not be able to appear live with her in the studio. He would be a Zoom guest instead due to the concerns over the pandemic. Who cares he convinced himself? Just appearing on her show would boost his career by leaps and bounds. He could hardly wait to call Berkley and share the news with him. One on one with Paula Wise; it didn't get any better than that. She had begun her career as a mere reporter and now look at her, the big time with a huge lion's share in primetime. That could be me before long thought Kitt. No more Nit Wit remarks from the naysayers. He fought feverishly against any potential head swelling. He refused to allow his usual mantra to be swayed by the potential of stardom. Smiling and humming a little tune, he speed-dialed Berkley Jay Patrick.

****

Camilla normally avoided television, especially most of the network news stations. The pandemic had changed her normal routine, now taking peeks here and there just to keep tabs on what was happening and how it was supposedly being handled. She liked the president's daily briefings, except for most of his boisterous unscripted rhetoric. She was more interested in the facts and stats being shared by the medical and scientific task force members. Even some of those she viewed as suspicious given her background in the field. Flip flopping, as in most political arenas, had been duly noted. She could read between the lines in many cases. Those blurred lines offered its fair share of scrutiny if you knew what to look for, and she did. The no mask versus wear mask reversal had been an obvious sign that the truth was being withheld or at least being optimized for one reason or another.

Camilla had her suspicions about the models being used to predict the number of cases and deaths. As data is collected, it impacts the stats and should influence the models. This wasn't happening as best she could tell. She began researching and compiling her own data, stats, and a proposed model. Hers was vastly different and not nearly as detrimental as those being shared with the public. No denying it, Covid-19 was real and was serious but the seriousness being portrayed was a bit over the top for her liking. Death tolls continued to climb as did the cases worldwide and on American soil. The reactions were a bit too theatrical and over the top as well according to her numbers. No one was asking her opinion. She was not a member of the coronavirus task force, not an active member in the scientific community. She was a mere bench warmer, sitting on the sidelines, observing the game being played. Still, she was a stake holder as were all Americans. For now, she would continue doing what she did best and compile her data, form her own opinion based on the stats. It was her escape, her birdhouse project and for now she would leave it at that.

George had grown weary of bird condo construction. He needed a new distraction. And since Melvin Meeker's construction business remained at a virtual standstill, he had to come up with a new outlet for his boredom. The perfect one just clicked, one that he knew C would appreciate. She had mentioned it numerous times and he had just as many times ignored it, feeling there was no need to change something that appeared adequate to him. Adequate! In the construction business adequacy was never accepted. Sure, you could recommend or try to sway the customer, but in the end, you gave the customer what they wanted. C was for all practical purposes a customer, even if he had never consented to the concept under their roof. Boredom had won out over that concept now. He would give in and do it, would love him for it once she got beyond rubbing his nose in it. In the end, she would be a happy customer and he would be an equally happy contributor. Win-win.

****

The United Broadcast Network continued posting running tallies on the screen of the cases being reported worldwide and nationwide, including the deaths attributed to the virus. Nothing but gloom and doom for the world population while not mentioning the origin of the disease by communist China. UBN did not shy away from blaming the president and his administration for the death toll. The bias media continued its relentless persecution of the sitting president as it had been for over three years of his term. Shamefully, they did not try to hide their contempt. There was no fair and balanced in their rhetoric. No reporting the news and allowing the viewers to decide. The canvas was painted with negative propaganda, giving this president no credit for any accomplishments, promises made and promises kept.

No denying it, the once record highs in employment and prosperity had been wiped out, those out of work climbing by the millions each day. The economy had tanked in the wake of the pandemic. There appeared to be no reasonable end in sight to the nationwide lockdown. A president that had been a shoe in for reelection now faced tragic uncertainty. The opposition party took every opportunity to discredit the presidency. The media supported their finger pointing as if every comment had been choreographed and read from a playbook. The first amendment was being broken according to the clergy. Freedom of speech was being denied by those wishing to worship. Churches had been ordered closed in most cities and states. Almost gestapo like, select mayors and governors threatened pastors who planned any church services, even if they gathered their congregation outdoors and social distanced. Practice of religion was deemed non-essential while liquor stores remained open. An uncivil war was on the brink.

15

Something struck Camilla as extremely puzzling as she sat at her laptop. Neither the government nor news segments had mentioned the status of the homeless. If indeed Covid-19 presented itself as highly contagious person to person and specifically deadly to those with preexisting conditions, then why hadn't the homeless population been decimated. Those unfortunate people would certainly be among the more vulnerable. The homeless would suffer from countless diseases, sanitation challenges, deplorable conditions with no social distancing or protection from masks. Why then, were they not being accounted for or extra measures being taken to protect them and the public from certain outbreaks? Could it be that the inner cities were allowing it to run its course unchecked to rid them from society? She could not fathom such an inhuman action.

Camilla further pondered these ramifications. What if the homeless had been minimally impacted by Covid-19? In theory, could this be interpreted as this population having an uncanny immunity to the coronavirus or might it be just the opposite; the person to person contact was unfounded? She had no data to support this either way, just questions. For the sake of argument, she reflected further; if person to person was not nearly as contagious as portrayed, could it be underreported or intentionally not reported because it did not fit the fear mongering narrative? Camilla shook her head, confessing she now sounded like a conspiracy enthusiast. Still, she felt compelled to follow up by asking questions but who could she ask? She highlighted the question in her notes. Overhearing the rumbling of George's truck in the drive, she closed the laptop.

She met him as he entered the kitchen from the garage. He certainly appeared more energetic than usual. Of course, any trip to Home Depot would do that for him. She hoped that more bird houses were not in the future. George smiled, kissed her on the cheek and then stepped past her to retrieve a can of diet Orange Crush from the fridge. After popping the top and taking a swig, he set the can on the bar and announced he had a surprise for her. No more bird houses, she thought a second time. To her amazement, not this time.

"Accompany me please, C."

"What are you up to, George?"

"Just come with me," he said grabbing her by the hand.

He opened the door to the walk-in closet in their bedroom and asked her to step inside. Now what, she wondered.

"How do you want it?'

"Want what, dear?"

"Your closet. I am going to customize however you want it. You have been talking about this for years, how you would love to redesign it. Well, I am ready to make that wish come true for you. We are going to give it an extreme makeover to meet your every whim."

"George, are you sure you are up to a project like this?" Not a birdhouse, she thought.

"I'm bored, C. I need something challenging and engaging to counter this China virus lockdown. Don't look at me like that, C. The president calls it the China virus."

"Call it whatever you wish. I am just concerned you are taking on too large a project by yourself."

"On the contrary, we are doing this together. You tell me what you want, and I will build it. And if I need a helping hand hear or there, you will be her to help, right?"

"If you put it in those terms then I will be your handy little rookie gopher."

"All settled then. Little gopher, you may assist me in unloading the truck.

"Your little buddy, Gilligan at your service, Skipper."

"We aren't shipwrecked, C."

"Close by your accounts though."

"Far from any three-hour tour but I get it."

****

An officer involved shooting in the Big Apple had gained national attention. It had been captured on someone's cell phone and then provided to The United Broadcast Network. UBN capitalized on the three-minute video blaming the president for the unrest in the country. The brief video painted an unflattering portrayal for the police officer and the department but what it failed to show were the events leading up to the incident. And the report failed to mention that the deceased was a convicted felon with outstanding warrants. The police brutality theme prevailed and served to rile the already restless and confined population seeking any reason to unleash their frustrations. Or so it had been portrayed once the first protests began in neighborhood where the incident had occurred. Quickly, peaceful turned ugly. Rioting, looting, and burning of businesses ensued. Innocent business owners were the new victims for an incident that they had nothing to do with. The police had been ordered to stand down and stay out of the way while chaos had its way on the citizens of the community.

Other cities erupted in chaos over the next few days in protest of what had been portrayed on the news. Several others had been killed in the melees, including an officer in another city. There is no justification for murder, plain and simple. One death does not right another. Screams of kill the pigs and burn it down were obvious for those willing to film and broadcast the severity of what was happening. UBN chose to play it up as peaceful protest and excluded any fires or looting in the images of their reports at ground zero. A handful of networks portrayed the reality of the destruction while others like UBN downplayed it as fiction being spread by the current administration and its minions. Something darker swam below the surface. Something more sinister and diabolical existed and festered. The pandemic served as the mere tip of the iceberg with America now the new Titanic.

Two groups were being pegged as domestic terrorists on American soil. The rise of PMG, People Matter Group and the ANTIAM, Anti-American Movement emerged as those fueling the unrest and promoting the violence. The administration insisted that both were well organized and were capitalizing on the situation to advance their socialist and communist agendas. Going further, without stating names, the president had all but pointed to at least one individual responsible for funding the so-called domestic terrorists. UBN painted the president as a racist and white supremist, comparing him to Hitler, accusing him of singlehandedly inciting the unrest in the nation.

Innocent people were being attacked and persecuted regularly. It had become unsafe to walk on the street in numerous cities, especially after dark. The looters were relentless, taking what they wanted, when they wanted, leaving burned business and destruction in their wake. Police personnel were fair game, bricks, frozen water bottles and other projectiles being weaponized against them by those intent on wreaking havoc. Governors and mayors of in some states and cities were being accused of standing by and allowing this to happen to their constituents. Most of these government officials painted the rioters as mere protesters or merely ignored the concerns of the people they were sworn to protect. Many scratched their heads; what had happened to this country? Too many cities resembled third word countries. The president insisted he and his administration stood for law and order and those sworn to enforce it. His hands were tied though if neither governors nor mayors requested federal assistance. In the meantime, the rioters, aka peaceful protesters, continued to burn cities down, their mantra roaring loud and clear.

****

Governor Anita Ming and Mayor Francis Kowalski stuck to the script; demonstrators were just exercising their rights. The mayor had even been photographed with a group of signs bearing PMG protesters in a show of solidarity. Excluded from the photo opt were the gutted and smoldering remains of numerous small businesses no more than a block away. Also excluded from the photographs were the boarded businesses nearby. As was the fact that the mayor was surrounded by nearly 50 police officers conveniently omitted from any of the shots. Hypocrisy had never screamed louder. Do as I say, not as I do.

One young man had infiltrated the mob perimeter and had attempted to film and interview the alleged protesters. He had been attacked and bloodied by those peacefully exercising their rights. He had given them an equal opportunity to explain to his viewing audience their concerns and the rationale behind their cause. Uninterested, they viewed him as a reporter, part of the problem and his attempt at being fair and balanced had almost cost him his life. They confiscated his backpack, cell phone and wallet like the common thieves they were. If not for a priest from a nearby church taking him in and fending off the unruly crowd, he might not have survived the onslaught. The priest had suffered a broken nose and black eye from the not so faithful believers in the Almighty and those that serve Him. Undaunted, he cared for the injured man as best he could, fearing no help would venture into the explosive environment.

Reverend Bobby Flowers made small talk as he offered the young man a cup of herbal tea. "Very bold of you, young man, venturing into the streets among such unrest in the city. Even I would not have been so bold to do so. My manners are terrible in these Godforsaken circumstances. I am Reverend Flowers."

Offering a hand and a thank you, the rescued young man introduced himself, "Kitt Whitt and my attempt at sensationalism did not go as well as I envisioned. They picked me clean, including my phone that I was using to video the experience."

"You are a reporter then."

"Not exactly. I have a pod cast, much safer surroundings; what on earth was I thinking? I had no business venturing here. Obviously, these people were not interested in voicing unscripted concerns to an uninvited guest to their protest. They never even allowed me to properly introduce myself, not that it really mattered to them. I should have known better, the media portraying this as a peaceful protest."

"Rioting, looting, and inflicting harm on innocent people is not the definition of a peaceful protest, my son. These are uncertain and equally angry times. I have witnessed it up close and personal. Too many are looking for any excuse to wreak unholy havoc in the streets. Rioters do not require much motivation to justify their actions of unlawful break ins and equally unchallenged pillaging. I have seen it too many times to count, working the various parishes of the inner cities."

"Why do you do it then?"

"I am a man of God, and this is my calling, to provide for those in need of prayer and guidance."

"Hate to burst your bubble reverend, but I am not sure those that I encountered are seeking what you have to offer them."

"Still, I must be here for those that do. The people in this neighborhood are not the ones out there on the street provoking and destroying."

"I am guessing no help is on the way for me or you or them."

"Sadly, the authorities have been instructed to stand down. Such is the norm in these situations."

"Just let it burn seems a bit unamerican. The honest taxpayers get screwed yet again. Thugs have their way. Stupid me. I sought to interact with them to better understand their grievances when obvious divides exist. According to you this is not complicated."

"What is happening out there has absolutely nothing to do with what happened in that officer shooting incident. Martin Luther King would never have taken this approach to resolve racial issues. Peaceful protests are legal. What we have out there is anything but. In case you have not noticed, I am black, older, and wiser as well. I understand racial divides and racial injustices. I lived through them as a child and young man. The America we live in today is a far cry from that time. I am ashamed of these self-appointed black leaders stirring the racial divide all for the sake of lining their pockets. Poke the beehive and keep it riled is their mantra. There is no room for brotherly love in their playbook."

"Same goes for many politicians, especially those making their careers of not solving the issues. That is why they hate this president so badly. He is the anti-politician, the problem solver and owes nobody any favors. Sorry, didn't mean to go all political but it is the basis for my pod cast."

"The clergy is fully aware of the political playing field and pros and cons of each party. I cannot speak for everyone of religious faith and leadership, but my eyes are wide open as it pertains to what our president stands for and what he has accomplished for the evangelicals. No president has ever spoken with open support for God, prayer and even Israel as has this president. He supports the constitution and our rights to the letter. And he is prolife and professes this publicly. He doesn't hold back any punches even when his rhetoric can be bit too distasteful and difficult to swallow. He was not voted into power to be the Pope or our Messiah. He is leader, not a prophet. I choose how I practice my faith and I chose a man who would lead us and do what is constitutionally correct to defend and protect our rights."

"Good stuff. It would be awesome if you would consider joining me on my pod cast and sharing your views."

"I am flattered, son, but I do not aspire to be an activist even for a good cause. I accomplish what I have been called to do from the bully pulpit."

"You could reach a lot more people if you ever change your mind. "

"Humbled, but that arena is not for me. How are you feeling?"

"Like…sh…I mean poorly but thankful you risked your life to save mine. How do we get out of here?"

"I would suggest you stay put until dawn. The worst will dissipate by then. The darkness emboldens them. Projectiles and unruliness are not so easily detected and there is less police presence to deter their vile activities under nighttime's cloak."

"Being on the ground and close to this makes me feel like I am dealing with the Night of the Living Dead apocalypse."

"Fair analogy. Chaos reigns."

What sounded like gunfire interrupted after their conversation. Reverend Bobby Flowers bowed his head and spoke a prayer out loud. Kitt half bowed, eyes slightly open, hoping the craziness remained outside. He had lost his desire for round two in what he had already experienced. Mentally he began preparing for what would be his most spectacular pod cast, reliving this and sharing the reverend's spin on things, anonymously of course. He respected Reverend Flowers' desire to remain out of the spotlight. He could hardly wait to share his latest with Berkley, his confident and ultimate sounding board. Better still, his session with Paula Wise would have fresh material up for discussion. All and all, he figured he had hit paydirt, venturing out into the world coming unraveled. His battered and bruised face would play well to his loyal following on his next visual podcast. He would squeeze these lemons into vintage lemonade.

16

Camilla, on behalf of George, had returned a phone call to Doctor Kyle Richardson's office. His staff was contacting patients recommending canceling scheduled visits unless they were considered emergences. They emphasized that there was no need exposing people, especially the elderly with preexisting conditions to others in an office environment. While Camilla frowned on George missing any of his appointments, he had insisted he was feeling fine and could delay it to when circumstances improved. Reluctantly, she complied with his wishes. She read George like a book though. He was so engaged in the closet customizing project that he could not be pried away for a doctor visit. She admired his tenacity, understanding that he was more pigheaded than anything. No denying it, the closet was taking shape nicely. Plus, it had weaned him off building the bird houses.

"George, I canceled your appointment. Currently they were not rescheduling any unless there is an emergency. The closet is looking splendid."

"Yeah, it is. I must admit C, it has thus far exceeded my expectations. It is encouraging to know I have not lost my touch."

"Thank you for doing it."

"And it only took me about ten years to get around to doing it, right? Don't look at me like that. I know what you are thinking, and I deserve the scrutiny."

Camilla just rolled her eyes. "Can I bring anything, dear?"

"Another orange crush would be great. How is your China virus research going? Don't act so innocent. You left your laptop open. I couldn't help but notice what you were up to. Don't sweat it. You did this for a living. Goes without saying that it would interest you."

"I know but I had not attended to become so enthralled by it. Too many of the circumstances are not adding up. Just thought I would compile my own data. Nothing more, something to do."

"If you figure out how to straighten out this mess, you have my permission to share it with the so-called experts botching it up left and right. I have said and I will say it again; their recommendations change with the wind. I find it hard to believe them anymore. Do this, do that, don't do this, never mind do it instead, don't wear a mask, do wear a mask. Stay home except for essential activities. The sunlight and open air are good but not in crowds more than six. Oh yeah, and the real doozy, shut down the beaches and parks. So much for enjoying the sunshine and killing the virus."

"George, no need getting worked up over it."

"Worked up, I am beyond that phase in my life. Keep telling you, C, they are preparing us for the future and a socialist America if we don't start fighting back with every breath, we breathe. I am done. I need to focus on these next cuts, so I don't botch up your shoe shelves."

"I will be right back with your soda."

George had a point she thought as she headed to the kitchen. Too much was going wrong simultaneously to be mere coincidence. Even she sensed an agenda in play, a hunch lacking the connecting piece of the puzzle unfortunately. And even if she had compelling evidence to debunk those leading the charge, she still had no forum to present it. Seemed unthinkable given the field she had worked her entire career. Her research had always been highly regarded until she had committed the cardinal sin by questioning those spinning the narrative. Her data undeniably supported what she had shared with her superiors. Instead, it had been shuffled to the bottom of the deck and she had been silenced, no threatened, by those not wishing to reverse what had already been publicized. Fragile egos take no prisoners. They merely silence those with opposing statistics. Not only had they silenced her, but they had also wiped clean any existence of her research. That incident had taken the wind out of her sails. Retirement became her only option, unwilling to ever be put in that precarious position again.

She reached inside the fridge. Last orange crush. She would have to venture out into the unclean world and buy more. She did not look forward to contending with those intent on following the rules versus those determined to break them. Masks were a prime example. Here were those that wore them properly and then those that did not, or even refused to wear them at all. And the worst of the worst thrived on confrontations. She had witnessed her fair share of confrontations gone badly. Social distancing always opened a festered sore for some. Some disregarded the six-foot recommendations and then there were those that absolutely refused to abide by the directional aisleways in the big box stores. She had tired of correcting the rule breakers, simply not worth the risk of reactions by those not interested in her alleged policing. Some of her friends avoided shopping like the plague, opting to order online and have merchandise delivered. She had not quite been pushed that far just yet.

As she made her way through the bedroom, she heard the unmistakable crash. Entering the walk-in closet, she immediately saw George lying on his back clutching his chest. Dropping the orange crush, she rushed to his side and reached in his pocket to retrieve the nitroglycerin. Camilla popped the top. The bottle was empty. George was gasping for breath becoming pale. She raced to the bathroom cabinet, opening his drawer, retrieving a second bottle. It was empty as well. In that fleeting moment it struck her, that Doctor Richardson always wrote him a new prescription during her scheduled checkups. It had been canceled. Her cell phone was in the kitchen, but George should have his. She checked his pockets but could not find it. Finally, she spotted it on a shelf near his toolbox. She called 911 and then Richardson's office, all the while trying to comfort her husband, his breath becoming shallower by the second. How had they become so careless as to allow his prescription to expire and to have run out of nitroglycerin? Trying times had caused them to operate abnormally and be too preoccupied with the pandemic and country being in lockdown. She remembered that aspirin is recommended in some cases if the person can chew and swallow one. It can help break up any blood clots. Offering him an aspirin would serve no purpose seeing he was incapable of chewing it. Camilla sat by George holding his hand talking nonstop to him, all she could really do given his condition.

****

Camilla sat in her automobile having just finished her last phone call to their children. Stoic and in semi shock she stared into space doing her best to come to terms with what had just happened. Life can change unexpectedly in a mere blink. Such had been the case this very day. The paramedics had arrived in record time given these uncertain times. Every precious second counts when cardiac arrest is involved. George had expired in route. She had not been allowed to accompany them inside the ambulance, new Covid rules in place to prevent her from doing so. She had driven herself to the hospital where she had not been permitted to enter. An emergency room staff member had delivered the message to her that George had died before arriving. He had died alone by all counts inside that ambulance with strangers by his side. Her world had been shattered by the news knowing this could probably have been prevented if only they'd had nitroglycerin on hand.

A tap on the driver's side window caused her to flinch. She opened the door and Berkley embraced her immediately, masked but tossing social distancing to the wayside. For the first time, Camilla allowed the floodgates to open, seeing the face of her dear friend. He patted her on the back as they embraced whispering his condolences. George was gone. He was really gone. How was this possible?

124

17

Reverend Bobby Flowers watched on the rectory television, the interaction on split screen between Kitt Whitt and Paula Wise, recognizing some of the rhetoric as his. As promised, Kitt had referred to him as an anonymous source crediting him for saving his life during the unrest that night. One thing for certain, conditions had not improved from that night. Protests, rioting, and looting had spread to other cities, especially since new footage had been released showing the officer basically execute the alleged suspect in the secluded alleyway. The source of the video had not been disclosed, the UBN host stating that it had been received by what else but an anonymous source.

Rioters and looters had stepped up their game, now tearing down statues, any statues, claiming history had been unjust and the slate must be wiped clean. One congressional leader, instead of condemning these actions, said instead, 'People will do what people will do.' More police officers had been injured by the alleged peaceful protesters doing what people will do. The president offered federal assistance to the cities where the worse was happening but mayors and governors of these cities, all from the opposition party, would not request help. Instead, they mugged it up for the cameras blaming the president and his policies for the 'protests.'

Paula Wise and Kitt Whitt were engaged in discussing the misinformation being fed the viewers of the various bias programs. Paula and Kitt shared the same perspective and each took turns laying out the facts that contradicted the portrayed narrative. Paula appreciated Kitt's resilience, venturing into the streets in search of firsthand reports. Even she had not dared do that yet. Why should she? She had deep pockets and resources to do that legwork for her. All she had to do was interview those on the front lines and rely on them providing compelling footage. This kid though, he took the risks to appease his loyal pod cast followers. No doubt, this little stunt would increase his viewership. The premise intrigued her. So much so that after they were off the air, she made a prepared pitch to the young rebel rouser.

Kitt, somewhere between being in shock and in awe, was almost giddy with the anticipation of sharing the news of this proposal with Berkley. He had informed Paula Wise that it would require further thought and consultation with his team before he could render a decision on her proposal. His team, right! He was his team. He was 95% sure where his rendering would fall but wanted Berkley's opinion for that final 5% of uncertainty. He had envisioned the appearance on her show would no doubt boost the viewership for his pod cast, but this had exceeded his wildest aspirations.

Exiting his building, and strutting now like the cock of the walk, Kitt made his way to his Mini Cooper parked a block away. He had a few errands to run before paying a call on Berkley. Rounding the corner, he came face to face with at least a dozen characters dressed in black toe to head, including their protective masks and hoodies. He recognized the posture, each strapped with matching backpacks. He had experienced it all too closely recently, their unwillingness to have a civil discussion. You either believed in their cause or were the enemy. Undoubtably, they recognized him as well, one blatantly pointing out that he was the one they had just seen on Paula Wise's show. Unable to detect if they were smiling or gritting their teeth underneath their face masks, there was no mistaking the hatred in their narrowing eyes. This was not going to end well, not for him. Glancing about there were few pedestrians in sight and no policemen. Given today's world it was doubtful he could have depended on either if they would had been present. So, he did what he usually did when facing bullies, he did his best to engage in constructive dialogue to potentially defuse the situation. Where was Reverend Bobby Flowers when he so desperately needed his rescue tactics.

****

Governor Anita Ming held a press briefing, shamelessly patting herself on the back for how she and her administration had handled the pandemic thus far. Even in the face of staggering deaths and increasing Covid cases, she professed that they had been doing an incredible job, much better than the federal government led by an incompetent president. Ironically, the governor had praised this same president mere months ago, stating as public record how he had come through for the state on every request in the pandemic crisis. Now being scrutinized for sending Covid patients back into nursing homes and assisted living facilities by her decree, she did what most politicians did when faced with bad PR, she deflected the blame to others. Nearly 60% of the deaths in her state had been the result of her bad decision, taking a specific toll on the elderly in those homes and facilities. She also included the mayor, a member of her party, in her blame game with most of these deaths occurring in the Big Apple. When convenient they even turned on their own.

Mayor Francis Kowalski had not taken Governor Ming's accusations lightly, firing back and pointing out her incompetence in several similar situations during the pandemic. The gloves were off. Anything was fair in an unfair fight. Both did take turns demonizing the president between personal jabs at each other. UBN did their best to protect both but their public bickering had not made it easy to stick to a concise narrative beneficial to them and the party. The president just took it in stride and fired back at them and UBN, nothing new in his three and a half years in office. He just took to Twitter as always and let it fly. He had learned to tell his story by circumventing the tainted version being broadcast by the bias media.

Senator Aaron Breeze, while appalled by the blame targeting the president, could not help but needle his old pal, Senator Charles Paulson, when she tossed the mayor, his party's mayor, under the bus to protect her butt. Paulson failed to see the humor or admit to the irony. At least he had only received the text and had not experienced a face to face berating by the senator from across the aisle. Privately, even he shook his head in disgust over the ugliness being demonstrated by his party. Feeding on their own, while uncommon, was still plausible in a CYA situation. He did not condone it, nor would he ever stoop that low himself. Then again, he had never faced anything close thus far in his young career. Might come the day. If so, would he cross that blurry line, he wondered.

A spokesman for the Global Viral Center was being interviewed on UBN and predicted deaths in the United States alone to exceed a million. The UBN hosts fueling the hype played on the public's fears, painting an apocalyptic portrait for America. Biased as usual, they pointed a finger to the president claiming these lives would be on his head. Those in the opposing party piled on demanding that the president step down and allow someone more competent to lead. What were they thinking? If the president resigned, his vice president would in charge. They hated her as much as they loathed the president. The GVC continued to push for more closures and even tighter reign over the businesses and people. Doomsday death threats currently carried a lot of weight in the growing debate.

A presidential election looming just months away grew uglier by the moment. A pandemic and crumbling economy continued to be at the forefront. This presidency had allowed it to unravel on his watch so said his critics consisting of the opposition party and their propaganda coconspirators, the mainstream news. Their persistence was paying off, the president's approval rating had continued to plummet despite his attempts to encourage reopening the country and a promise of an eventual vaccine. Tooting his own horn through his daily briefings did at least provide him an opportunity at a rebuttal even though UBN and other biased networks refused to cover them. Never had there ever been so much negative news coverage for a president of either party. For nearly four years every attempt had been made to discredit him, impeach him, or make him quit. Like water on duck feathers, he had managed to shed the worst.

Flattening the pandemic curve had been the objective, that, and the development of a vaccine. Many states were showing statistical signs of flattening the curve but the news media like the UBN refused to cover positive results for fear it might give the president positive momentum. Instead, they focused on the increasing number of cases and deaths nation and worldwide. Obsessed with keeping and presenting the score seemed a bit morbid for the taste of many. There were those who craved positive results, anything to hang their hopes for the survival of humanity. Those stories did not sell news and increase profits, or viewership for the millions following the epic event. Bad news was better PR. The opposition party professed a mantra of never allowing a crisis to go to waste and would use anything to discredit the president.

The riots and looting continued to spread like wildfires, those going beyond peaceful protesting wreaking havoc on the innocent. In most cases those creating the chaos no longer even attempted to hide their actions. Something sinister existed and it was not merely a concern for justice and law and order based on the police incident. Yes, they were attacking the police and, in some cases, committing cold calculated murder, but the incidents appeared too orchestrated, not random. Specific cities and areas were being targeted. Those perpetrating the crimes, and yes, they were crimes, mobilized with efficiency and the weapons to deliver destruction well beyond an act of spontaneity. The president continued to offer help but doing so required the request from a governor or mayor. Thus far those in charge of the cities being destroyed made no such requests. Instead, they blamed the president for what was happening. Ironically, these heinous acts were not being done by the president's base or party. Blame for everything going wrong was pinned on him exclusively. His opponent in the presidential race had the utter audacity to say that the president had been responsible for the deaths caused by Covid-19. He had even insinuated that global warming, wildfires, floods, and hurricanes were probably the president's doing. Not to worry though; when the new sheriff was elected for the country all that would change, including a vaccine and cure for the virus. Critics of the challenging party's candidate suggested that if he had a plan and cure for all that was going wrong under the current administration's watch, then he should share it now instead of waiting until he won the election. Saving lives and rebooting the economy should be acted upon with urgency if the cure or answer to both existed. This was no time to play politics if you had solutions. No solutions were offered. It is easier to just toss stones.

****

Berkley received news of Kitt Whitt's plight in a shocking manner. His face and name was splashed across the television screen shortly after he arrived home from comforting Camilla. Kitt had been brutally attacked near his apartment. He was in the hospital in critical condition. Police currently had no suspects in the assault. Berkeley switched off the television doing an about face as he rushed to the hospital. It seemed his dear friends were finding themselves in terrible situations lately. First the loss of George and now this. Berkley shook his head as he waited to hail a cab, thinking how glad he would be when 2020 came to an end. The streets were eerily empty including an absence of cabs. Never had he experienced just a ghostly presence on the Upper East Side in all his years of living here. The pandemic and the ordered lockdown had transformed a once hustling and bustling environment.

His impatience frantically increased with no cabs in sight. Walking the incredible distance to the hospital was out of the question. This was not his NYC. It had transformed into something ugly and untrustworthy. It was no longer safe to walk most anywhere now. Thugs and hoodlums ran rampart. Drug dealers and their derelict customers owned the territory. If this was not bad enough, toss in the rioters and looters for good measure. His home, his city, had vanished before his very eyes and it had done so extremely quickly. No one was protecting the people, the taxpayers. Even worse, the police were being persecuted and attacked. The mayor did not seem interested in standing up for justice. Instead, he given in to alleged protesters, specifically those rioting, looting, and attacking the city's police officers. Nope, this was no longer a happy place in Berkley's heart. Right now, he needed to get to the hospital in the worse way. He had yet to see any cabs or buses running. Why would there be when the city was a virtual ghost town.

18

Camilla sat in their bedroom blankly staring at the open doors of the unfinished master closet, the last place she had seen George. Stoic and emotionless she sat on a foot stool with her hands folded in her lap barely breathing as her mind struggled to process what had happened. She eventually ran her hands over her eyes and then through her hair, uncertainty rippling her moral fiber. She had never thought of a life without her husband, even given his extenuating health issues. Neither had discussed them, at least not after she had encouraged him to retire because of his heart condition. She figured that with minimal stress in his, in their lives, the risk had been minimized. Of course, this pandemic had introduced a new enemy to the battlefield. Neither of them had overly stressed about the threat. They had respected it but had not overreacted to the premise and they had taken every recommended precaution seriously.

Sure, they both complained about the ramifications and the ever-changing do's and don'ts issued by the science community, politicians, and media, but not enough to compromise their health. A fleeting thought ran through her mind; maybe George should have stuck to birdhouses. Possibly this project had been too large for him to take on. She quickly dismissed the premise and had seen the twinkle in his eyes. He had been thoroughly enjoying the makeover as he called it. If anything, the project had been a stress reliever if in fact stress had even been a factor. She did not think it had. Possibly, it was merely his time, his heart had taken him as far as it could. Obviously, he had left this world doing what he loved most, being engrossed in a construction activity. No, it would have been a sad way for him to go building mere birdhouses. This way had been more fitting for George.

The kids wanted to come but she had talked them out of it. There would be no funeral anytime soon and travel was not recommended, especially to and from New York right now. She told them she was fine, and they could continue what they had been doing, phone calls, video chat, text, email, and zoom for family gatherings. There was an arsenal of communication techniques at their fingertips. Luckily, she was a decent player on most of them. Besides, right now, she needed the solitude to grieve her way. There would be plenty of time for family later. That thought hung like a low settling fog. Time. No one was promised time. Proof in the pudding was never more evident. She kept those thoughts to herself. No need working up the kids over something no one could control.

Ironically, Camilla wondered who would finish the remodeling project. She mustered a slight smile, thinking how George would get a chuckle out of her prioritizing right now.

She stood, hands on her hips, wondering what now. Nothing seemed urgent nor important. There was no funeral to plan, no family coming to visit, no more vacations up for debate, and no more George. Just that quickly life had come to an abrupt screeching halt. No warning. Blink and the world as she had known it with the love of her life had ended. Camilla collapsed across their bed and cried. She had nothing more to give, no more thoughts to think; just a numbness overcoming her from seemingly out of the blue. Grief is but that. The process is never over. It will just evolve through stages, some worse than others. She had just entered her first of many yet to come. She would deal with them one at a time and she would survive for her sake and for George's legacy. Neither she nor he were quitters. Today she would mourn and then when the time was right, she would pick herself up and take the first step in the healing process. Right now, was not that time.

****

No cabs. Berkley finally remembered to utilize his UberApp on his cell phone. Even the Ubernation was not eagerly willing to venture out into this uncertain environment. It had taken several calls and transfers before finally locating a willing participant. Berkley was having second thoughts while waiting the driver's arrival. He had no idea what type of safety precautions the driver might be taking. Hindsight, he should probably have asked. While he had his mask and hand sanitizer, even a few Clorox wipes, he had no idea if the driver would be wearing one or if he had disinfected the vehicle since the last rider. Would the driver even be honest in his answer if asked? He would weigh the risks when his ride arrived. His urgency to reach Kitt at the hospital might out trump the ramifications of these concerns.

He would have his answer. The white Prius just arrived. The driver was a female, not that being so changed anything in his litany of concerns. Petite to match the tiny compact, she emerged from the vehicle seemingly fearless in today's world. Wearing a mask, she slipped it below her chin to display a sincere smile while remaining socially distanced.

She spoke first. "I am Melanie at your service. In case you have concerns, allow me to explain the precautions in place to warrant safe and germfree travel. I completely sanitize my Prius after every passenger. This includes a wipe down of the seat, all handles inside and out, and armrests, straps, window operational buttons. Masks are required for the trip and must remain on for the entirety of the travel, including if you decide to use your cell. Transactions for all fees including gratuities are accepted with credit cards only. A credit card swipe is provided conveniently. Sanitizer is also provided for you inside my vehicle and I expect you to use it when entering and exiting. I have not been ill, nor do I have a fever, or any other symptoms related to Covid-19. I have been tested for the virus as recently as a week ago. Do you have any concerns or questions?"

Berkley smiled. "I believe you have checked all the boxes, Melanie. Thank you for being so conscientious and for taking the precautions. My destination is New York Presbyterian Hospital. Not to worry. I am not sick. I am going there to visit a friend."

"You are aware that they are not allowing visitors, aren't you?"

"No, I didn't but this is quite the emergency. He was attacked by thugs and is in critical condition. He has no immediate family living nearby."

"Sorry to hear. Get in. Still, I do not think they will allow you inside the hospital."

Berkley smiled and nodded then entered the Uber. He followed instructions and used the provided sanitizer. This interior was spic and span, and he was confident that Melanie had been true to her word with the precautions being taken. There were no more spoken words on the commute, all business. Once they had arrived Berkley followed the process to the tee with his credit card using the sanitizer afterward.

"I hope your friend will be all right. You have my number if you require my services for the return trip."

"Thank you, Melanie. The pleasure has been mine and you will be highly recommended if anyone that I know requires an Uber."

As Melanie had stated, the hospital denied entry. It did not matter who he was, the rule applied to all. Somewhere inside Kitt supposedly remained in critical condition. He had no idea who his doctor was even though they had provided his room number. He tried phoning Kitt but there was no answer. Berkley did not know it had been stolen. He had no way of contacting ICU and obviously there was no family inside with Kitt. Berkley hopelessly sat on a bench not knowing what else he could do. Th ride had been a waste of time. Before contacting Melania again, he decided to check in with Camilla. At least he could reach her and even drop by and console her if she needed a friendly face.

This is a hell of a world we are living in thought Berkley. People in the hospital, especially those in emergency situations, needed family and friends by their side. Kitt had neither. It took what seemed like forever for Camilla to pick up after he had initiated the phone call. Even then, it was not her but instead her voice mail. No need to screen his calls, surely, she could see it was him calling. He left a cordial message expecting her to pick up, but she did not. This set off the alarm bells in his head. Next, he phoned Melania, the Uber driver. She answered promptly and was on her way. Whether she was prepared for company or not, Berkley's next destination would be Camilla's home. This would be a first. They never met at their...her residence, always at a restaurant or coffee house instead. Berkley was not offended by this arrangement because it was usually just, she and him, no George in tow. Not that George had not always been invited, he had just chosen to pass for whatever reason.

He had only been around George a couple of times, but he perceived George to be a likable gent. They did not have much in common, George in construction and him an author, however, George had always shown interest in what he was writing at the time. Berkley had to admit, he wasn't much of a conservationist when it applied to George's tools of the trade. He knew nothing about tools, machinery, or the construction business. Now, if ever he wished to know anything, the primary source for such banter was now gone. Dear Camilla must be in a dreadful state, thought Berkley. Mourning was such a dark and lonely state. Loss of a dear loved one can haunt a person forever. Some fare better than others when the grieving process challenges them to the core.

Berkley could relate having lost his mother three years ago. That loss had been quite devasting, him being an only child. His mother had lived with him after being stricken with pancreatic cancer. The stay had been brief. The cancer had been in stage four when it had been detected. It took her swiftly, within three months of her diagnosis. They had become quite close those final months, not that they were not before her illness. The two had always been close. Tragedies like this either bring you close or break you. He remained by her side as she drew her last breath under the care of hospice. The professions had been wonderful in preparing her for the end, as well as preparing him to face it. He could never do what they do. The endings were always the same, the ultimate ending of one's life. Special people they were.

He spotted his chariot down the street, the Prius turning the corner and heading in his direction. He wondered how his intuitive driver would react when he shared his destination, that of another person in need. Taxi drivers and Uber drivers substituted as bartenders, their customers seemingly with a desire to share their stories and troubles with a captivated audience. Like bartenders, most drivers were good listeners, as if they had nothing better to do on their commutes. Melanie seemed a bit different though, more of a conservationist and one to go above and beyond to share her opinion. Maybe he was stretching it a bit with his opinion. They hadn't actually exchanged that much conversationist during the last ride.

His thoughts briefly returned to Kitt. He had apparently been attacked outside his apartment. Here he was standing outside the hospital alone. This could easily have happened to him. Why Kitt? The poor chap had already survived one attack by an unruly mob. Like being struck by lightning, how is it possible for this to happen a second time so close to the first incident. What might be the odds wondered Berkley. The world was not the one they had lived in just a few short months ago. This virus had turned it topsy-turvy in a blink, so it felt. His New York City was no longer the same. The streets were deserted for the most part, no hustle, no bustle. All the restaurants were closed, many shuttered due to rioters and looters, either for protection or due to damages. Broadway and Fifth Avenue resembled war zones. Why had the world gone completely bonkers?

The Prius coming to a stop in front of him broke him free of the craziness circulating inside his head. Melanie greeted him with a cordial welcome back and sincere looking smile. Once seated inside she asked him how the visit had gone with his injured friend. He quickly admitted to her that she had been right, no visitors were allowed inside the hospital due to Covid concerns. When asked where to, she had not flinched when he had informed her of his next destination and the reason behind it. She offered no advice this time. Oddly, the commute remained quiet. She asked no questions, and he offered no explanations. He could probably have used a bartender's wisdom and guidance in a situation such as what faced him, but he never initiated the exchange. Yep, quiet and cordial, the ride ended in front of Camilla's home. She did ask if she should wait but he waved her off. Surely Camilla would not deny his entry, or better, his uninvited intrusion on her privacy. Hindsight, maybe he should have given it a bit more time and waited until she invited him here. Too late now. The Prius was gone.

Berkley rang the doorbell, waited a few seconds, and then knocked. She was not answering. Was she even here he wondered? He should have had Melanie hold the Prius. He eased to the side and felt like a peeping Tom cupping his hand against the window and looking inside. He could see a light on, maybe in the kitchen, but spotted no activity. He returned the door and tried the handle, locked, as it should have been. Next, he walked down the drive to where a side entrance doorway was located at the garage. Locked as well. Nothing to do now but venture to the back and complete his sweep. He hoped the neighbors did not notice an unidentified black man checking all the entryways. He surely did not wish to be the cause of another racial disturbance, especially with the city already in fear and paranoid about the state of society right now.

Backdoor, just try the doorknob. He did and it was not locked. Taking a deep breath, but not before looking around the backyard for any neighbors eyeing him from windows, he eased the door open and stepped inside. He was standing in a laundry room. One more door loomed ahead. He decided to knock on the door before testing to see if it was unlocked as well. No response so he slowly opened the door, only to be met by a broom in his face. It struck him hard enough to toss him off balance and on his butt on the tiled floor. On the other end of the witch's ride stood Camilla, eyes wide open and a grimace displayed on her face.

"Berkley Jay Patrick, what in the world are you doing?"

"Right now, I am thanking my lucky stars that New York has such strict gun ownership laws."

She offered the broom as a means for him to pull to his feet. "I mean, why are you here sneaking about in our backyard and sneaking inside our home?"

"I phoned. I rang the doorbell. I knocked on several doors and found one that was not locked. You should always lock your doors girlfriend."

"No. Why are you here?"

"I was worried about you and the fragile state you might be in."

"Since when have you considered me as being fragile? Yes, George's death is certainly devastating and unexpected, but I am not one to be pitied nor one that you should be worried about. You of all people should know that."

"Since I am here and currently stranded so to speak, could I at least come inside?"

"Sorry, excuse my manners and my loaded broom. By all means."

"Stranded you say."

"Uber driver dropped me off. Should have asked her to wait I suppose until I had finished casing the joint."

"Sorry about not hearing the phone or the door…doors, I was in George's shop. I guess I failed to lock the backdoor when I came back inside. My cell phone was on the kitchen counter."

"Are you okay, Camilla?"

"No one is okay in trying circumstances such at these. A little shock remains. It happened so quickly and by the time I got to him he was unconscious and unable to speak. We exchanged no final goodbye. But of course, you have already heard this Berkley, sorry."

"I have two shoulders and they both belong exclusively to you. Speak freely and repeat anything you feel deserves repeating."

"I'll fix us some tea. Please have a seat at the bar. Thank you for coming all the way out here just to check on me."

"Well, if I must confess, you were my second reason for getting out. My first was to check on Kitt Whitt. I don't guess you have seen the news."

"I am honored to be your second and no, I have not had the television on. Why were you checking on your friend and please tell me you did not break and enter his place too?"

138

"He is in the hospital. He was attacked outside his apartment apparently and is in critical condition."

"I thought he had been attacked when he was doing that piece for his podcast.

"Oh, he had. This is the second time. They did a number on him. Well, I can only assume they, whoever they are, did considering he is in intensive care. They would not let me see him, nor would they release any information to me about his condition. I am not family. Not sure if that matters. Hospital is not allowing family inside the building either. Covid restrictions were strictly enforced. I would not even have known he had been attacked if I had not seen the news segment. He had just appeared as a guest on Paula Wise's show. I watched it; a live zoom interview."

"I am so sorry to hear that. I know he is a dear friend. He was attacked after his appearance. Do you think that had something to do with it?"

"Your guess is as good as mine. He was so excited about his appearance on Paula Wise's show, and he can be quite outspoken on controversial matters. He and this Paula Wise share many of the same views. I suppose Kitt might be a bit more approachable and accessible than she if the wrong people were inclined to do something devious and hurtful."

"What now? How can you find out about his condition?"

"I don't know. The hospital, like most of the nation, is in complete Covid lockdown."

"Which hospital?"

"New York Presbyterian."

"No promises but I will see if Doctor Kyle Richardson, our doctor and close family friend, can find out his status. New York Presbyterian is his hospital."

"Super. Thank you dear. Now back to you, how are you really doing?"

"Day to day, minute by minute, the shock wearing off a bit. George and I did not have many conversations preparing us for a situation like this but we both agreed that neither of us would face any degree of depression over our loss. We are both strong willed and we have always been prepared spiritually. God gives us life, but death is inevitable. We have always cherished what we had, with each other, our kids, and grandkids. Neither of us feared dying. We both knew what lay ahead for us after we did make that journey. I am at peace with that fact and I am sure he is at peace with the outcome. My only regret, as I have stated, is we never had that final goodbye. It happened so quickly, Berkley."

"I wish I had a smidgen of the faith you have. It must be wonderful. Someday, maybe I can experience it."

"It is never too late to start."

"Got that. Thanks. So, what's next for you?"

"No funeral right now, leaves a chapter unfinished as you might say. Still must undergo the formalities one must face in situations such as this. We have wills and at some point, I will discuss his with our children. I will not deny that tough times are ahead. I will persevere though. It is the only way I know. Thank you for breaking into my home."

"The door was unlocked. I did not break in, but you did assault me with a broom. Might sue and claim I have been traumatized for life, a broom phobia now. I shall never be able to sweep again or view witches and Halloween the same."

"Drink your tea and then get out of my house, you conniving scoundrel."

"Tainted tea I bet. Poison me and bury me in your flower garden, the closing chapter in my life, one consumed by writer's block."

"Problem solved for you and me, right?"

19

Paula Wise sat in her studio, still finding it unbelievable that Kitt Whitt had been attacked so viciously after appearing on her show. She wondered if this had been provoked by his appearance. She certainly had received her fair share of death threats, especially lately. She had envisioned a promising future for the risk taker in her organization. He reminded her of a young Geraldo Rivera. She intended to have her producer arrange another interview with Kitt once he was well enough. Plus, by then, hopefully he would have had time to think over her proposition and agree to her offer. He held so much promise.

She turned her attention to her next show. There was no short supply of topics, the pandemic, the shutdowns, the crashing economy, riots and looting, and a presidential election year. One could easily draw lines and connect the dots to almost any if not all of them. It was her job to push back against the grain that represented the corrupt and biased media. She pushed hard against the socialist and communist uprising plaguing the country. Paula was obsessed with exposing it at every possible turn. Not on her watch. This country would never be ruled by socialism. Something undeniably swam just below the surface and was behind the evil surge America faced. She had her hunches, sure, but would not play that card until she had the undeniable evidence to support the bombshell. And, have no doubt, there were plenty of legitimate bombshells yet to explode on the scene. She did not believe in fabricating lies and false narratives. The truth and only the truth could defeat this evil. It was an evil like she had never experienced. True journalism had died except for a mere handful of fearless fighters, a virtual underground railroad battling insurmountable odds, so it often seemed. Stay true to the course and persevere was her mantra.

****

And if Covid, the shutdown, rioting, looting, and the destruction of cities were not enough, wildfire outbreaks were occurring in

California, Washington, and Oregon. Too many fires spreading rapidly were consuming the western states with vengeance. Firefighters from across the country were battling something never fathomed possible, so many fires in too many locations. Too coincidental, it had to be the work of arsonists. No suspects surfaced. The perpetrator or perpetrators had thus far been successful in staying a step ahead of the investigators. Only one brief sighting caught on a wildlife camera possibly offered a clue to a duo that might have been responsible for at least one of the fires. Three still frames had captured two hooded and suspicious characters out of place in the vicinity where three separate fires had begun, The Glass Fire. The fires added to the chaotic year plaguing America. Fires in major cities and now fires in the forest and rural communities were almost too much to comprehend.

****

Two police officers had been shot by a sniper as the local police department attempted to defend the city courthouse against a mob of rioters determined to set the building ablaze. In other large cities across the nation the rioters were throwing projectiles at the police. Numerous officers had been struck by frozen water bottles, bricks, and fireworks. Two state troopers had been injured when lasers had been pointed into their eyes. Two facist groups claimed responsibility too many of the destructive protests in the call for justice and defunding of the police. The president referred to these two groups as domestic terrorist for the billions of dollars' worth of destruction they were inflicting in major cities and for the threats of continued violence if he did not resign or if the election was lost by his opponent who stood for a socialist agenda and the new transformation of America. These radicals were vicious and unrelenting in their attempts to destroy the constitution, capitalism, and Christianity.

****

Senator Aaron Breeze stood at the podium on the Senate floor pleading with his party and that of the opposition to unite and denounce the chaos destroying the country. He delivered a compelling and inspirational speech at the Capitol, quite remarkable given the fact that he was a newbie on the scene when compared to the career politicians that had occupied the swamp forever. Partisan lines unfortunately held firm. While most in his party applauded his courageous attempt to tug on the moral apron strings, he was met with boos and jeers from much of the opposing party. Senator Charles Paulson tried to remain neutral until peer pressure from senior representatives prompted him to reluctantly toss out a few catcalls against his friend Aaron. It did not go unnoticed by Aaron, hurt by the display until realizing that Chuck half heartedly delivered the protest.

The Senate, unlike the House, had continued to hold in house sessions while wearing masks and practicing social distancing. The Speaker of the House only allowed video sessions and currently was in a stalemate with the opposing party over a stimulus package to aid businesses and people devastated by the shutdown. The Leader and her party demanded too many concessions in the bill that were unrelated to providing help for those needing it the most, the people and shuttered businesses. Too much pork was packed within the thousands of pages. The Speaker encouraged a bipartisan vote and then both sides could digest the content of the proposal. Never agree to a pig in a poke and expect to receive a fair deal so decried the Leader of the Senate. In this ridiculous and somewhat childish standoff, the American people suffered from the consequences of these politically driven actions. Where had the concept 'For the People' goneso badly wrong? The government was supposed to work for the people not vice versa. Big government had gotten out of hand and portrayed nothing like envisioned by the Founding Fathers.

****

Journalist Erwin Shipley, a veteran newsperson, could no longer report the biased narrative being pushed by his network, UBN, and resigned effective immediately. Shipley had recently spoken in opposition of these narratives on his weekly program and had been met with the utmost scrutiny by his producer and the network executives. After they had threatened to pull the plug on his program if he did not fall in line and report what they insisted he report, Shipley had promptly told them where they could shove their demands, but not before speaking his mind on their despicable deception to the viewers. Quitting had never felt so right and downright uplifting. Shortly thereafter he phoned a colleague and close friend to share his decision. His announcement was met with a simple reply, 'It is about time.'

20

Camilla had placed the birdhouse, the last creation of George's, on the kitchen counter. She had already phoned Pastor Roy Moony to ask if she could drop by the parsonage. She had not seen him since Abigail's or George's deaths. She remained in awe of him, at age 80, still persistent in preaching the gospel fulltime. Maybe with the church closure due to the pandemic and losing his wife he might consider hanging it up and enjoy his remaining years away from the pulpit. Doubtful though. Camilla missed those monthly scrabble games with the couple. Undeniably, Abigale's health had been noticeably declining rapidly. Roy had just recently admitted to her that his wife suffered from advance dementia. He had kept her going for as long as possible. He shared a few of the recurring episodes with Camilla, those portraying the once vibrant Abigale as one that at times did not recognize her husband. Camilla did not know what was worst, something like Alzheimer's or losing one's motors kills.

She placed her hand on the birdhouse as if trying to channel her husband's thoughts and essence. Of course, no spirits manifested, but still she drew comfort from knowing he had built it with his own hands and his vivid imagination. George had wanted it to go to Roy. She would make sure she abided by his wish and she had no doubt that Roy would cherish it just knowing that it had been the last one George had constructed. Selfishly she would loved to have kept it, but in her heart, she knew it had been bequeathed to Roy. She hoped the kids felt the same fondness for those their father had made for them before his passing. She had video chatted with Greg from Hawaii earlier. Almost every other day or so she chatted with either her other son Shay in Texas or daughter Margie in Vermont. She suspected they had agreed to some arrangement of alternating phone calls a bit too obvious by the consistency of the rotation.

Before heading to Roy's, she decided to review her spreadsheet for tracking the pandemic statistics. This had almost become an obsession of hers, an outlet and distraction from losing George. Her stats were not matching that of the Global Virus Center's, even though she supposedly was accessing the data from the exact same websites. She still surprisingly had access to sites she shouldn't have. Apparently, the administration had never deleted her logon and password. She should have reported this to them but until recently she had never tried to use them since her retirement. Now, she felt no obligation or loyalty for doing so. She perceived the GVC as corrupt and deceitful, especially in their dealings with the pandemic and what she believed to be dishonest reporting and recommendations. She was not sure what she intended to do with her analysis if she found compelling evidence to make her point. Right now, her research remained somewhat of a hobby and distraction.

She perused her data and could not connect the dots being shared with the public. The cases and number of deaths simply did not match. Both of hers were much lower. More disturbing was the fact that they were not sharing recovery rates, declining hospitalizations, and the mortality rate broken down by age. True to the facts being portrayed, the elderly and those with other existing conditions such as diabetes, heart conditions, and such were in the higher risk category. Mayors and governors insisting the elderly inflicted with Covid be placed back in nursing homes and assisted living facilities had been a death sentence for many living there as well as for those so carelessly sent to them. Camilla cringed at the hypocrisy of those officials not taking the responsibility for so many deaths that could have been prevented. Shameful!

Having had enough gloom and doom, she closed her laptop and headed to the bedroom to change and freshen up before heading over to Roy's. She found herself in a deeper funk when she stood at the doorway of the unfinished master closet where George had collapsed. If ever that was a such thing as ghosts, then her husband should forever haunt this space. She smiled, thinking that his paranormal self would be a welcome sight given the lonely confines of their home now. So far though, no apparitions had materialized, nor had there been any unexplained bumps and noises in the night or day as far as that goes. No restless spirits occupied the premises, only one restless alive and not so well person.

She still had not heard anything from Doc Richardson on the condition of Berkley's friend, Kitt Whitt. She prayed for the young man's recovery from his injuries. While she had seen the report of the attack on the local news, no mention had been made of it on UBN. She shrugged it off as not being worth national recognition maybe. But still, the kid had a huge following according to Berkley, even though she had never viewed his podcast. She had not even heard of him or his podcast until Berkley mentioned him. Still, it sure seemed senseless that someone would attack him like that and just leave him like discarded trash on the street near his apartment. Terrible and equally troubling times cursed this great country. Camilla had almost let time slip up on her. She sped up, not wishing to arrive late at Roy's.

On the drive to the parsonage, she was awestruck by the number of small, closed businesses while big box stores, grocery stores, and even liquor stores remained opened. She did not buy into the lines drawn for essential and nonessential. Was not everyone and their businesses essential to them and their families, their employees and the customers who depended on them being open? The Global Virus Center and factions of the government treated Covid-19 like some intelligent invader, as if it picked and chose what and whom it struck. Shaking her head, she scoffed at those who thought Walmart and Home Depot were safe, but a church congregation was not. If big box stores, grocery stores, and liquor stores could protect their employees and customers then why could none of the smaller businesses, restaurants, churches, and various other venues not follow the same protocol? Something was mighty fishy, just shutting down everything with no end in sight to flatten the curve. Diseases exist and will always exist. One cannot expect the world to live a shuttered life until a virus simply vanishes. First, it is not going on simply vanish and secondly, more harm is being inflicted to people quarantining them in this manner for months. Camilla understood the mental ramifications of long-term confinement, people not working, kids not going to school and no outlets being offered for them in this total lockdown structure.

The president was asking for some balance, for the country to reopen using guidelines of course, but open and return to at least some semblance of normalcy. Opposition called him crazy and a murderer for even thinking such irresponsible recommendations. Camilla, like many, could see through this ruse as political banner with the election growing nearer. Covid and a crippled economy was being used against the president. Camilla almost missed her turn off so engrossed in thought. Ten minutes later she parked in Roy's drive. She exited her car and felt she had arrived in an abandoned community. She saw no one outside, not even sounds of kids playing. Hindsight, the kids of today were not living in the same era she had grown up in or that her children had been exposed to. Too many children preferred staying inside glued to their social media devices and video games. Why would a pandemic force them outside any more than it would force them inside? As a parent she would have insisted they go outside for some fresh air even under these circumstances. She could envision herself becoming completely squirrelly if confined inside with her kids 24/7. Times had indeed changed for all the wrong reasons.

She rang Roy's doorbell and the door almost opened simultaneously. He had either seen her arrive or was sitting on ready when the bell sounded. In a world of masks and social distancing, she and her pastor hugged and then both removed their protective masks. One could not live and survive in fear, especially when she and he put their lives in God's hands. Some would view their actions as irresponsible and in the public's eye she would never have done anything to be perceived as reckless and endangering others. She wasn't where anyone could see them. Neither asked the other for a hug or requested that they keep their distance and mask on. What they did felt right, so they acted on it. No regrets and it felt wonderful, two humans sharing a normal embrace for a change.

"Please come in and have a seat, Camilla, dear."

"Hold that thought, I have something for you."

She returned to her car and retrieved the birdhouse and handed it to him. Roy looked a bit confused by her gift and gesture.

"Roy, this is the very last birdhouse that George made with his own hands. After her passing, he told me he wanted you to have it once you were up to us visiting. Obviously, he never had a chance to follow up on that, but I do. Look above the birdhouse door."

Inscribed was The Mooney Forever House.

"Simply perfect…I wish she and George were here to enjoy this extraordinary creation along with us. George was such a talented soul."

Camilla teared up, "I miss them both as I am sure you do as well, Roy."

"Please, have a seat. I have herbal tea ready and mint cookies, her recipe. I must confess it is my first time attempting to produce her little masterpiece mints."

"I get it. I am your guinea pig. Bring them on then."

"Trust me, I have already sampled them to make sure you are not poisoned by my attempt. They do not measure up to hers, but they are edible and not too disappointing to the palate, or I would not have dared offered you a sample."

Over tea and cookies, the two conversed covering most all subjects but the deaths of their spouses. Roy shocked her by saying he had been considering stepping down from his church but added that his prayers nor God had yet confirmed if this choice was the right one. He felt that the world needed God's word more than ever. He did feel like most people of faith, that the government was acting unlawfully preventing people from practicing their right to worship. What they were doing contradicted the First Amendment, Roy quoting that it stated that everyone in the United States has the right to practice his or her own religion. Roy did not understand why the religious sector was not standing united to uphold the First Amendment. Camilla nodded in agreement.

It was Roy who finally brought up the deaths, first expanding his wife's downward spiral and then providing graphic examples of her deteriorating mental health. Dementia in any form was indeed a terrible disease. He had witnessed firsthand the tragedy and decline that most outside the walls of their home had never seen. Camilla's heart ached for him and for what both had endured. Roy explained how some that had been impacted by this had found it too easy to blame God for the painful experience. He had not followed this path of course, but even he admitted that he was guilty of asking why her, why them and why this way given how they lived their lives worshipping God Almighty. He further explained that his had been a brief period of questioning, that prayer and his faith had overcome the adversary.

Camilla, taking the opportunity, finally asked him what had happened. She had not been prepared for the answer, expecting something more like she had passed in her sleep or with him diligently by her side. Neither. Poor confused Abigail had stuck a kitchen fork into an electrical socket after telling Roy that she had ironing to do and asking him to please set up her ironing board. It had happened so quickly, her electrocuting herself. Roy chalked it up to possibly God answering prayers, that his wife need not suffer from this dreadful disease. No, he did not blame God for what had happened but her dying in this manner had in a way been more merciful than what she could have possibly faced.

One thing puzzled him though and he shared this with Camilla. On her death certificate it mentioned that she had contracted Covid-19. He found this odd because neither of them had ever been tested for the virus. He shrugged it off figuring that evidence of Covid had been detected during the autopsy, an autopsy that the coroner had insisted not necessary. Camilla did something she would never have normally done in circumstances like this, she asked to see the death certificate. Roy retrieved it for her. She was shocked by what she read. It didn't merely state that Covid had been detected, it listed Covid as contributing to her death. She had been electrocuted for goodness sake. Covid could in no way have been a contributing factor. She did something even further outside her reactive scope. She asked Roy if she could have a photocopy. He without hesitation made her one. She expressed her concerns for the cause and explained she would like to check on it if he had no objections. Roy trusted anything Camilla said, adding he was a bit curious as well.

On her drive back home, Camilla listened to a talk radio station and the commentator was berating the president for his persistence in calling Covid-19 the China virus. She shook her head in disgust over the pettiness of the biased media. Evidence clearly pointed to China as the origin of this deadly coronavirus, accidently or not. The media and opposition preferred blaming the president for deaths on American soil all singing the same choreographed tune that he had mishandled it. Nothing was further from the truth to anyone that had an inkling of common sense thought Camilla. She thought the data she had been compiling and the narrative being portrayed just did not pan out. Abigail's certificate was just as troubling. A virus could not be the cause of someone dying by electrocution. If the coroner would have stated that dementia had possibly contributed to her confused judgement, she might be willing to buy that. Not this though. It was totally outrageous and misleading. More of a boldfaced lie to be blunt. Why was it so important to categorize her death in such a manner?

As she arrived home, she realized that she had missed a call on her cell phone. She switched off the engine and listened to it before exiting the car. It was from Berkley. He still had received no word about his friend Kitt's condition. She had not heard back from Doc Richardson yet either. She had not conveyed that the inquiry was an urgent matter. It had been less that 48 hours since the young man had been assaulted. Berkley's message indicated that he was heading back to the hospital to seek answers again. She felt his pain. There seemed to be no escape from the ominous grip lately; George, Abigail, and the tragic attack of Kitt Whitt were eye openers. It had to be even tougher knowing that his friend Kitt was so young.

She stepped from her car and stood there in the driveway looking at their home. For the first time she dreaded going inside, feeling the emptiness that awaited her and experiencing the emptiness inside her as well. Mourning a loss was not something to be wished on anyone. She, for the first time in a long time, considered returning to work, maybe volunteering as she once had. When the danger finally subsided, she also intended to spend some precious time with her children and grandchildren, maybe even head to the beach condo in

South Carolina. Her head was spinning with all these thoughts and none of them were making it any easier to enter the house.

"Oh George, why," she whispered.

21

Erwin Shipley had freelanced before so quitting the United
Broadcast Network did not stress him the least bit. He embraced his
newfound freedom by immediately pursuing the truth in the
controversy surrounding the pandemic. He had already titled his next
piece Fear Mongering Versus Common Sense. He opined how the
country could not come to a screeching halt over a virus. The
consequences of this direction were unhealthy and unamerican.
Shipley was not the type to hold back any punches, especially if
political motives were evident in the propaganda being flaunted. He
had seen too much of this political posturing during this president's
first term, more so than he had ever experienced in all his years of
journalism. He was old school, accustomed to reporting news as it
happened and allowing the viewers or readers in some cases to
decide. Genuine journalists did not edit the content, skew the details,
or ever interject biased opinions into the stories. Well, at least that
was how it was supposed to be done. Honesty and integrity appeared
to be past tense in today's world.

Masked and socially distancing as he entered the lobby, Erwin
Shipley stopped at the receptionist desk and smiled cordially, not
that the young lady could see his sincere attempt at being cordial. He
told her that he had an appointment. Sporting a mask that
coordinated with her blouse, she nodded and may have been smiling
as well. She pressed a button after picking up the phone and
announced that her 10 o'clock appointment had arrived. Anna
Williamson, according to the name tag she wore, instructed him to
please enter the doorway to his left. Shipley said thank you, thinking
how these masked exchanges sounded like the muffled fast-food
drive-in speakers did when the person on the other end was taking
your order.

"Erwin, how wonderful to see you. Please have a sit. Coffee, tea or
even though it is early, something a bit stronger?"

"Nothing for me, thank you. Nice office but I would expect the
infamous Paula Wise to surround herself with nothing but the best."

"Mere creature comforts to sooth those often a bit apprehensive when it comes to sharing whatever story they deem pertinent. Razzle dazzle them I always say. It loosens their lips and eases their conscience. Of course, this little charade is not for you. I respect you too much for that."

"No offense taken, Paula. We have known one another too long for that."

"How does it feel to be free at last?"

"Unemployment always feels the same. But honestly, I should have gotten out long ago. Frankly, journalism has died."

"Most, but not all."

"We are merely dinosaurs trying to survive in a world where the asteroid has all but destroyed civilization."

"We are survivors, you and I. Throwbacks maybe. We will always stand for truth and nothing but, no matter how sensationalized the story might become. That brings me to why I asked you here, Erwin."

"That's what I have always liked about you, Paula, straight to the point, no hem hawing. So, let's have it. Why am I here?"

"Your wheelhouse has always been your uncanny ability to infiltrate and obtain the scoop from the inside. Not that you aren't an excellent journalist, you are, but you have a gift that can not be taught or learned easily. Obviously, we share a similar passion, a quest to get to the bottom of what is happening, specifically what has been happening for the past three and a half years."

"Ah, the current presidential administration and America unhinged. Chaos has never been more rampant for sure."

"There is more to this than just a hatred for our president. You sense it as well as I do. The media bias is real, no denying it, but what intrigues and scares me is what is swimming below the surface. I think we can agree that the unthinkable is being cultivated by forces with hellish motives and even deeper pockets."

"Part of the reason I told UBN to shove it. I concur. Powerful forces are in play and beating the incumbent president is just one piece of the complex puzzle."

"I must confess, I did not ask you here to exchange theories, not that I would not thoroughly enjoy that conversation. Instead, I would like to make you an offer. Join me as an equal partner and then we collectively blow the lid off this, equal billing and credit. Our styles compliment each other. I will provide the smoke and mirrors via my show and you do what you do best from an undercover aspect. You remain out of the limelight until we have the final bombshell. We expose the truth as one."

"You do realize what you are asking and expecting us to do, don't you? This is as deep state as it probably gets, going where we need to go. My gut tells me that those that are ultimately responsible for what we both suspect they are up to, will not play nicely once they catch wind of what we are doing."

"So, is that a no."

"Hell no. I am in and it is exactly why I quit in the first place. Just wanted to make sure you fully understood the dangers of taking on something this huge. We are going to step on plenty of toes and piss off a lot of prominent people, not to mention exposing an element that prefers to remain out of public view."

"You know something already, don't you Erwin?"

"Let's just say I have my suspicions and a draft suspect list. Yes."

Paula reached into her desk and retriever a folder and slid it across the desk to Erwin.

156

"What's this?"

"I had my lawyer prepare a contract. Please review it and let me know if we need to amend it. Anything is negotiable."

"You were that confident, huh. Mere creature comforts to sooth those in need."

"On the contrary, I know you. This has been eating at you as it has me. It goes beyond mere sensationalism. You understand what is happening and why it is imperative to stop it."

"Got me there. So, when do we start?"

"Please, take time to review the contract."

"No need. Where do I sign? You have already so eloquently stated it. We are doing this for all the right reasons, end of story."

Paula's cell phone rang. "Excuse me just a second. I need to take this."

Erwin listened to the one-sided conversation observing Paula's facial tics. He was not liking what he was seeing in her facial expressions. Less than a minute later she ended the call.

"Not trying to pry but is everything okay?"

"Not really. I had asked my producer to have a matter investigated and I was not prepared for the outcome. Did you by any chance catch the news of the young podcast host, Kitt Whitt, that was brutally attacked near his apartment?"

"Yeah, that was very tragic. The kid seemed to have a promising future. Reminded me a bit of us and that is not something you see in today's generation."

"He is dead. Never gained consciousness. He had just appeared on my show moments before the attack. I had made him a lucrative offer to join my company. He had so much energy and promise."

"Puts things in perspective for where we are venturing, doesn't it?"

Nodding, Paula added, "Another interesting fact. Seems he was friends with Berkley Jay Patrick."

"The author?"

"One and the same. He was outside the hospital hoping to hear any news about young Whitt. Producer gave him my card and encouraged him to call and schedule an appointment to discuss a possible segment for my show. The least I could do to pay my respects for the kid, do an in-depth segment on his untimely murder."

"You get a two for, the kid's story and an interview with a famous author, not a bad angle. You have quite the Midas Touch."

"Like I said, me on the front lines and you in the trenches, they will never see it coming."

"Got to ask you, Paula. Are you buying this whole mask thing they are cramming down our throats?"

"Not entirely. The initial flip flopping raised my suspicions. If that wasn't enough proof, it has turned politically ugly. Your deep state hard at work. The virus is real enough but is it really any deadlier than other causes for concern? Diversionary tactics, sleight of hand, scare the bejeepies out of everyone while a more devious plan remains below the radar."

"And that is where we come in, right? Shock and awe!"

"Ready for that first chapter, partner?"

"Secret agent man at your service. Perhaps we should discuss our plan and initial targets for blowing the proverbial lid. I am currently available, willing, and able. Buckle up though. This is guaranteed to be one hell of a scary ride."

Paula Wise and Erwin Shipley thought they understood what they were getting into. Ultimately, they had no idea. An enemy deeply rooted would pose to be an extremely dangerous adversary. They were on the verge of discovering just how deadly evil can be once the nest has been disturbed. Poke a wasp nest and maybe you only get stung. Mess with killer hornets and face far worse circumstances. Too late for back peddling. Their journalistic juices were already in a frenzied state to reverse actions now.

22

Camilla sat in front of her laptop attempting to compile more data but only becoming lost in her thoughts instead. She was not one normally to succumb to melancholy, but these were anything but normal times. George's untimely death had been a forever gamechanger. She had not foreseen life without him. She felt for Roy Mooney as well, dealing with the loss of Abigail. Abigail, the mere thought of her prompted Camilla to refocus. She fingered the death certificate, again reading related cause of death, Covid-19. Not possible given Roy's explanation for her death. Electrocution and being pronounced dead at the scene, coronavirus had no place on this certificate. Juices flowing once again, she skimmed through her spread sheet. Just how many deaths were being miscategorized as caused by this virus? Even more troubling, was it intentional? It made no sense. What could be gained by misreporting these deaths. The medical profession would not manufacture false information. Then, she thought back to just how far the Global Virus Center would go to ensure their funding was sound. Fear of incurable diseases prompted those with deep pockets to reach even deeper.

The cell phone disrupted her further venturing down the conspiracy road. She glanced over and saw Doctor Kyle Richardson on the caller ID.

"Camilla, how are you holding up? Stupid question, I am sure."

"No denying it, hard to believe but I take one step at a time and will eventually arrive some place."

"I do have some news for you and your friend about the young man in question, Mister Whitt. Sorry, it isn't what either of you would have wished to hear. He is deceased, another tragic causality of Covid, I'm afraid."

"But he was attacked, Kyle, and no more than a couple of days ago according to Berkley. How could he have died of the virus?"

"My sources did not mention his injuries as contributing to his death, only Covid."

"Did you see the autopsy report?"

"I did not, but I have no reason to question what I was told. My source is quite reliable but for reasons you can understand, must remain anonymous."

"Thank you, Kyle. I will relay this to Berkley. I do have another question though. Do you find it odd that so many deaths are being attributed to the virus lately? It is rare to hear anyone dying of other causes."

"The virus is quite aggressive. Death is not uncommon. What is really on your mind, Camilla?"

"Sorry, too much time on my hands and an occupational hazard for an old, retired woman to be intrigued by this new strand. Thanks again for going the extra mile, Kyle."

"Not a problem. You call me anytime, day or night, if you need me. In time, this will be better or so they say."

"They have no idea what they are talking about, I can attest to that fact. Take care, Kyle. Say hello to Mildred for me."

Covid, Camilla was not buying it in this situation. First Abigail and now Kitt Whitt. Roy said his wife had died from electrocution not Covid. And then there was Berkley's friend Kitt who had been assaulted two days ago and now supposedly pronounced dead of Covid as well. It was as if anyone who expired magically did so by a single cause. No virus wreaked this much havoc so quickly and methodically. She added these to her spread sheet again reviewing what she had already been compiling. Camilla shook her head in disgust finding it unbelievable that someone was intent on painting a more disturbing scenario. She reached for the phone thinking she should reach out to her friend at the Global Virus Center but then just as quickly hesitated. He had made it clear that he could not become involved and she could not really blame him.

No, this was her cross to bear for now until she had enough concrete indisputable evidence to convince the proper authorities that what was being reported was a fabricated lie. Who could she trust though? This was above local jurisdiction. What was happening obviously had national tentacles. Her prime suspect remained the GVC. She reminded herself she had experienced it firsthand on a much smaller scale while employed there. Of course, a pandemic had never been in play while she worked for the GVC. Worldwide chaos existed due to Covid-19. Still, how could the world be deceived by such despicable consequences. All roads led back to the GVC, the one body that could pull this off. But for what purpose? Falsely reporting data, skewing the stats to depict a morbid outcome made absolutely no sense. Who had something to gain from such madness? Identify that person or organization and the rest should fall in place.

Camilla closed her laptop and expelled air like a deflating balloon. She tried to convince herself that this was not her problem, but the argument fell short. This was everyone's problem if such deceit was being purposely perpetrated and the American people and the world if truth be told. Back to square one, she contemplated the origin of the coronavirus, China. What did the communist regime have to gain by unleashing this deadly virus on the world and the Chinese people? She smirked. Since when did the Chinese government care about its people? Shaking her head, since when did I feel so compelled to become involved in a possible political powder keg? If George were here and I shared my suspicions with him, he would be all over this blaming the China virus for everything. But he isn't and never will be she almost mumbled out loud as a tear rolled down her cheek.

She stepped away from conspiracy theory central and returned to the kitchen where she poured a refill of herbal tea. Camilla stood at the sink gazing through the window, three birdhouses mounted on poles caught her eye. One was painted in the Rochester Red Wings Triple-A baseball team's colors. George so loved his baseball and supported the minor league team affiliated with the Minnesota

Twins. A second birdhouse sported a New York Yankee logo. He had been a diehard Yankee fan for sure. The third birdhouse was her backyard favorite, painted red, white, and blue. It had been the first one he built while confined under house arrest as he loved to call it. She smiled now thinking how obsessed he had been in his newfound hobby, a distraction from the horrors being unleashed on this great nation. Camilla had cringed after the completion of every masterpiece knowing George would gift them to people who did not need them. Feeling a bit guilty now about that, she realized this would become part of her late husband's legacy. No doubt, those possessing them would cherish them in his memory, especially the kids and eventually the grandkids. The cell phone ringing disrupted her nostalgic stroll.

"Hello, Melvin, so wonderful to hear your voice. Yes, I am doing as fine as one would expect given the situation. Sure, please come over if you would like. Noon would be fine, and you will join me for lunch. See you then."

What a pleasant surprise thought Camilla, having not seen Melvin Meeker since the Covid crisis had begun. He had battled his stint with the virus but had come out on the other side thankfully. Sadly though, his business still suffered from the mandatory shut down deemed necessary by Governor Anita Ming. The demonizing of perpetrated nonessential businesses drove poor George bonkers. In his humble opinion all businesses were essential. How could you pick one over the other, especially those in construction? She smiled thinking how George had professed that the nonessentials were in congress. He fumed at the audacity of the government, destroying the livelihood of the good hard-working Americans while they still earned a paycheck. He opined that congress should not get their pay until Americans were back on the job. Foxes watching the henhouses was a recipe for disaster.

Melvin wouldn't be here for a while and she knew how he loved her homemade pimento cheese, as did George. She had learned to make it from scratch as taught by her grandmother, a woman southern rooted in the Georgia clay. When she made George a toasted pimento sandwich for lunch, she always made an extra one for him to take to Melvin. She would even include a small container for Melvin for later knowing how much he enjoyed it. This time all the extra would go to him. She retrieved all the ingredients she needed and began preparing it, another perfect distraction.

Like clockwork, Melvin arrived on the button wearing a mask of course. She was taken by his appearance. He had lost a lot of weight during his bout with the virus or he was not eating well. Most people complained about weight gain during the pandemic confinement. His skin was a bit paler than she had remembered and his face appeared drawn. She withheld any comments on his condition. She tossed caution to the wind and hugged him. He had been a bit standoffish until she made the first move, her standing there unmasked after all.

"Melvin, I know George felt so bad that he could not visit you during your sickness."

"Wasn't his fault. They were not allowing any visitation while I was hospitalized. With this social distancing, it complicates everything. He stepped up and took care of the business in my absence; that's what counted. I will be glad when we can return to normal. My crews need to work. I need to work. Heck, this whole country needs it."

"How are you feeling?"

"I should be asking you that, Camilla. Guess I have felt better but being home and no longer on that ventilator is a God wink. I would not wish that experience on my worst enemy. This Covid is quite serious, worse than I ever envisioned. Made a believer out of me."

Camilla had considered discussing her findings with Melvin but after this, she did not feel compelled to do so given what he had gone through and survived. She knew the virus was real and she understood the ramifications of contracting it. The mortality rates she had compiled was not aligning with those being reported. There would probably be no convincing Melvin though. Why go there? Instead, they reminisced about George, Melvin sharing stories she had never heard. Stories George would have never shared with her, men stuff so he might call it. Melvin did not flinch in telling them, laughing loudly as he did, cherishing every single one as did she.

Melvin devoured two toasted sandwiches bringing joy to her heart seeing how he relished them. She could see a lot of George's ways in Melvin, probably from years of being his protégée. She almost chuckled out loud thinking how some say how old married couples grow to resemble one another. Might be applicable for longtime friends and working associates also. Of course, they say the same thing about people and their pets. She wished she had one of his birdhouses to give Melvin and even thought about offering one of the three in the backyard. No, a gift must be special. George customized his creations specifically for those people special in his life.

"Camilla, mind if I look at that closet-reno that George was working on for you? If you would allow me, I would like to finish what he started."

"You don't have to that, Melvin."

"But I do. He would want me to and besides, I am bored. I need something to do, all right?"

"Very well, this way but excuse the clutter. It is how he left it."

"There is no such thing as clutter in the eyes of a builder of masterpieces. I can see that George envisioned such with his gift to you. Let us walk through what you and he had in mind and I will do my best to honor those dreams."
Camilla and Melvin shared a few precious moments envisioning what George had failed to complete. She could tell that this unfinished project provided them both some closure and welcomed it wholeheartedly. They agreed on a time to complete the renovation. She packed up the remaining pimento cheese and some homemade fig preserves as well. She stood at the door watching until Melvin had driven his truck out of sight. Camilla then placed the palm of her hand on the glass door and sighed, "Oh George, I miss you so."

23

Berkley had arrived at Paula Wise's office, waiting quite impatiently to be summoned inside by the receptionist. He still was not sure why she had invited him to meet with her. The producer had extended the invitation after he had been recognized outside the hospital and after briefly chatting with him about his concerns for his friend inside. Kitt had appeared on her syndicated show shortly before he had been attacked. The wait seemed to be over. She told him he could enter.

"Please have seat Mister Patrick. Might I offer you something to drink?"

"No thank you and please call me Berkley."

"And likewise, call me Paula. Given the affairs of the world we now reside, how goes your writing?"

"Plenty of time on my hand like most everyone else. I appreciate your hospitality, huh, Paula. I apologize for sounding rude but exactly why am I here?"

"You were a friend of Kitt Whitt, so I was informed."

"He and I were extremely close friends. Yes, I saw him on your show...the last thing..."

"Yes, I regret what happened to him after his appearance. I certainly hope the attack was not prompted by that appearance."

"He received threats before doing your show. Goes with the territory for those being outspoken and dealing in the truth these days. Free speech is not so free if you do not agree with those speaking against it, so it seems."

"What a loss. Kitt had so much promise. I had just offered him a lucrative proposition to join my team. He was quite inspirational in his investigative approach. His last words to me were that he would discuss it with his associates."

Laughing, "Associates? Kitt was a one-man gang. He flew a lot of his ideas up the flagpole with me, but I was not an associate either. Unfortunately, he never had time to share your proposition with me. I am sure he would have though. That is who he was."

"What a tragedy, expiring in such a manner."

"Yeah, Covid doesn't discriminate for sure. Even the young are not out of bounds."

"Covid? My sources say he died from his injuries. Did he already have the virus?"

"Not that I know of. A friend of mine had a doctor friend of hers investigate his death for me. She said he died from the virus."
"Interesting. Guess it is possible but seems like a stretch to me given the severity of the beating he received."

"Seems you have a knack for digging in the dirt, Paula. Possibly your sources are not what they are cracked up to be. I apologize for saying that."

"My sources are quite reliable I assure you. It is my business to get it right the first time. Can you divulge your source?"

"I could ask you the same thing, but I think I know the answer. Mine was no deep throat, just merely a close friend that I asked to find out about Kitt's condition. I am not family so the hospital would share nothing with me. I could not visit him. I did not even know Kitt had died. It is kind of odd."

"Odd?"

"Yeah, my friend mentioned another person who had died recently. Seems there is a conflict in her death too. The woman's husband said she accidently electrocuted herself, yet her death certificate stated, she, too died from Covid-19."

"How long was she in the hospital?"

"She wasn't. She died at the scene. Boy, these hospitals are having a tough time. Guess they are overworked and understaffed. My friend has been compiling her own data and she thinks incidences like this are more than mere coincidence."

"Conspiracy theorist? Lot of them out there."

"My friend is not a whacko, if that is what you are thinking. She is of sound mind and grounded I assure you. She used to work for the GVC, retired now."

"Your friend was employed at the Global Virus Center?

"One of their resident experts in her day, I must add. She was a go-to person, a renowned virologist."

"Intriguing and she has been compiling data on the subject of mortality rates."

"Something like that. She is a firm believer that the data never lies. Stats all the way."

"You still haven't answered why you asked me here, Paula."

"I had hoped to do a piece on Kitt and allow you to plug any book projects you might be working right now."

"Your demeanor says otherwise."
"I must confess, I am intrigued by the conflictions in causes of deaths you have shared, and I am equally interested in meeting your friend, the retired virologist."

"I take it that Kitt Whitt nor I no longer interest you then."

"No, on the contrary, I still desire to pay tribute to young Mister Whitt and share any information about your writing, that is if you will agree to do so. It is my job to seek stories wherever they might lead. Often one door opens where another closes. Instinct tells me I should pursue this new angle. To be honest, it has potential links to other storylines I am pursuing."

"I understand. No promises though. I will share with my friend that you are interested in her studies and she can decide if she is willing to discuss them with you," Berkley said as he stood.

"Fair enough. Please prepare any information I can use about Kitt Whitt, as well as information about yourself. Make an appointment with my administrative assistant as you leave, and we will meet again to prepare the segment for an upcoming show. It has been my pleasure to make your acquaintance, Berkley. I look forward to your next best seller."

After Berkley exited, Paula phoned Erwin Shipley. "Stop by this afternoon. I have a new little nugget that might intrigue you. It requires your investigative intuitiveness."

****

Later that afternoon, Berkley made a phone call as well. He recapped his meeting with Paula Wise and her apparent interest in Camilla's studies of the virus deaths. He had to do some back peddling explaining that it had not been his intent to mention that to Paula Wise. It had just inadvertently happened. Camilla straddled the fence, not sure if she was prepared to share her findings and suspicions with a known news media celebrity. She had seen maybe a couple of Wise's segments but did not know enough about her to feel she was any different than the other biased media. The last thing she needed was someone to make a mockery of what she had worked so hard to compile and do so in a public format. She told Berkley she would think on it and pray about it.

She did find it interesting that Wise's source had conflicted with her own. Not much of a stretch though given she had already suspected something fishy about Kitt Whitt's death being blamed on Covid

170

after being so severely beaten and dying rather quickly. The injuries had been reported as not contributing to his death. She almost called Kyle again to ask him to dig a bit deeper but doing so would put him in a precarious situation. compromising his ethics further. No, she had gone to that well once, she could not go there a second time.

****

The rioting and unrest continued. Viewers would never know this if they relied exclusively on the media such as the United Broadcast Network. Rioting and the burning of cities and neighborhoods were just being blown out of proportion. Most were simply peaceful protests. The Matter Movement and Anti Movement did not exist. Both were portrayed as ideas, neither organized nor destructive. On the flipside, major corporations were donating billions of dollars to the so-called nonexistent ideals. Pay them and just maybe they would not burn the larger businesses. Police were being attacked, some killed in a cry for justice. There was no defense for killing innocent people to even the score. UBN looked the other way because it did not fit the narrative. Politicians opposing the president remained silent and would not condemn these supposedly peaceful protests wreaking holy hell on the nation. People watched as their livelihoods and businesses were burned to the ground, but only after loiters had taken what they wanted first.

Statues, any statues, were destroyed as symbols of oppression. These crazies were not historians because many of the statues stood against what they perceived as wrong in the nation. If it was a statue it was fair game. In some cases, the president had sent in federal forces to defend federal property, courthouses and yes, statues. He had just mandated by executive order a minimum ten-year prison sentence for anyone convicted of destroying federal property such as statues. Subsequently the destruction of statues had ceased because of his actions. The riots on the other hand continued. The world gone crazy never seemed to rest once darkness fell. The mayors of these cities did nothing to stop it. The president's hands were tied if neither the mayors nor governors asked him for help. The worst of the cities impacted by such distruction were governed by the opposition party. It was these same city and state officials that stood firm to the shutdowns regardless of statistics contradicting their decisions to do so.

Senators Charles Paulson and Aaron Breeze had all but ceased their civil conversations about the unrest. Political parties divided had claimed two more victims. Friends had been forced to draw party lines; having given in to the relentless peer pressure in the political arena. Both were appalled by the state of the nation and the politics being flaunted. The swamp had claimed two more victims caught in the quicksand of politic power. The goal was to get elected and then riches and fame would surely follow if you conceded to playing the game that was expected. Career politicians were just that; no term limits to deter them. Paulson and Breeze had known the ramifications of winning their elections even though both had thought they could bring change to the establishment. Unfortunately, the machine devours its enemies and its own if unwilling to fall in line. While Paulson could probably conform to the devious mantra, Breeze would not fair as well, too moral, and straight forward. He possessed Godly convictions and could never tow the line for those not believing in the power of the people they represented. His stint would surely be short lived, a one termer for sure if he lasted that long.

With the election and day of reckoning fast approaching for voters, the contrasting choice loomed large. Political pundits laid out the evidence and arguments. Socialism versus capitalism remaining on the forefront. Control of speech versus freedom of speech. Abolishment of religion or freedom to worship. Abortion all the way to birth or anti-abortion, no killing of babies. Open borders versus regulated borders. Free everything versus working for an honest wage and living, earning your way. Taxes, taxes, and more taxes versus tax relief. Confiscation of guns versus right to bear arms. Big government versus smaller government. The contrasts were staggering and mind boggling. Why would any sane or rational person wish to be owned, controlled, and prohibited from following the American dream? The wishes of the founding fathers were in serious jeopardy as was the constitution. Battle lines had never been so precisely defined. The analogy 'it didn't take rocket science to understand it' never spoke so profoundly. Yet, a generation of

172

people seeking to have everything given to them with no strings attached compromised everything. No strings attached, right! Once the dark side prevailed it would be too late.

24

Erwin Shipley did what he did best. He latched onto a trail and blood hounded it until he got answers. As unethical as it often became, the end always justified the means. He was good at it. Paula Wise knew it. Their alliance made perfectly good sense. Shipley was not a large guy, almost wiry if you had to hang a description on him. He had this chameleon gift, capable of transforming into the perfect individual to blend into any environment. A perfectionist, he took his assignments seriously. He researched and studied all aspects and, in the end, he mimicked the perfect portrayal, one that would ensure he infiltrated and completed all objectives. He had brought down the most infamous individuals and organizations in his wake.

The bone Paula had tossed his way was a piece of cake in comparison to where his reputation had usually taken him. Now the brass ring was something different. If what they both suspected was anywhere close to reality, this would be the blockbuster to top all. With it would surely pose unsurmountable dangers. Exposing something this large would not come without opposition and consequences. No, Shipley didn't shy away from a challenge or fear those consequences but even he understood the hazards of walking into the eye of a hurricane. After all, why wouldn't he, he was the epitome of a hurricane hunter.

First things first though, drop a line in the tiny fishing hole and see what nibbles at the bait. The bigger catch would come later. His goal for now, determine the identity of the virologist, friend of bestselling author, Berkley Jay Patrick. Paula did not seem to think that the virologist was going to come forth freely and share her findings. Patrick was perceived as a loyalist, not one to cough up his friend's name for any amount of additional fame or fortune. This called for circumvention. There were several ways to skin this cat. Go old gumshoe and simply follow him, bug his phone, or utilize numerous other tools as his disposal. Or he could lure the prey into the Venus Flytrap with a promise of tasty nectar. Today, just call him Venus. Celebrities had humongous egos that required regular stroking. The author would be mere putty in an expert stroker's hand. Loose lips can devastate the buoyancy of a drifting ship.

The pandemic did offer obstacles a bit abnormal and challenging. Normally, Shipley, or his alter identity, would assumedly stage a meeting with his mark at a venue such as a restaurant. With the closures of these he would have to be a bit more resourceful and keep it much less obvious. The waiting game began. He had camped outside the author's apartment building after already having researched his quirky patterns. A mom and pop grocery store nearby and still open, was a necessity given the current circumstances. Shipley, being the creative sole, had obtained information from a grocery employee that assured Patrick would be replenishing staples this morning. Paying for this information had been easier than ever given the current situation. And like magic, he exited the building in route. The rues now in progress but only after he exited the grocery.

Shipley had staged it perfectly. On schedule, Patrick approached, oblivious to what waited ahead. It would be a bit tricky, both he and the author wearing masks, but ego stroking knows no boundaries and can be quite shameful when orchestrated by a seasoned professional. The aggressive and well-placed bump, the spill, the stand back and excuse me, then the awe-struck fan speaks.

"I am so sorry. I should have been paying more attention to where I was going. Wait a minute. You are him, aren't you? You are really him. Even with the mask I would recognize you anywhere. I attended your last workshop, the one before this dreadful pandemic. It was amazing Mister Berkley Jay Patrick, sir. You are by far my most favorite author. No one compares. Your style is so unique. I must apologize for my blubbering, but I am in awe in your presence."

Shipley squatted and began assisting Berkley in picking up the scattered grocery items from the two bags he had been carrying. Eggs were obviously broken, as was a jar of preserves on the sidewalk. He again apologized profusely.

"I appreciate your enthusiasm and accolades, Mister…"

"Braden…Braden Peterson, sir. I am so sorry for being such a distracted klutz. You are a writer. You know how easily we can become consumed in our thoughts when visualizing a script."

"Ah, you write as well then, Braden? Genre?"

"I have not actually published anything yet, but I am working on a political thriller somewhat based on current events, the pandemic and craziness to be more specific. I have an outline but that is about it. Sorry to bother you with it though. Please, let me replace the items I have destroyed in my clumsiness."

"Thank you but that is not necessary."

"I must insist, the least I can do and allow me to buy you a latte or something if there is any place open around here."

"Very well then. The little grocery where I purchased my goods is just around the corner and does offer an assortment of beverages and a few outside tables. And I would love to hear about your manuscript. I always feel it is my obligation to reach out to those getting started in the writing arena. After all, I have been in your shoes."

"I am humbled and a bit embarrassed to share mine. It is rough around the edges, just a draft. Probably no more than a concept. A dream but a passionate one."

"It is a beginning. Besides, it is refreshing to meet and converse with an upcoming author who still possesses the drive and eagerness, something I have not experienced in eons."

An hour later, Shipley returned to his car, an old hat at this technique. This Patrick gent had been an easy nut to crack after he had spread his sob story so convincingly. The sap had been easy to reel in with his fabricated tale about a manuscript centered around Covid. Playing up his concerns to paint an accurate account of the virus had worked like a charm, the author adding he had even

176

considered penning a similar novel. When he had asked Patrick if he knew anyone who might be able to assist him in better understanding the virus, someone who might be a virus expert, he had confirmed knowing such a person, but had added he could not promise she would talk to him. He would check with her and let him know. He had let it slip though, her name, Camilla Richie. Now, Shipley had two viable choices. Wait and see if Patrick received permission from Richie to talk with him or locate her and cut out the middleman. It probably made more practical sense to allow him to try first. In the meantime, he could research her and complete the preliminary investigation, laying the groundwork for plan B if he needed it. He phoned Paula and filled her in on the progress he had made. She immediately opted for plan B.

Erwin Shipley, aka Braden Peterson, upon returning home, had no problem obtaining the information he needed on Camilla Richie. She had impeccable credentials as a virologist. She had retired from the Global Virus Center. Bingo. This gal was indeed an expert in the field and confronted with an occupational hazard could not help but conduct her very own study of Covid. Shipley had to devise a sure-fire technique to pry this information from her. Both he and Paula suspected it to be a valuable puzzle piece of the bigger picture. Politicians from both sides had been playing the 'listen to the scientists' card, each political party relying on their so-called scientific experts to woe or terrorize the people. Scare tactics were useful and powerful tools, especially when a presidential election was in play.

Erwin Shipley did his best to remain unbiased and intent on just following the facts. He refused to give in to the herd mentality, especially given the fact that 95% of the media narrative was against the sitting president. He had been justifiably pegged a renegade by most news affiliates for refusing to go along with them. He and Paula were cut from the same cloth except for one telling fact, her quest for stardom and the holy grail. Stardom did not interest him nearly as much as being factual in his investigations. Let the chips fall where they may. It was his job to compile the information and present it for the average Joe and Joanne to decide for themselves. It was not the judge or jury, just witness reporting it as it happened. He would do his best to prevent Paula from skewing anything he uncovered and shoot straight for her loyal audience. He was not overly concerned about it. Had he been, he would not have agreed to this partnership.

No doubt, journalism was more cutthroat now than he had ever experienced. More sickening, corporations owning the networks and little worker bees to the point they had no choice but to report the false narrative against the president and his party or they would be booted out and blackballed. He and Paula would no doubt be met with both barrels of a smoking gun when they dared to collectively challenge the preferred narrative. They really had nothing to lose, already on the outside of that window looking in. Paula had a leg up. She owned the rights to her syndicated program and the networks that broadcasted her segments could not be intimidated into dropping her. Yes, the format was an anomaly in today's world. A huge viewership craved honest reporting and a host that did not treat them like despicable mindless deplorables.

Taking all this into account, Shipley understood the ramifications of their actions. Their asses were clearly resting atop a political powder keg, short fused and mere seconds from exploding given any shift in the wind. Being right trumped lying any day. There was no justice in making people feel like they were stupid fools for believing in Christ, capitalism, and the constitution. Governor Mike Huckabee had penned a book titled *The Three Cs That Made America Great*, one that Shipley had thoroughly enjoyed reading. He had often pondered where the country might be if the Gov had won the nomination and had then been elected president. New person, same outcome, he suspected. The pack would be doing its best to rip him apart as well.

****

Camilla sat on the sofa in shock, rereading the death certificate, shaking her head, appalled by the cause of death. George Richie had died of a massive heart attack. She should know. She had been with him. She recognized the symptoms. She still ached from the fact that George had no nitroglycerin pills on hand all because he had put off contacting Doctor Richardson for a refill. Preposterous, George could not possibly have died from Covid-19 and a heart condition

178

placing him in the high-risk category. Did these pompous asses think that relatives, especially spouses, did not read the death certificate? Well, given the fact that she already knew the cause of death she could have easily filed it away without looking at it. Her eyes shifted to the coroner's name and then she immediately shuffled through paperwork in the desk tray until she located the copy of Abigail Moony's death certificate. One and the same, Franklin Hartsfield. She now wondered if this Hartsfield could be the coroner for Berkley's friend, Kitt Whitt. Did she dare ask the doctor for one more favor given these compelling circumstances?

She had just been on the phone with Berkley. Now, a second red flag stood out. Berkley had asked her if she would consider talking to journalist Paula Wise about her Covid data, apologizing for dropping her name, not once but now twice. An aspiring author had been seeking information about the virus too. A chance meeting with a gentleman named Braden something or other had also opened a conversation about her research or at least her experience dealing with viruses. Somehow this seemed a bit suspicious, more than mere coincidence, the two incidences occurring in a 24-hour period. Maybe she was overreacting, the death certificates prompting her to be a bit paranoid. No, paranoia was an exaggeration. Why should she feel paranoid about anything? Uncanny, yes, that the two death certificates appeared to contain false information and then the two meetings out of the blue focused on her. Obviously, Berkley had dropped her name. Still, something just seemed out of kilter. She struggled to shake it.

Camilla was torn between pursuing the death certificate situation or meeting with one or both individuals that Berkley had just met. The rookie author was a stranger. Why in the world had Berkley met with this guy, especially given the uncertainty of Covid? At least Paula Wise was credible, but she was not sure she was ready or willing to share her research with a newsperson. As for the death certificates, George's and Abigail's, that would require her confronting this coroner, Franklin Hartsfield. She could do that on behalf of her late husband, but she had no rights to question the cause of Abigail's death, that is unless Roy would agree to go along with it.

Camilla just shook her head mumbling, "Gal, where are you going with all this nonsense? What do you hope to accomplish?" It would not bring her husband back. Dead was dead. Still, he had died from an obvious massive heart attack and Roy had insisted Abigail had died by accidental electrocution. She had witnessed George's death and Roy had been present when Abigail had her accident. Covid-19 killed neither of them, fact is fact. What did Franklin Hartsfield have to gain by stating otherwise? Then there was Kitt Whitt, beaten in a horrific assault, dying less than 48 hours later supposedly of Covid as well. In his case, just maybe he had the virus and did not know he had it. In his weakened state maybe the virus had contributed to his death. No, Richardson clearly stated cause of death as Covid, not a contributing factor.

Camilla rubbed her fingers over her eye lids before then running them through her hair. She let out an exasperated sigh. Why was she allowing this to impact her so? Because right is right and wrong is wrong, at least as far as the death certificates went. Plus, these were incidences that both validated her suspicions and supported the data she had been compiling about Covid deaths. Decision made, she would call her doctor friend and ask one more favor but only after she was straight forward with him, sharing what she had discovered about George's and Abigail's death certificates. She would place contacting Paula Wise and the Braden guy on the backburner for now. The certificates won out as top priority. She had to know if Franklin Hartsfield had been the coroner. If so, just how many Covid causes had he been responsible for calling?

****

Franklin Hartsfield exchanged pleasantries via the video chat with the young lady stating that she could be assured that he had complied. Goal accomplished. She quickly reminded him that it was crucial on all fronts moving forward. He confirmed that he understood. There were no loose ends on his part. She almost smiled. Instead, she stated she would relay his progress, maintaining a professional demeanor instead of displaying a tone of giddiness. Franklin Hartsfield excused himself saying he had another fresh one requiring his undivided attention. She nodded, saying carry on as the chat ended.

Hartsfield closed his laptop feeling a sudden shift in the room as he heard footfalls over his left shoulder. Turning in the swivel chair he smiled and offered a cordial welcome to Doctor Kyle Richardson. Oddly, Richardson's facial expression was anything but cordial. The doctor looked as if he had a bug up his butt, the frown appeared somewhat out of character for him. Hartsfield waved him inside his office. Richardson closed the door behind him. Oh, what now, wondered Hartsfield.

25

Reverend Bobby Flowers did something uniquely different, delivering his usual fiery message to his loyal congregation virtually, New York not allowing church services, justifying the shuttered doors due to Covid.

"Human life must always be respected. Human life must be protected. Respect and protection begin at the moment of conception. This poses a unique question. If abortion is not murder, it must be explained why then when a pregnant woman is murdered it is categorized as a double homicide. Taking a life, especially that of an unborn child, is blasphemy and morally wrong. Children are precious and their lives are not to be taken lightly. Why is it unlawful to destroy the eggs of logger head turtles, destroying these unborn creatures and punishment as hefty fine of $100,000 and one year in prison? If a person intentionally kills an unhatched bald eagle that person can face a $250,000 fine and two-year prison term. To put this in perspective a mother can abort her unborn child and face no penalty. Abortion does not make a woman no longer pregnant; it merely makes the woman committing this sin the mother of a dead child. God, our Creator, grants our right to live. Government should have no say in this right and the liberty given to us by Him. Again, I say, life is precious, especially that of a child, born or unborn. Proverbs 21:21, Whoever pursues righteousness and love finds life, prosperity and honor."

After his blistering virtual sermon ended, Reverend Bobby Flowers sipped on a cup of decaf in the rectory, his time for reflection. He just did not understand the rhetoric of the party challenging the president. The support of abortion even up until the birth of the child seemed barbaric for a modern society. Scarier and most troubling, the reverend could not believe in his lifetime that he was witnessing communism and socialism being seriously considered in the United States. As if the political ramifications could not worsen, this pandemic had dismantled a promising economy while taking too many precious lives. Satan was indeed pushing his agenda, fire, and brimstone style. These were troubling times, the many signs making it a head scratcher for true believers in God Almighty.

What were the leaders of the Empire State thinking, ordering churches closed in a time when people needed God more than ever? Governor Anita Ming and Mayor Francis Kowalski stuck to their narrative, some saying too politically so, more intent on hurting the president instead of helping their constituents. The First Amendment protects the freedom of speech, religion, and press. Neither the governor nor the mayor appeared interested in what people had to say, unless they agreed with them. Blasphemy, closing churches and even worse, threatening those gathering to worship outside in church parking lots. Clergymen had been fined and even arrested for assembling their flock outdoors while protesters and rioters were given free rein. So much for protecting freedom of religion. The press on the other hand could do and say whatever they wanted. Spewing lies went unchecked and unchallenged. Persecution of the president was relentless and shameful, something the reverend had not witnessed in his lifetime.

Reverend Bobby Flowers mind drifted through the gambit of concerns; a world being challenged as never before. He said a little prayer as he thought about the young man he had rescued from rioters. Unbelievable, Kitt Whitt had been attacked a second time; this one costing him his life. Unfathomable, so much hatred in the world and specifically in this great nation. Sinners were indeed in no short supply and flaunting their hatred openly and in most cases unchallenged. The shutdown being enforced because of the pandemic contributed to the unsettled atmosphere. Drug and alcohol abuse levels were off the charts. The reverend had witnessed suicides and violent crimes increased in the neighborhood. Mental health concerns were on the rise as well, much of this hitting hard and taking its toll on the youth. There were no proms, no graduations, and no social interaction for those who thrive through peer interaction. Covid destroyed everything it touched or at least indirectly impacted what made the world prosper. God was still the answer at every turn. God's children must trust He who created it, the sooner the better.

There were those in his congregation that wanted to participate in peaceful protests. Ironically, any organized against abortion, support for the president, or prayer marches for the country were being shut down by the mayor or governor while the protestors and rioters were met with no opposition, deemed peaceful and justified even while neighborhoods were being burned to the ground. Turning a blind eye was the new normal by the state's political leaders. The silent majority remained quiet as church mice, fearful of deadly retribution. One thing for certain, local nor state government could be counted on to protect the innocent.

Reverend Bobby Flowers was anything but a crusader. Opinionated, yes; a challenger, not hardly. He did not possess the fortitude to be vocal except when in the pulpit. He shared his beliefs with his congregation while not encouraging organized opposition. God had not called on him to be more, or so this was how he personally framed it. Yes, freedom to worship was critical for evangelicals, for Americans, but he just was not the one to lead that charge. Old school, he chose to leave the fight to the young bucks, those with the energy and conviction to take the battle to the enemy. Too long in the tooth, he had paid his dues. Thinking back, he had taken a huge risk when he went out on a limb and helped Kitt Whitt. While that incident had been quite invigorating, it was not his usual reaction to such a dire situation.

Sunday, a huge sports day, but now there were no sports due to the Covid shutdowns. He should focus his energy on offering an alternative for the sports worshippers. Sadly, his spiritual stadium was closed as well. He had done his best to promote the virtual alternative, but it was tough to gauge the viewership. They had mounted a campaign on Facebook and time would tell if it was successful or not. Flipping through his calendar offered no relief. Weddings, funerals and even communions were taboo and forbid from happening due to the contagiousness of the virus and mandated limit on gatherings. The reverend took a sip of cold decaf, too much dwelling on the matters at hand had caused her beverage to cool. He opted not to refill it and instead decided he needed some fresh air. Fresh air in a pandemic shutdown, not going to happen. Masks and social distancing did not make for an exciting trek in the great outdoors, one governed by the social police. Instead, he opened his bible and read scripture, a welcome and much better escape from these trying times. God, after all, would ultimately decide the outcome of this perilous situation.

26

Melvin Meeker, as promised, worked vigorously to complete the closet project that had begun under George Richie's watch. A welcome distraction, Melvin tried his best to follow his predecessor's design while adding a few extra perks of his own. His heart still ached for Camilla; her loss still evident in her demeanor. He could certainly sympathize. He missed his friend and mentor as well. He cursed this awful disease and how it had devastated the country and his business. Selfishly, he resented the businesses allowed to remain open, those deemed essential by the local and state leadership. Everyone was essential in his book, no one any more important than the next. How could these idiots pick and choose so shamelessly while they still drew a paycheck, unscathed by their decisions? The madder he got the harder he hammered, drawing attention from Camilla in the kitchen.

Camilla chanced a peek inside the closet. All appeared to be okay. Melvin hammered vigorously and never noticed her standing just shy of the doorway. She almost said something but decided to leave well enough alone as Melvin seemed to have everything under control. If it had been George, she may have questioned if all was well. She appreciated Melvin wanting to finish the remodel that her husband has begun. She was sure George was standing vigil over his longtime friend. He had mentored him well, George being so proud of how successful Melvin had been after taking over the reigns of the construction business. He had even survived this dreadful virus after a stay in the hospital and assist by a ventilator. Persevering, Covid and the business being in shutdown, all things considered he looked to be handling all adversities. Camilla eased out of view and made her way back to the kitchen. Her cell phone rang. Caller ID identified the incoming call from Doctor Kyle Richardson.

"Hi Kyle. How is your day going?"

"Another day in the Covid trenches, always offering new adventures and more challenges, but that is not why I am calling. I was unable to access the corner's assessment. Whitt apparently has no immediate next of kin. I have no authorization as far as the death certificate goes and my source was not willing to share any additional information quoting the liabilities of doing so. Sorry."

"I understand protocol and the code of ethics. I should not have asked you to go out on that limb a second time, Kyle."

"You still believe cases are being miscategorized."

"Worse. I think too many cases are being intentionally misreported. I'm just not sure why."

"Could be for insurance reasons, if indeed your theory is correct. Incentives can drive situations like this unfortunately."

"Could be I suppose but wrongfully and willingly misleading the public is quite deceitful when so much fear exists during this pandemic."

"Have you shared your suspicions with anyone?"

"Only with you and a close friend."

"Friend, huh?"

"Yes. Like you, he respects my wishes and will not share this with anyone, not until I am confident the data supports the stats 100%."

"And when you achieve your confidence level, just what do you plan to do with it, Camilla?"

"I am not sure. I still have a few connections with the GVC."

"Would they accept your results? Understand, I am not questioning what you are doing; it would contradict what they are saying. Noses might be out of joint. Sometimes the hierarchy does not react well to their credibility being called out, especially in the world's eyes."

"I would never purposely showboat them. It would just be me sharing my findings, like old times so to speak."

"I would just caution you to be discreet when messing with those on the big stage."

"Point taken, Kyle. But fact, Abigail Moony and my George did not die of Covid. I have plenty of additional data to support the potential controversy brewing."

"You were a bit disgruntled when you retired, were you not? Hope this is not a vendetta. I apologize. I was out of line with that comment."

"Yes, you were, Kyle. Apology accepted."

"Just be careful before playing with fire."

"You know me, Kyle, I never jump to conclusions and would never intentionally attempt to upstage anyone at the GVC, no matter how we parted ways. It is not my style."

"Take care, Camilla."

"Say hi to Mildred for me. Maybe when this eases a bit, we can have dinner together like old times."

"Will do."

After ending the call, Camilla thought something did not feel right about the conversation. Kyle had never taken such a stance with her. It was almost as if he was warning her to stand down. Why would he do that? Why would she perceive something like that? Could be that the stress of dealing with the virus had worn on him. She tried to shake the feeling. Like George always said, sometimes you must go with your gut. Her gut was telling her something was not right with the conversation. She almost felt guilty thinking this way. Almost.

Camilla sat at the kitchen bar now reflecting, rethinking, something she did too often. Her mental rewind and replay buttons tended to be used more so lately than ever before. She sure had plenty of time to dwell on things given the house arrest scenario as George so boldly referred to what government had forced down America's throat. Sure, some common sense should be exercised. She had no issues with social distancing to some degree or wearing masks when you could not. Shutting down American though still seemed a bit harsh, especially when Americans had initially been asked to do it for just a couple weeks. Flattening the curve had lasted over six months so far. Too many major cities where the data indicated the curve had been flattened, remained in lockdown. The president and the opposition were at odds about this fact because those cities being crushed by the shutdown were run by opposition party mayors. Anyone with an inking of a brain could see through this ruse as a ploy to cripple the president and his once flourishing economy in a crucial election year. Like it or not, politics prevailed, politics failed, and the American people suffered through the political pandemic.

"Camilla...Camilla...CAMILLA! Something is burning," shouted Melvin.

Rejoining the world, she smelled it as well and saw the smoldering smoke emitting from the oven. "My breakfast casserole!" Quickly she grabbed her mittens and removed the smoking and somewhat charred catastrophe from the oven. Shaking her head, she then asked Melvin, "How do you feel about blackened cuisine?"

"My dad always claimed my mom utilized the smoke detector as her timer, further adding she invented the blackened concept. This never flew so well with her though."

"Sorry, lost in my thoughts, I ruined what I had promised you."

"Another valuable lesson learned in my household; the art of scraping and removing the outer layer of char from any dish to salvage the edible portion. What had you so lost in your thoughts?"

Camilla sidestepped the question and replied, "This pandemic has transformed us and now men have a taste of a woman's world. Masks are the new bras. As we have always proclaimed, they can be uncomfortable. Women are forced to wear bras in public. If ever we toss caution to the wind and opt for a bit of freedom, everyone notices we are not wearing one. Men, welcome to our world. The mask is your bra, Melvin."

"I can see why you might become lost in that one. I will surely have a lasting image every time I wear a mask or forget to wear mine." Melvin left it at that, not convinced that she was being completely honest with her thoughts. He suspected George played a larger role in her being lost in thought. He certainly could not blame her, given where he had just been, hammering like a wild banshee. "Guess I have not got beyond the toilet paper hording crazies myself. That and panicked people snatching up sanitizer and Clorox wipes. Guess I can be somewhat thankful that it is only me under one roof. Do you think these life changes are really working? I mean, all the sanitizing, hand washing, distancing from every human within your air space?"

"Washing one's hands has never been a bad idea under any circumstances. Sanitizing without succumbing to mysophobia is not necessarily bad until we have gotten a handle on the virus. Obsessive-compulsive disorder is not healthy though. As for the masks, I would advise anyone not to become exclusively dependent on wearing them to protect them from exposure to Covid or to prevent its spread if you have contracted it. Use common sense and weigh your risks. Utilize social distancing and wear masks as the situation deems fit. I must add that I am a bit disappointed in the Global Virus Center in their handling of the pandemic. They have created the distrust and uncertainty by flip flopping on their advisories and recommendations. They are the professionals. Their job is studying viruses. I know the protocol and the importance for getting it right the first time. It troubles me seeing how often they have gotten it wrong. I will just leave it at that."

"At least you are not there now and can not be blamed for the bad PR they are receiving, right?"

Camilla smiled and nodded. Almost tempted to share what she had discovered but decided now was not the time to disclose her suspicions. No, these were more than mere suspicious. The GVC had taught her to never deal in suspicions or hypotheticals. The data, on the other hand, never lied. That was the old GVC before billionaire investors became to involved in self-interests and tossing around their weight and demands to suffice their agendas. Money bought favors, insured dishonesty, and nurtured a corruptive environment. She had witnessed that ugly side firsthand. Worse, it had morphed into a more dangerous mutation. The president got it. He had begun questioning the center's integrity after it appeared. He accused them of siding and covering with communist China over the virus's release. He blamed them for the misinformation funneling from the communist country through the organization that was supposed to have the world's best interest.

"I should be able to finish the closet today if you don't mind me staying late. It isn't like I have anything pressing on my agenda."

"My social calendar is open as well, Melvin. That is if this burned casserole doesn't sicken both of us."

"Hey, I have already licked Covid. You think a toasty dish like that is going to finish me off; I don't think so."

"I do have a tossed salad if you would rather pass on it."

"I am a bachelor. I survive on baloney sandwiches and unthinkable things out of cans. This is a gourmet spread. Let me wash up first."

Camilla smiled. George would be so proud of Melvin Meeker, his manners and willingness to finish the closet project. She hoped his business survived the shutdown. He and George had worked so hard to make it what it had become. Her hubby had known what he was doing when he stepped away from it, leaving it in such competent hands. Dear George had walked away from what he loved due to his heart condition to no avail, his heart failing him just the same. And now someone had the audacity to claim Covid took his life. One thing for certain, thought Camilla, the coroner would not put his neck on the line if something more sinister was not involved. Honest mistakes can be made but toss in Abigail's misreported cause of death and a pattern of deception reared its ugly head.

****

Paula Wise leaned back in her chair listening to Erwin Shipley's reenactment with Berkley Jay Patrick. He had made short work of his first assignment. Camilla Richie was the mystery woman, an ex-GVC employee, one who possibly possessed key information in their ever-evolving investigation. Decision time. How would they approach her? And would she be receptive? She and Erwin had reviewed additional information received from various reliable resources. Critical pieces of the puzzle were fitting nicely. The facts were scarier than had been suspected. Laying the groundwork slowly and deliberately had never been more crucial. The ramifications, when exposed, would most certainly be explosive and dangerous. She and Edwin understood they were sitting on a potential powder keg. He was off dogging another trail as she pondered contacting Professor Richie, a recent widow.

She had retired from the GVC years ago. Maybe her data was accurate, maybe not. Question, how had she derived hers. If they were successful in bringing her on board, critics would scrutinize her data. Of course, they would not move forward on bits and pieces. When they played their hand, they would be prepared to do so in royal flush fashion. All the marbles on the line. Just how deep would this ultimately go was still up in the air. There were tentacles at every juncture. Deep state had taken on new meaning. Who could they ultimately trust? She did have a couple of contacts that had never betrayed her in the past, but she had never approached them with something as potentially explosive as this. Having Erwin Shipley in her corner should add more credence to the game changer if it did go where she suspected it would go. One thing for certain, this could not be spoon fed or handled haphazardly. Those perpetrating the atrocity would not play nicely once exposed. People vanished without a trace for less reason. She was not fearful of threats. She was fearful of promises kept if threatened. The media could be expected to aid and abet those she and Erwin exposed in the scandal. No, scandal was not harsh enough to describe what they

192

were up against. Deep pockets guarantee success at any expense. Two dead or missing journalist from the opposition side would not garner a blink in coverage by the biased bastards on most networks. Poof. Now you see us, now you don't, thought Paula.

****

Shipley had just finished meeting with the anonymous whistleblower, a person not willing to give up their identity at any cost. They had met in a remote countryside location, an old, dilapidated barn. No face to face contact, a barn door had separated the two. The person's gender had been concealed using a voice enhancement device. He was not permitted to record the conversation and had to rely on memory and quickly scribbled notes, the old fashion interrogation methodology. Fortunately, Shipley was comfortable with old school techniques. Given the circumstances he found himself in, they were the preferred and only viable methods. What he had uncovered exceeded his wildest expectations, even scarier than he could ever have envisioned.

He needed names, more leads to corroborate what the mole had just shared with him. Hearsay would not hold water. He sensed hesitation in the whistleblower to cough up what he perceived as high-level players in the unfolding atrocity. Puzzle pieces were obvious and falling into place nicely, but he needed more. The whistleblower knew more, understood the seriousness, and really wanted to spill the beans. That he could sense. The person was sincere and understood the danger involved; had not once asked for any monetary compensation or credit. Doing the right thing seemed to suffice. A whistleblower is protected by law, but this whistleblower understood that the law could not protect them from the powerful forces intent on quenching any flames.

"One name, one significant name is all I need."

"I understand what you are asking. I understand what I am doing. And I understand the endgame if I am exposed. I have family and

193

none of them will ever be safe if I am linked to what you plan to do, Mr. Shipley."

"I get it. I am in the same boat as is my associate. We fully understand the dangers. May I offer a different approach. I will toss out a few names and you just let out a little grunt if I mention any on your roster. Deal?"

The whistleblower mimicked a grunt. Game on. Name one, no response. Name two, silence. Name three, going nowhere, Shipley doubtful this was going to pan out. Name four, nothing and then a grunt. He stated the name a second time, a grunt ensued.

"Perfect and not surprising. He is top on our list. Care to try round two? I name countries." The whistleblower grunted to acknowledge.

Shipley randomly named countries, those under suspicious mingled in. The whistleblower identified two on their list and a third not on the list. When asked to play a round three, identification of political players, the person on the other side of the door declined.

"Do you know the counterpart's names?" A grunt sealed the deal. "Please think about it carefully. We can put a stop to this, but we do need your full cooperation."

"I understand. I will contact you if I change my mind. For now, I believe you have enough leads to pursue."

"I really need evidence to link these names, some we already suspected. Do you have evidence to support your claims?"

"Grunt...if I give you what you ask, those in question will connect the dots. Witness protection could never guarantee my safety or the safety of everyone I love. The world has a new foe, the likes never experienced. The extent they are willing to go has no boundaries. They do not buy favors or make promises. They take what they want. And to use the old cliché, *they take no prisoners* because they do not need them."

"What is next for you?"

"I remain silent and bide my time, hopeful your alliance can stop this or at least expose it and be taken seriously for doing so. Be careful my friend. Do not jump the gun or draw conclusions, and do not open Pandora's Box unless you are ready to face what escapes."

The voice on the other side of the door went silent. Shipley sat on a crate and contemplated what he had learned. Much of it they already suspected. Hearing it come from the whistleblower's lips made it real. Shipley had dealt with dangerous situations countless times. He had been an insider in drug lord scenarios. He had been behind enemy lines more times than he anyone should ever be to come out unscathed. This felt different. The sheer magnitude trumped all the others combined. Never one to question what he had gotten himself into, he now questioned it this time. He did not like this new feeling, the highest stakes he had ever faced before. Paula had not flinched when she divulged her suspicions. "In it to win it or until death do us part," whispered Shipley. "Vegas odds must be atrocious."

A black van barreled into the barnyard kicking up a dust storm. Before Shipley could react, the van spun to an abrupt stop near the opposite side of the barn, the back doors swinging open, automatic fire erupting. So much for a discreet meeting with an anonymous source. Luckily for him the gunmen had not spotted him. They had been too focused on where 'Grunt' had probably just exited. Shipley had parked his rental car a quarter mile back in a secluded overgrown logging road. Doors slamming and footfalls in the gravel alerted him that this was not over yet. The terrain around this side of the barn was wide open offering no cover to conceal a hasty retreat. He was royally screwed if they decided to conduct a perimeter sweep. He did not have access to the inside and if he did it would be a death trap. Two quick shots told him what he needed to know. They had just found or finished off 'Grunt'. Surely, they knew the snitch had not been here alone. He just hoped they did not know the identity of the other person, him.

Shipley searched desperately for an escape route or at least a better place to hide. The assailants were now inside. The barn door separated him from them, and it was secured shut from the inside. Grunt had utilized it as his buffer. Would it do the same for him he wondered. The door rattled. Shipley stood with his back against the barn wall to the left of the door, hoping there were no open slats giving away his location to those poking around inside. He chanced a peek around the corner and saw one of the individuals cautiously rounding that side of the barn. They were indeed walking the perimeter. Question, was the other one still inside or approaching the opposite corner? Only one way to find out given that he was out of options.

27

The Covid death rate in New York had surpassed 30,000, New York City accounting better than two thirds. The controversy continued, nursing homes and assisted living facilities taken the worst hit. Mayor Francis Kowalski was under fire for the mishandling of the pandemic where the elderly was concerned. Covid seniors had been forced back into the vulnerable community at his declaration. Governor Anita Ming continued to distanced herself from the mayor, allowing him to take the fall while Kowalski deflected blame to the president. Finger pointing while under fire was not anything new in the political arena.

California, Michigan, Illinois were faring better by comparison but were still leading all other states in deaths and cases behind New York. Florida, Georgia, and South Dakota were doing much better. South Dakota had not shut down their state and the strategy had been working. Florida had learned and adapted, focusing on protecting the elderly population. Georgia had adopted lesser extremes when it came to shuttering the economy. The media continued to praise New York's leadership while slamming the southern states for not complying with the mandatory closures. South Dakota drew their wrath as well with no data to support the reporting. If ever there was a conspiracy in play, look no further than the media and party opposing the president to clearly identity those in cahoots.

The president held back no punches, calling them like he saw them, fake news at its worst. The communist regime of China was ultimately to be blamed for unleashing the virus on the world and then trying to cover it up, or mislead with fictitious narratives, the worst lie being that it was not contagious person to person. The president kept his foot on the gas pedal, blaming the Global Virus Center for being a communist propaganda pawn and spreader of false and misinformation. The media and opposition party defended the communist regime blaming the president for misinformation and the murder of thousands of Americans. Paula Wise debunked the foolishness in one of her segments, sarcastically stating that this president possessed the powers of Almighty God and Superman combined, able to control climates, cause earthquakes and hurricanes, and direct this virus at will, while deflecting a barrage of bullets and leaping burning buildings and fallen statues.

****

Reverend Bobby Flowers met in his rectory with Police Chief Brenda Patterson. Her precinct had been overrun by rioters (aka protestors according to UBN) in a peaceful display of unity over recent officer involved shootings. The police chief was at her wits end dealing with attacks on her officers and the lack of support from the mayor and governor. Flowers had been her pastor for nearly twenty-five years, and she had known him even longer. In time of distraught she had turned to him for prayers and guidance.

"I see the anguish on your face, Brenda. It must be tough defending a city that shows you so little respect. Please be encouraged. It is not our neighborhood brothers and sisters that are disrespecting the police department and the city. They are suffering as well, watching helplessly as their businesses are ransacked and burned to ashes."
"Yes, and while I am being ordered to stand down and allow it to happen. Do you realize how difficult this is for me and my department to do? We are letting down those people that expect us to defend against this madness and protect them from the savagery. Many are our friends; most are like family. Lawlessness is the new mantra for these corrupt political officials, and I do not say this lightly. The governor wants my badge for being openly vocal about his actions and those of the mayor. A part of me is ready to hand it over."

"Brenda, I have known you since you were a mere child. You are no quitter. You have always faced off wrong for the belief in right. It is not in you to walk away from the fight."

"Once I might have agreed with you, reverend. I have always been proud of wearing the shield and don't take me wrong, I still do, but my superiors do not respect us or the job we do. They turn their backs and a blind eye to appease political factions. The matters movement and the anti-American phonetics have corrupted our youth. The streets are battlegrounds, too much like third world neighborhoods. I should know. I saw too much of this while serving in the army."

"You must rely on your faith, Brenda. God is on our side."

"Satan is holding a mighty convincing hand, herding the mindless sheep to slaughter. Communism nor socialism is the answer. People are not banging on America's doors for entry to fall prey to the same atrocities they are trying to escape. I apologize. It was not my intent to drop by and rant about failed politics and a regime headed toward hell."

"You are not alone in those thoughts or concerns. Christianity is under vicious attack, more so that I have ever witnessed. I agree, we are on the brink of losing this country and our freedom. I pray each day that we turn back these attacks. That the people of this great nation open their eyes and come to God as the only answer."

"I can not do this is any longer. I am spent. I do not have the fire I once had to take it to them. Them being the criminals. I spend too much time under assault of what we called friendly fire in the service, attacks coming from our side. In battle it was usually a mistake or at least a miscalculation when our own forces inflicted harm on our forces. Now, it is blatant and calculated, those who are sworn to stand with us, turning their backs on us, and worst of all, supporting the enemy and allowing them to have their way. I have been contemplating retirement. I know how it looks, me crying uncle, but I can't look the people in the eye knowing I am letting them down."

"Do you come here to pray about it or ask for my blessing in your decision, Brenda?"

"Both, neither, I don't know."

"I will pray with you that you do what God instructs you to do. If it is His will that you retire and walk away, I shall support you in that decision. I only ask that you allow the prayers to deliver to you that message. Trust in Him and he will guide you. Refrain from acting on emotions alone. You are a good person, Brenda, and you are an excellent police chief. Good will always defeat evil if one remains patient. Faith, family, and freedom are powerful tools in defeating God's enemies. Many battles and wars have been fought to ensure the kingdom stands. Remember, with Him on our side we never lose, no matter how bleak or winless it might appear. Old Satan works in deceit and illusions, taking advantage of every opportunity. Believe only in the Lord and the goal will become perfectly clear."

"Thank you, Reverend Flowers. My decision to come here was the right one. I will take your advice and continue my prayers as I hope you will do on my behalf as well. I promise I will wait for my sign to do what is appropriate no matter how long it takes for it to be delivered. You take care and stay off these streets, especially after dark. It is then that the demons wreak havoc on the innocents and, like I have said, the men and women in blue might not have your back given the current directives."

"I have no doubt if you witnessed this old relic in the streets in harms way you would disobey those directives and deliver me from evil," smiled the reverend.

"Indeed, I would but, still, do not hedge that bet."

****

Paula Wise had not heard from Edwin Shipley today and he had promised to update her after the meeting with the anonymous contact. She was not overly concerned given that he treaded on the edges in his investigations. He was fully capable of taking care of himself in any situation that might occur. She returned her focus to her next broadcast, one she hoped would hit home given the political shenanigans and misinformation being tossed about shamelessly. Honest Abe said it all and she would quote him in her opening to set the tone for the segment.

You cannot help the poor by destroying the rich.

200

You cannot strengthen the weak by weakening the strong.
You cannot bring about prosperity by discouraging thrift.
You cannot lift the wage earner up by pulling the wage payer down.
You cannot further the brotherhood of men by inciting class hatred.
You cannot build character and courage by taking away
people's initiative and independence.
You cannot help people permanently by doing for them,
what they could and should do for themselves.

Powerful and appropriate thought Paula. Would it make a difference
to those already under the influence of the socialism-communism
Kool-Aid? Maybe a few fence straddlers would see the light. All she
could hope for was to be honest and present a compelling and
straightforward narrative to debunk those being spewed by the
corrupt networks. Of course, anyone listening to the likes of the
United Broadcast Network would never tune in to her show or admit
it if they did. Those siding with the sitting president or believers in
freedom, capitalism and God were being viciously attacked verbally
and physically. She hoped the silent majority stood firm and would
rise when the occasion called, casting ballots to re-elect the
president. Only he stood between democracy and the country going
dark.

Paula would further make her case by pointing out what the
governors of New York and California were forcing on its people.
Covid-19 had given them the perfect opportunity to control every
aspect of their lives. First the shutdown, then regulating churches,
crowd sizes, except for rioters, shutting off power to those daring to
buck them, allowing no parks to remain open, all forms of recreation
forbidden. The California governor had ordered tons of sand dumped
onto a skateboard park to prevent kids from using it. Holiday
gatherings in California were being discouraged, even to the point
where individuals were being told they could not have family
gatherings, it being unlawful to do so. She would expose this
dictatorship being forced on Americans, especially those in the
larger cities being governed by the president's mortal political
enemies. America was being groomed for the takeover thanks to a
virus opening the door for the trial run.

She and Erwin would most certainly face their worst hailstorm when they had the evidence to pull back the curtain and expose the diabolic Wizard of Oz, names and faces to go with the evil being unleashed on the mindless sheep. She would not move forward without that evidence. She had one shot at this. Outnumbered and outgunned by the biased media, anything short and they would bury her. Who was she kidding? Even with indisputable evidence she would be debunked fast and furiously. Paula realized that the Lone Ranger approach, even with Erwin Shipley as her Tonto, would be futile at best. She needed the Calvary, big and powerful guns on her side when the time came. Sadly, too many swamp rats resided on both sides of the aisle. Who, if any of them, had the balls to stand shoulder to shoulder with her to save America? Maybe, only the president possessed the *cohones* to do it; not like she was best friends with the leader of the free world.

She shifted gears, now pondering her approach to contacting the Richie woman. Someone with ties and a credible reputation with the Global Virus Center, even if retired, could be an asset when the time came to present their case. She hoped she was not a disgruntle whack job. She would complete the vetting process of this Camilla Richie before reaching final judgment. Preliminary results had weighed in her favor, having found no skeletons thus far. Richie's research and disputing data intrigued her. Berkley Jay Patrick had the reputation of being a straight shooter. She had no reason to doubt that Richie would not pan out as legit. Still, she believed in doing the homework. She stood above most because the opposition struggled to discredit her once she put in on the line. Her enemies were vicious in their attacks and threats. She welcomed all challenges and made it a point to win.

****

Breaking News: Wildfires continued to devastate the west, northwest and southwest. Never had there been so many outbreaks seemingly simultaneously. Arson was suspected in several areas. Firefighters from across the nation volunteered to combat the wind driven infernos. The death toll was rising while the devastation to homes and property was climbing as well. Less than 10% of the fires had been slowed or contained. The nation could not catch any breaks, so it seemed. To add injury to insult, a third hurricane of the season bore down on the gulf coast, had reached Cat 4 status. Louisiana would take the blunt a third time, unheard of in one season. The rebelling opposition party supported by bias media pundits blamed the president for these natural disasters because he did not buy into global warming. God forbid if a volcano erupted or a major earthquake occurred on his watch as he would surely be the blamed as responsible.

28

Camilla, with much agony, organized the renovated walk-in closet after Melvin Meeker had completed the project. She had decided to nip it in the bud and sift through George's clothing, separating, folding apparel, and placing it in bags for giveaway. She only kept items that might mean something to the kids. None of their children wore the same shirt or pants sizes as George. She held back shoes worth salvaging along with socks, ties, and some selected hats. She could not help caressing and smelling some of his shirts, swearing she could smell George or at least the slightest fragrance of aftershave cologne. Obviously, this was only her imagination because his shirts had been washed and ironed. She slipped on his favorite ballcap, worn and ratty. Her hubby had been somewhat of a packrat. Getting him to toss anything had been a futile exercise.

She smiled as she went through the motion, realizing that he was not one to make a fashion statement, at least not one to keep up with current fashion. Some might argue that what he wore spoke loudly as a fashion statement, throwbacks to another era maybe. He was a no-frills guy. What you saw is what you got. There was nothing put on about George Richie, raw and rough around the edges. She sighed, aware of the void he had left in her life. The kids had wanted to help her do this, but she had pushed back on it. She had not seen the kids or grandkids since the onslaught of the pandemic. They had mutually agreed to honor and comply with the guidelines set forth for the pandemic. Camilla regretted that decision now. George never got to see them one last time. Realistically, she could not blame this on the social distancing. George had died from that massive heart attack. Visitation could not have been planned to compensate for that. In a blink, right there before her eyes, he had expired. No final goodbyes, just gone. No funeral either. Closure would not come easy for the family. They did not have the market cornered. Funerals, weddings, birthdays, and every other special occasion had been halted, postponed, or canceled.

Camilla opened a box containing several of George's favorite cigars. He had given up smoking them due to his heart condition. He had not tossed them though. Camilla retrieved one and held it to her nose. She envisioned George immediately. A devious grin spread over her face. She took a break and walked outside where she fired up the cigar. She took a couple of quick tokes and coughed. She held it between her fingers and took in the ambiance. A tear ran down her cheek as she extinguished it. It smoldered a bit before she finally forced out the last burning ember. She would save the last cigars for her sons and son-in-law.

She gazed at his workshop. His tools would be divided between Greg and George Junior. George Junior did not really follow in his dad's footsteps, but Greg had inherited some skills, more interested in it than his older brother. She wanted to keep something special out for Melvin Meeker as well. She probably should have thought about that while Melvin had been here. Today was not the time to delve into the workshop and treasures inside. She would save that special time for the boys when better times arrived. The New York governor discouraged out of state travel to and from the state. Camilla craved the ocean air of South Carolina, an escape to the beach condo a welcome distraction. She conceded instead, too much yet to do here. George was supposed to decide where they went on the next excursion, even if he had not really wanted to go, and had even told her to pick. Going now, this soon, felt as if it dishonored his memory, a silly notion indeed.

Sifting through George's belongings ionically offered a welcome escape from the rigors of the pandemic and political posturing. Alone, literally alone, not something she enjoyed, but she refused to succumb to anything resembling depression. Not her MO. Camilla was strong willed, head strong and independent. After all, she and George had both followed their careers, managing their homelife to make it work. Each had been quite successful while raising a family, sharing in this lifestyle while supporting each other. One blip on the radar, retirement had not gone as envisioned. Not that they had not done what they could to enjoy it; it had been short lived literally. No, George did not embrace the traveling but still they did it together. It had been important to her so George had made it important to him. Once into their travels he had enjoyed it, but was always ready to be back home once it was over. She loved him for being finicky yet forgiving and accommodating, even if it went against his wishes. There absolutely would never be another George Richie.

****

Berkley Jay Patrick parked in front of his laptop, creative juices flowing, somewhat inspired by the aspiring writer he had recently met. What was the chap's name again? Oh yeah, Braden Peterson, Berkley recalled. He wished him much success with the intriguing manuscript. He decided to stick with his depiction of the pandemic, more tongue in cheek, a satirical, sarcastic version, keeping it funnier than factual. Too much gloom and doom already existed. No need to recant it in a novel while the details were so fresh in everyone's mind. Regurgitating tragedy while capitalizing on tragic current events just was not his style, like what happened when America was attacked by terrorist, the Twin Towers collapsing, the planes targeting them as well as the Pentagon and other targets, the country was not ready to relive those horrors in a book or cinema production. It was all in the timing and the timing was not right for a Covid catastrophe in print.

Revitalized, he would focus on his little ditty, TPOCALYPS, a world where zombies craved toilet paper and paper towels resulting in a worldwide shortage, hoarders punished harshly. The walking dead could be destroyed by sanitizers or Clorox wipes, both weapons of choice in short supply as well with the collapse of the world due to the outbreak. Berkley envisioned survivors battling the infectious fens weaponized with water guns, spray canisters, and spray bottles loaded with homebrew sanitizers, direct hits to the eyes destroying them. The leader of the new opposition would be an American led movement, their mantra, striving to make America great again. Perfect, whispered Berkley, a fun romp dealing with the craziness of today. Zombies, not his genre, but with this twist he would make it happen. His publicist was not fond of his new brainchild, but she would get over it once it hit the best sellers list. Ultimately, it remained his decision to pen whatever he wished to pen.

****

206

Paula could not believe what had happened. A chance meeting with a whistleblower had gone awry and with such deadly consequences. The stakes had been raised. She interpreted this as they were onto something huge. Threats were one thing though; cold blooded murder raised the bar. It was not in her to backdown. This called for a change in strategy. Throwing caution to the wind was no longer viable, too reckless and with equally dire consequences. She took a deep breath before speaking.

"And you never met this person, never caught a glimpse during the entire ordeal."

"Like I said, altered voice and on the other side of that barn door. And based on what I heard, our whistleblower has blown his or her last whistle. Those men in black did what they were instructed today. Well, at least they snuffed out the perpetrator but lucky for me, the receiver of the information escaped unscathed."

"You acted swiftly under those deadly circumstances, Erwin. I will give you that."

"Lucky for me only one of them searched the exterior of the building. I managed to slip around the opposite corner and the one inside called it off before the goon reached that side of the barn. Sirens blaring somewhere nearby made them hightail it is my guess. I heard them haul ass. The emergency vehicle had been a firetruck. Beats an ambulance any day. The blood splatter I found inside the barn left no doubt that Grunt will not be contacting us for an encore performance. We are messing with a serious faction, Paula."

"I get that. Glad you escaped unscathed and with your identity in tack. Smart move, parking your rental car away from the rendezvous."

"Luck was with me on all accounts. How do you want to proceed now?"

"I take it that means you are still in."

"Contractual obligation, hell yeah. We must be close is my guess. I will follow the breadcrumbs such as they are."

"You know as well as I who is bankrolling much of this."

"Of course, but we still need the smoking gun, Erwin."

"This is more involved than even I suspected, Paula. Too many events cannot be mere coincidence. It is part of a grand plan, the ramifications unconscionable."

"Do you think the president knows?"

"Nope. He would call them out if he suspected what we do. It is not in his DNA to remain silent on matters like these, especially with the election pending."

"Do you think this has anything to do with the election outcome?"

"Partially, yes. There is more to this, I fear. Something we have not fathomed. Something maybe we cannot fathom."

"That huge?"

"Bigger. Too many smoke screens, too many false idols so to speak. Switch and bait at the highest level. The barnyard episode was mere peanuts in the bigger scheme."

"Do you think we are in over our heads, Ervin?"

"Absolutely. The Pulitzer Prize is a mere participation trophy by comparison."

"We are indeed facing extraordinary times, freedom hanging by a thread."

"A priest acquaintance of mine recently told me that 20/20 is supposed to be a sign of perfect vision. He then added his spin, that maybe the Lord is using 2020 so that man can clearly see He is in

208

charge and the only one that can save us. I am not inclined to be religious, but I cannot argue the point. I am absolutely a part of that generation that knew better than to disrespect your parents. As kids we drank from a garden hose when we got thirsty. We played with toy guns. We were spanked when we deserved it and we stood for the flag when giving the allegiance or during the anthem. We survived that time but, no denying it, the way things are looking now, survival might be a stretch if the wrong person goes in the white house."

"And if the wrong one does win, do you the journalist will become a propaganda machine for the party?"

"Been against this president for almost four years; don't see that changing, do you?"

"You and I will be an endangered species if it happens. We might have to go underground if we refuse to conform to the narrative."

"It took me too long to get here. I am not the type to roll over and be obedient. What about you?"

"I am in for the long haul, better or worse. I will always stand up for what is right."

"Trail blazers die the harshest deaths, Paula, especially when a communist is applying the chokehold."

"Communism, socialism, doesn't matter which, will spell doom if allowed to spread in this great country. My money is on the people who made this country great. I believe the foundation is more solid than is given credit. This war is far from being over. I am thinking four more years for this president to convert the naysayers still refusing to believe."

"Erwin, it is more important than ever that we expose this conspiracy before the evil has a chance to take root."

"All we can do is report on the facts as found and rely on the people to react accordingly."

"Tough case to make when the media will fight us tooth and claw."

"Makes for a good fight I always say. Best we continue our quest to lay out the groundwork. I will continue my excavating."

"And I will see if our virus expert is willing to share with us what she has uncovered. And I will evaluate if it passes the smell test. Be careful, Erwin."

Erwin winked and exited the office. Digging in this rabbit hole was going to be a dangerous proposition. Undaunted, the duo was not about to call it quits.

29

So called peaceful protests continued to be reported by the media nightly, turning a blind eye to the actual burning and looting of too many cities. Policemen were being specifically targeted even though anyone on the streets opposing the mob were fair game. Twenty-four-hour news coverage did not miss an opportunity to portray America as privileged and too rich for its own good. The richest were a cancer, an incurable disease infecting a corrupt nation, were the enemy, taking advantage of the poorest. Taxation of the rich would equal the playing field, free this and free that promised the constituents of a party leaning heavily against rewarding those willing to work hard and prosper.

Fearmongering continued. Covid spelled the end of the world and the president had botched up the handling of the pandemic. The propaganda machine thrived, terrifying the viewers with their rhetoric of gloom and doom. Death knocked on every door. Social distancing and wearing of masks were the only salvation. The opposition party held their cities in a death grip, refusing to allow businesses to reopen, claiming the shutdown and keeping the herd hemmed up inside was the only way to defeat the deadly virus. With a school year approaching, there was little talk of allowing schools to open.

Scientist formed their opinions, supposedly supported by the data. Wear masks, don't wear masks. Masks work. Masks offer false hope. Stay inside. Venture outside. Avoid crowds. No church. No amusement parks openings. Rioting and mass protests of no consequence. The president campaigning and having rallies were called super spreader events while protests were not mentioned. The pandemic had never been more political. The president continued to blame the communist regime and tightened the screws on the communist party economy. The president's enemies blamed him for the Covid deaths. Meanwhile, the fires raged in the west, northwest and southwest. Tragedies were in no short supply. In the face of it, the economy had stabilized, and wall street had made gains here and there. Too many Americans remained out of work due to closures.

Americans appeared to be becoming cozy and dependent on government handouts.

****

Camilla listened intently, a one-sided phone conversation thus far. The news woman had certainly done her homework, knew too much about her professional business. It seemed a bit suspicious given how long she had been retired from the GVC.

"Miss Wise."

"Please, Professor Richie, call me Paula."

"Miss Wise, please get to your point. You certainly know plenty about my reputation with the center but, like I have already said, I am retired and no longer have any affiliation with it. What precisely can I do for you? "

"Direct and to the point. I prefer that approach as well. I am intrigued by your research."

"Research? You must be mistaken. As I have stated, I am retired. I am no longer involved in research."

"I must confess, Professor Richie. I have heard about your theories concerning the virus."

"Theories? Where did you hear that if you don't mind me asking?"

"I am a journalist. I follow leads wherever they might lead, those worthy of investigating."

"I am sorry. Your leads have led you astray. What is it that you are investigating, Miss Wise?"

"It is a complicated matter."

"Complicated, I see. My life is not so complicated, and I prefer it to remain as such. Thank you and have a nice day, Miss Wise."

"I think we have gotten off on the wrong foot. Please, would you allow me to provide a better explanation."

"By all means…explain away."

"Not on the phone. Might we meet somewhere? A bit more privately."

"You do realize we are in the grip of a pandemic and social distancing is recommended. Meeting with a stranger is probably a bit risky."

"I understand your concern/"

"Do you? Why me? Why now? You have me at quite the disadvantage."

"Can we keep this simple? I can meet you at your home."

"And that is supposed to put me at ease, allowing a stranger inside my house. I am sorry. This seems a bit suspicious to me."

"We have a mutual acquaintance, an author friend of yours."

"I am listening."

"Berkley Jay Patrick to be more specific and no, he did not provide me with your name or physical address."

"I know he didn't. He is my friend and would not have."

"He did share with me a few tidbits about your research. In my business all I require are a few breadcrumbs. Intrigued by what he shared I utilized my resources and here we are. Let's just say your theories might corroborate some theories I have. I will gladly share more if we can meet."

"Why should your theories interest me, Miss Wise?"

"I envision you as one who loves this great country of ours and one who would do anything to protect our freedom and democracy. Even you can see that much is at stake right now."

"I have seen what the media has done, and it has nothing to do with protecting America."

"Exactly."

"Then why should I trust you?"

"Meet me and we shall further this conversation. I promise you I am not part of the propaganda machine. Do the research. Check me out and then decide."

"I am making you no promises."

"Fair enough. You have my number on your cell phone now. Call me once you have vetted me. I look forward to our next conversation."

****

"I promise you Camilla, I never mentioned your name in the one meeting I had with Paula Wise. She wanted to interview me because of my affiliation with Kitt Whitt. She had offered him a gig just before he was attacked. He had appeared virtually on her show. I met her producer at the hospital."

"I knew you had not mentioned my name. I told her that. Did you mention my research concerning Covid?"

"Maybe in passing but we really did not discuss it. She certainly did not quiz me for a name or anything remotely in that direction. What are you going to do?

"I'm not sure yet. What do you think I should do, Berkley?"

"You believe in your stats, don't you?"

"Yes."

"Maybe she could be the perfect conduit for making your case. You did say you felt compelled at some point to share it if the opportunity arose. Looks to me like an opportunity just knocked."

"Do you think she is trustworthy, Berkley?"

"I won't go that far but she is not like the drive by media. She is a journalist in the purest form and seems to report the news and allow her viewers to decide."

"Okay. I will think about it then."

"That is all she asked, right?"

"Yes, she was not overly pushy but persistent in an almost annoying way."

"Is your data still pointing you to the same conclusion, Camilla?"

"Undeniably so."

"Then what could it hurt to have someone of her caliber on board? You could remain anonymous as far as she is concerned."

"Now Berkley, you know how I hate the use of anonymous sources. Anonymous typically means there is no basis for the information if the source is not willing to stand by it. No credence, he said she said and then she told somebody else and eventually it is reported as factual anonymously so. No, if I am in, I am all in."

"Well, I will stand by whatever you decide."

****

"Good afternoon, Miss Wise."

"Professor Richie, please call me Paula. I brought an associate. Hope you don't mind me doing so without asking ahead."

"Touché, I did as well. Please come inside."

"Braden Peterson, I did not know you were an associate of Miss Wise. Now, we know the rest of the story, Camilla, just how I was convincingly deceived."

"Hello again Mister Patrick. I do apologize. Occupational dishonesty. As an investigative journalist I assume various personas to infiltrate and further advance stories that I am pursuing."

"You know him, Berkley?"

"Indeed I do Camilla. He claimed to be an admirer of my work. I bought it hook, line and sinker. I even mentioned you by name when he was interested in conversing with an expert on viruses for his manuscript. My bad. I was snookered royally."

"I owe both of you an apology as well. He and I are associates and I asked him to pursue this path to obtain your identity, Professor Richie. Allow me to formally introduce Erwin Shipley."

"Shipley, I have heard of you. You are the chameleon of investigative reporting, aren't you?"

"Mister Patrick, you flatter me. But yes, I am quite good at what I do. Years of honing my mimicking skills."

"I…we owe you an explanation. That is why I requested we meet person to person. There are those that would go out of their way to scoop us or discredit us for the sake of their greater narrative. We are the anomaly in today's journalistic approach. We refuse to follow the script, the propaganda agenda to support the cause opposing this president and one determined to transform the nation for all the worst objectives."

"So, Miss Wise, you are the anti-movement, those opposing the quest to socialist this country."

"Paula, please call me Paula. On the contrary. Erwin and I still believe it is our job to report the news, how it happens and when it happens. The readers, the viewers can decide for themselves if the evidence we present sways them one way or the other."

Berkley eyed them before speaking, "Then you are not really interested if this country is transformed into a socialist or communist regime? It is just another story."

"I do believe in freedom of the press, freedom of speech, all the amendments promised by the constitution. I just make it a point to keep my personal feelings out of my professional analysis. Old school journalism. I should be able to report the news without you knowing my political or personal preferences. Erwin and I have reported it both ways, ambiguously speaking."

Erwin nodded. "We follow the trail wherever it leads and present the facts as found. It is not our intent to be biased even in today's world of obvious biased reporting. We do not take sides even when undeniable lies are being portrayed. I, like my esteemed associate, do not wish to live in a government-controlled nation. The old USA offers everyone the freedom and opportunity to follow their dreams, as it should be. This said, we cannot argue that ominous clouds forecast a bleak change in the American dream. Speaking for myself, when possible, I do my best to even the playing field. No, I will not regurgitate lies to sway people one way or the other. We, as Paula suggested, deal in facts. Fact. Americans are being deceived by the media. It shames me to admit this but journalism, except for a few faithful outliers, has died. If the sitting president loses this election, the nation as we have grown to love is in jeopardy of going down a scary darkened path. And no, I am not the defender of the other side, the president's pawn in this war. Compelling evidence exists though, that will allow Americans to weigh the difference. The chips ultimately fall where they will fall, God help us all."

"Quite a speech," acknowledged Camilla. "It still does not explain this sudden interest in me. Why not pursue whatever information you desire with 'The Experts?' Any concerns you have about Covid-19 should be addressed with the Global Virus Center, not me."

"Would you trust their expertise on Covid, Professor Richie? Fair question. Please answer me honestly and if your answer is yes, we will leave promptly and pursue different avenues."

Camilla did not appreciate being placed in this uncomfortable situation. She had not asked to be involved in whatever these two were up to and had not invited them into her world in the first place. She had only agreed to meet with Paula Wise, more out of curiosity, wondering how she had obtained her name and address. She weighed her answer cautiously, but in the end, honesty had always been her policy. Data and statistics after all had been her life."

"No, Paula, I do not trust the center and what it is currently reporting. If I must be honest with you and myself, I retired earlier than I had planned because I witnessed firsthand the corruptive nature introduced by big money, corporate entities pulling the strings, skewing the data to meet their agenda."

"Thank you for your candidness and honesty, Professor Richie."

"Please, call me Camilla."

"And I am just Berkley. Should we call you Braden or Erwin?"

"My friends call me Shipley. Erwin sounds too geeky."

30

The presidential race, election of an incumbent, had never been under so much scrutiny and assault. The mainstream media despised this president and reported an unprecedented 95% negative portrayal of him and his administration. While credible details of corrupt dealings surfaced concerning his opponent, the media refused to report it or ask any questions about his questionable behavior. The accusations were ignored while the biased news people continued to fabricated dirt on the president. The opposition party and media worked from the Covid script, an administration they accused of killing Americans with their mishandling of the virus. Many Americans were not buying into the false narrative. Fake news had earned its name loudly and proudly, no longer even attempting to hide their bias.

Covid fear had crippled a once great nation and the world. The networks continued to run a live tally of cases and deaths in the United States and worldwide. They refused to cover any presidential rallies or speeches while drooling over ever word spoken or misspoken by the opposition candidate. Never had journalism stooped so low. One agenda for almost three and half years, discredit and destroy this president at all cost. So far, all attempts had failed. Carrying the Covid torch had become the new tool to bring the administration to its knees. Scare tactics, misinformation, and even the editing of the president's speeches was being telecasted to paint a deceitful picture. Shameful as it was, they were all in for the long haul.

Major cites were hurting. People were still forbidden to live anything close to resembling normal lives. Restaurants were shuttered except for those able to offer takeout and delivery. The streets of these cities were being infiltrated by the homeless and ruled by gangs. Lawlessness ran rampant. Governors and mayors of these cities allowed the worst to happen and refused to protect their constituents or support law enforcement. A taste of socialism loomed large. Americans were waking up but fearful of being attacked and further abused, most remained silent and on the sidelines. Freedom of expression no longer existed unless you were willing to spew the flavor of the day, the narrative being forced down everyone's throats by politicians and media with but one agenda in mind. Control the herd. Make them dependent on government. Banish thinking, doing, living for themselves. Covid-19 had served their purposes well. It had brought the nation to its knees. The mantra, never pass up on an opportunity to capitalize on a tragedy, had never being truer.

****

Senator Aaron Breeze sat at his desk at his home, astounded by the audacity of the media and the other party. There was no limit to how low they would go to take advantage of Americans in dire straits. Politics had become almost too deplorable to bear. The senator had never been more ashamed of the antics, terrorizing families and utilizing a pandemic for political gains. He refused to play part in the volley being engaged by both sides. The socialist and communist agenda was being covertly concealed by the presidential challenger and his party. His worst fear had never been more apparent. People were being persuaded to vote against the president because of too many false promises and lies being supported by an equally corrupt media and social network. Socialism never worked. History had proven that fact time after time. Communism surely was no answer. The Chinese communist party was the perfect example for these failures and terrible treatment of its people.

The senator shook his head in disbelief. The president had not caused this virus. It had been unleashed by a communist regime intent on destroying the world's economy and to influence the presidential race. It was plain to see if anyone just took the necessary time to open their eyes and examine the data to support fact. He could not fathom why his party allowed the opposition to run ram shot over them. Playing too nicely was not the best option for success. Getting down and dirty in the mud with pigs was not the best portrayal of a party always wishing to show diversity and morality. Sometimes you must toss fairness to the side to achieve the end game. Breeze rolled his eyes, now realizing just how far he had allowed himself to be pulled into the swamp's muck. No wonder congress's approval rating was in single digits.

He had not talked to Senator Charles Paulson in forever. Political lines had been drawn that now compromised their friendship. Peer pressure in Washington is much worse than the peer pressure that exists on the playground or in school, or life as far as that goes. Political assassination occurred frequently among the ranks. Covid had changed everything in a mere blink. A prosperous economy had been compromised. The president's countless accomplishments had been canceled by one 'oh crap' catastrophe, even if it had not been his fault. It had happened on his watch and the opposition had used it to their advantage.

The young senator had his suspicions as did plenty of others. Had this been purposively orchestrated? No denying it, this president had had every possible controversy tossed at him and so far, he had survived every attempt to overturn an election. Most attempts had been proven as bald-faced lies, well if you were not against him you saw through the deception and fabricated coops. This one had been a humdinger. It had impacted everyone, including the world. If communist China had purposely unleashed this virus on the world as had been suspected, it could go down as one of the most horrific world tragedies. Opportunist did not waste opportunities. To what extent would a corrupt government go to achieve the intended result regardless to loss of life or the destruction of prosperity? History had proved there were no boundaries.

Senator Breeze was not sure if he bought into all the conspiracy theories or not. Some were quite convincing though. He had been compiling a list of events, coincidences not easily brushed aside. Thus far, he had no shared his with anyone. His mantra never admit you have seen Bigfoot if you are not prepared for the consequences that transpires for speaking your mind. Blurry photographs are not credible evidence that a bipedal creature exists in the forest. Nope. He was not ready to go public with anything he had compiled thus far. The dots required connections, something he could not validate yet. Political suicide, as always, could be swift and terminal. A powder keg requires a fuse and a match, and he currently had neither. He had not even shared this information with his wife, someone he trusted to be honest and objective. His theories were mere distractions for now. Too many puzzle pieces were missing yet to make this worthy of boasting a finished project. Best leave well enough alone for now. He had another virtual zoom meeting commencing shortly. Time to venture back into the often-make-believe world he had gotten himself into and leave the theorized version alone.

****

Camilla, Berkley, Paula, and Shipley now unmasked both literally and figuratively social distanced at the Richie dinning room table. Paula had laid all her cards on the tables, at least those she could share without reservation of factual support. She had excluded pertinent people's names for now until she reviewed Camilla's data. She was a bit uncomfortable including the author in these discussions, but Camilla had refused to proceed without him being present. She had conceded knowing they had used the gentleman to get to her. It had been a sign of good faith to allow him to stay. He had promised not to utilize any information disclosed or discussed for manuscript opportunities. She had almost suggested that the four enter into a signed contractual agreement but figured it might suggest something counter productive instead.

Camilla sat back in her chair trying to absorb what had just been presented. If factual, and she had no reason to believe it was not, the premise and its repercussions were scarier than anything she could have imagined. Berkley had remained uncharacteristically quiet so far. She was not accustomed to this demeanor from her always outspoken and candid friend. She took this as a sign that he was as shocked and concerned as she. She did appreciate Paula and Shipley presenting their case first before asking her to share her data. It reinforced their integrity and willingness to expose what could be an earthshattering revelation if proven to be true. She had no reason to question its authenticity. The two seemed quite credible and forthcoming in their convictions to report the facts accurately and unbiased.

222

Now it was her time to shine. She fired up her laptop and began presenting the data that supported her suspicions as well. Covid cases, alleged Covid deaths, and the comparisons to the information being reported by the GVC thus far. Hers did not corroborate theirs. She even shared what she had discovered about the misreporting of George's death and that of Abigail Moony's batten fabricated cause of death. Neither could have been caused by the virus. Shipley dropped another bombshell. Kitt Whitt had not died of Covid either as had been reported by Kyle, her doctor and close friend. He had died mere hours after the attack from his injuries so had a reliable source told her remaining anonymous. Either Shipley's source had lied, or Kyle had. Given the circumstances, she leaned in favor of Shipley's. She would not be satisfied though until she confronted her old friend face to face to observe his reaction.

"Guess we have ourselves an unlikely alliance, do we not?"

"I cannot speak for Berkley, Paula, but yes, I am in this for the long haul. Injustices, especially when world recognized associations are intentionally misleading the public, they must be called out for their discretions."

"I am in as well. My only stipulation is that I have dibs on the book once we blow it out of the water."

"Berkley, I shall provide you with all the information you require for publication providing the four of us share equal billing, coauthors and contributors."

"Deal."

"Sounds good to me," added Shipley. "What's our next move?"

"We formulate a plan to get to the big guy himself," stated Paula.

"I have already been on that one. I have another willing contact. This one is embedded deeper than 'Grunt' supposedly. Surprised me. Grunt had disclosed the plans to cooperate with me, Apparently, he has gone missing as suspected. I would have expected anyone else to

223

lay low after that, any other deep throat contacts being fearful of falling prey as well. Not so. This person has already gone into hiding under the pretense of taking vacation time. Didn't even bother concealing their voice…female and willing to do the right thing so she said. Not sure if this will lead us to the head honcho. I will arrange a meeting ASAP."

"And you do not know the identity of the other person," inquired Camilla.

"Afraid not. Be forewarned again. These people are not to be taken lightly."

"I was just wondering because I had an inside contact, one that had been feeding me data, but he was feeling the heat and broke off further involvement."

Paula posed the next question. "Doesn't this seem a bit odd, so many people in one organization wishing to expose their bosses while surely jeopardizing their career?"

"We do not give people enough credit for wishing to do the right thing. Me for instance. I witnessed corruption on the smallest of scales, and it prompted me to opt out. Hindsight, I should have stayed and dug deeper. If I had, maybe I could have exposed them before the competition had an opportunity to reach such heights."

"You could have not possibly fathomed the depth of this, I'm sure," replied Paula.

"You are right. It was small potatoes compared to what is suspected now."

Berkley put his spin on it. "This darn quarantine has transformed me into nothing more than a hapless dog. Think about it. Like a dog, I find myself roaming my home all day long looking for food. Strangers yell at me 'no' if I get too close to them. I become all to giddy with the premise of an automobile ride or any excursion outside. I, like many others, have become trained canine,

224

programmed for idiotic yet predictable responses. My expectations have reached all time lows, willingly giving into submission like an obedient doggy."

"Herd mentality prevails," admitted Shipley. "Sadly, it is all about ultimate control in communist and socialist countries. America needs to open their eyes before there is no return to life as we know it. Much easier to maintain what we have instead of reestablish it once we have lost it."

"Thought you were unbiased," smile Berkley.

"In my journalism only. We have the best country in the world. That gives merit to everyone seeking our way of life, legally or illegally. There will be no need for border walls if the worst-case scenario happens. Nobody will want to come here."

"They might leave the walls intact to keep the herd corralled. Socialism requires cheap labor and sheep to rule."

"Are you gents finished? We can not save the good old USA from an enemy within without hard evidence to support it otherwise."

Camilla asked, "Paula, do you really think we can save our country?"

"It is not our job to save it. It is our objective to supply compelling information. If we do, then I have faith that Americans will see through the ruse and do what Americans always have done. Fight for the rights so valiantly earned."

"What if we are too late in that delivery? The election grows near. If we do not have those facts to present, the country is not promised a mulligan," said Camilla.

"We will present what we have before the election. Hopefully, we will have connected all the dots or as many as possible by then," replied Paula.

"Plenty of time yet," added Shipley. "There is no need to panic just yet."

Berkley was not too confident. "You forget, the media is in the bag for this movement. They will not go quietly. Plus, you cannot count on coverage from them even if the information is indisputable. If it goes against their candidate, it will be buried deeply and swiftly."

Paula smiled. "Not to worry, by the time we arrive at that juncture, we will have ample support to back us up. In this business we always have a few blue chips yet to play, favors owed and promised, right, Erwin…Shipley?"

"No good deed goes unpunished, has been my experience," Berkley quickly added.

"Paula and I have plenty of chips to play once we are confident that we have a winning hand. We never use them frivolously. Rarely do we bluff either, even though we do have quite the poker faces."

A foursome makes the perfect golf outing. Four in this case did not necessarily guarantee a successful round though. And, as already indicated, a mulligan would not place well on the scorecard this late in the game. At best, they would have one shot at this. If they fell short in making their case, they would most certainly not have another opportunity, at least not one that would be embraced by open minds. One and done. Make it count. There was no risk in being too cautious. Their next meeting would occur at Berkley's home. Camilla in the meantime would continue to compile her data. But first, she would schedule a little impromptu luncheon with Doctor Kyle Richardson. She would discreetly bring up the subject of Kitt Whitt's untimely death and poke the fire ant mound a bit.

Berkley would utilize his notoriety as a best-selling author to hopefully schedule a meeting with an activist for All Lives Matter that might have deeper ties than disclosed. Shipley said these types were publicity hounds, seeking any opportunity to represent the cause. A book deal would be the perfect lure. With Berkley using his real name, no one would suspect anything devious and undercover. It was a long shot at best. Shipley had gotten his most reliable leads from longshots. He hoped Berkley could pull it off flawlessly given his rookie credentials in investigative dumpster diving. The chap seemed to possess the posture to come across convincing. Paula would smoke and mirror their undercover mission by deflecting any suspicions in her syndicated show, discussing nothing remotely related to the avenues they pursued. Removing any scrutiny should ensure they were not being watched by the deep state.

Shipley understood the perils ahead. One miscalculated flounder would most certainly unleash a world of hurt like what had been the fate of the now missing Grunt. Thin ice to say the least, but all involved had confirmed they understood the severity of the circumstances and consequences once the cat got out of the bag. Shipley had firsthand witnessed the ramifications with Grunt going AWOL at that barn. He had barely escaped unscathed himself. Nothing to be taken lightly, the stakes were high. Losers lost everything.

31

Reverend Bobby Flowers watched from his rectory window the smoldering fires blocks away. The rioters had moved onto other areas of the city, always enacting on their so called depicted friendly protests after darkness fell each night. Police Chief Brenda Patterson remained handtied to intervene. Her disgust for the mayor and governor had eaten away at her like a cancer sucking the life from her body. She continued to struggle with remaining on the force or handing it up and retiring. She had not conversed with Reverend Flowers since their last chat. She contemplated calling him, but the world remained a hectic chaotic place, leaving few opportunities to act on her behalf.

Off duty after nearly twenty-four hours straight coping with a city under siege, she finally headed home. Rounding the corner, she spotted a Caucasian male lying on his back in the street being plummeted by five African American youths. Off duty but never really off the clock, she sounded her siren and switched on her blue lights as she came to a screeching stop less than thirty yards from the melee. She called for backup and then ordered the youths to halt their assault before exiting her squad car. They scattered as anticipated but not before landing a few extra kicks to the head of the gentleman no longer moving. Even from her position she could see the bloody mess that used to be his face.

She leaned down beside him and radioed for paramedics as she did her best to examine his wounds. The elderly gent was unconscious but still breathing. She shook her head, disgusted by her people doing these despicable acts, thinking how all lives matter. No, these were not her people. She was nothing like them. They were thugs, animals seeking any reason to loot and wreak havoc, and it had nothing to do with justice or revenge for that matter. So many broken homes, men deserting families, youths being lured into the promised life by drug lords. What a waste. It was at this moment her prayers were answered. She decided she would request retirement and maybe join forces with Reverend Flowers to start a youth program. Just maybe she could do more good out of uniform, a friendly face offering hope and encouragement. Being hated for being a police officer, a black one at that, had gotten old, especially when her superiors were not interested in enforcing law and order.

Shots were fired nearby. Brenda stood and touched her vest mic to call it in. The first round caught her in the left side of her vest, a stinging blow but the vest had done its job to protect her. She reached for her gun as the second shot struck her in the neck. Brenda wavered momentarily before falling face first across the body of the elderly man. It would be nearly half an hour before first responders arrived and located her lifeless body. Police arrived after the medic called in saying an officer was down. There would be no mention of the incident by the mainstream media. Her death did receive local coverage, one report even saying she must have been trying to shield the elderly guy. There were no suspects in her apparent assassination. A heartbroken Reverend Bobby Flowers mourned her senseless death. Due to Covid there would be no funeral. What irony: the protests and riots continued, untouched by Covid restrictions applicable for honest law-abiding citizens. Neither the mayor nor governor mentioned the untimely death of Police Chief Brenda Paterson. Fox News interviewed her family and Reverend Bobby Flowers to report the tragic event. At least her death was not blamed on Covid, not directly.

****

Camilla greeted Kyle and led him to the den. After social distancing themselves they both removed their masks. Camilla sat in George's recliner, more of a mental statement for her, while Kyle sat on the loveseat across the room from her. She kept it mostly small talk gauging when she would ease the conversation in the desired direction. She caught herself eyeing her old friend under a different light; unfairly maybe. Unsure why she leaned toward Paula's version of Kitt Witt's death over his. Her suspicions were somewhat warranted given the fact that the same coroner had presided over George's, Abigail's and Kitt's deaths. She would refrain from mentioning the coroner's name. Might raise a flag.

229

Over lunch Camilla shifted the conversation discreetly to Covid and the mounting death toll. She played the role of the grieving widow, not a stretch since she was still mourning George's death. She brought up Abigail Moony and how she missed her so and their game nights. Kyle offered his condolences for both agreeing that the disease was the worst he had ever experienced in all the years of his practice. Time to toss in the third death and she did so by saying how Berkley remained in disarray over the untimely death of his young friend Kitt Whitt.

"So young to have succumbed to this disease, wasn't he, Kyle."

"Some are more at risk than others. Possibly the young man had other factors no one was aware of."

"Berkley said he knew Kitt quite well and he possessed no other circumstances that might have placed him in a high-risk category. He was not diabetic or overweight. Berkley said he was extremely healthy, somewhat of a heath nut."

"Guess he and his doctor would be privy to that history."

"Does seem a bit odd that he expired after that horrific assault. Is it common for someone to die from Covid that quickly, Kyle? I have studied these viruses and have never seen one to react that quickly."

"I was not his physician. This strain is a new one, is it not?"

Camilla nodded. "Who did you say performed the autopsy?"

"I don't think I said. Look, Camilla, I overstepped by doing you that favor. Let's just leave it at that. This coronavirus is taking its toll at an alarming rate. We do not have all the answers. We are learning as we go."

"I just remembered the coroner's name. Same as George's. What a coincidence, same as Abigail's too. Something Hartford, was it not?"

"Sorry, I do not recall."

"Kyle, does it not seem odd that we are not hearing deaths from other causes? Well, suppose that is to be expected when the news media and political pundits are playing up Covid as the only show in town. Guess I am lucky my George died swiftly and did not suffer from coronavirus. No, that was an awful thing for me to say. I miss him and am not thinking straight."

Camilla had witnessed the slightest flinch when she mentioned George's cause of death. More of an eye twitch. Kyle had to know she had seen the death certificate by now. Maybe he thought she had not examined it closely yet. Preposterous, given her previous occupation. His next comment told her what she had suspected.

"Why the interest in the coroner? I am sure he is overloaded and doing his best to keep his head above water."

"Occupational hazard. I am retired but the subject matter still intrigues me. George would call me an armchair quarterback."

"This has been a pleasant distraction Camilla, but I must return to my world and put up the good fight. If I were you, I would not become too consumed by all this madness. Relax. Enjoy life such as it is."

"I almost invited Pastor Moony to join us. Roy is still mourning the tragic loss of his wife. Poor Abigail died in the most horrific fashion. Electrocution, but she suffered from dementia you know and accidently poked something into an electrical socket. She was spared from Covid as well. Crazy though. Roy mentioned to me that on her death certificate it referenced Covid. Imagine that. She had Covid but displayed no signs of the virus thankfully. Same hospital. Would they have had same coroner?"

Doc Richardson sidestepped a response saying, "Pass along my sympathy to him.

"All these deaths and we are not allowed to have funerals. Trying times indeed. Take care Kyle."

"Thank you for lunch, Camilla. Please, enjoy your retirement and leave all the worries to those still gainfully employed."

****

Kyle made the phone call to Franklin, a bit concerned about her curiosity.

"Look Franklin, I am not saying she is digging into anything. Your name just came up. She knows her husband died from heart failure. She has no reason to scrutinize his death certificate. Probably just filed it away. I am guessing the same goes for Roy Moony. He knows how his wife died. No need for him to read about it on the death certificate either. She did press me a bit on that kid Whitt's death. More curious than anything. She does not have access to his records, and she knows she has overreached her favors. She is a friend. No need to jump to conclusions."

Kyle listened to Franklin's response and then replied, "I understand where you are coming from, Franklin. Yes, you do not have to remind me of that. I get it. I will honor the arrangement. I do not appreciate that tone, Franklin. Is that a threat? Sounded like one to me."

Kyle frustrated tried to remain cool, "I will let you know if anything else transpires. No. I do not expect anything further. She is not a threat. Your secrets are safe. Yes. I received the envelope. Very gracious. Thank you."

****

Shipley and Paula convened in her office. Shipley brought her up to speed after the meeting with the new contact from GVC.

Shipley laid it out, "She held back no punches. She wants out, the sooner the better. Her name is Gretchen Houser, high up the totem pole, privy insider at that. She is willing to provide documents and leads if we ensure she and her family are protected against repercussions. She was not referring to lawsuits. She sincerely fears for her life. Get this. I now know the name of Grunt. He is…was a lab technician that got too close to the situation and Houser regrettably ratted him out before she realized what was at stake."

"Couple of choices then Shipley. We either hire protection on our dime or we kick this up a notch and if we do, we better be convinced she is shooting straight. I cannot afford getting the bureau involved unless we have the goods to convince them."

"I say we keep them out of it for now. I know a couple of gents that owe me. They won't gouge us and are reliable."

"Do it then, as she implied, the sooner the better. I heard from Berkley as well. He has made some headway. Not there yet but rushing it will only raise suspicions with that Matters Group."

Shipley shook his head in disgust, "Sad how so many major corporations have contributed to their bogus cause."

"Can you say extortion? Easier to fend them off, keep them from trashing their businesses. Plus, the media protects them and the party seeking the presidency cheers them on. What a country."

"Won't be our country for long is the dominoes keep falling. Tell me Kiddo, are you really just in this for the unbiased story?"

Paula leaned back in her chair. "I was. I try so hard to be what we are supposed to be. Report it and let the public decide. This is a different world, one that, if given half the chance, will devour us. Our democracy is at stake. I believe in this country. Does that make me biased? I'm sorry. Destroying and rewriting history is wrong."

"I look at it like this, Paula. History is not there for us to like or dislike. History exists so that we can learn from it. If history offends

233

us that is a good thing. Learning from the atrocities makes us less likely to repeat them, right? History does not exist to be merely erased. History is ours. It belongs to all of us, the good, the bad and the ugly of it. Destroying statues, changing names of streets and buildings serves no purpose except for the fragile snowflakes, the communist and socialist intent on making us forget the good parts. Biased. Nope. Americans, all in. Like you, I am tired of playing by the rules when they make their own. Let's take it to them. Take them down before they do far worse to us. Somebody has to save us from us, right?"

"Poetic and quite political partner, if we were deemed political in our journalistic quest."

"Keeping our eye on the ball, Paula. Sometimes the story is bigger than all of us. This one is the mother lode and no stakes have ever been higher."

"Guess we are about to go renegade then. Rebels with a cause. They go low. We go lower. Whatever it takes to prevent the beginning of the end. Contact your security team and let's get this show on the road while we still have a road to travel."

****

"This is Franklin Hartsfield. Call me at my other number. I think we have a mutual concern."

Moments later and after Franklin explained the dilemma…

"Mere Minions. We shall take care of it immediately. Hartsfield, must I remind you that you are compensated handsomely for your services. Keeping those under your fold from compromising the situation is crucial. Breaches are unacceptable. You do understand the consequences of any errors, do you not?"

"Clearly. Have I ever failed you?"

234

"Failure is interpretable and problematic. Do-overs and apologies nonexistent. Collateral damage happens." And with that, the line went dead.

Franklin nervously placed his cell phone on his desk. He had never delivered information such as this and by the tone on the other end, it had not been received well. How should he interpret 'take care of it immediately' and how had the situation impacted his status within the circle? Circle, he thought; he did not know the identity of those in this inner circle. He had been contacted anonymously and offered the opportunity to participate. No, not exactly offered. It had not been a choice proposal. Blackmail or better described, a threat, had sealed the deal to do their bidding. Making the only decision they had given him, he had been compensated well, no denying that. What he had been required to do seemed trivial in the larger scheme but no doubt, he was not the only coroner under their watch.

Franklin had not always colored within the lines as they had clearly reminded him. They did their research, he would hand that to them. It had made him an easy mark apparently. Now he felt as if he had bartered his soul to the mafia, figuratively speaking. Once in, there was no viable way out. You did what they said when they issued the marching orders. No debate, no argument, no deviation. What had Richardson been thinking? He had been compensated fairly to deflect any questions, yet he had blabbed valuable information to a friend. Obviously, he had no inkling of the bigger picture. Chump change can buy plenty. Unfortunately, chumps do not think clearly or fully understand the ramifications of their actions. Poor Richardson, what valuable lesson would he be taught?

32

Reverend Bobby Flowers began his virtual Sunday morning broadcast, still in denial about the tragic loss of Police Chief Brenda Patterson. He offered an inspirational prayer, mentioning her specifically, while asking God to protect all first responders and heal this nation under siege by such hatred. He added that if the Bible calls it a sin, your opinion does not matter. Flowers then delivered a blistering sermon, tiptoeing around the politically charged environment, further complicating the misery being inflicted by the pandemic. He did state profoundly that all lives and the liberty of those lives come from the Creator; no government can grant this for anyone. He called on those viewing the service to pull together and pray for those impacted by Covid-19, the shutdown, the rioting, and looting, which realistically included virtually everyone. He encouraged his flock while sanitizing and wiping their surroundings. He considered wiping any hatred from their hearts as it is as much a virus as Covid-19. He furthered his point by stating, consider the meaning of perfect vision, 20/20, adding that maybe the Lord was using 2020 to prompt those in the world he created to clearly see that He was in charge. Only He could help us by heeling and curing what man could not. Stop being fearful of those things that might go wrong and focus on what might go right instead. Be excited for goodness and Godliness. The reverend then quoted former President Ronald Regan, 'If we ever forget that we are one nation under God, then we will be a nation gone under.'

After the cameras went dark, Flowers retired to the rectory to reflect. Brenda and her family remained in his heart. He mentally recanted those church members lost this trying year and those hospitalized by the virus. His mind even drifted back to the young man he had once rescued from the street thuggery, Kitt Whitt. Senseless loss. The young man attacked a second time for just exercising his freedom to speak his will. The woke tolerated no opposition to their rhetoric. Censorship, what they called the cancel culture, had no place in the Lord's world. Threats and intimidation for those who dared have an opinion was blasphemy. Riots and looting, burning down businesses did not deliver justice for unrelated tragedies.

The African American community suffered the blunt for such retaliation. Black on black crime vastly outweighed any officer involved incidences. Flowers shook his head, disgusted by the media turning a blind eye to reality while stirring the racial pot. This was done all in the pursuit of a narrative that threatened the country, aimed at harming the president. One party stood out as the progressive plantation orchestrators aided and abetted by the media and Hollywood liberals. Keeping the blacks on the modern-day plantation, dependent on welfare, other government assistance and the promise of free everything guaranteed control over their constituents. The gentleman opposing the president in the election had been quoted as saying 'you're not black if you don't vote for me' and he even stated that the president's party was the one wanting to keep blacks in chains. Flowers despised the trickery being used to sway the black vote, treating them like mindless folks, easily manipulated by lies and rhetoric meant to create racial divisions. All lies, but he did not have the stomach or fortitude to be a counter activist. It was not his calling. People needed God and prayer in their lives, not activist or corrupt politicians.

Flowers remained pragmatic in his approach to the world created by the Lord. This said, he did have his suspicions and concerns though about what had been transpiring amidst the pandemic and events unraveling. Too organized. Too targeted. Too deliberate. Satan had a hand in it as well thought the reverend. The devil, like some politicians, never allow a tragedy to go to waste. People under stress and in the grip of misery are easier to manipulate. So easily, in times like these, God is blamed for allowing it to happen. Humans prefer not taking responsibility for their actions. Skeptics can easily use natural disasters, diseases and tragedies to make a case against the Lord as turning His back on the world. Skeptics and unbelievers are eager to point out, 'Where is your God, now?'

Flowers contemplated his next sermon, a message where he could paint the picture clearly. Satan was certainly using the tools available and pawns to do his bidding. Churches were closed nationwide. Those gathering to worship in any fashion were being persecuted by an adverse movement intent on snuffing out religion and the first

237

amendment. Professing that the cancel culture must be opposed would be a delegate tightrope to walk from the pulpit. It was not the church's place to wrestle with politics, even when those politics touched the home turf. There were members in the congregation representing all political persuasions. One could not show bias as had the current media moguls. God had a plan, and His plan did not cross these lines. All people were His people, even the nonbelievers. Flowers did his best to keep this in perspective, even though personally he recognized the political ramifications. He knew how he would be voting. This president deserved four more years, if for no other reason, his support for Christianity, the first amendment, and opposition to abortion.

Covid, Covid, Covid, thought Flowers. Had this horrific plague been unleashed knowingly by the communist country in question? Signs surely pointed to something quite questionable. Biblical plagues had certainly played huge roles in the trials and tribulations of God's people. Signs were difficult to ignore, especially as it impacted the world. National disasters were on the rise. Toss in political unrest and the radical agenda. Many in the clergy were peaching prophecy. Atheist cried foul, fear mongering most certainly. Flowers looked to God to guide him down the path most useful to bring the flock in His direction. For now, he prayed for the healing of the world and a cure for the virus, and only then if it was His will and His plan. Flowers stood firm, proud to be a Christian and an American. Too many were terrified to admit one or both.

****

Paula Wise multitasked, keeping her foot on the peddle of their ongoing investigation. She stood ready for the camera, her next telecast mere moments away. She had asked her producer to contact Reverend Flowers to see if he would consider a live interview, a clergy point of view on Covid, the closings, and how it had impacted the church. Thus far, no bites. The reverend preferred remaining on the sidelines and out of the spotlight so it appeared. There were other angelic holes to fish but no time to do so today. She hoped the reverend would forgo his stubbornness, feeling compelled to conduct this with him, her gut speaking volumes for whatever reason. Maybe it had to do with the reverend's intervention in the first Kitt Whitt assault. Paula felt she owed the kid something, just not sure what.

"You're on in 5...4...3...2...1..."

"Hi, I am Paula Wise. Welcome again to The Wise Watch. They tell you straight to your face that they will take your guns and will raise your taxes. Yet so many ignore the obvious. Riots, looting, the burning of major cities ignored by the media, ignored by the opposition leader and his party seeking to ruin our great nation. Aiding and abetting, when the law does not apply to the lawmakers and those elected to serve the American people, you are no longer being governed, you are being ruled. Covid-19 has given us a taste of socialist rule, a peek at a communist state, and a realistic view of the real face of a party intent on transforming our country for all the worst reasons. I do not say this for political gratification. The Wise Watch deals only in facts, not bias buffoonery.

Think about it, this pandemic quarantine has transformed us into
     canines. We roam in
our homes searching for food. Strangers yell at us 'NO' if were
     breach that six-foot safety
zone. We drool and tail wag at the mere mention of an automobile
     excursion. How
pathetic and predictable we have become.

Masks, now I am not going to take a stance one way or the other. Same goes for social distancing. Risks are individual preferences, rights protected for every American. The scientific community, the self-proclaimed experts, have floundered terribly, saying one thing then contradicting what they so profoundly professed as fact. How are we supposed to have any confidence in the integrity of the Global Virus Center after months of mask mandates? I can hardly understand some adults speaking with masks muffling their speech. It sounds like the Charlie Brown adults or someone on a speaker taking orders at a fast-food drive. I liken it to learning a space alien's language., I am culturally enlightened thanks to the pandemic and bureaucracy dictating that I comply or else."

Paula held up her mask, just to let the viewing audience know that she did possess one. "I do wear a mask when circumstances warrant, just as I practice social distancing as an option as well. I will admit, I forgo wearing it if I am distanced safely from others. Herd mentality grooms us for the greater control process. Ironically, many of the experts are against herd exposure for controlling the virus. We will save that argument for another day. Let's take a caller. Line 3, you are live on Wise Watch."

"Name's Caleb, old as dirt and proud to be still above it. Love your show Paula. Shoot straight. Like that. I am part of the generation that was taught to respect our parents, to respect our grandparents and speak when spoke to and to mind or else. As a chap I drank from the hose pipe, garden hose to you city slickers. I always stand for the American flag, kneel for our Lord. I played outside until dark thirty each evening, came in when my folks said I better, but did my fair share of kicking and screaming, wanting to play just a bit longer. I owned my fair share of toy guns. I shot my friends and got shot more times than I dare count. I died a mean death, award winning play acting. I got spanked by my parents, my grandparents, by teachers and by neighbors. A belt is no stranger to my behind. Even had to pick my own hickory switches. I reckon I deserved most of the whippings I got. What I am getting at is I survived all this. Not about to allow something I cannot see do me in and I am certainly not going to allow the government to tell me what to do and not do when it is my right to do otherwise. We are going to lick this virus and we are going to reelect our president for four more years, plain and simple. Take that to the bank. Keep doing what you are doing, Hon. The truth is hard to come by today. Those news folks on the other channels like UBN are a bunch of whiney, bed wetting losers and liars. Thank you for letting a man speak his piece."

"Thank you, Caleb, for your candid opinion and straight forward approach to making your point. Well, there you have it, unedited and uncensored, the way we prefer it on The Wise Watch. Switching gears, I find it quite appalling that these liberal run cities are allowing the destruction of every statue standing, supposedly by peaceful protesters expressing themselves. This is a cancel culture that deals by threats and intimidation. You are either with them or you are against them. Quite pathetic if one takes time to examine the wide variety of statues being destroyed. We are not dealing with a bunch of historians. Many of the statues ironically stand literally for what they profess they stand for. Maybe they despise marble and granite instead. These same hoodlums and thugs, and yes, that is exactly what they are, are Anti-America representatives. Thy are an extension of the biased Matters Movement, those with socialist, communist, and Marxist preferences.

Same anti-society is against certain movies, books or names linked to historic icons. History does not exist for us to like or dislike. It exists for us to learn from it. If it offends you, even better. We hopefully learn from our mistakes. When we do, we are not likely to repeat them. No one has the right to destroy or erase history. It belongs to all of us. It happened. You cannot make it un-happen. Tell that to academia. Schools and colleges are feeding the cancel culture and the willingness to erase all that offends. We have allowed a culture to procreate, one birthing a fragile and entitled insecure society. Promises of free everything is their rite of passage, a debt owed them by a world out of touch with their wants and needs.

Wake up people. Aliens do not cross our borders legally or illegally because we are governed by socialism or communism. They come to the United States because of the freedom and opportunity equally offered to everyone. We are the greatest country in the world. No, this is not a political add. I am stating facts backed by facts. We have possibly the most critical election ahead. There are clear distinctions between the candidates and parties. Shall we run the gambit. Killing babies or letting babies live. Defunding police or supporting them. Gun control or continued gun rights. More rioting and looting or law and order. Illegal entry into this country or legal immigration. Increased taxation or tax breaks. A weak military or the greatest in the world. More regulation or a strong economy. Allow anyone to vote or implement voter identification for everyone. Become a welfare state or working-class state. Poverty versus prosperity. More government or less government. Suppression or free speech.

Liberalism or conservatism. Communism versus freedom ad democracy. Socialism or capitalism. Defiance or patriotism.

Open borders are not the answer. Offering the world a free ride is not the solution. We cannot sustain nor support this pipedream. It would destroy this nation financially and socially. Christmas comes once yearly. It is not a year-round holiday. The United States cannot play Santa Clause for the world. As a society our focus should be to teach our children to work for the things they want, or they will never appreciate what they have. The alternative, they will always expect everything to be given to them free and without lifting a finger to earn it. Teaching them to respect this county and the flag for which it stands. There is something dreadfully wrong when we are threatened and ridiculed for respecting the flag and obeying the law. These are supposed to be good traits. Something is terribly wrong when Americans become angry by seeing a president holding a Bible but find it acceptable for people setting churches ablaze. Abraham Lincoln once said, 'Sir, my concern is not whether God is on my side; my greatest concern is to be on God's side, for God is always right.' Profound words if ever they were any.

I will leave you with this thought; not mine but one so profoundly illustrated just the same. A dog restrained outside had the length of its chain reduced one link every few days until the chain's length was so short that the poor dog could barely move. The dog never resisted because it had become conditioned to its loss of freedom, slowly and over time. Americans wake up. This is happening to us and only we can stop it by resisting. I am Paula Wise, and this has been The Wise Watch. Until next week, think and act wisely, treat everyone with respect, and be careful out there. Weigh your risks wisely. Good night."

Erwin Shipley clapped mockingly as she ended her show. He toasted her with a bottle of water and bowed to then queen. Paula curtsied and greeted him with the princess wave, all the while rolling her eyes.

"So ends another tragic episode of as the world turns over in its grave. Glad you have the stomach for it. I prefer the lows road

242

investigating and reporting it in a column, face unseen for those willing to retaliate and do me bodily harm."

"You flatter yourself, Shipley. I have seen you flaunting your goods on too many talk shows and news segments. You are not quite that guilt free."

"Early exposure and in a much different time when news stood for something to be proud of reporting. I am a dinosaur, long extinct, and you are the last glimmer of hope for a crumbling journalistic society, my dear. Dying breed just the same."

"I concede. What brings you here? Something tasty I hope."

"R.K. Soto is definitely behind much of this but…"

"But?"

"Our Marxist billionaire has deep pockets and many strings extended but even he has his limitations. I am not there yet but a blood trail, a mere trickle for now, might expose a fiercer and more dangerous predator trolling the grounds."

"Do I sense apprehension in moving forward?"

"Maybe. We could be breaching boundaries journalist should leave well enough alone, Paula."

"Are you suggesting that we step away from this?"

"Just saying we move forward with caution. One bad move and this will blow up in our faces. And I am not concerned about our journalistic future. I am concerned about any future."

"You are serious, aren't you?"

"Never been more so and I have been placed in many precarious and dangerous situation in my extraordinary career, some scenarios I will never disclose even today. Revenge works on no timetable. Paula, if we blow this thing wide open and I do stress, if, and if we have the support to even do so, it changes everything, and I mean everything in our lives. Specifically, our lives can and most certainly will be on the line. This is not an award-winning segment that is going to garner the envy of all. It might force us into witness protection and even then, I am not sure our safety will be guaranteed."

"I have never seen you act or speak like this, Shipley."

"I have never experienced the uncertainty or articulated the perils in this manner. Deep state is child's play compared to where we are potentially heading. It is decision time, Paula. Proceed or cut and run, count our losses and be thankful for our existence."

"Erwin Shipley you are scaring me, and I do not scare easily."

"Excellent. As intended. We have others safety that we are responsible far as well."

"Berkley and Camilla?"

"Yes, but your producers and crew as well. Anyone that has ties to you, to me, to them. Anyone is fair game. Colleagues, family, friends, anyone. We can discuss this with our two partners in crime or you and I can settle it. We can make the call."

"You sound as if we should make that call now."

"Exactly. Thin ice awaits us from this step forth. In this envelope I have information that I will not disclose if we call it off. There is no need for you to see it if we do. On the flipside, if I share it with you, turning back, while viable, will still expose you to matters that will most certainly endanger your life."

"Just what have you uncovered and how did you do it so quickly?'

"I am the best at what I do. No one else compares. You knew this. You would not have entered this partnership otherwise. This is no longer a mere powder keg; it is a ticking nuclear bombshell. I do not speak of this lightly."

"I feel like I am in Gotham City dealing with the likes of the Joker or Riddler. You speak in rhymes with few plausible reasons. I get it. This is dangerous. We knew that going in."

"No, you still do not get it, Paula. This is beyond anything we could have imagined. This is no longer a story. This is no longer a factual scenario we can share on The Wise Watch. This is the end of The Wise Watch. We will require heavy artillery running interference for us and all involved. I am probably royally screwed either way. Possibly I can guarantee your safety and everyone else's if we end it now."

"You know me better than that."

"Yep. Figured the conversation would go like this but you cannot blame a concerned citizen for trying."

"Let me pose it to you. If you were in my shoes would you step away from it? Or better still, if I call it quits, does that mean you will as well?"

"You got me by the short hairs. No on both accounts."

"Then you have my answer as well."

"What about Berkley and Camilla?"

"You heard my earlier segment. I am a firm believer in each person weighing their own risks providing they have the information to make sound judgement."

"Then I make these proposals. First, you do not peek inside this envelope before we talk to them. Secondly, we only share or vaguely stress the dangers, just enough for them to realize the deadly consequences if they remain in. Provide it then they can weigh the risks. Your words, not mine."

"Deal, but you better hide the contents from me until then. Temptation might get the best of me."

"Trust me. This remains with me and only me until decisions have been made. That goes for you too, Paula. Weigh your risks carefully."

****

Doctor Kyle Richardson and his wife were enjoying takeout dining at their home when the doorbell rang. They exchanged glances. Their doorbell had not rung in nearly five months. Nobody visited them, not under the lockdown and socially enforced distancing. Neither was expecting a delivery of any kind, not that UPS or FedEx ever announced package drop-offs any longer. Kyle made his way to the door after it chimed a second time. Someone urgently requested their attention apparently. Mildred had suggested maybe it was a neighbor, one concerned about some symptoms they were experiencing, possibly seeking his advice. It made sense that he should be the one answering the door. Peeping through the one glass pane at eye level, whoever was on the porch must be standing to one side of the door out of view. For the first time in a while, he regretted that he had not had a storm door installed. The darn pandemic had altered his plans to have it done. Nothing to do but open the door and face it head on. Nothing to fear. After all, they resided in a gated community. Just get it over with and then return to his taco meal.

33

Camilla rubbed her eyes. The strain of statistical data crunching and analysis had taken its toll. It had been a few years since she had applied her skills in such a dedicated and deliberate fashion. What she had managed to compile accessing the GVC database had been an astounding eye opener. Shocking as well, her presence had not been detected during the data excavation. She accredited this to her password still being valid and of no visible security breach. Often while still employed she worked from home, raising no eyebrows. After all, she possessed high level usage of the system. Still, she found it peculiar and a complete breach of security that they had not wiped clean any access by her, especially given the fact that she had been singled out as one opposing the system before she retired. The thought entered her head, could big brother be aware of her presence and might this be a set-up, revenge for her lack of compliance and cooperation with the center? She dismissed this premise. Too many years had passed for them to care about her now.

She sipped her tea and pondered what she had gotten herself into with this covert operation. Paula and Shipley had made compelling arguments, well beyond the normal rhetoric one would expect of mere conspiracy theorist. Even with what they had shared, she could sense there was much more they had not divulged. No doubting it, her research was but one puzzle piece to the larger jigsaw ahead. Was she ready and willing to be part of this at all cost? No denying it, she had uncovered indisputable evidence that reinforced her worst fears concerning the GVC. It was one thing to deceive knowingly and intentionally to advance one's agenda, but what they were doing went well beyond diabolical. Being privy to this information sealed the deal; she could not turn a blind eye any longer.

Apprehension did not begin to express her gambit of emotions. Something so sinister would not quietly go away without causing unrest. She wondered how deeply the corruption infiltrated the virus research machine. Paula and Shipley sensed that the center might be part of something huge, political ramifications obviously at the root of the evil. She had experienced it and agreed deep pockets pulled the apron strings. The data she had recently viewed supported the premise to an even greater extent. Deliberately manipulating data and the results to advance any cause turned Camilla's stomach. Too many good people were employed by the GVC. Certainly, some of them had not made a deal with the devil. Her contact, her once close friend and associate, had bowed out gracefully, or maybe not, when she had dug a bit too deep for his comfort. Hopefully, this had spoken volumes for his loyalty and not deep-rooted deceitfulness, bought and paid for.

Her cell phone signaled an incoming text. It was Berkley. *If you are home, turn on channel 13, local news.* She did and gasped as the on-scene reporter standing a block away from a smoldering structure explained to the viewing audience that the blaze had been brought under control. Firemen were sifting through the ruble, no longer a rescue mission but instead a search for potential bodies. While the reporter refrained from identifying those alleged bodies, she did mention the physical address. Camilla recognized it. The reporter clarified that first responders did not know if the residence had been empty at the time of the fire nor had they identified a cause of fire yet. A second text from Berkley read, *I recognized the location. Residents hosted a book club event there, one I attended for a charitable cause. Friends of yours I believe.* With trembling hands Camilla texted, *Doctor Kyle Richardson and his wife Mildred. Kyle was here recently.* Seconds later Berkley texted, *Wasn't he one and the same with links to that coroner?* Camilla confirmed but then phoned Berkley, too shaken to continue exchanging texts. Berkley did his best to calm her saying he was on his way. She watched in horror as the news segment finally ended.

****

Franklin Hartsfield poured another stiff drink, Johnnie Walker Blue on the rocks. He always stored a bottle in his desk. What had he done, confident that this had not been an accident? Sure, Richardson had done some serious botching up on his end but murdering him for it…he had not signed up for something so ruthless. No amount of money was worth being involved in cold blooded murder. He did not care what they were holding over his head. These people, whoever

248

they were, had taken things too far. If he could not get out, then he had no recourse but to cooperate with proper authorities that could guarantee his safety. He would ask for mercy, leniency, and immunity for his full disclosure. Franklin poured one more drink as he processed a plan moving forward. For now, he figured he was perfectly safe in his office adjacent to the morgue inside the confines of the hustling and bustling hospital. Besides, extra security measures were in place due to the Covid. He began jotting down notes that would paint a clear picture of extortion, how he had been forced into this arrangement by those who had anonymously contacted and threatened him, even though he had never felt personally threatened to the extent of being harmed, not until what had happened to poor Richardson. Second guessing, maybe it was just an accident. Accidents do happen. A fire does not necessarily equate to murderous intent he rationalized. Merely coincidental. Or maybe not, given the conversation with him sharing his concerns about Richardson. Better to err on the side of caution than be sorry later, maybe after it was too late to barter a deal.

He played the scenario in his head. If they contacted before he enacted on this new course of action, he would remain calm and agree to do whatever they asked him to do. They had no reason to question his loyalty. He had done everything they had told him to do. Loyalty really had nothing to do with it. He had no choices in any of this. He either did what they said, or they would blow the whistle on his inappropriate and somewhat unethical actions. Well, who manned the whistle now, especially if the experts determined the fire was no accident? Second thought, maybe he should wait it out and see if it had been an accident or arsonist before overreacting. Sure, he was basically being blackmailed to tweak as many autopsies as he could but, on the other hand, he was being compensated quite well. Up until the Richardson debacle, no one had raised an eyebrow as to cause of death, most buying into the Covid explanation. People were so fearful of the virus and its deadliness they would believe anything. Sit tight. No time to overplay the hand just yet. These people have been extremely pleased so far. Why rock the boat unless suspicions are raised about the fire. When the time arrived, if it indeed did, he would be prepared to CYA. He sloshed the ice cups around in the almost empty glass thinking Franklin Hartsfield a lot of things but is no murderer. He thought about how many cadavers had passed through this morgue under his watch, but none had arrived here because of something he had done. He cringed, wondering if the charred bodies of Richardson and his wife would end up here. Not to worry, if they did, they would be chalked up to two more Covid cases. Was he feeling more at ease or was it just the result of his longtime friend, Johnnie Walker, calming him when no one else could? It was good to be alive and somewhat wealthy he smiled before taking that last gulp.

Two men wheeled a gurney table into the morgue. Franklin recognized neither of the gents dressed in white, apparently interns. Lot of new faces lately with the pandemic disrupting normal flow. Covered from head to toe, there was no mistaking their friend, another Covid casualty, may as well skip the autopsy and document it as such to keep the peace and add to the count. He motioned to them where to park the deceased and gave them a courtesy nod. Franklin pulled double duty at the hospital, that of a diener, the morgue attendant responsible for everything from handling, moving, and cleaning the corpse and performing the entire dissection at autopsy. He served as county coroner as well. Double dipping, quite financially rewarding given his covert actions. He was even a qualified forensics pathologist if ever they needed one.

In his coroner role, he was the keeper of the gate, responsible for completing Form 100B, the 'Pink' form for the register stating the cause of death. He needed a Covid stamp to quicken the process. All the cadavers under his watch tended to be identified as Covid cases unless circumstances did not allow for this assessment. Most passed the coronavirus taste test though. Relatives never questioned the mention of Covid given the media and government fear mongering being force fed on them. When someone died, the first question, did they die of Covid? So easily the assumption was made and believed with little hesitation or doubt.

Time to cash in on another, thought Franklin as he pushed his chair away from his desk. He slipped on a pair of gloves before approaching the body awaiting him. A clipboard atop the covers always contained the personal information of his latest visitor. He retrieved it like clockwork and began perusing the form as he walked back to his desk. The form was blank. Sloppy work. Newbies had not been trained very well. Shaking his head, where do they get these people? He made his way back to the table, eased the cover back from the bottom looking for a John Doe tag, figuring this one had yet to be identified. The craziness continued. The cadaver still wore shoes. Never had this ever happened in the morgue. Personal items should have been removed. It was not in his job description to be responsible for such items. He hesitated to go further, thinking someone should see this. The last thing he needed was an unnecessary controversy given his skewing of the facts in these deaths.

Cursing, Franklin tossed the cover back over the shoes and returned to his desk. He began keying in the administrator's number on the morgue's phone when a commotion from behind alerted him that he was not alone. Fine, he thought, the newbies had returned to rectify their error. He would gladly grant them a pass, better than stirring the pot and opening the morgue to unwanted scrutiny. If procedures and protocol had been botched, then it might prompt an audit. Audits were never good. Too often other trails developed, and he certainly did not need an auditor following suspicious breadcrumbs. He decided it would be best for all to let it slide this time. He mustered up a fake smile and swiveled in his chair to greet the alleged perpetrators.

****

The cadaver, now safely secured in one of the body drawers, had been clearly marked as a John Doe. Under normal circumstances an identified body would be moved with 72 hours as arrangements were made for a funeral by relatives. These were not normal circumstances given the impact of Covid-19. With the premise of a funeral not likely anytime soon, bodies were being moved to refrigerated trucks for safe keeping. John Doe's received the same treatment, categorized as such, and stored away. The possibility of John Doe being identified were slim to none given the state of a Covid environment. Franklin Hartsfield's unethical and corruptive reign had now ended. Time off for misbehavior had been delivered mafia style, as Franklin might have framed it. Exit strategy delivered without remorse or fanfare, and no next of kin courtesy call. A replacement had already been recruited for another location, returning this one back to some semblance of normalcy.

A glass, a half empty bottle of Johnnie Walker Blue, and a typed note would be found on the morgue's desk. *Have had enough of this Covid catastrophe. I quit. Leaving for greener calmer pastures. Out of here,* signed *Franklin Hartsfield,* His apartment would be found later empty, personal belongings gone. Bank accounts had been closed and a one-way plane ticket had been purchased by credit card for the Bahamas. The man that boarded the plane possessed a passport that matched his likeness closing the last chapter in the ex-coroner's life. Loose ends guaranteed.

34

The time is coming when everything that is covered up will be revealed, and all that is secret will be made known to all. Luke 12.2

Berkley enjoyed playing the role of the host under any circumstances. It had been a day since Camilla's slight melt down over the Richardson deaths. This year had brought one tragedy after the next, losing her husband George, Reverend Moony losing his wife Abigail, and then there had been Kitt Whitt. Paula and Shipley had so far been unimpacted by tragic circumstances. The duo had requested this rendezvouses occasion. Berkeley sensed something forbitten in this meeting, an almost ominous presence. Excellent at body language observation, he eyed one then the other, scrutinizing their behavior. Shipley was the harder of the two to read. His stone-faced persona made it difficult to peel back any layers. Paula Wise on the other hand had those telling eyes and a barely detectable facial tic. Most would not notice but Berkley was not most. Something had changed. He could tell the change, an almost charged atmosphere, negative energy oozing like a festered fever blister on one's lip.

"Shipley and I have concerns about the two of you staying involved in this. We think it might be best that you bow out."

"I thought we had a deal, in it to win it, book rights and all," spoke up Bentley. "What has changed to sway this plan if you do not mind my boldness for inquiring?"

"Shipley has uncovered information that heightens the dangers."

"Explain heighten," inquired Camilla.

"I'll take this," spoke up Shipley. "We have not been completely honest with you. We did this to protect you, not to purposely deceive. One of my contacts disappeared. Possibly foul play involved."

"Possibly," inquired Berkley.

"Probably," replied Shipley.

Camilla asked, "When did this disappearance occur?"

"To be honest, before you were contacted," added Paula.

"And you are just now telling us. Why now? Why not before?"

"I understand your frustration, Camilla. I would feel the same."

"Not sure you would, Paula, given what you are sharing now."

Shipley tried to explain. "My contact was employed by the Global Virus Center."

Camilla raised an eyebrow, "Does this contact have a name?"

"I did not know his name until recently. I did not even know he was a 'he' until a second contact came forth."

"Camilla, we'd best not disclose any names. Doing so puts both of you at a greater threat."

"Paula, I still have friends that work there. If someone has been harmed, do you not owe me the courtesy?"

Shipley interrupted, "We are playing with fire, serious fire. We do not wish harm to come to either of you. The less you know…"

"We are already involved. You involved us, remember," insisted Camilla.

"Yeah. I agree. We are already committed to this cause," added Berkley. "Are you not interested in what I have found out snooping within the ranks of that alleged terrorist group. I have already put my neck on the line, and they know my real name. They think I am researching a book."

"He does have a point," said Paula. "Tell her his name, Shipley."

"I had only known the person as Grunt, a nickname I had given the contact based on a series of responsive codes we had agreed upon. My second contact, as mentioned, told me who 'he' was because she had been working with him, both fed up with the GVC and its deceitfulness. His name was…is Fritz McGinnis."

"Fritz," Camilla repeated in horror. "Fritz was my close friend. I discussed my research with him, and he had provided me with additional data and models until he finally broke it off, feeling his job might be compromised. He broke it off with me and then contacted you. And now you are saying he might be dead…murdered."

"Let us just frame it as vanished for now. I did not witness an act of murder. I only heard gunshots. Someone knew about a meeting we had scheduled at a deserted farm. They showed up and the rendezvous ended suspiciously. I do not feel they knew my identity, just that he was meeting with someone. I barely escaped. This is the reason you two need to bow out."

"Now we know the rest of the story, Paul Harvey," spoke up Berkley. "Names, places, a possible murder. Seems we are in too deep to exit."

"There is more," said Paula. "The coroner, Franklin Hartsfield, resigned and has let's just say, gone into hiding possibly."

"Suspiciously, if you ask me, given the fact that we have connected concerning dots to him, and his categorizing most every death as Covid related." stated Shipley.

"Do you think he is hiding or…" asked Berkley.

"Dead…no evidence but his exit seems a bit odd for my liking."

"Oh my," said Camilla, touching her hands to hear cheeks. "Doctor Kye Richardson and his wife Abigail just perished in a house fire. Remember, he is…was a family friend and knew Hartsfield. He seemed nervous to discuss the death certificates with me. Do you think?"

"Their deaths, the fire and Hartsfield's abrupt exit are related…plausible," said Shipley.

"Seems more than mere coincidence given what we know," added Paula. "See, this is exactly why we did not want you involved further."

"Too late for that I would say," said Berkley. "Hate to further muddy the water but our alleged terrorist group is being funded, by whom, I do not know yet. Get this. They are fully organized and move from city to city to cause chaos."

"You are telling me that these idiots told you this out of the blue," stated a disbelieving Shipley. "It takes months, sometimes years to infiltrate these organizations."

"You are not a million best selling author seeking material for a fictious novel."

"Maybe they just gave you fictitious answers," scoffed Shipley.

"I saw a copy of their manifesto, laid it out plain and simple. Of course, I was not allowed to have a copy nor photograph it. These people are seriously organized and structured. Toss out the premise of random and spontaneous involvement. And their cause is not the cause the media has been portraying. It is not about justice, an eye for an eye. They are opportunist as suspected by many."

"Did the name R.K. Soto come up by any chance?"

"No Paula, they did not share any sponsorship entities with me. That name does sound familiar though."

"Multi-billionaire, dark soul, the epitome of socialism and communism all rolled into one. It has been his mission to redefine this country," she explained.

Camilla tossed in her two cents worth, "It appears to me that we have more conjecture than fact. Unlike my contribution to this conspiracy circus, I can support my theories with concrete data and undeniable credible statistics."

"You have the floor, let's have it," smiled Paula.

Camilla did just that, compelling and straight forward, first stating that the information being spewed about an increase in Covid-19 cases was the result of increased testing. Compounding the misconstrued reporting was the fact that all tests were being counted, even retests of same individuals, and those testing positive and then negative were not being removing from the stats. Media announcing the number of people infected by state and by cities was highly deceiving. Those sharing this information wished to convince the public that these cases were the actual cases in any scenario when instead they were accumulative cases, none ever dropping off as people recovering. Some people, even though they tested positive, showed little or no signs of the virus. Further more, Camilla pointed out that obvious indicators were being purposely ignored; the drop in numbers of those being hospitalized and more importantly, the significant drop in deaths. The worst of the worst deaths were reported as being caused by Covid when they were not. George, Abigail, and Kitt were perfect examples. She had hundreds of others. Additionally, what has not been reported, the death rates by cancer, heart failure, car crashes, murder, you name it, had dropped dramatically off the radar screen. These illnesses did not simply go away because Covid had arrived. Statistically, she presented the data to support that Covid had contributed to these deaths because people were fearful of going to their doctor or to the hospital to get medical help. Suicides and drug use showed a similar correlation. One more obvious tidbit, survival rates in age categories were not as low as what the public was being led to believe. Even people in the highest age category had a greater than 95% chance of surviving the virus. Camilla was appalled by how Americans and even the world was being deceived, and for what purpose. Absurd that it could be only politically motivated, there must be something more to it.

"Mind boggling," commented Paula. "You are a statistical phenomenal."

"How do we bundle all this, or can we?"

"Berkley," Shipley now taking the floor, "This goes even deeper I am afraid. Soto has accomplices inside our government and outside our borders. Or should I say, he might just be a billionaire pawn in this chess game. He just thinks he holds a higher position on the checkered playing board. We are not ready to divulge that just yet. We need more data, to use Camilla's language."

"What now?"

"Excellent question, Camilla," smiled Paula. "For you, my dear, please continue to crunch the numbers, a most valuable component."

Shipley added, "As for you my best seller friend, cautiously dig in that hole but do it discretely. Do not be fooled by their generous sharing of insider info. Sounds like you are dealing with small fish. The bigger catch will be suspicious and not so naïve. Back away if you sense it is going south and do it quickly. Your name is not fictious in this scenario, remember. I have a meeting scheduled with contact number two and no, Camilla, I do not know her name yet. She has taken vacation time and she and her family are in an undisclosed location, one that I am not privy to either. She is in the hierarchy of the GVC, more so than Fritz McGinnis. Says she has what we need to blow the lid off the GVC's roll in this covert operation with extremely long tentacles, her words, not mine."

Camilla sighed then said, "This has gotten beyond intriguing and deceitful, has it not?"

"Dangerously so. All the more reason I wish you two would consider bowing out," advised Paula.

"Another best seller in my crosshairs," boasted Berkley.

"Crosshairs may not be so farfetched," added Shipley. "Those pulling the strings play for keeps. They do not intend to lose."

"There you go again with the scare tactics."

"Camilla, heed them as such and please reconsider."

Camilla shook her head no. If this impacted Americans and it obviously did, she could not sit idly by and not contribute where she could. She could not and would not speak for Berkley. He had to follow his conscience as well, book or no book in play. The concept of a tell all did not interest her. Stopping whatever this plot entailed was her only concern, even given the dangers involved.

They ended their powwow with specific and more detailed assignments. Paula would reach out to an acquaintance that might serve as a conduit for relaying this information to appropriate authorities once enough substantial evidence had been gathered. For now, she just intended to test the open mindedness and willingness for this induvial to consider joining them. She would divulge only enough to set the hook, after an oath of secrecy was sworn. If any of it trickled out it could endanger all involved.

****

Camilla had barely settled in at home when her cell phone rang. "Hi, Margie."

"Mom, just checking to see how you are doing."

"I am fine, honey. The better question, how are you doing?"

"The baby and I are fine according to the last ultrasound and check-up. That's part of the reason I called. You do still plan to be here for the birth, don't you?"

259

"Of course, I do. It would take more than a pandemic threat to keep me away."

"Another reason I called. Louis and I have been talking; why don't you come on up now? It might be good for you, for all of us. I mean, really, what's keeping you there? It would be so wonderful to have you here before the baby arrives."

"Good try, Margie. I am fine, really. Your father's death is tough on all of us, but I am coping with it my way. I miss you. I miss all my kids and grandkids. Please allow me to grieve my way. When the time comes, we shall be together."

"They will not even allow us to have a funeral. How can we ever get beyond this until then?"

'Your father remains in our hearts and memories. A funeral service does not deter these feelings or thoughts, a mere formality at best."

"What if I came there for a few days?"

"I appreciate that, really, but you need to stay put. There is no reason to risk the health of your child and you in these unpredictable and unprecedented times. A pregnancy places you at a higher risk, same as we old folks find ourselves facing. In due time we shall overcome all these difficulties and challenges."

"All right, Mom. But if you change your mind, we would love to have you here with us."

"I do appreciate that and will let you know if I decide differently. Give Louis a hug for me. I love you."

"Love you too, Mom."

****

Camilla smiled, thinking the switchboard is lit up tonight. "Hi John Junior. How are you, Nara and my grandboys doing in Hot-lanta?"

"All is well here. Better than most cities I suspect. We are lucky to live in the south and have a governor more in tune to America's needs. He has not clamped down on us like that New York scumbag has to y'all."

"We indeed live in challenging times."

"Mom, why don't you escape the craziness, come here and stay with us a spell. The kids would love it."

"Thank you and so would I but the timing is not suitable for me to do so."

"Timing? Now Mom, you are retired and there is no excuse for you staying in Rochester, especially with all that chaos nearby."

"And Atlanta has not had its fair share of chaos…son? You know me. I am fully capable of taking care of myself. I am not a helpless little old lady…not yet anyway."

"Mom, we have not seen you since Dad died."

"And we all agreed that it was best we stay put."

"Not forever, Mom. You could stay a few weeks with us then some time with Paul and Shay in Texas."

"I am not quite motivated to fly yet."

"Fine. I will come get you. Paul will do the same for the trip to Texas."

"Smart children George and I have raised and quite the conspirators you are. Margie is in on this too, isn't she?"

"What do you mean, Mom?"

"She called earlier. Similar strategy. I love all of you but really, I am fine, and we will still plan to spend Christmas together like we always do. Well, maybe we should plan having Christmas in Vermont instead of here. Your sister will be near full term by then and shouldn't travel."

"Consider coming here for Thanksgiving then."

"We will watch the pandemic and then make that decision."

"Okay, I know when to cry uncle. Love you Mom. By the way, expect a call from Greg next. Hawaii is a wonderful change of pace right now."

"Requires flying as well. Thank you for the heads up, Junior. I will plan to have a little fun with your brother."

"All right Mom. You call if you need anything. Miss Pop. Love you."

Like clockwork, son number three called on schedule. Camilla invited him for an extended stay knowing how he hated New York, even more so under these circumstances. She egged it as far as possible before finally admitting she had been stringing him along. He had almost agreed to her terms and stay. Both had a good laugh, Camilla warning him and his siblings they could not outsmart her. Afterwards, she regretted having turned down their requests, but not a lie, the timing was all wrong. She had to finish what they had started and break this attempted assault on the American way wide open.

Feeling extremely invigorated, she returned to her laptop and research. Not before thinking about what had happened to Kyle and Mildred, and that coroner, Franklin Hartsfield. Had foul play really been involved? If so, they, too could be venturing into perilously deadly territory. Undeterred, she stood firm to her convictions, seeing this to the bitter end. And then she considered her wedding vows, until death do us part. Profound indeed. She thought about one of her favorite sayings, *Stop being afraid of what can go wrong. Start being excited about what can go right.*

35

The presidential election continued at a furiously combative frenzy. The first scheduled debate had ended in what one pundit called a slobberknocker, referencing a football term. Name calling, interruptions, downright rudeness dominated the battle between the incumbent and the one vying to be the new king of the hill. Lines had been clearly drawn in the sand, never had two candidates been so extremely at opposite ends of the political spectrum. The president ended with these final words for Americans to ponder.

"Did you ever think you would be alive to witness an attempted socialist, communist takeover of the United States of America. We must stop calling them liberals. They are too far left for that. We are looking into the eyes of the new American Communist party, intent on destroying our great nation and for which it stands. Freedom must always ring loudly and clearly or there is no America. I will never apologize for saying Merry Christmas, God Bless America, for saluting our great flag and thanking our troops and first responders, for our freedom of speech and religion and our rights to own firearms. I will only kneel for our God Almighty. God bless the USA."

Senator Aaron Breeze quickly brushed aside the ugliness of the debate, inspired by the president's closing statement instead. He felt revitalized and determined more than ever to never become a Washington swamp dweller. This president, an outsider, was one who owed no one, loved his country and kept his promises. No wonder both sides of the aisle felt threatened by his actions. He boldly claimed he was not a politician. He got things done. He did what Americans expected their leaders to do. He led and raised the bar for others to follow. Words, threats, any attempt to take him down were ignored. Any mud slung his way never stuck. Was he abrasive and a trash talker? Sure, like none ever. He was no saint, but a saint was not needed for this job. He had created more jobs than any other president. More books had been written than ever before due to him being president. He joked, saying,

"See, I have stimulated the economy even from a literary standpoint. People who never considered penning a book have done so, for better or worse, facts or lies. I have made them famous. They should be thanking me instead of attacking me. Without me, where would UBN's rating be; probably tanked. Better than 90% negative but they cannot get enough of me. Even those good ay spreading fake information can profit under my reign as one of the greatest presidents to ever represent this even greater country. I am the people's president. God bless America."

The senator accepted the incoming call seeing the name of the caller on his cell phone's display and answered immediately. He listened intently both intrigued and astonished. He refrained from doing what most politicians did; he made no promises. He thanked the caller and said he looked forward to further discussions and disclosures. Senator Aaron Breeze prided himself with being logical and reasonable. He threatened people, even those across the aisle, with the utmost respect, even when they obviously did not deserve it. He was not sure if this approach would work in the swamp. Peers warned him that he would be devoured if he did not learn how to play hardball and if he refused to climb into the pen, wrestle, and wallow with the pigs. They insisted no one lasted in Washington without getting their hands dirty. Dirty in this case meant unclean morally. He heard them loud and clear but steadfast, he would not stoop to the level of those who had made careers of padding their pockets. He hated the term 'career politicians.' It implied that those elected to serve the people had done anything but. He would resign before ever stooping to that level. If he could not serve those who elected him and do it honestly, then he did not deserve to be here. Too many in Washington believed the opposite. Senator Breeze hoped to sponsor a bill suggesting term limits for congressional seats. He doubted it would ever sprout legs though. Foxes assigned to watching the henhouse would never agree to restraints minimizing chicken thievery. Pipe dreams for sure but it had been one promise he had made to himself. Plain and simple, there was no room for profiteering at the expense of those who had elected them to office. His mother would frame it as, 'You are as honest as the day is long, young Aaron, my eldest. Stay true to yourself always.' So far, he had and had been blessed for being so. He thanked God every day for allowing him another day in the world He had created.

****

Paula Wise sat at her desk, equally deep in thought. She had, since she was a child, been goal oriented, driven by achieving what she challenged herself to finish. She had never wavered in this approach, even now. What lay ahead was different though. It placed her in a precarious situation, a do or die scenario, one that could launch her to unfathomable heights or end her career, even her life if it did not go the way she envisioned it to go. One must weigh the risk and reward. Risks in this case were far more dangerous than anything she had undertaken before and the rewards were iffy at best. Nothing guaranteed. People were willing to kill to keep this secret. Had Richardson and his wife, and Hartsfield, lost their lives because of failing to follow the plan or disappointing those in charge? They had no evidence to support it, only conjecture. They did not even have names or faces to tie to the alleged murderers. The fire had not been identified as the work of an arsonist. That investigation continued. Until it did, they could not point fingers to it being orchestrated. Hartsfield supposedly had left a note announcing his resignation. Nothing out of the ordinary contradicted this scenario. No body. No proof. No reason to challenge the claim. Square one. Scenarios, mere suspicions with nothing to support them.

So where were they really going with this? Camilla had compelling data to support her statistics, but those alone did not support what they suspected. Funny, she thought, and just what do we really suspect? Hopefully, Shipley would excavate some answers to fill in these huge blanks in their narrative. She hated thinking in terms of a narrative given the false narratives the media had orchestrated against the president and the public. It turned her stomach thinking about how far journalist had fallen. Sure, she had used some questionable techniques while pursing storylines but never had she purposely deceived anyone with her reporting. She could profess her integrity was in tack when it came to that. Coloring outside the lines did not make her a bad person if in the end the truth prevailed. She

266

stuck to that conviction, integrity, and reputation in tack. Therefore, she was respected in her field by her peers and feared by those who knew she was relentless when on a trail. This one was different, quite unique from anything she had ever pursued. Putting it all on the line had never been so profoundly so. Putting other lives in danger had never been more stressful. Accustomed to being all in but she was not accustomed to having others placed in harms way. This troubled her tremendously. No prize was worth losing lives. Had she set her goals too high this time? To be determined. Treading in uncharted waters for sure.

****

Erwin Shipley sat in his flat, a modest dwelling, nothing fancy. He never strived for fancy or anything lavish. It was not his style. No frills suitable given how he spent little time in his humble abode. A man on a mission typically, his calling requiring him to operate remotely, blend into the environment and adapt to it as if he had always resided there. Mimicking was what he was good at, often his life depending on its success. His mission this time, much simpler; reassure and show compassion. Ensure he would not divulge the identity of this woman fearful of retribution. Not difficult to accomplish given he had firsthand exposure to the extent the opposition was willing to go to protect their agenda.

A neutral rendezvous had been chosen, the woman wishing to protect her anonymity. He fully understood her motives to do so. She had assured him she processed the golden ring and a cache of names to boot. She had forewarned him that he would be shocked by the revelations she was prepared to share, adding it would blow the lid off anything he could possibly imagine. Erwin wondered how she could possess so much knowledge from her role with the GVC. They delt in viruses, maybe capable of skewing the facts or misleading the public, but certainly not espionage. Agencies existed specifically solely for this purpose. Yes, with Camilla's assistance they were playing up the Covid angle, but it was but one piece of the assumed much larger picture. Could this person possess something beyond virus misinformation? And just who were these other players muddying up the waters?

Shipley had traveled the globe, weaving and bobbing, sometimes barely escaping what could have been dire consequences. If he had been born a cat, he would have already expended three times his allotted nine lives. Tippy toeing around explosive exploits had been commonplace, especially when he delved behind what he dubbed enemy lines. From the mafia to extreme Islamic terrorist, he had experienced it all, inside and out. This time felt different though. He could not quite put his finger on it but something evil and sinister existed out there with motives undeniably more diabolical and precisely orchestrated than anything that had ever challenged him thus far. He could almost visualize the wickedness in its rawest form. On full alert, the premise motivated him, a high he had never experienced in a career of unimaginable dangers. One regret, the author and virologist, were in over their heads. Accustomed to flying solo, he could not fathom how he would be able to protect them if the worst-case scenario materialized, and he did expect a worst-case scenario before this reached a climax. Too much appeared so obviously at stake, even though he did not know what specifically was on the line just yet. He just realized it was of the utmost importance that they stop it or at least expose it so others could.

****

Berkley Jay Patrick had finally shaken his bout of writer's block, felt revitalized. Best seller, he had already checked that box numerous times. This felt like he was part of something much more, something significant, something that warranted notoriety of an entirely different level. Spy games described the euphoria overwhelming his senses. Patrick…Berkley Patrick, shaken, not stirred, 007 style, almost infectious and quite exhilarating. Reborn. Purpose. To infinity and beyond. I am legend. The cape crusader, Gotham City beckoning him to the rescue. Berkley always assumed the identity of at least one of his characters in fiction novels. Sometimes it was the antagonist. Other times he was the protagonist. Seldom did he fill the shoes of a supporting cast member. They were dime a dozen. Good versus evil existed in most every novel. The hero had to be human, struggling and juggling something that haunted their past, something that misshaped their moral fiber, something that they must overcome to be successful by book's end.

Who would represent the hero in this developing story? Possibly it would be the A Team, Camilla, Paula, Shipley, and him? Maybe another would emerge to fill that void. Ah, but who would be the evil incarnate? A hero or heroes deserved an equally dastardly challenger. Heroes must be tested and pushed to the brink. Sadly, in novels there was no guarantee that everyone would survive. There were always casualties among the leading cast members. A good plot came with twists, one that kept the readers guessing, including a surprising twist they never saw coming. Reality mimics fiction unfortunately. The weakest link usually bought the big one first. Suddenly, Berkley did not like his odds given that scenario. He did not possess superhero qualities nor was he one likely to sacrifice his life for the greater good. He fell into the role of the geeky loser that too often fell victim in the early going. He suddenly regretted allowing himself to go down this rabbit hole. In his novels he controlled what happened and which characters survived. Not the case in real life, and he had never faced true evil or the pending dangers that might influence the outcome of this reality show. Sick to his stomach did not begin to describe his deteriorating mood. What had he been thinking? He was an author, a mere Stan Lee, not James Bond or a Marvel superhero.

****

Camilla Richie once again surmised that her participation in this dangerous situation was valuable or the journalists would not have sought her out and remained so persistent in gaining her research information. In her wildest dreams she had not seen this coming though. Finding out the truth had been a mere distraction at best, no clear path had existed for her sharing what she had uncovered. Voila, out of the blue, her path forward had been defined by unlikely means. Never had she envisioned her data would be lumped into an espionage reality. She certainly had not conceived that a diabolical plot aimed at the United States had been launched and that she held a key to preventing it from happening. She still was not sure how she felt about it. No doubt, this was serious business, much more serious

x

269

than identifying and studying viruses. Not that her role at the GVC had not been important. She sighed, thinking how George would have loved being part of this. In a way, he was. His death, one falsely attributed to Covid, ensured he would remain a viable piece of the bigger picture. Still, what purpose did it serve, the GVC insistent on deceiving the world about this virus, its origins, protecting the country that most likely unleashed it on the world without hesitation or remorse. It smelled of coverup, one much worse than what she had experienced while still working there. The center had been bought, had sold out, but at what cost to the world. Thankfully, there were those within the ranks that still possessed a conscience and moral obligation to expose them for what they were. Her stats would further support the existence of horrific corruptive misinformation being spread to an already panicky and stressed out population. Get out while she could they had warned. Still, she could not.

****

Reverend Bobby Flowers appeared on his Wednesday social media live streaming devotional. Modern technology continued to amaze him. With the church still closed technical experts within the congregation stepped forth and delivered, offering new means to reach out to those tech savvy enough to follow. Owen Gothelf operated the camera and linked it to the church's website. The reverend's devotional could be watched live or viewed later.

Wrapping up his ten-minute segment he ended it thusly,

> "One thing remains important. Please make sure you test positive for Faith. Remember, only you can ensure that you keep distance from all Doubt. Isolation includes isolating from Fear. Ultimately, you must trust in God throughout the storm.
>
> We are all God's people. Continue to give, even if you struggle in these troubling times. Remember those restaurants and businesses we have reached out to timelessly for

chartable donations. They need us now. Be generous. Answer the call in their time in need. Support them unconditionally.

There will always be things in our past that we would change if we could. It explains why life's rearview mirror is so small, and the windshield is so large. Where we are headed is much more important than where we have been.

Nightly, before your head comes to rest on your pillow, give thanks to the Lord for another day in the world He created for us. Pray for this country, for the World, and ask that He heal it, protect us, and lead us down the path of righteousness. Man does not have the cure. God does. Put your faith in Him. Nothing else matters if you commit to walking with the Lord.

Please step forth into this world and treat those as you prefer to be treated. Purge any hate from your heart and live life as He intended us to live. Amen."

The scene faded to black, Owen cuing him that he could breathe normally now. Both men laughed. The reverend certainly needed it, comfortable in the pulpit but not so in front of the camera. He found it concerning that he could deliver his message effortlessly in front of a church filled congregation yet struggle to compose himself in front of an audience of one while reaching greater numbers on social media. Old school really requires no explanation or defense. It is what it is. Now was time for him to rehearse his Sunday sermon off camera one more time before allowing Owen to record it. Flowers expected numerous restarts and edits, as had been the routine thus far. Unbeknownst to him, Owen had decided a new approach. He stepped out of the chapel but kept the camera running. If they were both lucky this would be a wrap in one take. Owen had insisted he stand in place and pretend the camera was rolling. Time would tell if this method worked.

****

Governor Anita Ming tightened her stranglehold on her state. Relentlessly she refused to allow dine in for restaurants. All parks were off limits. Any social gatherings exceeding ten was prohibited, and even these required masks and social distancing. She threatened the pastors of churches with fines and even incarceration if they dared disobey her and hold inside services. Outside services were prohibited as well. One pastor boldly confronted her boasting he intended holding his service on aisle 2 of the neighborhood big box store. Apparently, the virus shied away from social gatherings inside those stores. Another pastor, being interviewed by a local news station, suggested that his congregation might gather in front of the city courthouse for a friendly lawful protest where God's message would be delivered in contrast to those rioting and looting without just cause. A preacher with a church in rural America had assembled his flock in the parking lot of a nearby liquor store claiming they were present to quench their thirst. The liquor store proprietor had phoned the police complaining the saintly crowd gathered outside was preventing his customers from entering the store. The police if they were they using physical means to do so, and the store owner had to admit that they had not, but most people were gun-shy about being seen entering his establishment. Eventually law enforcement arrived but not until after the service had ended. The police chief, a devout church goer, had stood down until being tipped off that the crowd had disbursed.

With everything in place, the lockdown had not prevented the spread of the virus. The death toll in her state continued to be the highest in the nation. The Big Apple especially suffered, death tolls in nursing homes astronomical. Mayor Francis Kowalski deflected all criticism, blaming the president after previously praising the administration for doing everything they had asked to support the cause. Finger pointing is politically expected and acceptable, especially when under fire. At least she and the governor had made peace, agreeing to attack a mutual enemy. Ironically, the president had commissioned a hospital ship to the harbor and hospital facilities with hundreds of extra beds had been constructed in Central Park, mostly unused thus far. Ingrates possessed no integrity.

36

Erwin Shipley had met with the second whistleblower, this time face to face. For now, she used an alias. He had no problem with her doing this, possibly the wisest contingency given the circumstances. She allowed him to peruse various documents but was not comfortable with letting him photograph them. She did agree to provide copies but only if and when appropriate authorities were on board and when she and her family were under witness protection. Shipley had not reached that point yet, leaving him no bargaining options. What she had brought to the table implicated a vast network's involvement. She had provided viable leads as well. Another thing he had noticed; she was equally terrified and fearful of the consequences once the crap finally hit the fan. She did not have the market cornered in that category. Neither of them brought up Richardson or Hartsfield. Unspoken but understood.

Shipley texted Paula and suggested they meet, just the two of them for now. No need endangering the others further at this point he suggested. She agreed. The two rendezvoused at a café that offered takeout. Two tables outside offered a tiny sanctuary away from the chaos. No one occupied the second table. The usual hustle and bustle had been replaced by an occasional person roaming the streets. The street had few vehicles motoring about as the pandemic fear mongering had worked flawlessly on the population.

"And your meeting went as planned."

"Flawlessly so. She did not provide her real name nor allowed me to photograph any evidence. Luckily, I possess a photographic memory. Her evidence was quite compelling and damaging to the GVC. Goes to the top and beyond I must add. She would not share how she had obtained it though. For your protection I will withhold the names. Moving forward, the best policy is for none of us to possess all the puzzle pieces, agreed?"

"Agreed. Is there anything I can do?"

"Have you made contact with your political confidant?"

"I have. He understands that it is work in process. He has agreed to review the material once we are ready to share it. No promises. Not worried. He will be on board once we have what we need to make the case. What's next for you?"

"I have three new leads, viable ones according to her. Keys to unlocking Pandora's box. Unfortunately, it means I will be making an extensive road trip with stops in Denver, Lake Tahoe and Portland."

"How do you plan to pull this off, Shipley. Flights are grounded for the most part."
"Won't be flying."

"Are you planning to rent a car? If so, I will foot the expense."

"Thanks. Got it covered. An old friend owes me a long overdue favor. Melanie Finch is an Uber driver. I will cover it, discount rate. Not to worry. She will ask me no questions. She owes me big time. Something I did for her a few years back. We might be gone a couple of weeks at best."

"We could divide and conquer."

"My wheelhouse, not yours. My contribution to this partnership, remember."

"You always get the fun stuff, don't you?"

"Fun is my middle name; danger is my game."

"When do you plan to leave?"

"Immediately."

"You better see if this Melanie can accommodate you on such short notice."

"No problem. She will."

"She must owe you big."

"More so than you could ever fathom."

"Care to share?"

"Occupational confidentiality. I would only do so with her consent."

"And you are not asking it, are you?"

Shipley winked. "Just hope this little trip pays huge dividends. Not that I have never ventured down empty paths before. Our little canary's song seemed convincing and sincere."

"I trust your assessment and judgement. What should I tell the others?"

"Continue with their assignments and that I am pursuing hopefully the missing link. Caution Berkley again to not be overly zealous with his undercover antics. Might even be a better plan if we ask him standdown for a while. I am not sure there is much more to be learned from these ideological thugs."

"You could be right. I will talk to him tomorrow. Guess there is no harm in allowing Camilla to continue. She will not be crossing paths with anyone during her number crunching."

After finishing their lunch, they said their goodbyes, Paula wishing safe travels to her partner in criminal justice. She sensed they were close to blowing this thing wide open, whatever the endgame might be.

****

That night Berkley met with a new player in his imaginary fictional novel interview process. This gent from the Anti movement reversed rolls on him, rapid firing questions, almost so fast and furious Berkley experienced concern, unable to react with convincing confidence. Writing fiction did not compare with making it up on the fly and remembering what you said in case you were asked again. So far, he seemed to be holding his own in this unexpected inquisition process. The shoe on the other foot put him in a most uncomfortable role. With code name, Vlad, the twenty-five-ish Caucasian gentleman remained calm and collected as he pressed further. His only other contact had been an African American by the name of Jewel, maybe eighteen or nineteen. He had been a combination of spitfire and bravado with more gang swagger than this Vlad. He had eventually asked Jewel if he could meet with higher ranking members. Enter Vlad.

Vlad homed in on the specifics, book title, plot premise, genre, deadline for completion, all things that Jewel had never asked. Finally, he requested an opportunity to provide the foreword for the book, anonymously. He expressed that it would define the cause, fictionally speaking of course. Berkley agreed to all requests. Why not, it was indeed a fictitious book and project. Vlad asked the name of the publisher. Berkley did not want to use his and almost fabricated one. Instead, he informed he would be self-publishing it. The man did not blink. Hopefully, that meant he bought it or did not understand the concept. Short lived. Vlad asked why he had chosen to self-publish instead of using the company that had published his other books. The gent had done his homework. Berkeley sidestepped the question, stating his publisher was uncomfortable with the subject given the world we find ourselves in. Vlad's demeanor shifted. For the first time his expression changed and the tone in his voice indicated he was angry.

Vlad took a step forward, his face mere inches away from Berkley's. Berkley could smell his vial breath, a mixture of weed and pizza. Unmistakably pepperoni. He requested a copy of the manuscript for the next meeting. Berkley told him there was not manuscript yet, just an outline. Bring it then he demanded, a personal copy he added. He remained close, an intimidating posture to say the least. Berkley felt perspiration running down the back of his neck, forming above his brow and lips. You were not supposed to allow them to see you perspiring. It was not working for him, fear running down his spine. It did not go unnoticed.

Berkley offered his best courtesy smile. Vlad did not reciprocate. Instead, he pressed his nose directly against Berkley's and told him not to disappoint the movement. Berkley understood, heard the cancel culture decry loud and clear. The novelist was in over his head. He knew it. He sensed his adversary knew it as well. Berkley was no Shipley. He struggled to go off script once he had developed a plot in his head. He possessed no delete button, a chance to redo what had been done. A viable exit strategy momentarily eluded him. He edged backwards. Vlad smiled before placing his hands onto Berkley's shoulders giving him a slight shake.

"We understand one another, do we not, Mister Patrick?"

Almost gulping loudly, Berkley nodded.

"Very well. I look forward to reading your plot as it is. Be sure to pencil in a character in your outline that represents me, anonymously of course," he said managing a slight laugh.

He then grasped Berkley's shoulders firmly, shaking him a bit before then clutching Berkley's face in his hands. "It is not often I meet a best-selling author. In time, I hope we will become close friends. We could use someone of your status in our ranks. Please contemplate this invitation seriously. Complete access. A brother with a pen and a purpose. The perfect storm."

"Intrigued. Thank you for such a gracious offer," Berkley managed to speak with as much sincerity as he could muster.

"Be off then. You will be contacted by Jewel with a time and place for our next chat."

Berkley regretted having used his real name. These radical thugs obviously knew where he lived. If he did not keep up his end of the preposterous bargain, they could deliver a world of hurt. Peaceful protests equated to burning down buildings. He lacked the training to exit gracefully. He must consult Shipley at his earliest opportunity and before Jewel delivered the next scheduled appointment. No denying one thing, this was going to make one hell of a book. A shiver ran down his spine. He had the uncanny feeling he was being watched, maybe followed. If they knew where he lived why would they follow him. They wouldn't unless the charade was up. No, he argued that point down, thinking if they suspected a con, they would not have allowed him to leave. Unless…their intent was to seek out any others involved. Paranoia…compose yourself. He rallied his subconscious. Grow some backbone he encouraged himself. Pointless he countered. Heroes are born. Martyrs are revealed. Sacrificial lambs are a dime a dozen. Bah, bah, black sheep.

"I am no wolf in sheep's clothing," he muttered "My fleece is white as snow."

****

The next morning Paula phoned Berkley. He recapped the evening's events, painting a different picture from what he experienced. Berkley, as hard as he had tried, had not quite pulled off the version convincingly. Paula read clearly between the lines, sensing his little espionage was going awry. Didn't really matter. She was pulling the plug. Almost relived, Berkley did his best to express symbolic disappointment.

Paula expressed her concern. "Given that they know your identity and your address, I would suggest that you temporarily take up residence elsewhere."

"You are asking me to vacate my premises?"

"You said it yourself, you thought you were being followed. If you fail to deliver to this Vlad what he has requested, I fear they might pay you a little visit. These are not people to be taken lightly. Their involvement in inciting riots, looting, and burning buildings can not

278

be taken lightly. I do not put anything beyond what they might be capable of doing to advance their wokeness narrative. Do you have somewhere safe to go?"

"Hotels are closed thanks to our governor and the virus unleashed by the communist regime. I know of no author safe houses. Not to worry, I will come up with something, I promise."

"Do not procrastinate, Berkley. This is serious. By the way, Shipley will be out of the picture for a couple weeks."

"I hope he hasn't come down with something. It is not Covid, is it?"

"Sorry, did not mean to mislead you. He is not sick. He is following several leads. Please do not ask me to elaborate further. The less you know right now the better, as we have all agreed."

"Life in the danger zone, fair lady, I understand and I oblige."

37

Melanie the Uberqueen awaited Erwin Shipley's return, having dropped him off at the location he had requested. They had departed New York three days prior. She had never been to Denver. Truth be known, she had not ventured further than Buffalo westwardly, more north westwardly if plotting it on a map. Erwin had not shared the reason for his east to west coast excursion and she had not asked, aware of the newsman's unorthodox exploits. She had unintentionally found herself center stage four years previously while he had been in high pursuit of one of them. That unexpected meeting had changed her life, a welcome second chance from a life with seemingly no hope of escaping. For that she owed him everything and more.

Melanie Horovitz had just celebrated her twenty first birthday, a feat worthy of much fanfare given the unlikelihood four years ago of her ever reaching this ripe old age. Like much of her young life, she had commemorated the accomplishment alone; no confetti, no horns and no birthday cake unless you counted the cupcakes, she had splurged on from the one grocery store near her modest apartment. Her favorite one had been looted and burned to the ground. The owner had been gunned down while trying to protect it from the rioters that far outnumbered him. Three months had passed, and the police had not arrested anyone for his heinous murder. The neighborhood resembled nothing like she remembered, gutted, and burned buildings for blocks, a few boarded up and abandoned. Melanie had firsthand experience, an insider's perspective that evil knew no boundaries.

Just when her life had looked so promising, Covid-19 had jerked the rug out from under her. She had managed to lease an automobile and had begun a promising career as an Uber driver in the Big Apple. It had gone far better than she could have ever anticipated. Her earnings had paid for her apartment and the modest lifestyle she required. She had not missed any lease payments yet. This was bound to be impacted if the city remained in shutdown. The two-week excursion with Erwin would buy her some precious time, even with the discount she had offered. Erwin had paid for her gas, her room and meals, a pleasant surprise. He had a heart of gold and had been there for her when no one cared a rat's ass if she saw another day. Truth be known, even in the dire straights she currently found herself, she would have done this for free, probably spending every dime she had. Melanie could never do enough to repay his kindness and thank him from rescuing her when he could just as easily have turned a blind eye to her plight.

She tore open the wrapper of the Reese's Peanut Buttercups, a luxury she afforded herself weekly. As a child, in another time, she had been rewarded with this treat when she completed choirs or performed well in school. Those days seemed an eternity ago. Her past, the worst and the best of it, remained in her rearview mirror. She vaguely remembered having a mother but could not recall her name, first or last. Horovitz had been a name she picked off a billboard advertising a law firm. She had scrambled when asked by Erwin, figuring it sounded as good as anything she could make up on her own.

Melanie sipped through the straw, it bottoming, out making a loud noise that seemed even louder inside the confines of her Prius. Her root beer was caput. Still, there was no sign of Erwin. He had sure been gone for a long time or so it seemed. Sitting alone, one can lose touch with the ticks of a clock. For years she had possessed no sense of time, only wishing it would end when she was forced to do despicable acts. Nope, she shook off that notion, refusing to fall backward, thankful that those days were long gone, thanks to Erwin Shipley. A tap on the driver's side window caused her to drop the cup and what remained of a peanut buttercup.

A gnarly bearded face pressed against the glass, foggy from the breath being expelled. The eyes widened as he knuckled a second rap, this one more urgent than the first. He placed an open palm to it now, mouthing something incoherently. Obviously homeless, her heart urged her to engage the window button, but her head encouraged her to switch on the engine. Her head won out and she mumbled she was sorry as she eased the Prius forward and eventually away from the poor man apparently in need. She could not take that chance though. All homeless people were not harmless as she had learned the hard way. Brutality existed on the streets. Survival of the fittest never loomed larger than it did among those struggling to make it through another day.

A block away Melanie pulled the Prius to a curbside stop, still eyeing the rearview mirror to make sure the guy did not follow her. He had not. To her relief he had shuffled off into the opposite direction. More troubling now, she had deserted her pick up post. Erwin Shipley counted on her being there. She waited until the homeless guy had disappeared around the corner before shifting the Prius into reverse and retracing her route. Just as she pulled to a stop, she spotted Erwin exiting the alley, the same one he had entered earlier. He waved and she eased forward meeting him halfway. Erwin slipped into the passenger side and without exchanging words, she drove off, waiting for his next instructions.

"Option one. We can stay one more night here and head out early toward Lake Tahoe. Option two. We can head in there now and stop later."

"You rest. I will drive. I am good for a long haul yet."

"Very well. Drive, James."

Melanie smiled and nodded. Shipley made a quick phone call and reported to the person on the other end that he had experienced a no show; maybe Tahoe would come through for them. Curious yes, but she did not pry, and Erwin offered no information. Denver to Tahoe was just over 1000 miles, a 16-hour drive and at least one overnight stop. She just did what she was expected to do and drove while enjoying the breathtaking scenery. Erwin had settled into the backseat and was engrossed in his laptop with conversation at a bare minimum. She had learned long ago that, while compassionate, he did not talk much except when making a precise point. Apparently, he lacked having any points to speak of right now. She almost switched on Sirius but thought better of it. This was not her road trip. Melanie was still thankful for the gig and the experience. It was great to see Erwin again as well, this time under much improved circumstances. She could cope with him being quiet and secretive, feeling a sense of comfort in his presence. Sure, he remained all business but underneath she had experienced the real person that existed beyond the shell he presented to most. If not for the extreme age difference, she might have pursued something romantic with him. Who was she kidding? He knew her past better than anyone. Age difference or not, he could never be attracted to her, not romantically for sure. Better to just focus on matters at hand. To Tahoe and beyond.

****

Bummer thought Paula. Strike one. Hopefully Lake Tahoe and Portland would come through for them. If they did not, it would be tough for her to make a compelling and convincing argument. Maybe argument was a bit strong. She merely required the facts, supportive facts, to present a case that would stick, something beyond a wild conspiracy theory. Fact trumped fiction any day. No denying it, they were onto something and keeping it a secret had already met deathly consequences for those willing to risk sharing the truth. She kept telling herself that the national interest was at stake and just prayed that she would eventually have the compelling evidence to support the theory.

Paula had checked back with Berkley to make sure he had taken her seriously. He had but, of all places, he had taken up residence with Camilla. She had insisted and had plenty of room. Maybe it was for the best, she figured, the two laying low together. Surely, no one would be aware of their friendship in case things escalated. Paula found herself in virgin territory, unsettling as it seemed, deadly forces capable of doing the needful to quiet all opposition. She secured what she could to a thumb drive and then deleted the information from her laptop. She had never gone to such extremes before. She even deleted any texts that might be meaningful. Pertinent information from emails had been included on the thumb drive as well before deleting them. She wondered if she should acid wash her devices or use a hammer on them. She chuckled, envisioning Hilary Clinton's solution to covering her butt. Maybe she was overreacting, taking such extremes, but better to be safe than sorry her mother had always taught her.

Paula began perusing social media and news websites for the latest updates, screening out the bogus and fabricated narratives. Covid continued to wreak holy hell havoc worldwide, or at least according to the data being shared. Knowing what she knew, just how badly were these cases and deaths really being blown out of proportion? It was amazing to the extent they would go to discredit the president all for the sake of winning an election. Destroying the once booming economy and spreading fear seemed of no consequences for those lacking moral fiber and a conscience. Witnessing such a collapse was a tough pill to swallow. She jotted down various leads and scenarios on a notepad, bullet pointing what she knew, what she suspected and what she figured they hoped to gain. It was quiet the ugly picture given the facts as they stood. She quickly ripped the paper from the pad and ran it through the shredder. She just wanted to see them in black and white even though they were vividly etched in her head.

Her next program would have been in two days. Promos for the segment had already been recorded and were being run. Simple, the topic, Freedom. With the election looming large, the future of America would be decided. She would begin by quoting Ronald Regan yet again,

> 'Freedom is never more than one generation away from extinction. We did not pass it to our children in the bloodstream. It must be fought for, protected, and handed on for them to do the same, or one day we will spend our sunset years telling our children and our children's children what is was once like in the United States where men were free."

She would bring it home with another favorite quote, that of author and intellectual giant C.S. Lewis,

> 'You cannot go back and change the beginning, but you can start where you are and change the ending.'

And toss in a bit of John F. Kennedy for good measure,

> 'Let us not seek the Republican answer, or the
> Democratic answer. Let us not seek to fix the blame
> for the past. Let us accept our own responsibility for
> the future.'

It was not her job as a journalist to appear biased but to instead
provide her viewers with thought provocative facts and the choice of
scenarios and potential consequences. This election would be the
most critical in her lifetime. Americans would be encouraged to get
out and vote as their given right, a right that should not be taken
lightly. She knew how she would be voting but her viewers need not
know that. Her job was to provide the compelling evidence on both
political sides of the aisle. Choose but choose wisely for you and the
majority will be making the choice that impacts every American for
the foreseeable future. In her heart there was but one choice. Let
freedom ring.

****

Berkley met with Reverend Bobby Flowers, curious about his rescue
of Kitt Whitt, the untimely death still haunting him. He had learned
about Flowers involvement through Paula. Instead of laying low he
had chosen this, needing closure but unsure why he thought this man
of God could offer it. They sat in the rectory both masked and
distanced, following the protocol of the day, one that had changed
several times since this had begun.

"Thank you again for agreeing to humor me," spoke Berkley.

"I find nothing humorous about this, Mister Patrick," answered
Flowers.

"I did not mean it to come out like that. What I mean is that Kitt was
a close friend and he died so suddenly after that second attack. You
saved him from the first and for that I am sincerely grateful. He was
a good kid, so talented, a future of possibilities."

"I met him only once, but, I agree, he seemed quite gifted. How can I help you with your grief, son?"

"I suppose I seek answers, maybe answers only a man of the clergy can provide."

"I will do my best. What is it you specifically seek?"

"My chance or intervention, however it is best framed, you saved my friend Kitt by bringing him inside your church. A noble thing to do I might add."

"Thank you. Nothing noble in my actions. I saw a man in distress, and it was my obligation to assist in any way that I could. I am sure you would have done the same. God does not turn his back on any of His children, nor would I."

"Then please answer me this. Why did God allow Kitt to survive that attack only to allow him to be attacked a second time and not survive? Why would He grant one reprieve to simply cancel that out with a more brutal attack? Purpose, I just cannot fathom the rational in God allowing this. Second chances I get. I do not get this though. Like dangling a carrot and then yanking it away. Why? And please do not give me that 'God works in mysterious ways' baloney. I need something a bit more valid than that."

"I understand that you seek answers. It is quite common for anyone to have questions when someone passes, especially in such a tragic manner. I do not have those answers for your friend's death. Nor can I explain the timing of any person's passing. Allow me to share this with you, something I read and have retained for times like these."

A Butterfly

Has only 14 days to live,
still it flies joyfully.
capturing many hearts.

Sometimes it is not how
long we live but it is
how we live it.

Each moment in life
is precious, use it to
glorify God.

Be a channel of joy.
Be a blessing to others.

"Profoundly quoted, I will give you that. I appreciate a good metaphoric analogy. I am not sure it explains Kitt's untimely death sequence though."

"Death, especially the death of a loved one or close friend poses its fair share of puzzling questions. Sometimes you must look beyond it. God does work in mysterious ways, often delivering a subliminal message to those who need more than mere answers."

"Like what, reverend? God justifies his actions."

"No, God does not have to justify any of His actions for us. He has already given His son to pay for our actions, our sins."

"I must admit, reverend, I did not come here to discuss theology with an expert. Thank you just the same. I have probably taken up enough of your valuable time."

"It is said that one's faith does not always take you out of the problem, but you can count on faith taking you through the problem. Faith will not necessarily take away the pain, but it can offer you the ability to handle the pain. Faith will not always take you out of storms way. but faith calms you during the storm. I cannot take credit for theser either, but can I at least have an amen?"

"If ever I require divine collaboration for one of my novels, I will certainly be calling on you, Reverend Flowers. Matter of fact, I might do just that given the chaos we find ourselves in and a manuscript I have in mind." Berkley could envision working some of these angles into it, a world gone mad.

"The world that He created has fallen on hard times, no denying the signs. Satan may be winning a bunch of the smaller battles but be assured, God always wins the war. I hope something I have shared will assist you in finding the answers you seek."

"Like a butterfly, I must be fluttering along and on my way. You stay safe as well, Reverend Flowers. Covid-19 is a bear, so they keep saying."

"Rioters and looters are equally terrifying. All we can do is pray and trust in God. Safe travels, Mister Patrick and may God protect you."

38

Shipley and Melanie were a couple of hours away from Lake Tahoe, now six days since their departure. Shipley remained hopeful that this lead would offer substance. At least he hoped the whistleblower's contact would rendezvous with them as planned. He sat in the backseat of the Prius while Melanie freshened up at one of the few truck stops they had found open in the past seven hours. This was not a time to travel for sure. The lockdown in full force in most towns and states. Takeout could be had but finding bathroom facilities to use or open hotels were in short supply. Some remote mom and pop establishments risked coloring outside the lines, a means of survival outweighing the consequences of their actions. Unfortunately, they could not Google ahead. Instead, they had to rely on sheer luck stumbling upon them.

Melanie had been a trooper, not one to complain at all. Shipley credited her tenacity during the current situation being a far notch above the environment she had been exposed to before he had offered her a means of escape. He would forever be indebted to her. She had just smiled saying it was she that owed him. After this maybe they could call it all square. He spotted her heading to the car, two drinks and a plastic bag in her hands. More artery clogging cuisine no doubt. Not like he had not lived on grease droppings before. She slipped inside, passing him a soda and something scrumptiously wet and stickily, wrapped and feeling weighty like a double patty burger.

"I have called ahead and confirmed our destination. You still think we can make Tahoe in a couple of hours."

"According to the GPS. Do we need to be there sooner? I can make that happen if we do."

"No. Told my contact I would call when we were close. Proceed when ready."

She nodded and pressed the engine button. Keyless still amazed her. Melanie did not question the specifics of the next stop, figuring he would tell her when she needed to know. Yes, she was curious, but it was none of her business, leaving it at that. As the norm, extraordinarily little conversation occurred during the next two hours. Erwin remained engrossed in his laptop, only once making a phone call and even then, keeping it short. He sounded as if he might be speaking in code, little substance to give away to the subject matter. Again, none of her business.

****

Berkley had settled in at Camilla's home. Uncomfortable did not begin to express how he felt. Not that she had not welcomed him with open arms and had insisted he make himself at home, he sensed he was intruding on a life, one that had been occupied by her and George. He could not explain it, but he could still sense George's presence. A worn black leather reclining chair had obviously been his. Positioned at an angle to the large big screen television was a dead giveaway. In contrast, Camilla's was a flowery patterned swivel chair with a matching foot stool. A small wood round table separated the two. George's side was worn and scratched. Hers was blemish free. The spare bedroom that he had been assigned was a treasure-trove of memories, kids and grandkids framed photographs occupying ever nook and cranny. Berkley perused the many photos envious of the family personified, a life that had eluded him. Never married and with very few relationships he had a rather uneventful existence. He had never suffered any remorse or regret for the path he had chosen, at least not until he now found himself emersed in the family phenomenon. Warmth and love oozed loud and clear. He had no explanation for why he had chosen the lifestyle he had until now. His writing had been his escape, all that he had ever required, the essence of happiness. He looked back now thinking how foolishly he had deceived himself. He whispered, *"Sometimes it is not how long we live but it is how we live it. A Butterfly has only 14 days to live…"*

"Beautifully said. Is that yours or from a favorite quote?"

Berkley's face reddened. He had not realized he had spoken it aloud or that Camilla had been standing behind him in the doorway. "Not mine. Just something someone shared with me recently. Just a portion of it anyway."

"Profound just the same. Are you ready for dinner?"

"Whenever you are. Again, I cannot express my gratitude enough for the graciousness of your hospitality."

"A safe house hopefully, given what you have shared and what Paula has suggested. Did you ever imagine we would find ourselves playing cloak and dagger?"

"Only in one of my novels. This has been a bit surreal yet quite exhilarating to say the least. It has elevated my appreciation for uninhibited research. I fear for our world if ever these woke cancel culture extremists gain a foothold, rebellious with radical causes indeed."

"Thankful you stayed out of harms way while taking such a risk, Berkley."

"Did not reach a risky level until Vlad entered the scenario. This movement is well organized and funded. These are not random spontaneous and peaceful protesters the media would like to convince us that they are. I sensed viciousness in their intent."

"Do you think they will seek you at your place?"

"Paula seems to think so. I did feel as if I was being watched when I returned there."

"Do you think they could have followed you here?"

"I don't believe they did. I utilized techniques from one of my novels. Switch and bait, I changed cabs once, Uber drivers twice, and took an evasive route here. They might be good, but I left no breadcrumbs in my wake. I am famished. What specialty awaits us, my dear?"

****

"My son, how can I help you?"

"Got this friend in trouble, just asking for him. I think you might know him."

"And does this friend have a name?"

"Famous guy, he writes books."

"I see. He is an author friend then."

"Writing a book about me, about us but strange thing, supposed to meet him at his place but he was not at home. Thought you might know how I could get in touch with him, preacher."

"Again, his name?"

"Goes by Berkley Jay Patrick. Jay-berk is what I call him."

"And you are?"

"He calls me his Jewel of the Nile, catchy, ain't it?"

"Yes. I am acquainted with Mister Patrick."

"Thought so. Seen him here recently. Did he confess his sins or something?"

"You are confusing us with the Catholic faith."

"Sinful people can confess to any preacher, can't they?"

"I am sorry, son…Mister Jewel…I cannot assist you. I am not privy to his address or contact information."

"Is this like a doctor keeping his mouth shut about what ails you or a lawyer not being able to say if his client is guilty as charged."

"Obviously, I would not disclose any personal discussions I would have had with anyone seeking advice. In this case, I reiterate, I do not know how to contact your friend. Sorry I could not have been of more help."

"Wrong answer, preacher. He was here and he was here for a while. More than simple chit chat, right? Confession time. You talk. I listen. Nothing but the truth, the whole truth, so help you God."

****

Melanie parked the Prius in the parking lot of Bert's Café. The café was closed but it had been the address Erwin had given her to enter in the GPS. There they just waited, the usual absence of conversation deafening the vehicle's close quarters. Dusk crept closer. The parking lot remained empty except for the white Prius. Melanie almost asked if this was the correct address but instead chose to remain silent, almost obedient, and submissive; thoughts that immediately repulsed her. Defiant she found the courage to rebel against her subconscious fears.

"How long do you think we should wait?"

Shipley sighed, "As long as it takes. This cannot be happening, not a second time."

Darkness had fallen and the lone occupants of the vacant parking lot continued to stick out like a sore thumb. Noticeably so. A blare from a siren and blue light alerted them they were no longer alone. A spotlight blinded Melanie. An instant fearful reminder ran down her spine. Never trust the cops. They are evil. Blinking and breathing heavily she managed to dismiss the misconception, something she

293

had been brainwashed to believe. A tap on the driver's side window interrupted her train of thought. This time no homeless bearded man stared at her through the glass.

"Miss, is everything all right?"

She lowered the window. "Yes sir."

The officer using a flashlight suspiciously eyed the passenger in the backseat. "Are you sure everything is fine young lady?"

"Yes sir. I am an Uber driver, and he is my passenger." She presented the officer with her credentials.

"New York. Nevada is a long way from New York."

"Officer if I might explain," spoke up Shipley.

"Please do. Might I see some identification."
Shipley passed the policeman his driver's license. He eyed it and then handed it back. "New York too. Care to explain why you are parked in Bert's parking lot, conspicuously I might add?"

"Sorry officer. I commissioned her to bring me here. I am supposed to meet a friend shortly. He gave me the address."

"Curious. You have a valid license. Why didn't you drive instead?"

"Automobile mishap. My car was in the shop. No flights. Seemed to be my best option. "

"Is this correct, Miss Horovitz?"

"Yes sir. With the shut down and businesses closed, a girl must seize any opportunities to make an honest buck. Not much going on in the Big Apple to make ends meet. Mister Shipley made me an offer that I could not refuse. It will help keep me afloat in these trying times."

"Officer, as soon as I meet with my friend, we will be off."

"Very well, but if you are still here when I make my next round, we might further this conversation. Enjoy your stay, Mister Shipley. By the way, given the closures, just where do you plain to stay?"

"We have reservations at an Airbnb. I hope this isn't an illegal arrangement in Nevada."

The officer smiled, "Welcome to Nevada. We do things a bit differently. Please finish your business with your friend. This could be considered trespassing, especially after hours."

"After hours," questioned Melanie. "The place is closed due to the shutdown, isn't it?"

"Just make sure you and your…passenger…clear the premises soon, Miss Horovitz. Vagrancy is still an illegal offense."

After the officer vacated the premises, Shipley leaned forward and told Melanie, "Ten more minutes."

Melanie giggled. "I think he thought you were a john and…"

"You are a legitimate Uber driver. Honest pay for an honest day's work. Ten more minutes and you are off the clock."

Melanie smiled, thinking how liberated she felt. No place she would rather be than with Erwin Shipley, her knight in shining armor."

Shipley fumed inside. More dead ends. This trip had been a bust so far. The whistleblower had apparently purposely misled them. What had she to gain by lying? She feared the situation enough that she had fled. Or had that just been fabricated to throw him off the trail. It had certainly worked, sending him off on a two week cross country witch hunt. An expensive lesson. Wasn't his first.

****

Berkley had missed a call. He checked his phone and it indicated he had a new voice message. He retrieved it and played it.

'Mister Patrick, this is Reverend Flowers. Felt compelled to inform you a young man going by the name of Jewel of the Nile paid me a visit. He was interested in where he might find you. Obviously, I had no idea but had your number saved on my phone. Be warned. I fear his intentions are questionable. He did not harm me. I shall alert you if he returns.'

Camilla eyed Berkley as he listened to the message. After ending it, Berkley shook his head saying, "Not good. Jewel dropped by Reverend Flowers church looking for me. Paula was dead right. These terrorist thugs can be relentless in their efforts. Infiltration comes with a cost. Vlad is quite determined so it seems. The jig is probably up."

"Do you really think their agenda is linked to everything else?"

"Camilla, I fear we are on the far reaches of what everything else really is. Speaking of expired jigs, we deserve answers from Paula. Keeping us in the dark is no longer a negotiable option."

"As my George would say, gut instinct cannot be ignored."

"I wish I had gotten to know him better."

"George was a tough cookie on the outside, but he had a tender heart. Men in his family rarely displayed emotion. His father instilled in him and his two brothers that emotion signaled weakness. Real men do not cry, nor do they gossip like a flock of hens. Mr. Richie came across extremely stern, a gruff voice and an almost bully persona. I saw through it though and had him eating out of the palm of my hand. He maintained his false imagine until the end. Inside he was a good man, a Godly man. He raised three young boys alone after his wife died in a car accident. He never remarried. He did what was expected of him and then some. He taught his kids values and belief that a hard day's work never harmed you. I will forever miss Mr. Richie."

"And you are still grieving for George, aren't you?"

"Grief is not the end of the world. Memories are precious. Everyone deals with them on their terms. I will forever miss my wonderful husband, but life does not end in the death of those you loved. One must mourn and move on as best one can. There is no set time for this process. And yes, steps backwards are part of the healing."

"Each moment in life is precious. Use it to glorify God. Be a channel of joy. Be a blessing to others. Such is the butterfly."

"The butterfly again," smiled Camilla.

"As spoken by an extremely wise gentleman. Applicable in troubling times and it is here we find ourselves, our version of a fourteen-day lifespan, metaphorically speaking."

****

Paula Wise listened intently to Erwin Shipley's latest news.

"Unlike our Denver experience, number two eventually made the appointment, but only after the Tahoe policeman exited the premises. Dead end. The guy was a disgruntle ex-employee, one with a serious axe to grind. I sensed nothing credible in the information he shared."

"Why so?"

"No evidence to support his claims. Nothing substantial either. You could glean the internet and find a s much on the infamous Global Virus Center."

"Maybe Portland will be more of the same. Why not cut our loses and head back?"

"We are less than 600 miles from our last stop. May as well complete the cycle. Better to know how it ends than forever be doubtful I always say."

"I will keep my fingers crossed, Shipley."

"I am not one to believe in miracles or luck. Anything on your end, Paula?"

"I have one of my reliable sources following a lead. Has deep ties to our old friend, R.K. Soto."

"Mister Deep Pockets with an illicit and destructive agenda, huh. Do you think it is anything substantial or new?"

"My source seems to think so, but it is sketchy at best for now. Berkley has taken up residence with Camilla, safety in numbers and an undisclosed location to our friendly protesting community. Seems our author friend might have gotten a bit too close for comfort. They were questioning his integrity and honor, the premise of a book unlikely."

"Rookie mistake. Concerned me from day one. He is not experienced in dumpster diving in the backyards of those astute in garbage harvesting. Tough to con a con convincingly. Will they be safe at her residence?"

"I believe they will. Some henchmen were initially searching for Berkley, but it appears they have discontinued their efforts. I will hand it to him though; he did manage to connect a few interesting dots. We shall discuss potential new trails upon your return. Otherwise, has your little excursion being enjoyable?"

"Notable best describes it. Amazing viewing this country under a new microscope. The new shuttered America is like nothing I have ever experienced. Puts things in perspective. We are heading in the wrong direction, Paula. The transformation is under way. Never in my life would I have ever imagined we could be so incredibly close to witnessing our nation go to hell in a hand basket. Socialism is at our doorstep. Katy bar the door."

"You sound like a crusader for justice, Shipley."

"True journalism has been flushed down the toilet as we both are aware. The media is but a mere propaganda tool for those with our best interest not at heart. Do we pick sides or continue playing it straight down the middle? I am just suggesting we proceed with an open mind and equally open heart. Call me an old softy with a moral compass given what stakes are in play. I will simply leave it at that."

After the call ended, Paula reflected on what Shipley had said. She, too struggled, straddling a fence she had never balanced on before now. A journalist absolutely did not choose sides. Report the news and allow the viewers to decide, nothing more complicated than that so she continued to try to convince herself. Could she realistically sit idly on the sidelines and watch the game play out, the ultimate winner of no consequence? There were winners and losers in every sport. This was unlike any sport ever played. All the marbles reached new levels. Freedom had always been the ultimate wager, wars fought hard and furiously, precious blood spilled to protect its net worth.

Paula remembered something profound, a quote by Jake Remington, that spoke volumes and seemed appropriately in play, *Fate whispers to the warrior, 'You cannot withstand the storm. The warrior whispers back, 'I am the storm.'*

39

Welcome to Portland. A welcome sign thought Shipley. Last stop and possibly equally last hope with this debacle going south quickly. Her admired his companion and chauffeur. She was such a gamer, never a complainer. The young lady had come a long way since he had first met her, blossoming into an astonishing successful woman. Shipley took pride in his role of freeing her from the worst world anyone should ever had to endure. Melanie Horovitz, doubtful that was her real name, had turned out all right indeed.

Once one of his favorite cities, Portland was now a war zone, one of extreme unrest. Riots, looting, utter destruction had consumed the city under the pretense of friendly protests. According to news being shared by the media, the opposite was in play. Like other major cites under siege, governing political officials turned a blind eye and allowed the citizens to suffer under the cancel culture reign. Melanie drove the Prius through ravished neighborhoods, shells of once thriving businesses burned and unrecognizable, ghost towns now. The address of the last secret meeting place had been entered in the Prius GPS. Within the hour Shipley would find out if this one would pan out. His confidence level had diminished considerably. Melanie in contrast appeared unfrazzled by the ordeal, personified as the Uber driver just doing her job.

They were nearly 3000 miles from home and had zig zagged their way across this great nation in search of truth. Someone was behind this orchestration of evil. Conspiracy theories were just that without evidence to substantial the premise. Shipley remained confident that ugliness existed if only he could overturn the right rock. The pandemic's timing months before a presidential election just felt more than mere coincidence. While the virus impacted everyone, the mandated shutdown and destruction of a once prospering economy challenged a popular president seeking reelection. The false reporting based on Camilla's research of Covid cases and related deaths pointed to sinister origins. The million-dollar question, who was willing to unleash a deadly virus, destroy an economy worldwide and take down a sitting president and to what end?

Seemed a bit extreme but wars had been waged forever for seemingly horrific causes. Not one to throw in the towel, Shipley found himself wondering if it was even possible to trace the origin of this tragedy.

Thankfully, the timing of their arrival had offered them somewhat of a reprieve. Daylight presented some measure of safety. The rioters and looters preferred the element of darkness to conceal their cowardly antics. Bold and defiant, they wreaked their havoc when the fireworks could be deployed to terrorize neighborhoods and keep any challengers at bay. Not that anyone in Portland really challenged their reign of unbridled terror. The police had been for the most part ordered to stand down and stay back, allowing the unruly to have their way too long. The loyal taxpayers and business owners were receiving no protection, no compensation for their hard work and faith in a system that was no longer functioning to work on behalf of the voters, Americans believing in a nation that promised them freedom and prosperity.

Erwin Shipley had ventured countless times into regions ruled by communist and socialist regimes. He had firsthand experienced it, seen it with his own eyes. He had interviewed those suffering in the most horrid conditions and had hunkered down with the locals being unmercifully attacked. This was the United States of American, his backyard, not some third world country being ruled by tyrants. One would not recognize it as such. Is this how it started he asked himself. Was he witnessing the unraveling of democracy, the American dream? Surely not. We are stronger, better than that. The constitution, the declaration will not stand for this. Americans will not tolerate this transformation. Americans are fighters. Liberty and justice for all reigns true, doesn't it? Shipley hated struggling with these emotions, uncharted territory for a usually reasonable and clear-thinking individual. The evilest seed had been cultivated. Given a chance, it would grow and flourish. The challenge facing him, would he fight it or merely report it. Stay tuned he thought. Do not change that channel. To be determined, a cliff hanger in the making.

Melanie, awe struck and almost in shock, could not believe her eyes. She had never seen such destruction. Those that had transpired in New York had been small by comparison. Never had she experienced something of this magnitude. This was America. How could anyone allow it to happen here she wondered. Her heart ached for those impacted. She thanked her lucky stars, even given the circumstances of the pandemic shut down for how far she had climbed from the ashes of her past. She thought about a passage she had read and forever remembered after her emergence into freedom.

Not once in the Bible does it say worry about it, stress out about it, figure it out, but often it says for you to put your trust in God Almighty.

Melanie encouraged everyone to remember all the restaurants and small business owners. She fell into this category as well. Support them throughout these difficult times. They were the true victims, every day working people. Initially Americans had been asked to self-quarantine for two weeks and the virus would be brought under control. Seven months later she and her fellow Americans were being forced, not asked, to comply with government mandated restrictions. Melanie was far from being an expert on politics but, on every level, this seemed wrong to her. She had Googled dictatorship after hearing cries from acquaintances in her building, people who had escaped such rule in Cuba and other communist countries. It is explained as a government or social situation where one person makes the rules and decisions without input from anyone. It implies absolute power of a political party. Shocked to say the least.

She trusted the president. He had followed the experts' advice and had asked Americans to give the two-week thing a try. Cities like New York had taken liberties and ordered citizens, no threatened them, to comply with even tighter restrictions. The president had urged these cities to allow their businesses to reopen. They had not. Mini dictatorships sprung up across the nation. Rule of law had reached complex abnormalities. Melanie struggled to understand the rationale behind the madness. A woman who owned a hair salon had been arrested for reopening her business, a matter of survival simply explained. Big box stores remained open.

Melanie wondered how this virus knew when and where to go. It apparently thrived in the bar scene or in church congregations but shied away from Walmart, Lowes, Home Depot, and grocery stores. It seemingly could not survive in crowded protests, riots or in the presence of looting. Melanie was no expert, but it did not take an expert to recognize BS piled so high. She recognized control freaks, those wishing to have power over innocent people. She knew it all so well. She had lived among such people and appreciated the simple perks freedom offered. Sadly, she wondered how Americans would escape the prison that had been forced upon them. She had blindly submitted once. She was not ready to be so easily and ignorantly submissive again. She had discovered a rebellious side, one that would not be deceived and lied to again under any circumstances.

Caught up in her thoughts, she shook her head, a means to return to the current situation. Waiting for Erwin to return should be the norm. Far from it. As each minute expired, she nervously perused the landscape for any sign of his reemergence. No harm had come to him thus far, but she just could not shake the feeling that something sinister lurked out there. These dreadful times had brought out the ugliness and evilness in the world. She for one recognized evil. She possessed an almost expert intuitiveness. Experience speaks volumes. Whatever had driven him to travel across the United States was not something of pleasure. Erwin had purpose. He was on a mission of extreme importance. She could feel it even if he were not willing to share it with her. She paused to again whisper a little prayer for his protection in whatever situation he found himself. Glancing about again. No sign of him. He had now been gone for over an hour. Neither of the first two stops had taken this long. Well, the first one had been in his words, a no show. The second, she had observed while he met with someone in the shadows. At least in those he had not been out of her sight.

Supposedly, this would be their last stop before heading home. She had mixed emotions about returning. Melanie had embraced the experience, seeing a world she had never seen before. The Big Apple had lost much of its appeal. A world existed beyond its boundaries, something more wonderous than she could have ever imagined. That is until they arrived here. Portland had disappointed her. Much so after breathing in the panoramic views of Lake Tahoe. The drive had been a splattering of natural wonderment from snow covered mountains to endless plains, wild animals dotting the land, some she had never seen before, except in zoos. Bison, elk, antelope and even a grizzly bear had crossed their path. Natural beauty of this great nation had captivated her like no other experience in her young life.

For now, though, she waited, her patience getting the best of her. Where was Erwin and why was this taking so long? She found herself almost tempted to venture out and search for him. Almost. He had cautioned her to stay vigil and wait for him to return. She trusted him and against her better instinct would do as he had asked. She did not necessarily have to like the predicament, but she would stand on ready if the situation required a hasty retreat. She wasn't sure why she was even thinking in these terms. Something just felt off. She checked behind her through the rearview and side mirrors suddenly edgy, feeling like she was being watched. She saw nothing to indicate danger lurked nearby. Still, she could not shake the eeriness and sense of foreboding danger. She reached for her cell phone. Tempted to call or at least text him. No. She could not. It might compromise his situation and place him in an even more dangerous situation, if indeed he was in danger at all. More on her, not anything he had ever indicated. She popped a Reese's peanut buttercup in her mouth, her means of regaining composure, the treat that comforted her when nothing else would.

****

Camilla reviewed her data, the latest statistics substantiating her previous findings. Covid-19 as it had been portrayed thus far bared no resemblance to her models. Cases and related deaths continued to be drastically exaggerated. Worse, her stats painted an even dire scenario. Suicides and drug abuse were on the rise more related to the social disfunction being forced on humanity. Too many people were putting themselves at risk by refusing to seek treatment or routine follow up for cancer, heart disease and countless other common diseases, fearful of exposure to Covid in hospitals and their doctors' offices. Fear mongering had reach epidemic proportions.

Someone willed the misconception of this disease on the world for unthinkable gains.

"Here you go, Camilla, brought you a cup of hot herbal tea."

"Thank you, Berkley."

"How goes the wonderful world of germ warfare?"

"Staggering. We are the victims of relentless lying. I find it difficult to understand why our government would knowingly deceive us. Well, allow me to rephrase that. The Global Virus Center is behind this. I cannot confirm if our leaders are willingly coconspirators. The data does not lie. It does not conform to the information being broadcasted 24/7 on the airways."

"Do you think the news media is in on it?"

"Whether they are or not, they are supporting the narrative as always."

"You look tired my lovely. Why not give it a rest? You cannot change their portrayal, at least not yet."

"You are probably right. As Paula and Shipley have pointed out, my analysis is but one part of the puzzle they seek to assemble."

"When is the last time you talked with your kids? Better still, when is the last time you visited them? I will answer for you. Too long. Why not give this a well-deserved break and go visit some of them?"

"There is nothing I would love more. As crazy as it might sound, what I am doing I am doing because I love my kids and grandkids. This deceit must end now to secure their future. I am referring to the bigger picture of course. There are those intent on transforming this country into one more skewed toward socialism and even communism. We see it every day. Maybe Covid-19 is related to this collapse of our nation. Who can really say for sure? If what Paula and Shipley are pursuing provides evidence to wake up a sleeping giant, then so be it. I cannot pass on an opportunity to contribute to its demise. What about you, Berkley, why are you really in this?"

"Of course, the premise of my next bestselling novel being a sure thing is reason enough to saddle up with you bunch of rebellious renegades. Ironically, I may have seen the light and am more willing to appreciate a greater value in our little merry band of misfits merging to thwart the evil seeking to destroy our country and possibly the world."

"A bit overly dramatic even for you. This is not that butterfly and cocoon inspiration again, is it?"

"I never insinuated cocoon or a rebirth of any kind. Honestly, I suppose I am experiencing one of those life altering moments though. What could I have done differently or what can I do differently moving forward?"

"You impact plenty of lives with your writing. Is that not enough?"

"I am thinking something more epically proportioned if not merely morally subjective. Face facts. I have lived my life selfishly."

"There is not a selfish bone in your body, Berkley."

"Thank you for the spirited reply. Not what I mean, lovely. I have never been a person of faith. A believer that something spiritual exists in my not always so humble universe."

"Why Berkley Jay Patrick, are you trying to tell me you are truly seeing the light, seeking a relationship with God?"

"Let's not expedite my emboldened awareness to that level just yet. I will confess though that I am open to other interpretations of my awakening state."

"Face facts and, in my world, facts trump opinions. You are caught in the pull."

"Pull? I have no earthly idea what you are insinuating."

"God's pull, silly. Us, banning together as one, has obviously shoved you into the pull, a push or a nudge, whatever, but the pull has definitely snagged you."

"Pulls, pushes, God snatching me up, I don't know if I buy into all that. I am a practical man. I do not function in any orbital spiritual gravitational pull, pushed or otherwise. While I do appreciate your candidness, I must move at my own pace to better understand the so-called awakening, if indeed, that is what this is."

"Pastor Roy Moony once told his congregation that it comes naturally to be caught in God's pull and it can be caused because of something tragic or life changing. Those circumstances often push one in the direction of the Almighty. He added that there is no timeframe for arriving in a relationship with God and no right or wrong way to get there."

"Thank you for your spiritual intervention. I am not quite ready to submit to a personal revival. Can we just change the subject?"

"Whatever you say, Butterfly. I have two ears for listening whenever you feel so inclined."

"And when and if I become compelled to tote the Bible and sincerely speak of the gospel you shall be my first choice as a mentor."

"Just promise me Berkley that you will listen to and follow your heart."

"Can not make any promises, Lovely. My head usually rules my body when it comes to complicated decisions. My heart has been more of a bench warmer."

"Trust me, when the time comes, your heart will become the quarterback in the game of life.'

"You have such a profound way with words. Have you considered writing your memoirs?"

"My focus is on maintaining an ample supply of toilet tissue. Rationing is not good for anyone. The stress of a shortage constipates my thinking process."

"See, there you go again. Reminds me of something my grandmother once said. She told us that she hoped we never had to endure what she had to during those hard times of long ago. She up until the day she died, washed, and saved used aluminum foil, jam and condiment jars and various plastic containers. She even saved her bacon grease for reuse and seasoning."

"Berkley, your grandmother was wise beyond her years. My parents and grandparents did the same. I tend to dabble in some of these quirky thrifty ways. Coffee cans and Cool Whip containers make excellent storage cannisters. Confirms my southern roots."

"Pure southern belle you are."

"Thanks for the distraction but I have a program running that should be finished. Oh no!"

"What's wrong?"

"My use name or password has been denied. Correction, I no longer have access to the Global Virus Center database. Big brother has discovered the covert breach."

"What does that mean?"

"Beyond being denied access, I am not sure."

"We still need to have our little discussion with Paula and Shipley."

"She blew us off when we tried, saying to wait until he returned, but I am not sure we can delay it now."

"Do you fear legal repercussions for accessing the GVC without authorization?"

"That and who knows what else they may be capable of doing. And no, I am not implying they had anything to do with what happened to Kyle Richardson and Franklin Hartsfield. A fire does not equate to murder. Hartsfield resigned. There is no indication of any foul play in either situation regardless as to what our cohorts might believe."

"They are on to you just the same."

"Could be just a routine computer security breach. Phone Paula and tell her what happened. We will sit tight until then."

"Sit tight? Are you suggesting what I think you are suggesting?"

"New ballgame, and above my paygrade, is all I am saying."

40

Paula, exasperated by their progress thus far, swiveled around in her chair, mimicking a kid in a playground amusement park. She spun one direction and then the opposite way, all the while thinking would Shipley had hit yet another dead end in what once seemed to be promising leads. Covid-19 raged, nothing implemented apparently stopping its spread. The election had been tossed into chaos, unbelievable given how just months ago had been a dropkick for the president. One step closer to the unthinkable. Could America be headed down the darkest of paths? Socialism had reared its ugly head, a formidable opponent gaining momentum.

Paula, holding on by a thread, held firm to her ethics. She was not an activist or political pawn. She was a genuine journalist, a dying breed. Paula had never crossed that line, the line fading just the slightest for the very first time. Outgunned and outnumbered, politics had taken on an ugly darker stance. The media, in the bag for one party, spelled doom for those striving to remain credible. She had ventured down this path too many times recently. Playing the what if game got her nowhere. Report it. Just report it. Let the chips fall where they may, even if the scenario scared the crap out of her.

Play fair. Be consistent. Remaining true to who you are, who you have always been, on the surface seemed easy enough. No way Jose, did she want to see this country, her country, the greatest country in the world, shift politically toward socialism. Juggling right versus wrong never got her anywhere. One must hold firmly to one's values. Values are not worth having if one allows the worse case scenario to develop and dig its claws into the land of the free. Why was she debating herself? Simple. Change is not always good. Transformations are not always for the greater good. Socialism does not work as proven countless times in countless countries for countless years. Back to square one. Crap or get off the pot as her dad would often say. Was it her time to get off the pot? She could not make this decision alone. Others had a stake in it. After all she convinced herself, this is a democracy and majority rules, right? Well, the one political party seemed to be ruling dangerously for everyone. She reminded herself that a lie does not become truth. Wrong does not become right. Evil dose not become good just because the majority accept it. Where did that leave her then? Still sitting on that proverbial pot so it seemed, toilet paper in short supply at that.

Her phone ringing stopped her in mid swivel. It was Erwin Shipley. Hopefully, he had good news for a change. Taking a deep breath, she accepted the call.

"Mother load, my dear, we have stuck it rich. I have only enough time to share a few interesting bullet points. I possess a bundle of evidence I am going to send you via express mail."

"Why so urgent? We have plenty of time to talk."

"Not so. My meeting with whistleblower number three may have been compromised. Melanie spotted them first, just before I arrived back at her car. An ambush maybe if not for her quick thinking. She is trying to ditch them as we speak, not easily done in a Prius on deserted streets. I will share with you what I can so you can prepare for a chat with your senator pal. This is huge Paula. HUGE! Far beyond anything we could have imagined and a threat the likes never experienced in my humble opinion."

"Please, Shipley, stifle the drama and tell me what you have."

"Not good. Sorry. Will have to wait. I will phone you once we have handled our little dilemma."

"Shipley? Shipley! SHIPLeY!" The call had abruptly ended. "Not good," Paula whispered.

Her phone rang almost causing her to drop it. "Hello, Shipley?"

"No, Paula, it is Berkeley."

"Berkley, it is an emergency. I cannot talk right now."

"Yes, it is indeed a potential emergency. Just listen then."

"You don't understand. I can't, not now." With that she ended the call with Berkley.

Berkley shrugged, looking over at Camilla. "She cut me off, babbling about emergencies. Must be a pandemic of them as well. Appears we are out on our proverbial limb solo or duo in our case."

****

Melanie wheeled the Prius through uncharted territory. Something out of a movie. Ditch those tailing them. An Uber driver, she had no experience in such matters. Erwin confirmed her efforts had gone unrewarded thus far. The black Mercedes had them outpowered with a professional behind the wheel. Her white Prius was no match for those intent in overtaking them. Erwin urgently beckoned her to speed up, turn this way, that way. Undaunted, the Mercedes was swiftly gaining. What would they do once those in pursuit overtook them? Her Prius was her livelihood. She had not paid off her loan yet. Crazy thoughts. These people were not in it to destroy her car. Much worse scenarios were in play. Not knowing *the what, why and who* loomed large in her brain. Still, she remained silent. Not the appropriate time to ask questions. Her job was simple. Lose them or else.

****

"What should we do now, Berkley?"

"I am not experienced in such matters. Your access has been denied. Question of the day, do you fear any repercussions from your previous employer?"

"Define repercussions."

"Legal matters, possible arrest, physical threat, you pick."

"Until recently, maybe legal, but now I am not sure what they might be capable of doing. We have no evidence that the center is linked to what happened to Kyle Richardson and his wife or if it were anything more than an accident. As for Franklin Hartsfield, who is to say whether he had any ties to the GVC. I do not know the gentleman, nor have I ever heard of him until now. His resignation does not indicate foul play regardless of what my cohorts might suspect. Honestly, Berkley, I am not sure I am buying into scrupulous characters or organizations willing to do anything to protect a hoax being pulled on the Americans or the world in fact."

"Politics is a dirty business, deals cut, promises made, lies told and who knows what else. I have said it and I will declare it yet again these shenanigans are clearly over my head. I am not sure any book deal is worth these risks. I fared much better when I flew solo and spun the manuscripts from inside my head."

"I am with you, merely a humble retired virologist, one who should have kept her nose out of the business of those in charge. No. All wrong. It is not in me to turn a blind eye when there is data to support a lie being fabricated and so much deceitfulness being spread. No regrets. At least not yet. Perhaps we should stick to our original plan and consult Paula and Shipley before we possibly overact."

"That worked so well on our first attempt. She cut me off practically in midsentence."

"Something is apparently going on that we are not yet privy to, Berkley."

"You ask me, I believe we are being purposely kept in the dark more so than their hokey explanation of merely doing it to protect us. Camilla, there is some serious deep diving going on by them."

"Changing gears slightly, I recently read an article that ironically supports my stats and theory. A famous athlete was recently quoted as saying he knew two people whose parents had died from something other than Covid and unnamed people were asked whether their deaths could be changed to Covid-19 and they declined the request. The eighty-year-old golfer explained that he knew hospitals were getting more money with Covid deaths than with deaths categorized as something not virus related."

"I bet no one called him a crazy senile old man or conspiracy spreader."

"Adds much credibility to what I am seeing."

"Maybe you should contact him and inquire as to whether he is willing to be your spokesperson. What a platform that would be, you and the legend who has won 18 majors and 117 tournaments."

"Fat chance he would endorse a mere nobody, a controversial conspiracy theorist at that."

"My lovely, you sell yourself short. You possess statistical evidence, the data to support it. Facts trump theory and mere rhetoric."

"An extreme uphill climb. The experts do not tolerate opposition to what they have clearly stated as fact worldwide. The Global Virus Center will not recant nor walk back what they have already made public. Apologizes are nonexistent. This much I do know from experience. If ever the time arrives, it is probably best that I remain as a contributor and an anonymous expert in the field."

"You are a credible virologist. How could anyone dispute the evidence once presented?"

"I am an unknown and a retired virologist. Their mission would be to discredit me. Their angle might be that I am an angry and disgruntle former employee out for revenge or compensation. I have witnessed this firsthand from their playbook. They would have witnesses to falsely testify just to raise doubt. Investors, shareholders in the organization are quite devious and greedy."

"What do these investors and shareholders have to gain by deceiving the public?"

"Monetarily, maybe nothing. Protection possibly. If the communist party is truly behind the virus release, accidently or intentionally, then saving face is a critical aspect. The president continually calling Covid the China virus and vowing retribution sends the wrong message to the world, They thrive to be the new world leader, control supply and demand. They dominate the pharmaceutical industry."

"For some one supposedly naïve to politics you certainly have your finger on the pulse."

"Common knowledge within the medical circle, the United States has forfeited ownership of three essential drug ingredients to China. Capreomycin and streptomycin used to treat tuberculosis and sulfadiazine used to treat trachoma and other things. China has nearly 3500 drug companies. They are many other key drugs manufactured in China. Medicines for blood pressure, Alzheimer's, Parkinson's, epilepsy, and depression. The United States no longer manufactures penicillin. China accounts for much of the 80% of active ingredients found in America's medicines. They will not lose face and jeopardize their role as stakeholder. Essentially, in my humble opinion, they also own the GVC, bottomless pockets supporting research. Corruption running amuck, shamelessly but discretely except for insiders who have witnessed it as I."

"Enough so to murder?"

"That I can not answer, prove or disprove."

"I for one prefer not to become statistical evidence to support the fact that they are capable of such heinous acts."

"Maybe we should try calling Paula again, Berkley."

"Maybe you should this time."

"Very well. Guess it is my news to share, me being the one that no longer has access to the GVC database."

"Here, use my cell phone."

"My, you are becoming quite paranoid, aren't you?"

"I prefer framing it as common sense. Goes to figure if they have cut you off and have the means, they might try to monitor your devices, phone, computer. Who knows what else? The communist regime controls much of the electronic world and what I understand, their surveillance techniques are quite superior. Espionage is second nature, stealing intellectual property common practice. If they are connected at the hips to the GVC then I suspect they keep close tabs on everything, and everyone associated."

"Point taken. Very well, key in her number for me."

"As simple as pressing recent calls…here you go."

Paula answered on the first ring.

"Paula, it's Camilla. Please do not end the call this time. It is important."

"Please apologize to Berkley for me. Quite rude but urgent at the time. No excuse just the same. Is anything wrong?"

"Possibly. My access to the GVC database has been severed. Could be the result of a routine computer security verification software. Doubtful though. My password has been in tack since I retired. I suspect recent activity raised someone's eyebrows in the IT department."

"Do you think they could have been monitoring your activity to determine what you were up to?"

"Feasible I suppose. Berkley felt strongly that I use his phone instead of mine for that very reason. He feared surveillance from the communist community and maybe others involved."

"Othera?"

"Longer story."

"Make sure you back up everything."

"Already have."

"Do you fear for your safety?"

"Not currently. More concerned of legal action, I suppose."

"You had a legal and functioning password. Not your fault that they failed to follow security protocol."

"I stole data. I am sure legalities a plenty exist. Not your cross to bear. I fully understood what I was doing and take full responsibility for my actions. I had suggested to Berkley that I should remain in the shadows as a whistleblower if the time comes to use what I have excavated."

"That cat might already be out of the bag. We have other developments."

"Other developments?"

"Too early to confirm but my intuition is on high alert. Is there somewhere else you and Berkley can relocate? Somewhere safe?"

"George and I own a beach condo in South Carolina. Obviously, it is presently unoccupied. No rentals given the pandemic. The New York governor is discouraging any travel though."

"Governor Anita Ming has much bigger problems on her plate. I do not think she will keep tabs on your vacation plans. Long drive."

"Not really. We always commuted there by car. Beach front view will be a pleasant distraction."

"Camilla, do not tell anyone where you are going, including your kids. Tell Berkley to continue his stint out of the public eye."

"Not to worry, old hat to him now. Paula, just how serious has this gotten?"

"I will know more once Shipley and I talk. As we have stated…"

"The less we know the better. Yes, we understand or did. That situation has grown exponentially, I fear. Have your conversation with Erwin Shipley, then we wish full disclosure of the activities. Until then, my contribution is null and void. We are either in it for the entirety or we are not. And before you ask, yes, Berkley feels the same as I."

"No promises, Camilla. Shipley and I will consider your requests. It has always been our desire to protect you and Berkley. And your contributions are quite important and instrumental. And for that we are extremely appreciative. Please sit tight once you are settled in and we will further this discussion at the appropriate juncture."

"Be careful, Paula Wise. Something tells me this is venturing into uncharted and rather dangerous waters."

"Safe travels. Please leave as soon as possible. Keep your eyes open for any suspicious activity."

"Define suspicious."

"Anything and everything. Peculiar phone calls or text messages, strangers snooping about, any vehicles spotted nearby too frequently to be merely coincidental, the normal being too abnormal."

"Covid already has the abnormality aspect covered. We will be mindfully careful and watchful. Godspeed as well, Paula."

41

Reverend Bobby Flowers eyed the activities of the political arena. While it was not for the clergy to openly take sides, he was still after all an American voter. The leader of the United States carried a big stick and politically speaking, too much bias had gone against Christians for way too long. The sitting president had done more for Christians than any other president in history. His reelection was of the utmost importance given the support for Christianity in general under his watch. Flowers stood firm on his belief that those who were willing to kill the unborn should never be trusted to govern the living. The opposing party made no apologies for such utter disgusting believes.

Flowers, still remaining strong when it came to abortion, had just included one of Dr. Mildred Jefferson's quotes in a recent sermon. 'Today it is the unborn child; tomorrow it is likely to be the elderly or those who are incurably ill. Who knows but that a little later it may be anyone who has political or moral views that do not fit into the distorted new order?'

All was not gloom and doom in God's kingdom as the naysayers would like to persuade anyone willing to listen to their misguided and hateful rhetoric. The reverend instead told his virtual congregation, "All of you have a choice. This choice exists everyday of your lives. Do not doubt God's love and power. Choose to feel blessed. Chose to remain grateful. Choose to be excited and forever choose to show thanks and happiness over everything darkness offers."

> *Beloved, believe not every spirit,*
> *But try the spirits whether they are of God:*
> *because many false prophets*
> *are gone out into the world.*
> *1 John 4:1*

The reverend was on a roll. He encouraged those streaming to believe in only two defining forces that had offered to die for them.

The obvious was Jesus Christ. The other he professed was the American soldier. Looking directly into the camera he said "Jesus died for your soul. Our mighty fighting men and women died for your freedom. Never forget either. Pray to God for our president and our country. Amen."

Long after the telecast, Flowers sat alone on a pew, consumed by his thoughts while immersed in prayer. He asked God to give those in need the wisdom to develop a cure or a least a vaccine for the invisible enemy delivering unfathomable destruction and death on the world, while specifically dividing a nation, people reaching new lows led by Satan to deliver evil on thy neighbors, unremorseful and relentless in their behavior. He asked God to guide him, use him as a tool in such challenging times. Deliver us from evil had never been needed more.

The church door opening behind him prompted a quick amen. Standing he turned to greet anyone who might be visiting the sanctuary during these troubling times, even though the church was officially closed for business as decreed by the governor. Two gentlemen had stepped just inside. He recognized the young man on the right. Not one to be naïve, he realized this would not be a spiritual visit, seeking guidance or forgiveness from the Lord. Leaning on his faith he met the challenging circumstances head on. Not once in the Bible does it say worry about it, he reminded himself. Quite simple. Put your trust in God. No sacrifice is too large.

****

Three days had passed, and Paula had still not been able to reach Erwin Shipley. His cell phone no longer went to voice mail. She was not sure how to interpret this. He had ended his previous and only call saying they were being followed. She had no idea who 'they' were and what had happened. Nothing good obviously. Forever the optimist, her faith in a good outcome had begun to dwindle. Shipley would have contacted her if he had the means to do so. Whatever he had obtained from the Portland contact prompted someone to intervene, forcefully it seemed. She tried to dismiss the premise but denying it felt unrealistic.

She had not contacted the authorities. What was she supposed to tell them? She had no idea where in Portland he had rendezvoused with the alleged whistleblower. She did not know the identity of the person either. Shipley had not even shared with her the name of the person who had chauffeured him on this little cross county excursion. Being too focused on segmenting the mission, minimizing sharing names, places and such had proved to be a fatal and flawed tactic. Here she was in New York. Camilla and Berkley in South Carolina and Shipley's last whereabouts in Oregon. This could never be more disjointed and out of control.

She felt helpless. Shipley had not been able to share an inkling of what he had uncovered. Even the senator, her contact, had become nervous and wary of anything she might have in the works. The election of the next president loomed large, just two weeks remaining. The stakes had never been higher for the American people to chose wisely. The million-dollar question, had Shipley uncovered anything that would impact the election or had the mystery been purely related to the virus conspiracy? Not knowing was driving her a bit squirrelly, not an emotion she was accustomed to experiencing. Nothing she could do by working herself into such a frazzled state, so she had decided to go home.

Upon arriving at her apartment building, she discovered the express delivery envelope. Excited, she quickly went inside and placed it in front of her at the kitchen bar. She picked it up and stared at it, flipping it over before placing it back on the counter. It had Portland mailing address. Shipley had made good on his promise. Still, it did not begin to explain where he was and what had happened. She struggled with wanting to rip it open or wait until he returned to open it in his presence. No, he had meant for her to do this and share the contents appropriately. Opening it or not did not change Shipley's situation. She owed it to him to utilize what he had found and act on his sacrifices. Sacrifices. Seemed final and morbidly real.

321

Paula had agonized long enough, another emotion new to her. Observation. The shipping envelope had been retaped, clear adhesive tape at that. A jagged edge indicated it had been torn open and then taped afterwards. What did this mean? Maybe nothing. Could have been Shipley's doing. Possibly he had forgotten to include something or needed to review something already packaged in the sealed envelope. Procrastination, not her style either. She grabbed a pair of scissors from the side table and proceeded while whispering, "The envelope please, and the winner is."

A hefty bundle of papers was secured inside a manilla folder with a large rubber band. She slipped it from the shipping envelope. "Drum roll." Taking and then releasing her breath nosily she removed the rubber band and opened the folder. Must have been at least a hundred pages in the mystery manifesto given the thickness. The Holy Grail came to mind. Mother lode Shipley had referred to it. She wished he were present to enjoy the official unveiling and to narrate what he had discovered. She paused momentarily hoping Erwin Shipley had not been harmed, realizing the odds and likelihood that he hadn't were doubtful at best.

Paula flipped over the first page. The second one contained no information on the front side. Nor the back. Third, fourth, fifth, sixth, nothing, all blank. She rapidly began thumbing through more pages. All were blank. Now shuffling as if she were preparing a deck of cards for dealing, same result, all were blank. Mystery solved. Someone, somehow, had gotten their grimy hands on it, ripped it open, stole the originals and then replaced it with blank papers. Paula leaned back on the loveseat running her hands through her hair, totally exasperated, and angry by what she had not found.

Something seemed off. It made absolutely no sense that someone would take great measures in locating Shipley's express mail envelope, remove the contents, and replace it with worthless printing paper. Possession is 9/10th of the law. If whoever had it, game over. Take it and run with it. Why take the time to perpetrate a farce? Unless, purposely so, a gotcha moment. It suddenly struck her like a thunderbolt. The perpetrators knew the mailing address, her address.

Post marked and from Oregon three days ago gave them plenty of time to already be here. Panic was delivered by the next lightning strike. They must be here and were waiting for her to open it. She launched from the loveseat and double checked the locks on the only entrance door. Ten stories up ensured that no one could scale the building for an ambush attack.

What now? No Shipley. No evidence. No story. Worse, maybe no way out of this.

****

Berkley smiled and took another sip of dark brew. He breathed in the glorious salty air and embraced the magnificent sunrise, the sun seemingly emerging from the ocean like a giant glowing orb. Nothing could be finer than to be in Carolina in the morning. He almost stood and belted out the tune to those seven floors below.

"Ah, good morning Camilla and a glorious morning it is indeed."

"You are quite chipper. Breathtaking sunrise I see."

"I do not get it."

"Get what, Berkley?"

"Why in the world would you prefer living in Rochester, New York when you could reside here and wake up each morning with a beach and the Atlantic Ocean as your backyard? No brainer. This is where I would be year-round. Never ventured to South Carolina before but this, what did you call it, oh yeah, Grand Strand, would certainly be my cup of tea, given the option."

"I agree. Love it here as well. George was never fond of coming here. George did not like traveling anywhere. Work was his life, his escape, his hobby. Nothing made him happier than being on a work site. The beach never held his interest. As he would say, if you have seen one sunrise you have seen them all. Even before we bought this condo, he made it a point to remind me that New York also had views of the Atlantic Ocean."

"Nothing like this, my Sweetness. I am glad we utilized this little escape pod as our safe house. Might just be what I need to kick start my creative juices. This breathtaking scenery and the ocean air are quite invigorating for my brain and soothes my soul. I know that look. Confess. Something troubles you."

"Crazy as it sounds, being here makes me miss George. We never made any great memories here. Guess even knowing how much he hated coming here was still always a part of it."

"All memories are good memories, I say. There is something else though?"

"We have not heard from Paula or Shipley. Do you not think that is odd?"

"Yes, I have caught myself dwelling on that very fact. I tried to dismiss it, hoping they were allowing us time to get settled."

"Sufficient time has passed. Perhaps we should phone her."

"She did request that we sit tight and contact no one, not even your children. Possibly we are overreacting."

"My children! I have a grandchild due next month and I promised I would be there for them before, during and afterwards."
"Then maybe you should fulfill your promise, my lovely."

"I can't. It might put them in danger if the worst-case scenario exists. Refill?"

"Certainly. Thank you."

Moments later Camilla returned and sat down on a chase lounger next to Berkley. She had always enjoyed lounging on the balcony soaking in the sun with a good read in hand. George had not possessed the patience to just sit on the balcony and breath in what life had to offer. Too fidgety, he would make up excuses to go venture out and explore the area. Sometimes he would pretend to go golfing. She knew he did not ever go to any courses but never let on to him that she knew he hadn't. Knowing him as she did, she had envisioned him locating a construction site and hanging out there if he could, just watching the heavy machinery and productiveness of the workers in hardhats. Harmless, and his little white lies never harmed a fly. If he was happy so was she.

"Camilla, do you ever find yourself going to a room and then wondering why you went there in the first place?"

"Rite of passage. We all arrive there sooner or later. I take it you have experienced it as well."

"More frequently than I dare admit. I have a theory though. What if when we walk into a room, we are not just merely forgetting why we entered. Maybe there is a more plausible explanation. Stick with me and keep an open mind. Say, for instance, I leave the balcony and end up in the kitchen and it suddenly dawns on me, why did I come to the kitchen. What if I crossed paths with an alien creature, something not of our universe, maybe from a different dimension? Don't laugh. The alien does not wish to harm me but cannot allow me to divulge its existence. The space visitor erases my memory, thusly, I am standing in the middle of the kitchen like a complete idiot."

"Berkley, why would an alien be in anyone's kitchen?"

"Munchies. Alien weed. I don't know."

"Okay, explain why these visitors from space end up in all parts of my house. Seems to me once I had already stumbled upon them, they would learn their lesson and go someplace differently."

"Scientist! I thought you might be a bit more openminded. Could be that they are different visitors, just saying."

Camilla just smiled and shrugged. "I wish more places were open. I would love to show you some of my favorite venues. This pandemic and all the craziness have put a hurt on so many businesses. This is not Broadway, but the Carolina Opry and Alabama Theater are fun filled entertainment options. Sadly, they are shuttered due to the fear of spreading the virus. Great restaurants here as well. Takeout doesn't do them justice though, the ones that have managed to remain open."

"Sooner or later, we will lick this godforsaken virus. During the middle ages they celebrated the end of the great plagues by throwing orgies and dinking their fill of wine. Maybe the government will fund the granddaddy of all toga parties for us once we have gotten beyond the social distancing and shutdowns. We are due for some drunken uninhibited nakedness for a change."

"This has certainly been a year to top all years and for all the wrong reasons. Best quote I read somewhere, 'This is not the year to get everything you want. This is the year to appreciate everything you have.' A bit profound for me to quote that given the fact I have lost the love of my life this year."

"I hurt for your loss as well, Sweetness. Crazy does not begin to define the year. I have never seen one party work so hard to get an elected president out of office all the while ignoring the threat of illegal aliens, drug dealers and child traffickers. Speaking of quotes, I have one as well. Albert Einstein once said, 'The world will not be destroyed by those who do evil, but by those who watch them without doing anything.' Defines the fake news media does it not? Peaceful protests. No looting, burning, and rioting. Evil speaking mean of a president. No recognition for all the good things he has done, and the promises kept. Remember that feeling you got when those airplanes crashed into the Twin Towers and it finally dawned on you what was really happening. I am feeling that way again with what we are going through and what some are hoping to achieve in the presidential election. I never thought in my lifetime that I would be witnessing socialist/communist takeover in plain sight and without more opposition. Oh yeah, all the while taking advantage of this virus smoke screen,"

"Tell me how you really feel, Berkley."

"I am as serious as a heart attack. Sorry, poor analogy."

"Heart failure happens. Do not apologize."

"Governors and mayors of one party, and you know the ones I am referencing, are using this pandemic to test drive socialism. They are telling us what we can and can not do. They are even suggesting that we will be prohibited from celebrating Thanksgiving and Christmas with family and friends. We can not attend church or any social activities publicly but that was not good enough for them. Now they are invading our homes telling us we cannot have people inside our houses to celebrate the holidays. I say, Governor Anita Ming and Mayor Francis Kowalski, when you begin paying my bills, you can tell me how many people I can have in my home. Until then, Happy Thanksgiving and Merry Christmas you bunch of power hungry, socialist hypocrites."

"Another reason I love the southern states like Georgia and South Carolina. Southerners do not take kindly to being told what they cannot do on their own property. God, family and freedom, is not up for debate. And do not and I repeat do not even consider taking a good ole boy's guns away from him. If the government wishes to incite another civil war, threatening to take away people's guns will surely guarantee that outcome. My, a peaceful morning on the balcony observing a glorious Grand Strand sunrise has suddenly awakened sleeping giants so it seems."

"If the cancel culture can experience a woke moment, then the quiet majority can feel the burn as well, an alternate awakening that will not play nice if pushed too far."

"Not exactly spoken like a true Yankee, Berkley."

"I am a northerner, yes, but I am not a corrupt power-hungry fascist. As I have previously shared, I am not an African American. I am an American, believer in the constitution, the declaration of independence and one who stands for the red, white, and blue and national anthem. Cue the fireworks and stand clear of my awoken ways."

Camilla stood and applauded and then placed her hand over her heart. "More reasons I love you so my dear friend. My heart aches for the children. Schools and colleges were forced to close in March, and they were not able to finish out their school year, go to proms, sign yearbooks, or attend graduation ceremonies. High school and college sports were halted. Look at us now. We are approaching November and many schools and colleges remain closed. Those that have opened are under constant threat of closure due to outbreaks. I cannot imagine how I would have coped with this if it had impacted my children."

"What did they ask us? Give us two weeks. Just two weeks of disciplined social distancing and closures and everything would be fine. That was nearly nine months ago, and they have kept us in the bubble for the most part the entire time and now threatening to do it again, especially if we end up with that new presidential candidate. Same leaders, same states, same cities. A chief of police was just terminated because she arrested dozens of vandals caught red-handed on video destroying statues and looting businesses. Her detectives did the leg work and apprehended the culprits. How did the mayor reward them for their hard work? Fired the chief for racial profiling and dismissed all the cases. And now the Holiday Gestapo have positioned themselves to spy on our grocery purchases. If we buy a turkey capable of feeding more than six, they will storm our homes and break up the festivities, issue citations, levy fines or arrest the family for giving thanks during a thankless period in modern history. I find myself morphing into a rebel with so many causes I lose count of them."

"Our poor overworked first responders, doctors, nurses, those who have worked around the clock are ignored for their sacrifices. Berkley, this will only get worse if our president fails to be reelected."

"I do not recall who penned this, but I will attempt to state what I can remember. It plays well into the situation and our conversation. Good thing I have somewhat of a photographic memory, Here goes.

I am sick of Covid. I am sick of blacks versus whites. I am sick of the political parties bickering. I am sick of the bias media. I am sick of the mask wearing and social distancing. I am sick of one group having freedom of speech while the other is attacked for exercising the same right. I am sick of those that justify their looting, burning, killing with a false premise. I am sick of the world being blamed for the sins of so few. I am sick of people being persecuted because their beliefs differ. I am sick of fearing sickness. I am sick of watching my country implode for the sake of those who are weak, needy, and unwilling to work for what they get and support those who sacrificed their lives so that we can live free and worship as we wish. I am sick of remaining quiet because I fear persecution. I am a person, an American and will forever support my great country."

"How in the world were you able to recite something like that from mere memory?"

"Might I remind you that I so easily forget why I entered those rooms."

"You blame that on alien erasers or have you forgotten that too," laughed Camilla.

Berkley's cell phone rang. He did not recognize the number, but it was a 718-area code, New York calling, "Hello."

"Mister Berkley Jay Patrick. I am highly disappointed. I thought we had an agreement."

"Vlad, how did you get this number?"

"I do not feel you are in any position to question me, my good man. However, to show good faith, I shall answer. Your pastor friend cooperated with Jewel. He can be quite persuasive. I must say we had to make numerous phone calls from his phone's index before reaching you today."

"Tell me you did not harm Reverend Flowers."

"Very well, as you wish. I did not harm any flowers."

"You did not hurt him then?"

"You asked me to tell you I didn't, did you not?"

"Let me speak to him."

"No can do. You listen to me you conniving, lying piece of..."

"Where is Reverend Flowers?"

"There is no manuscript, is there? Just what is this game you play, Mister Former Best Seller? Might I suggest you honor your commitment. We have much to discuss. I will gladly meet you if you would be so kind to tell me where you have taken up residence."

Berkley ended the call and quickly filled Camilla in on what had just transpired. Playing a hunch, he located and pressed the call button of an unsaved number. Three rings and no one answered. Panic stricken he was about to end the attempt when someone answered.

"Reverend Flowers?"

"Might I ask who is calling."

"Berkley Patrick. May I speak to the reverend."

"I am Katherine, his sister. Bobby has mentioned your name. I am sorry, he is unable to speak to you right now."

"Is he okay?"

"No, I am afraid he is not. He is at my home but sleeping."

"Your home?"

"My brother was savagely beaten and spent a couple of days in the hospital. He is here with me now but not doing well."

"Did he say who attacked him?"

"He has not. He has only repetitively said, 'God chose the color of your skin. You chose the content of your character.' The detective, based on this, has called what happened a racially motivated hate crime, a black pastor in an explosive environment, rioting and looting ravishing the surrounding neighborhoods. My brother did not deserve this fate."

"What are the doctors saying? Will he recover?"

"With head injuries comes so much uncertainty. I am a registered nurse and, because I am, I was able to convince the doctor to release him to my care; that and the fact Covid has the hospital pushing out patients that are not Covid related. It is terrible how people in need of normal care are being ignored for the greater good of this pandemic. The world has gone mad. I apologize. I did not intend to vent."

"Venting I understand. This crazy world, not so much. Is there anything I can do?"

"Pray."

"I will check back later if you do not mind."

"Please do."

"Katherine, I am sorry."

"Sorry? You have nothing to be sorry about. He was attacked. Doubtful, given the rampant lawlessness, his attackers will ever be brought to justice."

"Not so sure about that. Have faith, Katherine. The one above moves in mysterious ways, so they say."

"Faith is something we do not lack. Thank you for your compassion and concern, Mister Patrick."

"Please, just Berkley."

"Berkley, I will call you if he becomes alert."

"I would like that."

After ending the call, Berkley fumed and vented as Camilla listened.

"These worthless bastards cannot be allowed to go unpunished."

"We are not in a position to retaliate or seek retribution, my dear friend."

"Never underestimate an author scorned. Many characters exist in my mighty imagination. Superheroes, sleuths, innovation the likes never experienced in times that have thrown everything but the kitchen sink in our direction. From the cocoon births the butterfly, a creature entirely diverse from the one that existed before. Hold onto to your britches, Sweetness, a bumpy ride is nothing more than ruts in the roadway."

42

Paula had slept on it, slept extraordinarily little actually, not yet convinced she should pack up and flee. No unscrupulous feigns had burst through her door nor had she received any peculiar phone calls or threats of any kind. What did that mean? Were they just biding their time, possibly waiting for her to leave here and then pounce? Was she just being too paranoid? She certainly had reason to be cautious. No word from Shipley. She had even tried calling again. Nothing. She could not simply do nothing. Police? Still not an option given so little information she could offer. She would more than likely open herself to more questions and much scrutiny if she dared bring the situation to light. She had not contacted Berkley or Camilla since they fled. She should probably check on them given the uncertainties.

This had gotten totally out of hand. She had taken risks plenty of times and had found herself in dangerous predicaments, but none compared to this one. Powerful players were involved, yet to be identified participants capable of unimaginable consequences. The stakes must be extremely high, far beyond the death and destruction being waged by the pandemic. The virus was a piece of the puzzle but something more sinister existed, more aggressive goals in mind. Did this include the total collapse of the world economy, the removal of the president or something far worse if that was even possible?

Maybe she was overthinking the situation. Maybe it was not as bad as it seemed. She quickly dismissed this premise. Dire straits with no foreseeable path forward better framed it. She was an excellent problem solver, astute in tackling her assignments head on. This was not a typical assignment. Her producer nor any of her crew were aware of this investigation. She had simultaneously prepared an alternate agenda for her telecasts, mere smoke, and mirrors lately while she diverted much of her focus to something deemed critically important. In due time she had planned to drop the bombshell but only after she had secured the assistance of the senator if evidence supported getting him involved. Now everything was up for grabs, an unforeseen game changer. Question. Did this mean Erwin Shipley was indeed dead?

Decision made.

"Hello, Berkley, is everything all right in the Palmetto state? Not to worry, I am on a secure phone. One of those disposables."

"Yes and no."

"I'll bite. Explain."

"We thus far have encountered no menacing foes here but…"

"But?"
"I did receive a disturbing phone call yesterday. It was from one of the anti-America thugs, the one requesting the manuscript or at least some synopsis to validate the authenticity of my intentions."

"How did he get your number? Does he know your location?"

"Reverend Flowers was attacked. They apparently downloaded all his contact information. The reverend did not have my number cataloged so they worked the list until they reached me. We are safe. He does not know where we are."

"Comforting."

"There is more. I called Reverend Flowers. His sister, Katherine, answered. She is caring for him. He has suffered a head injury. I realize you requested us to remain low profile, but I had to breach that request to check on him. I do not apologize for my action."

"Very well. I understand. Is that it?"

"Afraid not. Vlad, the one making the demands requested that I meet him to further discuss the project he now suspects as false research."

"And…"

"And I ended the call and then phoned the reverend."

"Has he attempted to contact you again?"

"Not yet."

"Berkley. It is imperative that you destroy your phone immediately. Now that they have your number, technology exists that might allow them to trace your location. Use a hammer and have at it. Use Camilla's phone or purchase a disposable one."

"What have we really gotten ourselves into, Paula?"

"I wish I knew. Erwin is missing."

"Missing?"

"Destroy your phone first. Then call me using Camilla's phone."

Berkley filled Camilla in and asked if she had a hammer. She checked a toolbox located in the owner's closet. Her hubby had already maintained quite an assortment of tools, something for almost any unforeseeable situation. A large hammer was used quickly. Little remained of the device once Berkley had worked out his frustrations on his expensive cell phone, forgoing any thought of the expense and aggravation of replacing it. All his contacts and many memorable photos were in that phone, irreplaceable but, undaunted, he realized the urgency involved to ensure their safety.

Paula waited for his call once the task had been completed. She hoped it had not been too late. Did this terrorist group possess the capabilities on doing what she had described? Better err on the side of uncertainty than be sorry later. She agonized over whether to have him contact the police. Doing so would create an avalanche of questions though. All fairness, she would ask him what he wanted to do. She would support him even if it jeopardized the ultimate endgame. She could not place him or Camilla in any further danger.

Her conscience would not allow that. Everything had basically blown up in her face anyway.

"Hello, Berkley."

"I can report that there is not a piece that remotely resembles my phone now. Anger management accomplished as well."

"Place me on speaker. We have much to discuss."

****

Camilla and Berkley had ventured out for pick up, a local pizza place, even though dine in was possible with minimum capacity at a few places. They had much to discuss and even more to think about given what Paula had revealed. The scariest aspect being the disappearance of Erwin Shipley. The situation had rapidly deteriorated. Objectives had changed. The consequences hung in the balance. Threats were real. Nefarious individuals were deadly serious about concealing secrets that could have far worse ramifications.

Now back on the balcony, the hotel complex casting long shadows over the beach below, Camilla had opted for the veggie pizza while Berkley settled on a slice of his selection, the meat monster deluxe. Not one to skimp on artery clogging consumption, he stuffed his face rather sloppily, result of nervous clumsiness when he was stressed. He had never been more stressed for sure. Camilla reached over with a napkin and wiped the paste from the corners of his mouth. Mother hen compulsiveness in play.

"Given the unnerving new development, where does that leave us, Berkley?"

Choking down a mouthful, he held up a finger, indicating to give him a second. Sloshing it down with a swig from his beer, he mustered a reply. "I cannot simply walk away from this, my Lovely. My conscience would be a wreck if I ignored what has already

336

transpired under our somewhat helpless watch. Where do you reside on the most difficult fence line on which we find ourselves?"

"My concern is foremost for my family. What happens to them if we persist? I can not jeopardize their safety for something with intentions so disturbingly unknown. I have no doubt that a great deception is being perpetrated against our nation, even the world, as goes the misinformation being reported about Covid-19. The numbers are incorrect. The death rates have purposely been skewed to instill panic and fear for reasons I still do not understand nor can explain. Is it so critical and important that people would murder to protect it? Your guess is as good as mine. I follow the data. It is the only way I know, Berkley. I have seen no credible data to insinuate murder is in play. No denying it, the Richardson's died in a fire. Accident? Intentional? The coroner resigned, left a note stating it. Nothing substantial points to foul play. Rehashing it once again does not present argument otherwise. Erwin Shipley is an outlier possibly. Paula is convinced his vanishing is a result of diabolical intervention. Assumption does not equate to fact. No body. No evidence. No data to support it. We do have your Reverend Flowers. He has been attacked and hospitalized, evidence and documentation exist. Assumption, the group that you befriended appears responsible. Even so, we have no evidence to support that either. Are they a threat to your safety? It appears to be founded but cannot be proved either."

"You haven't answered my question, Sweetness. Where does that leave you moving forward?"

"I do not take this lightly."

"I never felt you did."

"That's not what I meant. I feel that what I have uncovered needs to see the light of day. I fear I will be met with full frontal opposition by the GVC if I try. They will destroy me and discredit my findings. Of this I have no doubt. I had hoped Paula had the connections to keep me out of it. Given the original plan has badly unraveled, I see no path going forward now."

337

"Never give up hope. We will figure a way to make this happen if you are determined to rectify the wrongs. I for one cannot sit idly by and allow those responsible to go unpunished."

"I do not like the tone in your voice, Berkley. Data or not, this is not a time to play hero."

"Me…hero? I only pretend to be characters playing those roles in my novels."

****

All the dirty tricks one would expect in a presidential election were in play. The president had lost ground, the pandemic wreaking havoc on what was once a shoe in for reelection. The economy had begun a slow rebound, but continued shutdowns in major cities compromised everything. His rivals had portrayed him and his administration as incompetent and uncaring concerning their handling of Covid-19. Increasing cases and deaths were the evidence they used against him. The unethical and biased media supported their efforts, the new propaganda tool at their disposal. Due to the pandemic numerous states run by his opponents were mailing out millions of voting ballots adding more chaos to an already chaotic year. Fear of voter fraud and manipulation ran rampant. Well, the administration shared these concerns. The corrupt media refused to support it. With less than a week remaining, the nation's uncertain future hung by a thread. Mail in votes had reached epic numbers.

The political polls favored the challenger. Undaunted and in the middle of a virus crisis the president continued having enormous rallies. Of course, his opponent, as supported by the media, dubbed these as super virus spreaders, portraying him as evil and a killer of Americans. People were afraid and out of work. No. It was not the president's fault. It was not anyone's fault, except for the country that unleashed this invisible enemy on the world. False narrative according to the media, the president refusing to take responsibility for mishandling its spread. They held him solely responsible for every American that had perished while ignoring the people were dying in every country and their leaders had not been blamed. The shameless hypocrisy knew no boundaries.

43

Paula poured a glass of Chardonnay, second guessing her decision to be completely honest with her remaining two partners in crime. It rested on their shoulders now, an option to exit the original agreement. Only Camilla possessed any credible information worthy of a news segment. Berkley's interaction with the anti-America movement was eye opening but he had no evidence to support the findings. Verbal admissions could and would be denied. It still troubled her that these terrorists were obsessed with seeking vengeance. Especially given Berkley was a well-known bestselling author. Harming him in any way would bring attention to them. Well, except the political opposition to the president and the media in utter denial. Maybe harming someone with such notoriety was what they wanted. It would establish them as an organization to be reckoned with.

Any way she played it this was over. Drop it and move on she tried to convince herself. The argument remained an even bet at best. Paula was no quitter. Something huge loomed just out of her reach. Dropping this would equate to Erwin Shipley's death or disappearance going for naught. His life meant more than to be merely forgotten, swept under the rug as if it never happened. She owed him, even if it meant placing her reputation on the line. Still, she had absolutely nothing credible to link his vanishing to anything criminal. Dead ends, nothing but dead ends. What a waste this had been. Waste? Shipley had not seen it as a waste. He believed in their cause. She had believed in it as well. Still believed. That and four bucks would buy her a cup of coffee.

A knock on her door prompted her to flinch. Had they finally decided to finish her off now she wondered. Why would they bother knocking? Why not kick in the door and get this over with? No, they would lure her to the door and then make her disappear too. She pressed 9 then 1 on her phone, her finger hoovering over the 1 button. Would the police even respond given the way they had been treated so unfairly? Paula eased her way to the door and eyed through the peephole, finger ready to press that last number one. At first no one was in view then a shadow appeared followed by a face. The face did not resemble that of a killer, but hit persons probably came in all shapes, sizes, ages, and genders. Plenty of people out of work right now. Why not just refuse to answer the door. Seemed simple enough. Against her better judgement, she instead asked the person to announce their name and intentions.

"I have something for the person living at this address," came the reply.

This sounded like something someone with ill intentions would say, didn't it?

"Not that easy. I have my cell phone and with a final press of the button I will have the 911 dispatcher on the line." Stupid, she thought. I would be long dead or abducted before anyone could come to my rescue.

"Please don't call the police."

"Now that sounded exactly what someone would say if they meant to do me harm," yelled Paula. "Just go away and leave me alone or I will make good on my promise."

"Do you know Edwin Shipley?"

That got her attention but concerned her even more. This person had a connection to him. The threat loomed larger given that fact. "What have you done to him?"

"Nothing. I have done nothing."

"What do you intend to do to me then. Remember, one digit away from calling the calvary."

"I wish no involvement with the police."

"I bet you don't. One last time. Why are you here? Make it quick and convincing or else."

341

"I have something for the person at this address."

"How is it you have my address in the first place?"

"It was written on the envelope."

"What envelope? Let me see what you are talking about."

Paula could make out an envelope through the peephole.

"What does the envelope contain?"

"No idea."

"Then why are you here to deliver it to me?"

"I told you. This address is on it."

"Do you work for the postal service?"

"No ma'am."

"Who told you to deliver it then?'

"No one specifically told me, but it had this address on it. I did not know what else to do with it."

"This is getting us nowhere. Leave it and then you leave."

"I am afraid."

"Why should that concern me? Afraid of what?"

"Them."

"Them, who are 'them'?"

"I don't know."

Paula rubbed the back of her neck with her free hand. "Let's try something different. How do you know Edwin Shipley?"

"He is my friend."

"I asked how you knew him."

"I would rather not say."

"How about this, where is Edwin Shipley?"

"I do not know."

"You don't seem to know much about anything except you want me to have that envelope. I am sorry, I am not buying it and I am not going to simply open my door to retrieve the mystery envelope without you even sharing your name or real reason for being here."

"My name is Melanie."

"Okay. Melanie. If that is really your name."

"Melanie is my real name. It has always been my name. And to whom am I speaking?"

"You came here to delver this envelope and you don't even know my name."

"No. The address on the envelope is the only reason I came here. I think it is important. Erwin thought it was important."

"Set it in front of the door then please step away. Keep both hands in the air so I can clearly see them."

Melanie complied. Paula opened the door but kept the lock chain in place to gain a better look. The young girl did not look threatening but what did she know about such matters. She closed the door and then removed the chain, reopened the door just enough so that she could bend and retrieve the envelope. The girl remained in place; hands held above her head. Paula quickly closed the door and examined the envelope. It was indeed her address, and she recognized the handwriting. It was Shipley's. She chanced another glance through the peephole. The mysterious stranger, Melanie was not in sight, not where she had just been standing. No way was Paula going to open the door again and risk being jumped.

She yelled out to this Melanie. No one replied. She looked again through the peephole. The girl still was not where she had been standing. She shouted again but received no response from the other side of the door. Tossing caution to the wind, but not before retrieving a baseball bat she kept around for protection, she opened the door. Slowly she peeped one way and then the other. The hallway was empty. Melanie, if that was really her name, had vanished. Paula closed and locked the door. She then sat at a barstool in her kitchen examining the envelope. It was an express mail envelope like the one she had previously received. Why the first one, empty at that, and now this one, hand delivered? It felt about the same weight as the previous one. More blank pages?

Paula retrieved a kitchen knife and opened one end. Slowly she removed the contents. The first page was blank just like the last one. What kind of sick game was being played she wondered. Here goes, she thought, flipping to the second page. This one was not blank. Instead, it was handwritten. Written by Shipley. She began reading it out aloud, somewhat of a habit she had.

Paula, if you are reading this then it means (1) I met with unfortunate circumstances, a scenario I feared given what we found ourselves facing. (2) Melanie delivered it to you as I requested given the uncertainty of our predicament.

Melanie is a friend, the Uber driver that drove me to my various destinations. Not to worry, she knows nothing. Not who I met or the contents of this care package. Did this on purpose to keep her out of danger. My last contact delivered the goods. Someone else intervened. They were out to intercept us. Melanie gave them the slip

344

at least for a brief time. I realized we were still in danger, being followed. I stuffed two identical envelopes. One is a decoy. The decoy goes with me just in case they nab me before I mail it. The real gem goes with Melanie. She will deliver it to your address if I do not return. The contents will knock your socks off.

Please proceed with caution once you have it. Trust no one. Stay alert. We are dealing with the deep state and beyond as you will soon realize when you review the material. The documents and evidence speak volumes. Worse than either of us could have imagined possible. Hopefully, we can see this through together. If not. Be assured I have no regrets. What a ride! And for reasons you will understand, I did not sign my name to this. Take care my friend and blow this thing wide open.

Not one prone to showing emotion, a tear ran down Paula's cheek. Did this mean something afoul had happened to Erwin Shipley? The abruptly ended call, no further contact with his cell phone and now this. Too obvious. The bad guys had gotten to him but not before he had mailed the decoy. She retrieved the first envelope and examined it again. Maybe not. Deep state he had said. Someone had somehow intercepted the envelope, opened it, and examined the contents. Then they resealed it and allowed it to reach its destination. That meant but one thing. They were watching her. If they were, they had most certainly seen this Melanie person deliver the second one. It suddenly dawned on her; what if they had already snatched Melanie. If they had, they would be coming for her next. It might even be too late. These people, whoever they were, were quite efficient and precise in doing the unthinkable. Ordinary commoners did not think or operate in such covert operations. The deck was stacked against her for sure. Dillydallying would only aid in their success. Time to act, to get the hell out of Dodge if it was not already too late for an escape strategy.

****

Berkley and Camilla diligently stayed put in their Palmetto State coastal safe house. Thus far nothing suspicious had warranted their attention. Vlad had not called again. Hopefully, they could interpret this as him not knowing their location. It seemed a stretch that someone residing in New York would dare venture to South Carolina simply to even a score. Sure, secrets had been shared with Berkley, but they had been shared knowing that he was penning a new noel. Worst case scenario though, these terrorist urban thugs were obviously aware that Berkley knew they were responsible for the assault on Reverend Flowers. This posed a serious problem for them, him knowing. Anything might be possible for them to rectify that blunder. Berkley keeping a low profile was of the utmost importance. She should be safe. They did not know she was involved. What was more concerning, the ramifications of what had possibly happened to Erwin Shipley and Paula's concerns moving forward.

"My dear, you have been quiet, too quiet. We should probably discuss this ever-evolving dilemma we have found ourselves in, don't you think?"

"Berkley, I don't know what to think about it. I find it difficult to think, period. I just wanted to expose the artificial manipulated Covid information, somehow, someway, but I never contemplated finding ourselves in such dire circumstances."

"I get it. Like something out of a spy novel, espionage and maybe germ warfare. Sadly, we do not know the identity of the enemy. Well, except for your previous employer, who seems to be deeply vetted. And of course, the anti-American group, who might be working independently of all this other chaos."

"More serious than that, given Erwin Shipley appears to be missing. Whoever is responsible plays by no rules or laws. I fear we have gotten in over our heads."

"Paula explained why she has kept us in the dark up until now. For our protection. She insisted again that we bow out. I think we already know too much. Tough to turn a blind eye."

"Where does that leave us then, Berkley?"

346

"Heroes survive in my novels. I control the narrative though. Here, much of it is out of our hands. Might be that this goes beyond mere heroism. Patriotism seems more appropriately applied. If Covid 19 was launched, released intentionally, then why? Can someone be so evil that they would jeopardize the world population?"

"If it was unleashed intentionally, those responsible knew exactly what they were doing. Yes, it would have a devastating impact on the world's population, but the manipulation of the cases and deaths have had far more dire impact, fearmongering, instilling turmoil and uncertainty."

"Hoarding toilet paper, devious beyond belief, the world at the evil doer's mercy."

"Besides the self-inflicted shortages, the coronavirus has singlehandedly collapsed the booming economy. Unemployment like we have never seen. Maybe, that was the intent all along. Destroy prosperity and then attack us while we are vulnerable."

"WWIII was expected to be a nuclear apocalyptic ending for the world. Instead, we are taken down by those who control sanitizers, Clorox wipes, paper towels and toilet tissue. Who could have seen that coming? Top that off by scaring people from working, no sports, no movies, no concerts, no church, no school, all social functions brought to a screaming halt. We have an incredible mastermind out there, don't we?"

"Where does that leave us, Berkley? In or out?"

44

Paula opted for the stairwell instead of the elevator. unsure why she thought it might be safer. She had packed light, a canvas satchel tossed over one shoulder and a leather brief case carrying her laptop and documents looped under her arm. She carried the envelope in the other hand, in much need of a pack mule. In her hasty retreat she had not taken time to peruse any of the information Erwin had uncovered. Paula feared going to the parking garage and instead decided to exit on the street side and hail a cab. That is if her exit plan worked. Hindsight, she should probably have called a cab, but she feared using her cell phone given the intrusive powers of the deep state who most certainly knew her identity. She had left the phone on the kitchen counter, having watched too many detective shows and spy movies, those indicating that the powers to be could track a person's location via their cell phone.

She had reached the exit door but paused, wondering if danger awaited on the other side. Paula placed her ear to the door and listened. She was not sure what she expected to hear. Not a sound. Should she interpret it as a good sign or pending ambush? Taking a deep breath and then letting it out noisily, she panicked, thinking someone outside could have heard her or maybe someone above on the stairwell now knew where she had gone. She listened for a few seconds but heard nothing to indicate she had lost this round of high and go seek. Now or never. She pushed on the door bar and slowly opened it, fighting back the urge to shoulder her way through and run as fast as she could.

Chancing a peek, like a tortoise from its shell, she looked one way and then the other. The street was vacant of pedestrians and vehicles. Good sign or bad? No one would be around to hear her scream if the bad guys were lurking nearby. She slipped through the door and headed southward toward an intersecting avenue that might offer better cover, more people and traffic. To get there though she would have to travel nearly three blocks and pass several alleys. Anyone of them would be the perfect hiding place for would be abductors.

Hopefully, they would be either in the garage or already breaking through her doorway.

Paula approached the first alley. She considered crossing the street to avoid it, but another alley awaited her on that side as well. Pick your poison. She stayed close to the wall, not sure what it really gained her. Just seemed logical given the uncertainty. Less that ten feet away she paused. Thankfully, it was daylight, midday to be exact. She gathered herself, regripped her belongings and did the unthinkable. She sprinted past the alley and never chanced a look. She did not slow her pace until she was nearly a half block passed it. She then slowed and peeked over her shoulder. Nothing. All was clear. Second guessing now, she wondered if she had blown this out of proportion. No. She could not be too careful given what Shipley had relayed. Halfway there. She spotted the first signs of traffic as a truck passed through the intersection clearly in view now. Paula quickened her pace, adrenalin inspired by the sight of a vehicle.

The next alley was less than ten yards ahead. Ambush opportunity number two. She engaged the same strategy, sprinting even faster this time. Just as she reached the alley a figure stepped into her path. She found herself entangled in arms and legs and falling to the sidewalk, falling atop the intruder, the assailant breaking her fall. Instinctively Paula began clawing and flailing wildly seeking any opportunity to escape. Freeing herself she rolled to her left and quickly got to her feet, preparing to roundhouse her adversary with the canvas satchel. It was then that she saw the fear in the eyes of the homeless woman, arms crossing over her head to fend off the attack. Paula managed to stop in mid blow and whisper, "It's okay. I'm sorry." She then helped the lady to her feet and retrieved a twenty, placing in her hand before vacating the area.

Walking briskly, she could not help but think how stupidly she had been acting. Overreacting possibly. A bit too paranoid even given the circumstances. Still, something told her to push onward. No time to drop her guard. The intersection was now just a block ahead. A cab passed through it. A good sign. It was then that she heard the footfalls from behind. The sound could not have been that of the homeless woman. These were heavy, more than one set and approaching fast. Nothing to do but chance a look. Two, no three figures were running in her direction and gaining fast. Paula ran as fast as her legs would carry her. Thirty feet more and she would be at the intersection and could yell for help. A car pulled into the street blocking her exit. Trapped.

A horn sounded. Headlights blinked. They must be signaling those in pursuit that they had her. An arm extended through the driver's side and seemed to be motioning to her. The horn sounded again, the hand motioning more urgently. What did she have to lose? Paula sprinted toward the vehicle. Mere paces away she recognized the person behind the wheel of the Prius. Melanie, the Uber driver, Shipley's friend. She looked behind her and saw the three men were almost on her. She would never close the ground in time. She turned, stumbled, and dropped the envelope. It ripped open on impact, the wind scattering the contents. Nothing to do be keep running. Somehow, she made it, the passenger door already open waiting for her to dive inside. Melanie slammed the Prius in reverse. Like a deer in the headlights, Paula watched as two of the men scrambled to gather the papers while the third had just reached the hood of the Prius. Melanie accelerated, causing the man to lose his balance and fall face first to the pavement. The young Uber driver wheeled the car into the intersection and then shifted it into drive. No one pursued them. Men on foot were no match for the Prius and its stunt driver.

Neither Paula nor Melanie spoke for what felt like an eternity but had only been less than two minutes. Paula broke the silence first. "Thank you but how did you know?"

"Saw them enter the building after I reached my car. I know the type. Could tell they had concealed weapons. I hung around just in case."

"Why didn't you call the police?"

"Don't trust the police."

"Don't trust the police?"

"I have my reasons."

"What if they would have gotten to me? Seems you did not have my safety in mind."

"Figured you to be the resourceful type, like Erwin."

"Mighty big gamble."

"Life is a gamble. Sometimes you win. More often you don't."

"I owe you one."

"Where to now?"

"Not sure."

"Sorry you lost the envelope. It was important to Erwin that I deliver it to your address."

Paula smiled. "No need to fret. That envelope is safe and sound inside my briefcase. The one I conveniently dropped was a fake one, a decoy that Shipley had mailed me."

"Oh, that was the second one he had. He did not tell me it was a decoy."

"By the way, Melanie, I am Paula, Erwin Shipley's cohort in this little caper."

"Any friend of Erwin's can be considered a friend of mine as well."

"What happened to him, Melanie?"

"Can't say."

"Can't or won't?"

"Can't, I don't know. Haven't seen him since Portland. He gave me the envelope and said to deliver it to the address marked on it before he exited my car. Said it was important. Told me to head here. Not to worry about him."

"And you just deserted him like that?"

"I did what he asked me to do. I trust him and I trust anything he says. I have no reason to doubt him or his intentions. Have you decided where you would like me to take you?"

"Are you opposed to going to South Carolina?"

"I drove Erwin to Portland, didn't I? No questions asked. Anywhere specific in South Carolina?"

"Just drive. I will provide an address when we get closer."

"Yes ma'am. I am fueled and ready."

"One stop first. I need another cell phone. You may want to ditch yours too."

"It is my business lifeline."

"Those people who were chasing me probably followed you to my place."

"No one followed me. Trust me. I can make a tail with one eye closed."

"Then how did they…damn it! Never mind. The decoy. They knew exactly where to find me. Odd, they never showed up until after you delivered the second one. The sneaky bastards! They already had me under surveillance. They saw you arrive with the second one and then moved in. They had no reason to play their hand before then. Change of plans, head to Washington while I read the contents of Shipley's material."

"Washington it is."

Camilla answered her phone and then whispered to Berkley, "It's Paula"

She listened to Paula, jotting down some notes during the conversation. The call was brief but filled with pertinent information.

"What gives? Any news on Erwin Shipley?"

"She did not mention him. She has obtained a wealth of information that our missing Mr. Shipley apparently sent her."

"Care to share, my lovely?"

"She did not elaborate, saying best we did not know the full details. She did say it would change everything."

"Meaning?"

"Everything. She gave me a new email account and wants me to send her everything I have. Said she would take it from there and advised us to remain where we are and keep a low profile."

"Intriguing, I am fascinated and most curious, aren't you?"

"Undeniably, but she does not wish to put us in further danger."

"Always kept in the dark. Quite disappointing. Outcasts we are."

"For our protection, remember."

"Who are these evil doers and what are their intentions?"

"Not knowing might save our necks, Berkley, given what Paula is not willing to tell us."

"Nothing to do but follow her instructions I suppose. I think I will contact Reverend Flowers' sister and see how he is doing."

****

Paula had skimmed through the information provided by Shipley. It was jaw dropping indeed. The tentacles reached unfathomable origins. Paula sat in the backseat ringing her hands and then rubbing them through her hair. Melanie eyed her curiously through the rearview mirror, concerned but remained silent. Paula rubbed her eyes before asking to borrow Melanie's phone a second time.

"Hello. Yes, it is me. I have it. It is unbelievable and is a national security bombshell with global ramifications."

Paula listened and then responded, "Yes, I have it with me and I am Washington bound. I can meet you wherever you think it is safe and inconspicuous. Others have tried to intercept and relieve me of this material."

"Yes, most certainly. I did feel my life was being threatened. My associate, the one who obtained this, is still missing."

"Yes. I am certain. No one else is privy to it. I have the only copy."

After Paula ended the call, she handed the phone back to Melanie but not before deleting the phone number. Oddly, the young girl made no comment concerning the conversation. Maybe it was just Uber driver etiquette. Paula gave her a new destination, a site capable of printing Camilla's research material, the final piece in the precarious puzzle.

"I apologize for getting you involved in this matter, Melanie."

"Involved? I am but a mere Uber driver taking my passenger to their requested addresses."

"I appreciate that, but as you have already witnessed more than once, motoring us about comes with dangerous consequences. It saddens me what has happened to Shipley."

"What makes you think something dreadful has happened? Erwin is quite resourceful."
"He has not contacted me in days. His last call was extremely concerning. I fear the worse. I still find it difficult to swallow that you left him there."

"I did as he asked. It is not for me to question his intent."

"Everything is black and white to you, isn't it? Care to share with me how you and he know one another?"

"Not really. You have your secrets, so it seems. I should be allowed the same curtesy."

"Touché."

Paula resumed her focus on the contents spread about on the backseat beside her, still finding it tough to digest. It was imperative that this information be disclosed before the election, now less than two weeks away. She remained confident her contact would elevate it to the highest level. Then it suddenly dawned on her. Who could really be trusted given what she now knew?

"We have arrived at your destination."

Paula had saved Camilla's research to a thumb drive. Printing it would be monetarily costly and time consuming, but little did that matter right now. She would add it to the pile of evidence that would shatter the democracy and beyond. The enemy existed outside and within, probably always had. Paula still struggled with what had been uncovered. Everything she had once believed in had been a pipedream, something evil and sinister just biding its time. That time had arrived and what had been unleashed would redefine this country and the world if not stopped. Hard to fathom just the same.

"Melanie, this will take a while. Here take this," she said handing her a twenty. "Please grab us something to eat. It is going to be a long night."

"Any preference?"

"Whatever you can find works for me."

"I will be parked out front when you have finished inside."

"Here's an extra twenty for gas."

"Thanks, but I drive a Prius. We are good on gas."

Gas, thought Paula, something that could be compromised. One of many game changers given half a chance. She exited the Prius and headed inside, looking about as she did, wary of any devious presence intent on stopping her. No one intercepted her. She safely arrived inside and accessed a printer. She opted to use cash for all transactions, fortunately keeping a reserve on hand. A credit or debit card would allow those seeking her to find her. She was learning to play the game. Technology offered too many avenues for tracking people. To think, Covid 19 was being used to propose embedding chips in people for contact tracing of coronavirus exposure. Just another attempt to control and tract people, Big Brother thumping his chest and overreaching. Never more clearly than right now given what she had read.

While waiting for the printer to complete its task Paula diverted her thought to Melanie, a needed distraction. She wondered what the connection was between her and Shipley. She was obviously loyal and quite protective of him. Shipley had trusted her as well, enlisting her help for the across country trip. Melanie expressed little emotion and dealt in conversation as a matter of fact and not just mere chit chat. At times she almost seemed robotic. One could only imagine what the young girl had experienced in her short life. Had Shipley been involved somehow in helping Melanie find her way out of a world that had done her wrong? The scenarios dancing in Paula's mind were endless.

The printer completed its task. Paula payed the clerk and stepped to the entrance. The Prius was parked within view. The gal was flawlessly loyal. She understood why Shipley had entrusted his trip in her hands. Shipley had sacrificed everything for this story. Everything. Paula opted for the backseat again, not because she considered herself a fare for the Uber driver; she required a bit more room to spread out and organize Camilla's research within the contents acquired by her missing associate. Melanie passed her a soda, a double cheeseburger, and fries before asking where to now. Onward to Washington, address now programmed in the GPS.

Paula perused Camilla's stats and graphs. Impeccable and compelling they were. The virologist knew her stuff inside and out. What she had uncovered left nothing to mere opinion. It laid out the deceptiveness of what the so-called experts had stated as fact. Warnings unfounded. Misleading guidelines. Recommended shutdowns total BS. Americans were being jerked around royally by power hungry control freaks. This only exposed the tip of the iceberg. What remained beneath the surface was terrifying on a scale the public might struggle to comprehend.

From a journalistic perspective it had always been Paula's job to report the facts and allow the viewers or readers to decide how it impacted them. This was extremely different, overwhelmingly so. In this case Paula decided she would place it in trusting hands and allow the powers that be to decide how much information should be shared with Americans and the world. Powers that be? Back to that trust concept. Who within the United States government were trustworthy and just how many were involved in this travesty? No doubt the roots were deeply embedded.

As experienced thus far there was little chit chat between her and her escort. Not that Paula hadn't attempted numerous times since their initial meeting. Melanie guarded her private life. Maybe, it was again just Uber privilege, never become too comfy with the paying customers. Unlike a bartender. Paula's occupation, on the other hand, prompted her to ask questions. Hard habit to break. No denying it, the young girl was quite intriguing. Solving the mystery dogged Paula. She did her best to respect Melanie's privacy, often biting her tongue to remain silent. Reviewing the material again served as a distraction, a gosh awful scary one at that. Judgement day would come soon enough when she met with the senator.

Paula remembered a time when opposing political parties running the country did not hate none another. If they did, they did not openly display it. Most Americans did not vote party. They voted for ideas that came from both parties, the intent that both parties were Americans first, looking out for Americans and America's interests. Neither party was identified as racists, sexist or Unamerican. Americans accepted election results. They did not scream 'burn it down' and then riot and destroy businesses. 'We the People' was exactly that. Being an American meant supporting closed borders and entering the country legally to become a citizen. There was but one national language – English. Americans were proud to be Americans and respected the flag, the anthem, and God. How had it gotten so crazy, disrespectful, and so biased? It wasn't easy for Paula to remove her journalist hat, but she did believe in America and the American way of life, or at least what it used to represent.

****

Governors of New York, California, Michigan, and Illinois were tightening the thumb screws on restaurants, bars, and churches. Owners and operators were being fined and arrested for not following strict pandemic guidelines. Officials were even threatening to fine and arrest people in their homes if they had huge family Thanksgiving gatherings. Socialism and communism test driving persisted. Big government's hunger for power and control had reached a feeding frenzy as Americans continued to suffer under their reign while looters and rioters were immune and allowed to wreak terror and lawlessness whenever and wherever they wanted.

Some feared Americans were reaching the tipping point. Could a rebellion or even a civil war be brewing? There were those that professed enough is enough. If government and the law were no longer going to protect them and their businesses, then possibly it was time that those being harmed would unite and fight back. What did you have to lose once you had virtually lost everything? Pride and dignity meant something. Government was supposed to serve the people not the other way around. A reckoning seemed inevitable. Push and be pushed back. Too many of the same government officials enforcing the shutdowns and restrictions were being caught not practicing what they so vocally preached. Tolerance levels of the people were wearing thin. It was time to reclaim America went the chants in peaceful gatherings. Oddly, police were in full force at these peaceful gatherings while missing in action during the looting and burning of neighborhoods. Government bureaucrats were drawing their paychecks and living their lives fat and happy while destroying the lives of their constituents. Don't think blue blooded Americans were not taking notice.

45

Camilla sat on the balcony with a glass of chardonnay reflecting on the events that had so drastically impacted and changed her life in recent months. Obviously, the death of George topped the list. At their age and with George's heart condition there were never promises of another day. She had never even dwelled on that fact nor had she realistically taken their lives for granted. She and George just lived in the moment and did not fret over the future. For that she had no regrets. Sure, she regretted silly stuff that they did or did not do but she accepted the fate every human faces. You are born and one day you will die. One does not get to pick the time for the latter as it should be.

As for the situation she had found herself in, that had been her choice as had the decision to research the coronavirus. No one had twisted her arm or forced her down this path. She had no regrets for her actions. It had been her choice as well to become involved with Paula Wise and Ervin Shipley. True, they had used deceptive tactics to seek her out but after they confessed to it, it had still been her decision to share her research. While she now had some reservations as to how this might play out, she had no regrets. What troubled her more was what she and Berkley did not know. For their protection she understood that but she was an 'all in' type person. Her research had given her a vested interest in the outcome. She deserved to know the whole enchilada. She did regret she had not pressed Paula harder. She could even have leveraged her research as a bargaining chip. Too late for that strategy now.

"Ah there you are, my lovely. Penny for your thoughts."

"While you are up, Berkley, a refill would be wonderful. Pour yourself one and join me. The view is breathtaking as always."

"Back in a jiffy."

Poor Erwin Shipley, what had become of him, she wondered. And that Reverend Flowers, so brutally assaulted by the same individuals Berkley had infiltrated. Then there was Doctor Kyle Richardson and his wife Mildred. What a tragedy, dying in a fire, accidently or intentionally. Berkley had suffered as well with the loss of his dear friend, Kitt Whitt. So much gloom and doom this year. The virus was real even if a conspiracy existed, intent on destroying the livelihoods of innocent, hardworking Americans. How could something so evil exist? She reminded herself that God is always in charge and has a plan.

"Here you go, the vineyard's nectar to sooth a troubled soul."

"What makes you think I am troubled, Berkley?'

"Frown lines, deep contemplation, concerning eyes, take your pick."

"Okay, I admit, I was reassessing the events that have impacted my life this year and those that have shifted the sand in the world in which we live."

"Care to share."

"Not really. I have already completed that part of the journey and need to just move on."

"Berkley-ology 101. Everything always happens for a reason whether we agree with it or not. Somewhere down the line we will eventually see and understand it. Reverend Flowers told me that God will eventually reveal to us why he allowed things to happen as they did. You know me, I have never been a full-fledged believer in these heavenly matters but maybe, just maybe, I am coming around a bit. Far from converted mind you, but more openminded than I once was. Flowers did add that God's way is better than our way and His will is beyond our will. It has to do with trust he said."

"Sounds to me that you have turned the corner further than you thought, recalling such significant conversations."

"A bit too optimistic, Sweetness. Remember I have a photographic memory. Writer's gift. I still remember the world's best toys of my ancient youth. Sticks, rocks, water, dirt, rope, and buckets."

"Interesting youth you must have had. Reverend Flowers indeed impacted your life. Something to add to your little devotional mantra; remember, there is a purpose for everyone you meet. For reasons beyond normal explanation, there are those who come into your life to test you. Others are teachers. Some will use you while others will bring out the absolute best in you. I believe this Reverend Flowers is responsible for checking all those boxes even if you are not prepared to admit it right now."

"Your reflection has taken you deeply into the biblical world, so it seems."

"Not so, Berkley. Your journey has inspired me to give you a friendly little push. You opened yourself up to this. Be patient and listen. I admit, in these trying times I tend to turn to the bible. Take Psalm 18:2-3 for example. The Lord is my rock and my fortress and my deliverer. My god, my strength, in whom I trust, my shield and the horn of my salvation, my stronghold. I will call upon the Lord, who is worthy to be praised; so, shall I be saved from my enemies."

"Profound indeed, Camilla. I must take time someday to read the bible."

"Believe in this my dear friend. When you and I draw our last breath, only one thing will ultimately matter. That our names are written in the Book of Life."

"I am not familiar with any published work titled 'The Book of Life.' Who is the author?"

Camilla shared a gentle and sincere smile, "The Book of Life serves as a testament to those saved who will enjoy eternity with the Lord. It is referenced in the New and Old Testaments of the bible. In other words, my friend, if upon your death your name does not appear in that book, you could end up on the short end and destined for a life in hell instead. "

"Is it the wine or the ocean view that inspires you so, my lovely?"

"Neither. I draw my inspiration from God All Mighty, the creator of the vineyards and the oceans and everything we have been so graciously provided."

"Remind me to seek Him the next time I am inflicted with writer's block. Just kidding. I respect you and your beliefs. Maybe one day I will experience what you cherish unconditionally."

"I hope and pray so, Berkley."

He nodded and then took a sip of his wine. "Do you think Paula has met with her person yet?"

"Hopefully, whoever this person is, he or she can be counted on to utilize the material to seek justice."

"If so, how do you think the public will react? I would be quite angry if I had been led to believe what you have uncovered. Well, I guess I have, haven't I? People are being driven to the brink on false pretense. People have lost their businesses, their jobs and freedom because of this virus and the lies being spread. To what gain still eludes me."

"And add to it what Shipley and Paula have discovered; this could be far worse than what we suspect."

"I fear one bottle of wine is not going to suffice for this deeply troubling conversation. Not like we have anything better on our schedule, I suppose."

"I miss George."

"I know you do. I miss my friend, Kitt, as well. And I will be damned if we are going to allow their deaths to be attributed unjustifiably to Covid 19."

"Here, here," said Camilla, clanging her wine glass against Berkley's.

****

Melanie parked the Prius outside the building complex as instructed by Paula.

"I am not sure how long I will be."

"Not a problem," replied Melanie.

"Thank you, Melanie, for doing this."

"No sweat."

Paula opened the door, the envelope concealed inside her laptop's briefcase. She had just reached the building's entrance door when a voice from behind said, "Be careful." She turned and nodded to Melanie. Melanie smiled and winked back; the first time she had seen the girl show any sign of emotion.

Inside Paula walked through a small empty lobby. No desk. No security. Very modest surroundings. She approached a single elevator and pressed the eighth-floor button. She watched as the elevator descended from the eleventh floor. The doors whooshed open. The elevator was empty. Once she reached the eighth, she searched for apartment number 827. Taking a deep breath, she then knocked. The door opened.

"Paula Wise, please come in. I assume your travel here was without any misfortunes."

"Thank you, Senator Breeze. All went well."

"Please, call me Aaron. Senator makes me feel too much like the old establishment."

"Then, by all means, please call me Paula."

"I apologize for my humble abode. I am quite frugal by nature. I do not require the luxurious lifestyle that some seem to cherish here. I am here to serve not rule or take advantage of taxpayer money."

"Like your style, Aaron."

"Might I offer you coffee or a soda. Sorry, I have nothing stronger. I don't drink."

"I am fine. Perhaps we should move on to more important matters."

"Certainly. I am quite curious to see what you have uncovered."

"You may wish you had a drink once you review what I have in this folder."

"Very well, let us sit at the bar where we have more room."

Paula laid it out piece by piece, noting the senator's expression and sweat beading up on his forehead and upper lip. Several times he sat back on his stool and simply shook his head in disbelief. Almost three hours expired before they reached the final piece of evidence.

"Astounding. You were right about that drink. How can all this be possible?"

"You read it. You saw the evidence. It is credible and deeply rooted. That is not fabricated documentation. The question now is how are you going to ensure it gets into the right hands, someone you can trust, someone not part of this. Time is not on our side, and in some incidences, it might already be too late to undo the damages."

"This will require considerable thought. And you say this is the only copy."

"Everything but the Covid research by a credible virologist."

"And your friend…"

"Erwin Shipley…he has vanished. As previously stated, others have tried to make me vanish as well while getting their hands on it. They know I am involved."

"Not to worry. I will make sure you receive protection. Curious though, why me?"

"You were gracious enough to grant me an interview when you were running for office. I saw something in you then, something new, and quite refreshing. I sensed your honesty and sincerity, one who had yet to be corrupted by the political machine. You were not in the political arena prior to your run, were not a power-hungry career politician. You walked onto the scene as a person concerned and one loving your state and this country. Simply put, I reached out to you not because you are the best at what you do, more so that you are real and not a put-on, not a chosen one, but a person of dignity and pride, and not one who can be bought. Please don't prove me wrong, Aaron."

"I appreciate your honesty as well and hope that I will not disappoint you. Why not go public with this yourself? You already have the viewership and following. This would define your career forever."

"The deep state machine would never allow that. The media would crush and discredit me, no matter how much info I presented. There was a time that an honest media would have run with this and exposed it. Not now. Social media, big tech, Hollywood, and your party would never stand for it either. And, before you ask, no, I am not afraid to take them on, have done so plenty of times. This is different. The stakes have never been higher. My life has already been threatened and my colleague has probably been murdered to prevent this information from seeing the light of day. No, I am the wrong choice to delivery this. You must get this in the president's hands. Do not trust anyone in your party. Go directly to the top and circumvent typical protocol if you have any chance of seeing this through."

"You paint a compelling yet bleak scenario. Paula, I must confess, I have never personally met the president. What makes you think I can reach him now?"

"You have reviewed what is in that folder. That should be all the motivation you require. I do not have a second draft choice in this matter. You are it. Your country has never needed you more, senator. Is this not why you chose this path, to make a difference, to work for the people and not become a swamp creature? You will find a path forward. You have no choice. Failure to do so dooms this nation, forever changes the world's landscape. We cannot allow this to happen. I have always prided myself as being a credible journalist, unbiased, just report it as found and allow the viewers to decide. I find myself in uncharted waters because of the contents of that envelope. I am an American first. We cannot allow this covert operation to tear apart our country and the world if truth be known."

"You missed your calling, Paula. You could have been a politician."

"Afraid not, I don't have it in me to lie, manipulate the public and become wealthy off the people who have entrusted me to work for them, to support them, to protect them. And no, I am not lumping every politician into that pile. There are a few good ones left like you."

"I will do what I can."

"Not good enough, senator. Make it happen."

"What about you, Paula? Where does this leave you?"

"When the time is right, I will support you and the president on the airways. Doing it prematurely will doom us to failure."

"Allow me to do what I can to offer you a safe house."

"Thank you but I do not trust anyone in this broken system to guarantee my safety. No knock on you insinuated. I will take care of that part and contact you when I see signs that the tide is turning."

"Again, I appreciate your confidence in me seeing this through."

"One last thing."

"Name it."

"Once this does hit the fan and the corner has been turned, the nation and world has been convinced to believe in the worst attempted travesty in history, please do what you can to find what happened to Erwin Shipley and bring them to justice. I owe him that much."

"You have my promise, one sealed with a handshake, the way I was taught to do by my dad and grandfather."

"Take care, Senator Aaron Breeze and be extremely careful. Evil exists and will kill to protect this information."

Paula took the stairs instead of the elevator, a routine of late. She quickly spotted the Prius as she reached ground level. Melanie had seen no suspicious activity while waiting for her return. As usual, she did not ask who Paula had met with or the nature of the meeting.

"Now, we head to South Carolina. We can swap up driving duties if you would like. You could probably use a little rest."

Eyeing Paula through the mirror she replied, "I am fine. You rest. You look exhausted. I have already called ahead for an Airbnb midway, your treat."

Paula smiled, "My treat indeed. Thank you, Melanie."

****

"Hey. It's Aaron, can we meet? Now if you can. Your place will be fine. Not on the phone. I will explain when I get there. See you within the hour."

46

"You are not going to believe this Camilla. That was Paula. She is on the way here. Should arrive late tomorrow."

"How are things going?"

"She did not say. Short and directly to the point. The more the merrier I suppose."

"Sounds a bit suspicious, her traveling all the way down here."

"Why so? We did."

"Exactly, Berkley. We did not come here on vacation. We are in hiding, remember. Sounds to me she may be coming here for the very same reason."

"You think she is on the run."

"Maybe. Guess we will know the rest of the story when she arrives."

"I would not count on that, Sweetness. We have been spoon fed from the get-go for our protection supposedly. Putting all the eggs in one crate seems a bit dangerous from my perspective if our protection is so important."

"Excellent observation. Perhaps we should turn on the television and keep a vigilant watch on late breaking revelations."

"Not a bad idea. She is a journalist and makes sense that she would use her platform to expose the ugliness."

"Scary thing, Berkley, we don't know the full ramifications of this yet."

"We know enough. This is huge, enough so that people have died or gone missing to protect it."

"What have we really gotten ourselves into, Berkley?"

"Cloak and dagger antics. My next book will obviously be my best published ever."

"Hope it and will see that light of day, my friend."

****

"You have the same expression I am sure I displayed when I read it."

"And you still won't tell me how you got your hands on it, Aaron."
"In due time. So, what do you think?"

"Shall we recap this. Maybe by doing so I can better digest what I really read."

Aaron nodded, "Works for me. We now have undeniable evidence that communist China is responsible for Covid 19 and the deaths of nearly two million people worldwide. The virus was not accidently or intentionally released by a lab nor is it transmitted person to person. Thanks to the Global Virus Center we were misled over and over. First there was no person to person, then the opposite. We were not to use masks then we must wear masks. We must socially distance and initially isolate for a few weeks to flatten the curve. The world came to a standstill under lockdown. The GVC's involvement with communist China was never a conspiracy theory. Masks nor social distancing were ever going to save us either."

"The implemented travel band did absolutely nothing to prevent coronavirus from spreading according to this documentation. We were the primary target, but the world's destruction was intended as well. Communist China dominates the global supply chain. They utilized this to spread the virus. Pharmaceutical and other goods were intentionally infected by Covid. We never had a chance. Everything we used, touched, or consumed guaranteed the spread all

371

the while the GVC lied to us. The compiled data and stats support the compelling evidence as well."

"Masks nor social distancing prevented the spread. It was just a well-orchestrated distraction. Shutting down the economy and confining people did nothing. The virus, the invisible enemy, has been among us the entire time. Still is, allowing China to control too much of our supply chain and routinely used products doomed us from the outset."

"Aaron, these documents place enemy corroboration within our borders."

"It confirms that R.K. Soto, the billionaire extremist, along with others, have funded all groups associated with the protests, the rioting, looting, and burning of our major cities. These movements were utilized to distract us from the greater scenario, racial divide, defunding the police, politicians turning a blind eye and refusing to protect Americans were merely smoke and mirrors. These groups and the politicians have been pawns in the game as has the battle over the border and legalizing the millions of Hispanics already in our country. It is political banter and chest thumping, no more. Communist China has been purchasing businesses and property in this country in record numbers, infiltrating academia and political positions posturing for the final demise. We have documents linking the forest fires to R.K. Soto as well, just another distraction and form of chaotic behavior for our country. Those police officer shootings were bought and paid for too."

"This is unbelievable, Aaron. I cannot begin to fathom the depth of deceit and corruption. We have been led to believe that Russia, North Korea, Iran, Muslim extremists in general were our ultimate enemies."

"The communist regime of China has used these countries as a distraction while they orchestrated this ruse. They have never been in cahoots with any of our enemies. They want total domination and control over the world population. They needed us out of the way first."

"Tough to digest, Aaron."

"Worse times ahead. Covid has covertly introduced an even greater opportunity. It has changed the dynamics of the presidential election. Millions of unsolicited voter ballets have been mailed out. You read what I read. Voter fraud is the plan to oust the sitting president. Like him or not, this is wrong."

"Guess you are blaming my side for this, aren't you?

"Senator Charles Paulson, get over yourself. I did not come here to argue politics nor point fingers. This is not democrat versus republican. This is about saving America. Like this President or not, he loves this country. We can not allow China or any conspirators inside the United States to succeed in deciding our elections by illegal means. Ultimately, given what we have in front of us, we must expose this now and prevent further damage. I could have gotten this into the president's hands myself but, pardon me for saying this, your side would have done everything it could to debunk it. The media, your side's propaganda machine, would have given it no coverage. If you and I deliver this to the President it would offer credence to the material, bipartisan support."

"The leaders of your party and mine will have our political heads for circumventing them."

"Charles, you and I are newbies on the block. We do not owe anyone except the American people that we swore to serve and protect. We are not swamp creatures. We have a chance to save the greatest country ever. I am not in this for political gain. I am a patriot, and we are under attack from outside and within. I need you by my side in this,"

"I get it. I am honored you considered me for the task at hand. Can I ask you to give me a little time to review these further to ensure we are not overreacting?"

"We are not overreacting. These are legit. What has already transpired is beyond horrific. Time is of the essence."

"Twenty-four hours. Please allow me just twenty-four hours to review these documents. I perused them but would like a bit more time to scrutinize them, somewhat of a sanity check before we go gung-ho. You do fully understand that once we venture down this rabbit hole there is no turning back. Plus, neither you nor I have a direct path to the president. We have some work to do to make it to his doorstep."

"Understood. All right, twenty-four hours but you promise me that this information does not leave your sight."

"Just having it here is terrifying enough. And no one knows about it or you are coming here, right?"

"This is mine and your cross to bear. For the record, others have been trying to get their hands on it. Lives might have already been compromised as well."

"Now you are scaring me, Aaron."

"And scared you should be, Charles. This is no Micky Mouse operation. Who can say how far or where the tentacles go? My party? Yours? The agencies that are supposed to protect us…anything and everything are possible. Twenty-four hours and the countdown begin now."

"Holy crap, Aaron, what have we gotten ourselves into?"

"The survival of this nation and the world I fear."

"One final thought. Why haven't you or I been infected by Covid if the supply chain is infected?"

"Probably wasn't prudent to infect every product, component or shipment. Surely there is a method to their madness to minimize

374

detection. Plus, you have the GVC running interference to keep us on our heels."

"Just the same, I will now be paranoid over everything I touch or take."

"Sanitize and continue washing your hands. If you are not on any prescription medication, maybe avoid over the counter for now."

"Too crazy. Just way too crazy to be possible."

"Charles, twenty-four hours, no more."

"And what are you going to do in the meantime. Aaron?"

"Pray. Pray a lot. God is in control and has all the answers. We are mere conduits for his bidding."

47

A rap on the condo door caused both Camilla and Berkley to flinch. Camilla peeked through the door's peephole, something installed by George. She turned to Berkley to announce the arrival of their guest. When she opened the door, to her surprise, Paula was not alone.

"Hi Camilla, hope you have room for one more."

"We can make do. Please come in."

"This is Melanie. She drove me here and is a friend of Shipley's."

"Melanie, meet Camilla and Berkley."

Melanie smiled and nodded.

"Melanie is an Uber driver by profession. Quite indispensable I assure you and trustworthy as well."

Berkley asked, "An Uber driver drove you from New York to here?"

"Not much of a stretch considering she escorted Berkley to Portland."

"I see," commented an inquisitive Camilla. She then offered them use of the facilities and a bite to eat afterward.

Berkley uncorked a bottle of wine pouring everyone a glass except Melanie. She declined, even after Paula reminded her she was off duty. While Melanie opted for a shower and change of clothes, Paula caught them up to speed, much of what had transpired in the last 48 hours. She did not disclose everything though, only the bare minimum of what Shipley had uncovered. Enough to express national interest was in play. She shared that she had enlisted the help of a young senator but refrained from providing his name, again insisting it was for their protection. She reinforced the dangers lurking, recanting the near escape and crediting Melanie with saving her life. It was a waiting game for now she insisted, adding that everything at stake hinged on the senator successfully delivering the goods to the president.

Unlikely allies found themselves facing a perilous situation, any chance of normalcy returning in their lives in considerably unnormal conditions bleak at best. Paula added that Melanie did not know the severity of their dilemma but did understand the danger involved. She had witnessed it with Shipley and with her close call. Melanie had been the last person to lay eyes on Erwin Shipley. Paula said it was unlikely that her colleague was still among the living, having had no contact with him since Portland when he had set out on his own.

Paula, like Berkley and Melanie, were first time visitors to the South Carolina Grand Strand. She found the oceanic view breathtaking and wished being there had been under more desirable circumstances. At best, the beach condo was a hideout, for how long yet to be determined. She had made the conscious decision to keep Melanie close by in case of saying she was basically keeping her on the clock. Melanie had not flinched when agreeing to the arrangement. Paula sensed that the young girl sought belonging someplace and drew comfort from being around her. Maybe she was giving herself too much credit, but it just seemed right having Melanie around.

Camilla had attempted small talk with Melanie but quickly discovered she was not the chit chat type. The girl answered questions with minimum words and did nothing to advance any discussions. To each their own Camilla finally decided. The three-bedroom condo offered two options for their extra guest; bunk with Paula in the bedroom with twin beds or opt for the den sofa with a hideaway bed. Paula made the decision, saying she could share the room with her. Melanie agreed.

Berkley decided to take a brief walk on the beach, the late afternoon sun already casting long shadows on the sand and turf. He asked if anyone cared to join him. To his surprise Melanie took him up on the offer. Little conversation transpired during the elevator ride. Berkley had already noticed the standoffishness of their new arrival and had not pushed in spite of his inquisitive nature. They maneuvered around the pool, pausing only to remove their shoes before venturing onto the sand. Berkley preferred barefooting it, enjoying the sand between his toes and the opportunity to walk in the tiny ocean waves rushing onto shore.

Berkley could stand it no longer and broke the silence. "Melanie, do you enjoy your chosen occupation, that of an Uber driver?"

She replied with a simple yes, offering no additional dialogue.

"What prompted you to choose that profession?"

"Necessity. It prevented me from being homeless and a wanderer of the streets."

"No family?"

She shrugged leaving Berkley perplexed. Should he interpret this as a yes or a no or I don't really care?

"I apologize for so many questions. By nature, I am no nosey busy body I assure you."

"Are you a cop?"

Berkley smiled. "Guess I sound like one with the third degree. I am an author. I am accustomed to asking questions, especially when I am working on a new project."

"You write books?"

"Yes, mostly fiction."

"Fiction…made up stuff?"

"I guess it could be described as such, but authors do utilize real places, situations, and sometimes real characters to form the foundation of fictional literary work."

"Do you write about stories that are true?"

"Nonfiction...sometimes. Much tougher though. It requires a level of detail and research that can be quite time consuming. Accuracy is of the utmost importance. One must always make sure a person's quote is precise and on point."

"Would you write my story?"

Berkley mustered another smile and tried to frame his reply without sounding condescending. "Biographies are not my genre." He could tell by her perplexed look that he had not framed his response very well. "Why is it that you would like your story told, one so young, Melanie?"

She sighed and appeared to be hesitant to answer.

"Biographies are usually reserved for old fogies like me, long lives and much to tell. Perhaps you should give it a few more years before penning your life for the world to read."

"I was used in sex trafficking."

Berkley stopped dead in his tracks, mouth ajar and staring at the petite thing standing beside him. "Did you just say..."

"Sex trafficking. I was kidnapped. I think I was eleven or twelve, not sure though. Nice man. Looking for his lost dog. Asked me to help him find it."

"Your poor thing. How old are you now, my dear?"

"Seventeen, eighteen, maybe a little older. I don't have birthdays. Haven't for a long time, so it is kind of hard to know for sure."

"How long were you held captive?"

"Until Erwin helped me escape."

"Our Erwin Shipley?"

"Yes. He was underground, researching a story. He is a journalist, you know. He found me and helped me get away. It made Max terribly angry. He tried to get me back. Tried to hurt Erwin. We got away. Erwin called the police and they busted up the ring. Killed Max too. He was an awfully bad man."

"What compels you to wish to tell your story?"

"If other girls like me read what happened to me then maybe it will not happen to them."

Berkley wanted to hug the girl but in times like Covid it was not the proper thing to do even though neither he nor she was wearing a mask or social distancing on the beach.

"That is extremely admirable, Melanie. I commend you for wishing to educate others."

"They must be warned."

"And you drove Shipley to the west coast?"

"Erwin is my friend for life. I owe him everything. There is nothing I wouldn't do for him."

"By all means then, Melanie, it would be my honor to write your story."

"Is Berkley your author name?"

"Berkley Jay Patrick is the name on my novels. Can I let you in on a little secret?"

"Sure. I am excellent at keeping secrets. Just ask Erwin."

"That's not my real name. It is my pen name. My actual name is Pat Jason. Our little secret, remember. Even my dear Camilla does not know this, so it must remain our little secret."

"Pat Jason is a nice name. Can I let you in on a little secret? My last name is not my real name. I did not know my last name. I am not even sure Melanie is my real first name, but it is the only one I remember and what Max called me. Erwin, after rescuing me, asked my last name. I saw a law firm sign and picked the name Finch as mine. It stuck."

"Have you never considered searching for your past life, your parents, any connection before you were abducted?"

"No, not really. I have a new life as Melanie Finch, Uber driver. My past is in my taillights. My future in my headlights. I live for the moment. I have a safe place to sleep and have food and clothing. In owe no one. I am no longer used to favor a lustful fancy. My life is perfect now."

"Melanie Finch, it would be my honor to pen your biography, the perfect deterrent for other wayward girls. And if you ever change your mind, I will assist you in locating any relatives you may have and reclaiming your childhood memories."

"To be honest, Mister Jason, sorry, Mister Patrick. Erwin has already offered many times."

"Let us keep it simple. Just call me Berkley."

"When do we start my book?"

"Let us chat as we continue our stroll and collect our thoughts. Share with me what you wish. The process begins now. A wise woman shared this with me, Melanie: *There is a purpose for everyone you meet. For reasons beyond normal explanation, there are those who come into your life to test you. Others are teachers. Some will use you while others will bring out the absolute best in you.*"

Melanie giggled and said, "I get it. There is a purpose for me meeting Erwin Shipley. He saved me. There is a purpose for me meeting you, Berkley, so that I may help others as I have been helped already too. I am being tested by yet another, Paula Wise. She trusts me, yet she is in trouble. Toby Reichard, another Uber driver, taught me how to drive and earn my way. As for those who have used me, I no longer have a reason to fear them. That leaves me with one yet to fulfil, someone to bring out the absolute best in me."

"You have already found that person, Melanie Finch. Merely look in the mirror. You have been reborn. You are that person, and I am gazing upon the absolute best life has to offer."

"Can I hug you, Berkley?"

Berkley embraced the young lass, already experiencing a lasting bond. Before releasing him, Melanie said, "You are the second man I have hugged since those awfully bad times. Erwin was the first."

"I am honored in this case to play second fiddle. Your story will be a spectacular one and an inspiration to all. Not to brag my dear Melanie, but did I mention I was a bestselling author?"

Berkley Jay Patrick was no longer interested in writing the book about Covid and all the madness that accompanied it. He had the perfect inspiration, one that would surely dismember any threatening writer's block. Melanie Finch would be the perfect conduit to bring out the best in him. He reached out and she clasped his hand as they finished their walk and discussed the perfect biography, one that would be filled with tears and tribulations of horrific proportions, but one to certainly end with the absolute best happy ever after and save many from falling into the trap of sex trafficking.

48

Twenty-four hours had expired two hours ago. Aaron had not heard a peep from Charles. He did his best to stifle the urge to call him, realizing that he had not absolutely demanded an answer in this timeframe. No doubt, the evidence and threat were daunting and unimaginable. Together, a bipartisan approach offered the best path forward. They owed no one any favors. Still, leapfrogging protocol and going directly to the president, if successful, would unleash a firestorm on both sides. He expected that he and Charles would be censured and blackballed. Probably, Charles was putting his head on the chopping block more so than he by siding with a republican senator and president. Second guessing now, he should have given this more thought before putting his friend in such a tough position.

Another hour passed. Aaron had reached his tipping point. He phoned Charles and after a few rings it went to voice mail. Leaving a message was out of the question. He ended the call. He toyed with heading over to Charles' apartment. Instead, he tried the phone again. This time Charles answered.

"Hey Charles. You were making me a bit nervous having not heard from you yet. So, what do you think? Are you in and up to this? And I understand if you are reluctant."

"Aaron, we can't do this."

"We? I have no choice. You understand. Fine, I will head over to pick it up. Best you pretend you haven't seen it when it hits the fan."

"Aaron, I'm sorry."

"Sorry for what? I put you in a tough position. We will remain friends, I promise. I can be there within the hour."

"No need."

"It would not be fair for you to bring it back. Plus, I need some fresh air. Been cooped up too long. Of course, once this sees the light of day, we can end the lockdowns. Well, your side will still try to stay the course."

"Not what I meant. I don't have it."

"What the hell you mean you don't have it, Charles? I thought we agreed. You were not supposed to share it with anyone."

"I didn't. I kept that promise."

"Then what's the problem?"

"I destroyed it."

"You what?"

"I destroyed it, Aaron."

"It was not yours to destroy, Charles. Tell me you are just yanking my chain."

"I am sincerely sorry."

"You had no right. I trusted you. Who got to you, Charles? You are lying. You showed this to someone, didn't you?"

"Aaron, it is gone. There is no evidence. There is no need for us to argue about it. I don't expect us to remain friends. Shoe on the other foot, I would be done with you over something like this."

"You asked me if this was the only copy. You planned to do this all along, didn't you? The swamp has claimed another victim, hasn't it?"

"We are at an impasse. You can not accuse me of getting rid of something that you cannot prove it ever existed. And if you do, I will deny it. My word against yours. Just another perpetrated republican conspiracy theory."

"Where is your loyalty? This is our country. We are both Americans. Why would you knowingly allow this to happen? Never mind, your party wins the White House, ousts the incumbent president, one term and done. How can you do this all for the hatred of this president and ignore everything else in those documents? Communist China, R.K. Soto and others will destroy this great nation. You do get that part, don't you?"

"Goodbye Aaron. It is just politics. Nothing personal."

"Screw you, you piece of…" the line went dead.

****

After her phone call Paula returned to the balcony where her three cohorts sponged in the beach below as the last signs of daylight dwindled. She paused at the doorway and downed the bourbon shot before speaking.

"It's over," she sighed.

Camilla looking perplexed asked, "What's over?"

"Everything. We have been betrayed. A senator has destroyed the evidence."

"Destroyed the evidence. I thought you said your senator could be trusted," spoke up Berkley.

"My senator did not destroy it. He enlisted the help of another senator. That senator destroyed everything. Refused to help."

Camilla fired another question, "Why would another republican senator betray his own?"

"Because he wasn't a republican. He was a democrat."

"Why would yours trust a democrat?"

"He sought a bipartisan approach and never suspected betrayal."

"I think it is time for you to share with us exactly what those documents contained and what is really at stake here, Paula. We know there is more to it than just my research."

"Yes, Camilla, indeed there is. And yes, I do owe you. Before I begin, we need refills."

"I will do the honors," replied Berkley as Melanie waved him off and started to exit the balcony.

"Melanie, please stay. You are part of this. You have taken the risks with Shipley and with me. Welcome to our merry band of losers."

The captive audience remained mesmerized throughout Paula's recap of all the events and the contents of Shipley's discovery. Words could not begin to express their shock. Melanie sat emotionless as usual but inside was equally overwhelmed by what she had just heard.

Camilla broke the silence saying, "We still have my research. We can use it to prove Covid is not what they wish us to believe it is. Sure, it is deadly, but it is being used for control purposes."

"And if we do, Camilla, it will only serve as a distraction while all else transpires, that is if the media decided to cover it, which I doubt they would."

"Paula, given what we know, we can't just do nothing."

"Proverbial rock and a hard place, Berkley. Without evidence our words mean absolutely nothing, not even if we each testify under oath. Just words, nothing more. Without those papers we are no match for deep state, a corrupt Washington, special interest with deep pockets and a communist regime. IT IS OVER."

"You do realize it is never over until the bad guys say it is."

They all turned to Melanie, shocked that she had weighed in and even more caught off guard by what she had said.

"They do not forget or forgive. They get even, dish out the punishment, and remind you to never try it again. Sometimes they make examples of others to instill fear."

"Listen to her, folks. She is the voice of experience and I will leave it at that," added Berkley.

"Voice of experience, she is just a young girl," said Paula.

"Trust me on this. She has endured more in her young life than most of us endure in a lifetime. You will have to read her biography to learn more," he winked then elbowed Melanie.

"Fine, I concede. Maybe we are not out of the woods just yet. Perhaps we should lay low a while longer."

Camilla asked, "How much longer? My daughter is giving birth shortly and I promised to be with her. I am supposed to spend Christmas with my family as well."

"Not to make light of your family circumstances, but the presidential election is next week. The president will lose reelection if their plan works. The president elect is bought and paid for by people wishing to make this a socialist country. The transformation has already begun with Covid as the catalyst."

"Paula, you said it was over. You said no one knows of my involvement. My name has never been linked to the research, remember."

"You quickly forget that you were caught red handed inside the GVC network. Do the math. I'm sure they already have."

"How long then must we hide?"

"Camilla, I have no quick answer. Perhaps we wait it out a bit longer and see what happens."

"You are suggesting that they, whoever they are, will try something here eventually."

"Berkley, I am not insinuating anything. I hope nothing happens. Face the facts. They know about me and what I attempted to do. Your terrorist friends are still looking for you. While there is a connection to them and those pulling the strings, we do not know how much this Vlad and Jewel know. Probably not much but they still want you just the same. I have already made my point concerning Camilla. That leaves Melanie. Logic says they have made the plates on her Prius and are aware of her identify too. That is why I was compelled to share everything with her."

"Are we not sitting ducks now then? They must know about this condo. Anyone could figure out that George and I own it. It would be a matter of record."

"I agree with Camilla. Here we are, boxed and wrapped with a big red bow. They burst through that front door and have all of us, end of that chapter."

"Good point, Berkley. We should distance ourselves. Go our separate ways if it is not already too late. I fear we are already under surveillance."

"I'll bet this condo is bugged. It was probably bugged even before we arrived. Spy technology knows no boundaries," added Berkley. "I am having that same feeling I had after the second plane hit the second tower."

"Well, if that's the case, expect that crash through the door any second then," warned Paula.

Everyone diverted their stares to the door anticipating the worse. Ten agonizing moments passed, and nothing happened. Time to pack and exercise an exit strategy. As agreed no one would disclose their destinations just in case. Camilla would travel to Vermont to be with her pregnant daughter, Margie, and her husband Louis. Safety in numbers opted out over fear of retaliation on the entire family. Melanie would stick with Berkley. They planned to ditch the Prius and lease another vehicle. Destination unknown. Paula opted for a trip as well, securing a private jet. After completing their sad and apprehensive farewells, they departed without any hitches. Deep state did not intervene and as best they could tell, none of them had been tailed.

****

Election day came and passed. As choreographed, on election night it appeared the president had been reelected given the numbers being tabulated and shared on television. By daybreak, the game had taken an ugly turn. Hand ballots had materialized in key battleground states, all seemingly going for the president's opponent. As planned, the sting was on. The electoral college had been flipped by an election that was never intended to be fair. Cries of foul and election fraud followed. The president and his legal team fought a valiant fight. Sworn affidavits poured in, professing fraudulent behavior by pole workers, observers, even truck drivers. Most cases were tossed by judges in corrupt cities and states, an insurance policy being cashed in to oust the president. By late December, the president finally conceded the election.

Senator Aaron Breeze sat in his apartment reading his bible. He had prayed for a miracle that never happened. The plot that had been laid out loud and clear in those documents was playing out as perfectly orchestrated. It could have been stopped. Should have been stopped. What have you done, Senator Charles Paulson, he thought as he pounded his fist on the sofa? This should never have happened, not without giving us a fighting chance to stop it.

Across town, Senator Charles Paulson held his glass high to commemorate a toast made by one of his colleagues, a toast to him. Those gathered in the room, none wearing masks nor practicing social distancing, praised him for intercepting the documents furthered the cause and guaranteed the election would be theirs. The inauguration just hours earlier had sworn in the new president. Transforming America and reclaiming the swamp were next on their agenda. Open borders, then legalizing the millions of illegals would increase the vote counts in their direction. Defunding the police and backing the supreme court would fulfill just a few of their promises. The only thing standing in their way was a runoff for two senate seats. All they had to do was win those and then the vice president would possess the deciding vote for anything they posed. They had maintained the control of congress by the slimmest of margins.

Mere steps away from a socialist society and two weeks into the new president's term the unthinkable happened. Video surfaced incriminating the new president. He and his son had been exposed parlaying a multibillion-dollar deal with Iran granting them access to nuclear technology that would advance their program for developing a nuclear weapon much sooner than ever conceived. Labeled a traitor he was removed from the White House in handcuffs. His son was currently on the run and thought to be in North Korea where a second deal had been brokered and caught on camera.

The vice president stepped up and was sworn in as the new president for the full first term. A socialist agenda had been replaced covertly by one directed toward communism. One missing piece of the puzzle, the perfect duel double cross. The intent had never been meant for the new president to serve. Unbeknownst by all, the vice president had been groomed for this position by Communist China. The nation celebrated the new president's immediate downfall, sensing some skin in the game. Nothing was further from the truth.

49

Camilla held her new granddaughter, Chloe, rocking her as she gave the newest member to their family her bottle. She had watched in horror as the president had been escorted from the oval office in handcuffs. A chill had run the length of her spine, shaken by the revelation, and now wondering what next. Replacing the corrupt president with a running mate that probably possessed a just as evil agenda seemed moot at best. She sensed this was far from being a utopian proposition. Still, she remained thankful to the Almighty that she and her family had been spared from any persecution by the deep state or whoever had been responsible for murdering Erwin Shipley and pursuing Paula Wise. There had been no contact with the journalist since they had departed the Carolina condo.

It troubled her that she had not heard from Berkley either. She missed her dear friend, but they had agreed to go their separate ways and remain socially distanced until the uncertainty of retribution vanished. Covid continued its rule, conveniently utilized to break the will of Americans, the plan in full force. She found it difficult to swallow knowing what she had uncovered. Even more difficult to cope with was the guilt, having had an opportunity to stop this dead in its tracks. No, she did not blame herself personally but still, the group possessed the evidence that could have thwarted this and would have ensured that the president had a second term. No, nothing guaranteed that they would have succeeded. It would have provided a fighting chance for those capable of exposing the lies and plan to overthrow America. Camilla looked into the eyes of Chloe and wondered just what hope her future held.

****

Paula Wise had come out of hiding and begun a pod cast after the demise of her syndicated show. She had been deemed a liability after she had walked away from her last gig. No one trusted her nor wished to invest in her return. She settled for the podcast to gradually return to the light of day. Her following had grown only marginally, her audience having lost interest as well. Banished from the land so to speak, deep state had won again. She believed the powers that be had conspired to further discredit her just in case. It had been another long unproductive day. She sat in her modest flat in Texas half a wine bottle into forgetting her troubled path when someone knocked at her door. One thing for sure, it could not be opportunity, she thought as she figured she may as well answer the door. She opened it and almost stumbled backwards.

"I know what you must be thinking. Make way for the walking dead."

"Shipley! You are alive!"

"Relatively speaking. Might I come in?"

Paula stepped aside, still in semi shock. "You look like crap. Where in the hell have you been?"

"Pour another glass and I will have one as well, please. Then you better have a seat and strap yourself in. This is going to be a bumpy ride, wild and crazy, with an ending I believe is worth the price of admission."

Shipley recapped his ordeal. After mailing the decoy those in pursuit were relentless. On foot posed its share of challenges. He had given them the shake and was hiding in an empty burned out shell of a building waiting for the coast to clear. His hopes had been dashed. He heard them talking nearby. Eventually they were just on the other side of the barrier where he was hiding. Suddenly, the brick and mortar walls began crumbling around him and on top of him. Thinking back now, Shipley was certain they had sniffed him out and caused the avalanche.

He woke to find himself in a hospital bed. One hitch, he had been in a coma for weeks. His emergence among the living had been less than a week ago. The owner had found him in the rubble. Her family business had been ransacked and destroyed by what the mayor insisted had been just friendly protestors. No identification or cell phone had been found on what they assumed to be a homeless street person. Upon regaining his strength and gathering his wits, Shipley accessed his accounts to obtain some cash. He later heard Paula's podcast and tracked her down. Now, here he was, alive and kicking, once again.

"I am glad you are all right given what we previously thought. I have bad news to share though. I have failed you. I lost the second envelope. Well, lost isn't exactly correct. I entrusted my political contact with it with a promise to get it into the president's hands. He enlisted bipartisan help to legitimize the delivery to the president. His democratic friend deceived him and said he destroyed it. I am so sorry you went through this ordeal for nothing."

"I figured something had gone badly wrong after catching up from my deep sleep, discovering that the election had not been stopped and there was no mention of the bogus Covid numbers or communist China conspiracy."

"We decided to go our separate ways just in case we were still targeted for elimination or revenge. Seems they are done with us. We also decided to sit on Camilla's research figuring it alone would just be stifled."

"All was probably for the best considering. Appears there was a double cross among the corrupt. They turned on the new president quicker than expected, the quest for communism replacing the threat of socialism."

"You don't sound surprised."

"It was part of the plan all along."

"I saw nothing of this mentioned in the documentation."

"It wasn't, not in that version."

"There is more than one version?"

"Not exactly, just an add on to the original. All is not lost, Paula. After emerging from my deep sleep, I was contacted by the whistleblower again. Obviously, there was some concern and confusion as to why the original information had not been used. Of course, I did not know what had happened, so I improvised saying it had been intercepted in the mail. Not exactly a lie. Not so surprising, they were angry about what had happened to the election and what lay ahead for the country. Everyone involved in producing the initial evidence are willing to swear under oath and produce the material in a congressional hearing. Nearly twenty individuals. As the info commercial goes, but wait there is more. The additional evidence incriminates the vice president and numerous congressional representatives as well as high ranking CIA and FBI officials. Of course, it still takes down R.K. Soto and a treasure trove of the elite. Communist China stands at the top of the heap as the orchestrator, instigator, and ultimate loser."

"Unbelievable!"

"It should be a slam dunk to now arrest the vice president and relieve him from his presidential duties. Once done, the Speaker assumes control of the White House, a republican, and as far as we know, not involved in this coup. That said, a swamp rat will always be a bought and paid for as a swamp rat."

"Where does that leave the fraudulent election?"

"Once the dust settles, I would expect the supreme court to make a ruling and eventually turn it over to the senate utilizing electoral votes. There is a good chance the president will complete his second term."

"And businesses will no longer be sacrificed with these bogus shutdowns. Sadly Shipley, many will never return, financially devastated."

"Don't count them out. If the president regains his place in the White House, I would bet the bank that he cuts a deal to ensure those with their American dream squashed will be compensated to give them a fighting chance."

"A lot must happen to undo this mess, Shipley."

"My money is still on Americans. I also envision a political house cleaning, dumping the worthless trash on both sides of the fence. It is time to restore the intent of the constitution and the declaration, the government working for the people once again."

"I hope you are right, and these people make a compelling argument."

"Undeniable once it hits the fan. I failed to mention that several major networks and their news media are culpable as well, the evidence taking them down a peg or two. Fake news will get what has been coming to them, a reality check of enormous proportions."

"What about us, Shipley?"

"What about us, Paula Wise. We report the news and, as always, allow the viewers and listeners to decide, right? Are we still partners?"

"A perfect pair we make. It will be tough to top this one, though."

"Don't know about you but I could use a little less heavy lifting and return to normalcy."

"Amen to that. I forgot to tell you. Melanie is with Berkley. They are penning her biography."

"Wow. The butterfly has emerged. Good for her and for him."

"Camilla has a new granddaughter."

"That child will have a chance now in a world still fighting to survive."

"One more thing if you haven't already read about it; Covid 19 vaccines were launched under the president's watch before the inauguration. He delivered as he promised yet again."

"Can hardly wait to get mine. Now it is time to totally unhinge the guilty political party and the media, and restore law and order, capitalism, and the American way."

"All in!"

50

Berkley waited nervously. It had been his decision to do this, but heroism had always been reserved for characters within the pages of his novels. He controlled the outcome at his fingertips. Here, he felt helpless and exposed. No amount of research had ever been worth putting his life on the line. He kept reminding himself that this wasn't exactly research, not that he wasn't beyond using any experiences or characters encountered. All fiction had a basis for existence. It required tweaking at best to mask reality and protect the identity of those not responsible for the actions within the chapters. Footfalls echoing somewhere within in the cathedral alerted him to the fact that he was no longer alone.

"Author, author, come out come out wherever you are."

Berkley fought off hyperventilating and chickening out. No, he must see this to an end and have this behind him, he almost spoke out loud. He cocked his head listening, trying to determine where the sounds were coming from, but they had stopped. He gulped and retrieved his handkerchief, wiping perspiration from his brow and upper lip. Goosebumps appeared on his arms and a shiver tingled down his spine. You can do this is mentally coached himself.

"Must I remind you, you conjured up this little powwow. He had all but given up on our little project, disappointingly so I must add."

Berkley, more out of nervous habit, flattened any wrinkles in his trousers with his hands before standing from the balcony pew. "I am here."

"And here is where? Come out where I can see you."

"You first. Walk to the alter."

"Very well, we shall but I must warn you, I will not tolerate a sham."

Once they reached the alter Berkley gave the command to turn around. Vlad, accompanied by his righthand henchmen, did just that.

"I am here, in the balcony."

"Oh ye of little faith. I assure you we do not bite. This is, after all, the Lord's house, is it not? I am glad, after all this time, you have reconsidered and have brought me an outline of your next greatest novel."

"I find that comment quite satirical given that you did not honor God when you ruffed up Reverend Flowers in this very house of worship."

"Jewel can become a little overzealous when a friendly discussion does not go well. The good reverend refused, to, should we say 'rat you out' prompting the conversation to get a bit out of hand. Please do not fault Jewel nor I nor the reverend for this. If anyone is to blame it would be the man in your mirror for failing to follow our original agreement. I do hope the reverend has mended completely since our little prayer meeting a few months ago. Now, let bygones be bygones, if we can focus on the agenda of the day. If you would be so kind as to join us here, we can conclude our contractual proceedings. A handshake will seal the deal, a gentleman's agreement I always say."

Another figure stepped into view in the balcony. "Yes, those are the two men that assaulted me."

"Reverend…"

Police resembling stormtroopers arrived from all directions. Vlad and Jewel were forced face down on the floor and cuffed as their rights were read to them. The police captain nodded to the gentleman in the balcony acknowledging they had recorded the confession.

"Thank you for having the courage to do this Mr. Patrick."

"Thank you, Reverend Flowers, for agreeing to identify them. I am so happy you have recovered from the ordeal prompted by my failure to meet with them as they had requested. They were correct, if not for me this travesty would not have occurred."

"I will lift up mine eyes unto the hills, from whence cometh my help. My help cometh from the Lord, which made heaven and earth, Psalm 121:1-2. All is forgiven I assure you."

"Still, just the same, I am guilty as charged."

"And I am thankful more than you can imagine. The Lord is my rock and my fortress and my deliverer; My God, my strength, in whom I will trust; My shield and the horn of my salvation, my stronghold. I will call upon the Lord, who is worthy to be praised; So, shall I be saved from my enemies...Psalm 18:2-3."

"I must read these words from Psalm sometime. Thank you for opening my eyes to so many things, Reverend Flowers."

Flowers smiled. "I sense your heart has been breached as well."

"Maybe so. One thing has surely been changed in my life. Traditionally, I have always purchased a Christmas ornament signifying the year. Last year I ended that tradition wishing no part of a 2020 ornament hanging from my tree. My version of a leap year I suppose."

Flower laughed, "Can not say I blame you for that one. Might I add, you always have an open invitation to join us here."

"Might surprise you."

Flowers winked, "Might surprise you, not me."

****

Camilla sat on the back deck sipping hot herbal tea, the spring morning sun warm and inviting. Birds took turns carrying new nesting material to one of George's birdhouses. Little blue birds, a mating pair. She would forever miss him, but for the first time life almost felt normal and a tad bit hopeful. Tomorrow she would close on the selling of their home and begin the next chapter with a move to South Carolina. The condo had been removed from the rental circuit. She had decided, after staying there while they were in hiding that it felt like home and the perfect place for a new beginning. Plus, living at the beach would be a sure guarantee that her children and grandchildren would visit often.

The threat of Covid 19 had drastically diminished with the vaccination of most of the world now complete. The president had delivered another promise delivering a vaccine for Covid-19 in less than a year, something that had never been done. People were still contracting the coronavirus just as people still come down with the flu. Fewer were dying and no longer were the number of cases or deaths being falsely skewed. The presidential election had been rectified and the president now focused on his second term. America had indeed undergone a transformation but not the one that had been envisioned by communist. The Chinese communist regime had been overthrown and for the first time showed signs of an emerging democracy. America had reopened for business; the small business owners having been given a fighting chance.

Camilla, Berkley, and Melanie were scheduled for brunch at The Owl House after , one of their favorite restaurants that had reopened and was flourishing. Berkley and Melanie had completed the first draft of her biography titled *Save the Butterflies*. The deaths of Doctor Kyle Richardson and his wife Mildred had been deemed murder but thus far those responsible had not been identified. Kitt Whitt's attackers had not been brought to justice; the case remained unsolved. Franklin Hartsfield, the corrupt coroner had been buried in a gravesite reserved for John Does.

Paula Wise and Erwin Shipley, along with investors had bought the United Broadcast Network at a bargain basement price. It had been rebranded WTP for the We The People Network, the truth and nothing but. They were in the process of renovating it, transforming it into a reliable and reputable news agency, restoring the premise of real journalism. Berkley would be a literary contributor. Camilla would be utilized as a medical consultant for segments requiring her expertise. Senator Aaron Breeze had been tapped to offer political analysis.

Reverend Flowers also had his rightful place on the new network. He appeared weekly to offer hope and guidance to those seeking God and for those already in a relationship with the Lord. In his first appearance he put things in perspective for the viewers including this appropriate quote he felt compelled to share:

"The Eagle does not fight the snake on the ground. It picks up the snake and changes the battle ground, and then it releases the snake into the sky. The snake has no stamina, no power, and no balance in the air. It is useless, weak, and vulnerable unlike on the ground where it is powerful, wise and deadly. Take your fight into the spiritual realm by praying and when you are in the spiritual realm God takes over your battles. Do not fight the enemy in his comfort zone. Change the battle ground like the Eagle and let God take charge through your earnest prayer. You will be assured of a clean victory. Pray without ceasing.

These are not my words, but they are powerful ones to ponder, are they not, given where we have been and where we are headed. On a lighter note, more hindsight than anything, we should probably have vaccinated the politicians first instead of the health care workers, first responders and our precious elders. Losing a few politicians would not have mattered to most of us. I do jest. I love everyone. Even the unclean…I mean politicians."

Paula and Erwin had found a national treasure with Flowers and God had been returned to America's schools and churches were now filled with believers. Peace on earth had found its place once again, the pandemic cleansing the world like the great flood of biblical times, proving that God Almighty does indeed work in mysterious ways. God Bless America, the anthem and the flag were respected, not disgraced. Taking a knee meant kneeling before the Lord. Those doing otherwise were booed and shunned. Being politically correct had worn out its welcome. Sports figures and Hollywood actors and actresses were no longer recognized as role models if their messages were anti-America and anti-God. The great woke had taken on new meaning. All lives mattered in a world proudly representing the red, white, and blue. United a nation stood, one under God as the founders had envisioned. Covert 19 had failed as only God knew it would.

About T. Allen Winn T. Allen

Winn began writing in 2003 while being cooped up in hotels during business travel. Completing a 650 page so called novel he became hooked. The homegrown Abbeville, S.C. boy embraced the experience completing one novel and then leaping into the next one, fun and therapy at the time. That changed in 2011 when a chance encounter brought stranger and new neighbor Bob O'Brien to his Pawley's Island doorsteps. Bob didn't realize the neighborhood home had been sold and apologized when Tom greeted him instead of the man he had expected to see. Book in hand, Bob had just published his first novel, The Toppled Pawn and explained the previous neighbor had shown interest in writing. Tom remarked he dabbled in writing to which Bob asked, do you have a manuscript? Tom replied ten. Bob had just started Prose Press, a publishing company and suggested publishing one. You cannot make this stuff up.

T. Allen Winn's first novel, Road Rage joined the ranks of the published a few months later, and he owes a special thanks to Bob O'Brien for making this possible. His first seven books were published by Prose Press. In 2016, T. Allen Winn established Buttermilk Books, his publishing company and has now published twenty two books under the brand. He and his wife reside in Myrtle Beach, South Carolina.

Ole T does not write under any specific genre. He writes what strikes his fancy. If you don't see something that fits your reading wheelhouse, just tell him what you like, and he might just write it for you.

Books are available on Amazon or online where books are sold. Select books are available at Southern Succotash on Washington Street in Abbeville, S.C. and in Tabor City, N.C. at Grapefull Sisters Vineyard. Or *Message* T. Allen Winn on Facebook to arrange delivery of signed copies, or to schedule him to speak at an event or book club.

Fiction from T. Allen Winn

The Detective Trudy Wagner series

Road Rage
North of the Border
Tithes and Offerings

Bigfoot Trilogy

Foot, Tree Knockers and Rock Throwers
Another Foot, What Really Happened to D.B. Cooper

More Fiction from T. Allen Winn

The Perfect Spook House
Dark Thirty
Lou Who
Raw Ride, a Wild West Zombie Apocalyptic Shoot'um Up
The Man Who Met the Mouse
Mister Twix Mystery, a Cat Scene Investigation
Come Here, Getouttahere, Tyler's Tail Wagging Tale
The Tenth Elemental
Last Stand on the Grand Strand
The Lord's Last Acres
Covert 19. 2020 A Devil of a Year

Non-Fiction from T. Allen Winn

Being Bentley, A Dog Like No Other
It's All About the 'A', Faith, Family, Football and Forever to Thee
with coauthor, Benji Greeson
It's All About the Angels in the Backfield, Dawn of a Dynasty
with coauthor, Benji Greeson
December's Darkest Day, While I Breathe, I Hope
The Hardwood Walker of Port Harrelson Road (based on true events
in Bucksport, S.C.)
Cuz, My Brother, Life is Good, God is Good

Pushed into The Pull, Thank You Cuz

Memoirs

The Caregiver's Son, Outside the Window Looking In
Cornbread and Buttermilk, Good Ole Fashion Home Cooked
Nostalgic Nonsense
Don't Sit Naked in a Grits Tree, More Nostalgic Nonsense Vol 2
The Endless Mulligan, Short Shots from the Golf Whomper

Biographies

Clay Page, Somewhere In Between
Screw It, Let's Ride, The Legend Bub Lollis

Short Stories

For Your Amusement featured in Beach Author Network's book titled 'Shorts'

Ciled Me a Bar featured in friend and author, Danny Kuhn's Headline Book's *Mountain Mysts*, Honorable Mention in Fiction at the 2015 London Book Festival and the book is endorsed by *Joyce Dewitt* of the sitcom *Three's Company*

Short story about Granny Bowie in friend and author Robert Sharpe's book, *The Heart and Soul of Caring*, about caregivers and their challenges